The Codex File

Miles Etherton

City Stone Publishing

ISBN: 978-1-915399-00-7 (paperback)
ISBN: 978-1-915399-02-1 (ePUB)
ASIN: B06XRN2SL1 (audiobook)

A CIP catalogue record for this book is available from the British Library.

Miles Etherton | www.milesetherton.com
City Stone Publishing | www.citystonepublishing.com

First printed: February 2012
Second, revised, edition: February 2022

For my sons, Ethan and Milo.
I love you both very much.

"If you want a picture of the future, imagine a boot stamping on a human face—for ever."

—— George Orwell, *1984*

Contents

CHAPTER ONE

THE FLICK KNIFE SNAPPED open with frightening ease, its serrated edge glinting in the light of a passing street lamp. The weapon was standard issue for CODEX operatives, along with most of the contents of the canvas bag that sat in John Kennedy's lap.

One by one, he scrutinised each item of equipment—preparation was vital; nothing left to chance. The first object was a transparent bag containing an assortment of plastic ties, designed to restrain his victim and bite into her flesh if she struggled. A length of rubber tubing was next, followed by duct tape and a can of spray paint—everything he required for the job.

Vincent Trevellion sat next to Kennedy in the driver's seat, navigating the blue Mercedes through the dark, quiet streets of Hersham. A right turn led into a long tree-lined road that stretched around a gentle corner and there, the 1930s pebble-dashed house they sought, came into view.

Trevellion pulled the Mercedes up alongside the pavement a few houses down from their destination. Apart from some parked cars, the street was quiet, intermittent street lamps illuminating the darkness.

From his jacket pocket, Trevellion pulled out an electronic device. The screen blinked, and a menu of options appeared. With a stroke across the screen, an intelligence file containing a photograph of a woman appeared. She was smiling, walking hand in hand with her husband, their daughter running along behind.

He didn't need the photograph. He knew what she looked like.

He scrolled down past the photograph to the text about Colette Robertson, technical director at a leading web technology company. Past the biography, his eyes scanned the last line of text accompanying the picture:

Objective: Colette Robertson to be eliminated under Phase 1 of CODEX operation OP09/ST.

Trevellion closed the file and opened a second intelligence report attached to the data on Colette Robertson. A picture of her eight-year-old daughter, Clare, flashed up on the screen: a pretty girl with long blonde hair that fell over her shoulders and down her back. Once more, he scrolled past the image to the biography and objectives. And again, read the same order:

Objective: Clare Robertson to be eliminated under Phase 1 of CODEX operation OP09/ST.

Trevellion closed the files and placed the electronic device back in his jacket pocket. The murder of the child would guarantee the nationwide media coverage they required.

Even if a camera or passer-by captured their registration plates, any investigation would be pointless. The stolen plates would only lead to a long-deserted warehouse in rural Scotland; whilst the police were chasing their tails, they would vanish.

Trevellion tapped his opposite jacket pocket to confirm the two high-capacity flash drives were still there.

They were special issue for CODEX operatives, not the standard multi-gigabyte versions you could buy on any high street. These could handle terabytes of data and weren't for public consumption.

The two men exited the Mercedes and began the approach to their victim's house.

Colette sneezed for the umpteenth time, reaching for yet another tissue. She winced as she dabbed her nose, red and sore from wiping away the non-stop proof of her cold. If only she had bought some of the balm tissues that were always being advertised, she thought, stroking her nostrils.

Colette hated being ill, and this was the third cold she'd picked up in as many months. Maybe it was the flu, she considered, since she'd begun feeling worse as the day had gone on. Her muscles ached, the throbbing headache was pounding now more than ever, and her streaming nose showed no sign of stopping. With her best aim, she tossed the damp tissue in the general direction of the bin, watching as it bounced off the side and landed next to her cat. He eyed her with suspicion, awoken by her latest sneeze.

She hoped she'd be well enough to return to work tomorrow. But she doubted it as she felt her head, bunged up with cold, throb again.

The TV remote control sat in her lap, and she began channel-hopping, looking in vain for something half-decent to watch.

Maybe she ought to do some work, she wondered. There were always meetings to prepare for, reports to compile, and strategic IT problems to solve. Yet the thought of sitting in front of her laptop seemed to make her aching head throb further.

What she needed more than anything else was a bit of TLC, she mused. Everything seemed to have gone wrong. On today of all days. It was their wedding anniversary, after all. But where were the people she cared for?

She welled up again as the bitter exchanges over breakfast came flooding back. Deep down, she knew it hadn't been Michael's fault. His managing director had invited him to an important corporate dinner.

'Look, you know what these work functions are like, I have to go. I can't get out of it. I'm really sorry,' he'd said.

'If you were sorry, you would have said no and made some sort of excuse.' Her eyes had flared as her voice grew louder with each word. 'I can't believe you didn't realise what day it was.'

'I'll make it up to you, I promise,' he had said, before returning to his toast and avoiding her probing gaze.

Attendance hadn't been obligatory. They never were, were they? You only didn't go if you wanted to stay in the same old job for the rest of your career. Michael hadn't mentioned the fact that she'd done the same many times on her way up the career ladder at SW Technologies. She'd remembered and had kept that fact to herself.

It hadn't mattered this morning. It was their anniversary, and it had pissed her off. With her horrible cold too, it seemed the entire world was conspiring to ruin their special day.

She couldn't even seek comfort in their daughter. Clare was at an important ballet rehearsal. The performance was on Saturday, after all. The mother of one of Clare's friends would pick her up after the rehearsal tonight. Any other week, it would've been Michael. But not tonight, all because of that bloody dinner. It just wasn't fair.

At least she had Harry with her, she thought, feeling a little comforted when he jumped onto her lap and began purring.

Her eyes, heavy with the weight of her cold, began closing again, her thoughts drifting away to happier things.

Before they reached far, she was aware of a distant ringing, somewhere in a different consciousness.

Have I started dreaming? Am I asleep or awake?

She didn't care until Harry leapt from her lap, clawing her thigh as he used it as his launch pad.

The ringing was much louder now, and nearer. Her eyes opened with a start, and it took her sleepy mind several moments to realise it was the doorbell. Maybe Michael had forgotten his key in the heat of their argument in the morning?

A glance at the antique clock on the mantelpiece told her it was too early. Unless he'd skipped the function after all. Had he come home to surprise her on their anniversary?

In the hallway, she could see two figures through the glass of the front door. One was tall, the other shorter and stockier. The shorter man was carrying some sort of case.

When the porch failed to illuminate, she blinked with surprise. The figures on the doorstep remained in darkness as she flicked the light switch.

Colette opened the door far enough to see who was standing on her doorstep. The men, who had been looking away, turned to face her. For a long moment, all she could see were their silhouettes and the outline of their faces. Just before the taller man spoke, she noticed the porch light bulb was missing.

'Mrs Robertson? Mrs Colette Robertson?' The voice was low and unfamiliar.

Within a moment of confirming her identity, the stocky man's fist crashed into her mouth and nose. A ring tore into her lip.

She was thrown backwards, landing on the oak floorboards with a dull thud. Unconsciousness took her as she was aware of the tall man closing the front door and bending over her.

SOMETIMES SHE WOULD HAVE a terrible nightmare and wake in a cold sweat. Michael would be there to cling to for security, and she'd soon breathe an enormous sigh of relief she'd been dreaming. Colette knew this wasn't one of those times.

Even through the semi-consciousness of waking, she could feel the intense burning of her chest, although she felt cold and restricted in her movement. Before she opened her eyes, she knew they had bound her to something.

Her eyes shot open as the rasping pain burned into her waking senses again. Through bleary eyes, she could see a figure hovering above her. The flash of metal, the spectral white hands, the pain getting unbearable. Sleep was replaced with frightening consciousness.

She could see everything. A stocky man in dark blue overalls.

Blood.

The blade of the flick knife snapped shut.

It's my blood.

The white surgical gloves were coated, her blood running everywhere.

She tried to scream, but her mouth could not move.

Duct tape

Her panic threatened to escalate. She lifted her head to look at herself. Her feet taped together around the ankles, preventing any movement. Hands tied to the bedstead with white plastic restraints.

It wasn't that which concerned her most. It was the pools of blood running from her chest, staining the white sheets of the bed. Her screams echoed in her head as through wide, frightened eyes she looked at the bloody mess that had once been her chest. She felt sure she could make out a handful of individual wounds as her eyes flitted between the blood and the man in the dark blue overalls circling above her, his gaze tracing a line over her.

John Kennedy looked down at Colette's bloody, restrained body, his expression blank. Vincent Trevellion watched with no discernible interest from a chair to the right of the bed. Kennedy was quite pleased with his handiwork, although the full effect wouldn't be visible until she was dead and the bleeding had stopped. It served his purpose. Trevellion's suggested mutilations had been inspiring and would send a chilling message.

He studied the woman's bloody chest, a thin smile crossing his lips. It wasn't bad at all, considering it was the first time he'd carved a message in human flesh.

His eyes moved across her exposed, blood-drenched breasts. Above them, it read *Fuck the Net* in jagged letters.

His gaze rose above her stained body to the message he'd smeared on the wall. Daubed in her blood, it said:

Reclaim the World

Trevellion stood up and approached the bed; peering at the bloody message carved in flesh. He admired his macabre suggestion. Their work was nearing its conclusion.

Whilst his accomplice had been torturing Colette Robertson, he'd copied all the SW Technologies state network tender project data and wider semantic web development information from her laptop. The priceless flash drive sat in his inside pocket.

The ransacking of the house had also yielded a few more useful hard-copy files for him to study. The final satisfying act had been to format and infect her laptop, removing all the SW Technologies data forever. It was too risky to steal the machine. He knew it would contain a tracking device given her line of work, and they didn't have the time to locate and remove it. He smiled as he tapped a second flash drive in his jacket pocket containing the virus that had forever wiped her computer of its secrets.

All that remained was for the others to complete their jobs. A break-in at SW Technologies' premises would be a formality. Once the information was theirs, they would torch the building.

The anti-net activists would be blamed for her death. After tonight's events, they would have nowhere to hide.

Trevellion checked the digital video camera erected on its tripod was still recording. He smiled as the red light continued to beam, the intrusive lens capturing the death of Colette Robertson.

He turned to face his colleague and nodded before returning to his seat to watch the last rites. As he sat, he saw the flash of the flick-knife blade snapping open, blood sticking from its earlier work.

Colette struggled, pulling in vain against her restraints, as the bloody blade flicked into position. This couldn't be happening. She'd wake in a minute and wrap a comforting arm around Michael's sleeping body. But she knew this was it. No waking up in a cold sweat. No relief at the vividness of her dreams. No escape.

She struggled more violently than ever as the man leant over her, careful to avoid the bloody sheets, the blade moving towards her face.

Tears streamed down her cheeks. For the first time, she studied the face of her attacker and then the man sitting nearby. She didn't recognise the assailant in the overalls, but the other, taller man was a different matter. The dark hair, well-defined features and high cheekbones made him about forty. It was difficult to be certain. He seemed older because of his manicured black goatee beard.

She couldn't be sure, but there was something familiar about him. She'd seen him before. As sheer terror overtook her senses, her heart pounding in her ears, she couldn't remember where or when.

The blade was at her lips.

She sank back into the mattress as far as it would allow. It wasn't enough. She closed her eyes and winced as the sharp blade flashed in front of her mouth. She waited for the intense burning pain, but all she felt was a slight trickle of blood seeping into her mouth.

Colette opened her eyes again to see the stocky man in his overalls had moved away to one corner of the room. Her wide eyes scanned across, stopping in alarm as she saw her digital video camera propped up on a tripod.

All her muscles tightened, burning from the effort, and she clenched her fists. Her eyes narrowed as her anger rose.

As if what was happening wasn't enough. They were going to kill her. She was certain of that. But the sick bastards were filming their work for all time.

What sort of fucking animals are you? What are you going to do when you've left me butchered on the bed? Go home and get a hard-on watching this?

Her gaze once more fell on the taller man and her anger faded as tears spilled down her cheeks. She would never see Michael or Clare again. She was going to die alone, never having the chance to hold them again.

Her sorrow evaporated as she looked back to the familiar-looking man, aware of him moving to her right. He was placing something in a leather-bound briefcase, open on the dressing table.

Is that a flash drive?

Her confusion rose. She needed to be rational despite the waves of terror and nausea rushing over her. She had to understand why this was happening to her.

The bastard must have copied something from my computer. But that's all work-related. How could that be of interest?

Her thoughts trailed off. The bell in her head was ringing loudly. So this is what it was all about.

This is about my work. And the tender I've spent so many hours on.

She knew industrial espionage was a dirty game, but this was beyond anyone's worst nightmare.

And now she realised why the man looked familiar. She had a vague recollection of meeting or seeing him at an industry event the year before. He'd been presenting on advancements in...

The answers and images in her mind faded as the stocky man approached the bed again. This time it wasn't the knife menacing her, it was a long length of rubber tubing and a large white plastic container. Her eyes flicked from the man to the plastic container, attempting to read the words on the label.

The man forced the rubber tubing through the slit in the tape in between her swollen lips, and she caught sight of the label.

White Spirit. He's going to pour White Spirit down my throat and burn out my fucking insides.

She clenched her mouth shut, shaking her head. The rest of her body continued its losing battle to break free from the restraints.

Within seconds, the fist that had first greeted her at the front door had smashed into her face three times. Unconsciousness consumed her before she could register her nose being smashed, her septum splitting, and teeth breaking. Had she been able to think, she would have welcomed it rather than face what was coming.

As she succumbed to the black unconscious, she never felt the rubber tube slide into her throat.

THE LIGHT BULB FOR the porch was missing. It was the first thing Michael Robertson noticed when he approached his front door. Frowning, he reached into his jacket pocket for the key, groping about in the darkness, sure the bulb had been there the night before. *Perhaps it had broken that evening and Colette just hadn't got round to replacing it.*

Another thought crossed his mind, one he hoped was too petty to be true. Was Colette still pissed off enough with him to have removed the bulb to annoy him when he arrived home?

Michael dismissed the idea and exhaled, hoping the bunch of red roses and bottle of Lindeman's Bin 65 Chardonnay, one of Colette's favourites, would help smooth over their fight at breakfast. Even now he couldn't help but feel Colette was a little hypocritical in making a fuss about him attending. How many meetings, conferences and overnight stays had she been on in the last few manic months?

Trips to London for emergency meetings with zero notice were almost as commonplace as her going into the office.

There were weeks he wouldn't see her at all; not once had he made a fuss or made her feel guilty about the fact that their eight-year-old daughter Clare missed her so much when she was away.

Although, as Colette had been keen to point out, none of those meetings had taken place on their wedding anniversary. Not only that, but she'd got a nasty cold and needed looking after.

It was no surprise she had the flu, given how hard she'd been working.

He knew the timing had been dire, but there had been nothing he could do. The managing director had made it clear she would take a dim view if all the senior insurance brokers didn't attend the annual dinner. And he'd toed the line, incurring Colette's wrath.

The key slid into the lock, and the front door opened into the dark hallway. Glancing at his watch, lit up by the full moon, the time was a little after eleven. Most evenings, Colette would still have been awake, working on her laptop, but all the downstairs lights were off. The only illumination came from the upstairs landing.

Michael flicked the hall light on, and his gaze dropped to the assortment of letters strewn across the carpet, just beyond the doormat. Colette prided herself on her tidiness. Letters and bills would be in a neat stack on the side of the hall table, not lying in a mess on the floor. Maybe Harry, their cat, had taken a walk across the narrow table, he thought, closing the door behind him, careful not to let it bang shut.

For a second, he considered calling out to Colette but rejected the idea in case she was asleep. Despite the recriminations at breakfast, he hoped she was still awake. Perhaps they could enjoy some of the remaining evening together with a pleasant glass of wine.

He placed his keys on the hall table and headed into the kitchen to retrieve two wine glasses. Before he reached there, he stopped, his gaze on one of Colette's slippers, discarded on the bottom step of the staircase. Several steps further up lay one of her gold-encrusted earrings, a present from their last wedding anniversary.

A quizzical look crossed Michael's face. He frowned and turned to climb the stairs. Even when she was ill, Colette wouldn't just dump things on the stairs, especially not her favourite jewellery.

With the roses in one hand and the wine in the other, Michael walked up the stairs, careful to avoid the creaky step at the top.

The upstairs of the house was just as quiet as downstairs. Too quiet. There was no sound of life from the bedroom. No mumblings from the television. Not even the whistling of the wind coming in through the bathroom window, which was always open, even in winter. And no sign of their cat Harry keeping guard at the top of the stairs; his nightly ritual.

Upon reaching the landing, one more thing wasn't as it should have been. Their bedroom door was closed. They never closed it, just in case Clare needed something in the night.

Without further thought, Michael turned the door handle.

The bedroom, like the rest of the upstairs, was in darkness. But there was something else. The smell. A metallic chemical cocktail hung in the air, invading his senses as he grappled to decipher what it might be.

His heart pounded, and he could feel himself perspiring. There was something wrong; as he reached for the light switch, his sense of dread was rising.

The air was sucked from his lungs as artificial light bathed their bedroom. For a few long moments, he stood, unable to move, a sea of blood filling his vision as he looked at their bed.

Even as he stared at the sight before him, his confused thoughts couldn't process what he was seeing. The duvet was on the floor at the foot of the bed. The sheets were stained crimson, not a spot of white remaining. On the bed was Colette, her wrists fastened to the bedstead, her ankles taped together.

Michael felt numbness and nausea creeping through him as he took in every detail of the horror before him. Bloodied duct tape was over Colette's mouth, and what looked like a piece of rubber tubing was hanging like a limp rag from her swollen lips. A discarded white plastic canister was on the floor next to the bed. The words 'White Spirit' just visible.

The acidic taste of bile burnt the back of his throat as his gaze dropped to Colette's exposed chest, her shirt torn and crumpled beneath her. Savage markings and lacerations marked her pale flesh. The blood now dried into a gruesome message that made no sense.

Fuck the net.

And on the wall above the bed, more blood, smeared in large letters, spelling out another message.

Reclaim the world

Unable to hold back nausea any longer, Michael vomited hyperventilating.

That can't be Colette, his mind was pleading.

But he knew it was. His eyes traced the lines of blood running from the wounds in her chest, matting portions of her long brown hair together where it had impeded the blood flow.

As unconsciousness crept upon him and he slumped to the floor, one more terrible thought filled his head.

Where was his daughter?

CHAPTER TWO

THE SHADOWS WERE LENGTHENING as the dark blue Mercedes ground to a halt alongside a deserted playground. Two men exited the car, following the path around the edge of the play area. One wore a smart black suit, the other dark combat trousers and a thin jumper, carrying a black holdall.

Swings creaked, rocking in the breeze as the men turned onto a narrow path running along the back of the houses on the small estate. Vincent Trevellion looked around him, ensuring no one else was on the path. The only sound was the gentle crunching as their shoes trod down on the gravel.

The men strode up the path while Trevellion counted the houses, making sure they reached the back of their intended location. Conservatory after conservatory loomed up over the tall fences, the wooden structures decorated with a mixture of trellises and climbing plants, all backing onto the path.

At the seventh house, Trevellion stopped. They'd reached their destination.

Above the fence, they could see the upstairs of a large mock-Georgian house.

A vast conservatory ran along the entire back of the building. In front of them was the back gate of the garden, shrouded in ivy hanging down from the bricked arch above.

Trevellion watched as his stocky accomplice prised open his holdall. Kennedy handed him a pair of white rubber gloves before pulling his own pair over his large fingers. With no words spoken, the two men pulled on the gloves.

Kennedy returned to the holdall and slid out a well-used crowbar, a glance confirming they were still alone on the path. Confident the high fences obscured any view of their activities, he inserted the crowbar in between the gate and its wooden frame and leant his bulk against the tool. The lock creaked and buckled and gave way to his weight. Beyond the gate was a tidy, manicured garden. A vibrant mixture of flowers and shrubs subdued by the twilight.

Once inside, the gate was closed and a nearby shovel propped against it, hiding the evidence of their entrance. The two men stole up to the back door of the house, Kennedy still with the crowbar in his hand. With the tool raised to the glass, Trevellion nodded as it punched a jagged hole through the glass above the door handle.

Kennedy returned the crowbar to the holdall and slid his hand through the hole in the glass, turning the key lodged in the lock.

A smile cracked Trevellion's face as they entered the empty house. They both knew the owner would be back soon.

Trevellion looked around the large galley-style kitchen until an item on the tiled wall opposite caught his eye.

'This should be very persuasive,' he said, lifting the meat cleaver from its hook on the wall and passing it to Kennedy.

The meat cleaver glinted from its newness. Trevellion smiled as he studied the sharpness of the edge while his assistant gripped it. Eight inches of metal so sharp it could slice a wrist off in one vicious strike.

The kitchen sparkled from pristine clean work surfaces, a well-stocked wine rack with excellent vintages, in sharp contrast to the shards of glass from their forced entry decorating the polished wooden floor.

Armed with the meat cleaver, the two men passed from the kitchen into the study, careful to avoid making unnecessary sounds. The room contained what they were expecting—a touchscreen computer, mounted at 45 degrees, and shelf upon shelf of paper files, computer disks, DVD-ROMs and flash drives. A lifetime's work of a man dedicated to developing computer technology. The location as tidy as the mind that had arranged it.

The bookcase along the adjacent wall was full of manuals on advanced programming techniques and the online world into the twenty-first century. A filing cabinet sat beside the bookcase, doubt-less containing more technological secrets, Trevellion thought, his gloved hand stroking the top of the storage unit. Their briefing had been accurate. The contents of the room were exactly as expected.

The sound of the 7 Series BMW pulling into the luxurious gravel drive filtered through, and Trevellion glanced at his watch. On time, as predicted, he thought, as the second hand moved to 7.10 a.m.

Kennedy placed the meat cleaver on top of the bookcase before slipping his hand into the pocket of his combat trousers. He pulled out a thin rope, about a metre long. The key in the front door turned and Kennedy wound the rope around his fingers. Just inside the doorway to the study, both waited and listened.

With the front door opening, the sound of creaking hinges filled the quiet house. David Langley trudged into his darkening hallway, dropping a heavy briefcase onto the thick-pile carpet.

A sickly odour of stale aftershave and a day's sweat permeated the hallway. Langley tossed his keys onto a wooden table before closing the door. A hoarse, asthmatic cough echoed. Pausing, he reached into his pocket for his Ventolin inhaler. The heavy briefcase from the car had stirred up his asthma yet again.

Two pumps on the inhaler eased his breathing, and he looked down at his stomach. A mountain of flabby flesh hung over his waistband. A puddle of sweat stained his Yves Saint Laurent shirt where it clung to his skin. He should lose weight, he thought, replacing his inhaler in his jacket pocket.

Langley wiped the perspiration from his face and bent over to collect the post congregating on his doormat, and began gasping for breath again. The thin rope bit into his flesh and tightened around his windpipe. Duct tape wound round his head and over wide, fearful eyes as he struggled.

'Oh my God, if it's money you want, I can get you money.' Langley's voice rose in panic as he gasped for air, the rope constricting his windpipe.

'Shut the fuck up, fat man,' Trevellion said.

His clenched fist smashed into the man's right kidney. Through a stifled cry, Langley crumpled as his legs gave way. For a moment, he hung like a limp puppet; the rope cutting into his throat.

Kennedy's grip loosened, and the man slumped to the floor. Motionless, his reddened face began turning blue.

'Great, where's his fucking inhaler?' Trevellion asked, his polished shoe thudding into the man's back.

Still with a grip on the rope, Kennedy rummaged through Langley's suit pockets. His searching stopped as his fingers wrapped around the inhaler.

Kennedy yanked Langley into a sitting position before loosening his grip. The man's face had turned to a darker blue as he fought for every precious breath. Trevellion shoved the inhaler between his quivering lips and pumped five rapid squirts into Langley's mouth.

You're not allowed to die yet, fat man.

The man spluttered for a few seconds before his colour returned.

'On your feet,' Trevellion said as Kennedy hauled Langley into a standing position.

'Look, what do you want?' Langley panted, sweat oozing from every pore.

'I'll ask the questions.'

Bundled into his study, the assailants shoved the man into the swivel chair. For a moment, he sank into unconsciousness as Trevellion ripped a vicious blow across the side of his face.

Kennedy moved in and wound the silver duct tape around Langley's ankles, fastening his chubby arms and wrists to the thick wooden armrests. The man's fleshy fingers were next, each digit taped to the chair.

Trevellion stood close by, looking down at the balding, middle-aged man before him. His face was bright red, sweat congregating in his furrowed brow. His stomach hung over his pressed trousers, rising and falling as his body shook.

'Who are you? What do you want?'

Trevellion didn't reply. Instead, he walked to the bookcase and picked up the meat cleaver.

'I want access to ACE Solution's records relating to the state network tender and everything that's in your company's R&D pipeline.'

Trevellion approached the chair, passing the meat cleaver to Kennedy.

'You must be bloody joking. I can't give you that.' Langley's eyes were wide with shock. 'I don't even have access to all that data.'

As he finished his sentence, Trevellion lurched forward and brought his hand over the man's mouth as Kennedy drove the meat cleaver down. Langley struggled in his chair as his little finger shot two feet in the air, blood gushing from the gaping wound.

Trevellion pulled his hand away. Langley whimpered.

He felt nausea well up inside him. The smell of his sweat and the metallic odour of his blood filled his nostrils. His shirt was drenched in perspiration as he writhed in vain against the restraints.

'Oh Jesus, oh fuck. I'm going to bleed to death. Oh God, no.'

Kennedy wound the thin rope back around Langley's throat and tightened the grip.

'Don't fuck with me, fat man. It'll only get worse.'

He paused, looking down at his polished shoes. The fat man's wound had dripped blood onto the Italian leather. With the slightest shake of the head, he wiped his spattered shoes on Langley's trousers.

'Listen. We know you're the project manager for the state network tender at ACE Solutions. That means you have access to the project information and the R&D pipeline. Tell me where it's stored and this will soon be over.'

'I can access some of our network through a secure VPN connection from my computer here. But I don't have access here to everything,' Langley lied.

The meat cleaver whistled again, slicing through the air, severing the man's thumb at the knuckle. A sickening sound of metal ripping through flesh, tendons and bone drowned out by the fat man's screams.

Trevellion leant in again, closing his hand over Langley's mouth.

'Well, you won't be able to jerk off anymore with just three fingers. And if you don't start talking, you won't have anything to jerk off because I'll cut your dick off and fucking feed it to you.'

Trevellion removed his large hand and stood back.

'Alright, alright,' Langley's words slowed by asthmatic gasps for breath. 'All of our developmental state network and intranet projects are on a suite of secure remote servers. I can access all of it from my machine here. We don't keep hard-copy files at ACE Solutions. It's not company policy. It's part of our push to the paperless office and meeting the needs of the Freedom of Information Act.'

Sweat continued to pour down Langley's reddened face. A thin smile crossed Trevellion's.

Trevellion tapped the "On" button of the tablet computer. Within seconds, an array of software options filled the uncluttered desktop.

'Where am I going from your desktop? Via the VPN link?'

The man nodded and Trevellion noticed the duct tape across his eyes was working itself loose because of the continual sweat seeping from Langley's pores.

With a gesture to his accomplice, Kennedy slapped a fresh piece tighter across the man's eyes.

Trevellion slid his index finger across the glossy screen and tapped the VPN icon.

'User name and password?'

Langley flinched, anticipating being maimed by the meat cleaver again.

'Er, ace497#dl and home794#fv.'

Trevellion keyed in the details and the screen transitioned to display further options:

    1. Connect to ACE Solutions Email services
    2. Connect to ACE Solutions corporate LAN

Trevellion grinned, his narrowing eyes scanning the screen. Within moments of selecting the second option, the rapid VPN broadband link had connected to ACE Solutions LAN.

A fresh menu of user options appeared. In the screen's corner, the company's logo: a defined sphere, rotated with a smooth motion. Six buttons ran along the bottom of the screen.

Trevellion glided his finger over "Advanced user options" and pressed the screen.

He sighed annoyed, as a further dialogue box popped up. A cursor flashed in the centre of the screen.

'What's the PIN for "Advanced user options"?'

The fat man's resistance left him as rapidly as his finger and thumb as he divulged the password. More waves of nausea swept through him as Trevellion entered the code.

Trevellion scanned the new on-screen options:

    1. Upload information
    2. Copy information
    3. Help

The thin smile returned as he pressed the second option.

'Please specify the destination drive and directory' a further dialogue box insisted.

Trevellion's hand hovered over the on-screen keyboard. The fat man's hand continued to ooze blood that dripped onto the dark blue carpet.

Trevellion retrieved a flash drive from his jacket pocket and slid it into the USB port before turning back to Langley.

'How many files are on your LAN?' He checked the time on the antique clock above the monitor.

Langley jumped a little, stirred from momentary unconsciousness.

'I don't know. Three or four terabytes, I suppose.' The asthmatic pauses for breath were growing.

Fuck it, Trevellion thought. It wouldn't all fit on a single drive.

His focus returned to the screen; he continued to type and watch the small red light on the flash drive flicker. Less than five minutes later, the technological secrets of ACE Solutions sat on his flash drive. The entire operation had been easy. And with a couple of finishing touches, everything would go to plan.

A second flash drive completed his data theft, and he slipped the usurped information into his suit pocket.

The screen in front of Trevellion had returned to its previous options. With a wry grin, he selected the 'Upload information' option.

As the FTP application opened, Trevellion again turned to the bound man.

'OK, it's almost over now,' he said almost soothingly. 'I just need your FTP username and password for the company server.'

Langley replied, the words slow and laboured, a stream of sticky sweat sliding between his swollen lips.

Trevellion typed on the command line, smirking as he accessed the heart of the system. And the area where they would wreak most long-term havoc.

Now he'd confirmed Langley's login details, he'd pass them on to his technical specialists. From there, it wouldn't take long to wipe the server clean and render it unusable. With their skills, no one would ever retrieve the lost information. And with all the ACE Technologies' backups being destroyed in a further covert operation, it would put the company's R&D pipeline back years. Just as they'd planned.

From his jacket pocket, he pulled out a fresh flash drive, inserting it into the USB port. The irrevocable formatting and scrambling of the hard disk with a virus would suffice for Langley's computer, he thought as the drive flashed up an option on the screen.

One of his team had developed a destructive virus that ensured no one would ever retrieve data from any machine it was installed on, no matter how technologically gifted.

After clicking the "Run" option, the storage device whirred as his program disassembled the hard disk.

Trevellion rose from his seat, reached into Kennedy's holdall, and pulled out an aerosol paint can. In less than a minute, jagged, black words daubed the wall.

Fuck the Net. Reclaim the World.

His stocky colleague grinned as he stood close behind his prisoner, poised to strike if required. Trevellion looked down at the tortured man, who was shaking in his chair.

Langley sensed the strangers' attention had returned to him.

'Please don't kill me.' Tears ran down his reddened cheeks as he heard the meat cleaver slide across the surface of his desk. 'Why are you doing this? What do I have that you want?'

Trevellion paused as he studied the bloodied man.

'A piece of the future.'

Kennedy slapped another piece of duct tape over Langley's swollen lips. Trevellion smiled as his colleague raised his right arm.

The meat cleaver tore through the fat man's left wrist, severing the hand. Langley's arm shot free, flapping about, arterial spray staining the carpet. The severed hand remained attached to the armrest, the duct tape keeping it in place.

Langley howled in muffled pain; his lips split as he fought the duct tape.

Trevellion watched motionless, careful to stay out of the arcing arterial spray as the fat man's restrained body thrashed about in the chair.

One more glint of the cleaver severed Langley's other wrist with equal clinical precision.

How long does it take a man to bleed to death?

He watched as Kennedy stepped back from the dying man, the widening pool of blood spreading across the carpet.

By the time the flash drive was collected from the computer, Langley had stopped bucking in his chair. Unconsciousness had taken over.

Trevellion grinned. What a pleasant neighbourhood this was.

CHAPTER THREE

DIGGER CURLED HIS STUBBLED top lip into a grimace, snorted, and spat on the ground in disgust as he read the newspaper article. They were coming. He knew it. They all knew it. Even Moley had said so, and he wouldn't bullshit them.

The last time Moley had gone into town to get some food and supplies for the group, he'd seen it on the front page of a newspaper. And not one of the crappy tabloids, mind, which always reported alien abductions or royal bleeding rubbish no one cared about.

No, this had been one of the quality rags, always moaning about whether Britain should fuck Europe or get fucked by it.

The words of warning had spread through the camp quicker than flies on shit. The suits that were going to destroy the countryside, yet again, were coming. One more road carving its way through woods, hillside and the 'natural land' as they called it.

They'd already ploughed on through Winchester and Newbury.

Concrete monstrosities for ignorant fuckers whose only interest was to make a quick profit. If the countryside got in the way, fuck it. That was tough luck as they bled the "natural land" dry.

No more. They'd put up good fights in Winchester and Newbury. Kicked a few arses.

This time the bastards won't get their money-making way, Digger thought grimly as he ran his grubby fingers across his chin. His fists clenched and unclenched as he thought about their imminent arrival. This time, they weren't playing by the rules.

Sure, in the past the suits from the government had quoted by-law violations. They'd even re-written the Criminal Justice Act; they'd been so desperate to get rid of them. This time, it was different. The rules had gone out of the window.

What the fuck do we know about the internet, anyway? Or care about it?

Yet Moley had seen it all in that rag. Two important bastards from some rich computer companies were dead, and they were getting the rap for it.

Digger flicked open the pages of the tabloid Moley had picked, pausing on the buxom blonde on page three. His eyes burned with rage as he reached the offending page. The story wasn't just in the quality rags.

The headline read:

Anti-Net activists implicated in gruesome murders

His eyes scanned the text, coming to rest on the fourth paragraph.

In both cases, police have confirmed the murder scenes exhibited the words: 'F*** the Net, Reclaim the World.' In the killing of Colette Robertson, the words being written with the victim's blood police reveal. Detectives have said...

Digger looked up, scowling, before hurling the pages away.

It's a bleeding setup, he thought, surveying the countryside before him.

Their camp was in a forest on the edge of Brookwood Heath, a former protected site of special scientific interest with a vibrant and diverse eco-system. But that status had gone thanks to a government U-turn and chasing the pound signs UKCitizensNet would bring. Once the bulldozers came, parts of the open heathland and much of their forest would go, and countless habitats lost. His gaze moved to the camp of platforms amongst the trees, his resolve hardened.

He looked back at the newspaper and the murdered executives and scowled again. What the fuck was going on? Their agenda had sod-all to do with the internet. Sure, their war cry was 'Reclaim the World,' always had been. But 'Fuck the Net'?

This time, the suits from the government had an alternative plan to get rid of them.

At Winchester and Newbury, there'd been a fair amount of support for their cause. Who wanted a road instead of the countryside?

But if the suits pinned a brutal set of murders on them, any sympathy would soon ebb away. With no public sympathy, the pigs would have a free hand to use strong-arm tactics to get rid of Digger and his group.

He thought about the tabloid article once more, looking down from his high tree perch at the scattered pages below. They were building a link road to new headquarters for a company developing semantic web technologies.

'Digger, the bastards are coming.'

Moley's warning broke his concentration. On the horizon, he could see a gathering of vehicles heading in their direction.

Right where the fucking road would go.

Behind him, the chatter of voices and boots thudding on the ground filled the air. He watched as the rest of the group climbed the trees to their well-constructed lookouts or went down into their labyrinth of underground tunnels.

The approaching hordes were closing in; his eyes widened in surprise.

No, this is wrong.

Instead of the normal police vans, pursued by a mass of hungry hacks looking for a story, were a strict formation of army lorries, two tanks, and a long black limousine.

Where's the fucking press? Who's going to record our fight to protect the countryside?

He looked again at the procession of army vehicles. For the first time since he'd chosen the life of an environmental protester, over twenty years earlier, butterflies began in his stomach and he felt himself perspiring, his breathing becoming heavier.

The bastards could do anything to them. Without the cameras, who'd find out? The government suits could hide behind the Official Secrets Act and no one would ever know what happened.

This entire area must be pretty fucking important.

The procession of vehicles ground to a halt at the edge of the trees.

'Wankers.'

The words echoed through the dense formation of trees. It was Harmony, a veteran of conservation causes.

An officious-looking officer climbed down from one lorry and looked up at Harmony's lofty position.

'Take that bitch down first as a warning,' Digger heard the officer order.

Two further soldiers leapt from the back of the lorry. Both carried bulging rucksacks and approached the base of Harmony's tree fifty feet away. Digger squinted to see what they were doing, but the early morning sun blinded his vision.

Within a minute, the soldiers returned to their lorry, uncoiling a long length of something he couldn't quite identify. His mouth dropped as the soldier raised the detonator plunger.

'No,' Digger's word was only a whisper. 'Harmony, get off the tree, use the ropes. They're going to...'

An orange flash and a deafening explosion filled the forest. The sound of groaning and splintering wood sliced through the air. Harmony's tree swayed for a few long seconds before crashing down in front of the army congregation.

Harmony. Oh, fuck it, no. Harmony.

Digger looked down from his tree perch and into the swirling cloud of smoke hanging over the fallen tree. He couldn't see her. He couldn't see a thing. All he could see were more soldiers rushing into the smoke, punishing batons raised.

His eyes closed. He bowed his head as the dull thuds echoed through the trees.

To his left, more branches swayed and creaked under pressure. Within seconds, Moley swung onto the lofty tree perch. His cheeks were flushed, eyes brimming with tears, as he tied the rope to one of the sturdy branches and turned to face Digger.

'Harmony...' he forced the words out.

'I know. The bastards killed her.'

'Harmony,' Moley said again, shaking his head.

Digger placed a comforting arm around Moley. He wasn't the most articulate, but he was a damn good tunneller. The best.

Digger looked into his stubbled face, his eyes wide with fear, dreadlocks hanging around his chin. Behind the grimy exterior, from days in the tunnels, was a frightened young boy.

It was easy to forget Moley was only nineteen. He'd been with them for four years. A runaway and reformed intravenous drug user from Birmingham. All he wanted was to 'Reclaim the World' from a bloodsucking, poisonous establishment. Never mind all the 'Fuck the Net' bollocks. Their concern had always been the countryside.

His fists tightened once more. The scowl returned as he surveyed the scene below, fear giving way to anger.

Behind him, he could hear the startled voices of his friends amongst the trees. But what was in front of him was more concerning. Five teams of soldiers, all with the now-familiar army rucksacks, were approaching the edge of the woods. For the first time since he had chosen this life, Digger prayed.

Sebastian Tate and Vincent Trevellion sat in the soft leather seats of the black limousine. The sound of explosions and batons subduing the protestors, one by one, bounced off the reinforced glass with soft thuds.

They needed the land, and the protesters were trespassing. The most recent amendment to the Criminal Justice Act, which Dr Marcus McCoy had pushed through Parliament, gave validity to this punitive action. Not that it would ever come to light. They'd ensured the media hadn't got a whiff of the ejection.

Tate gazed through the black-tinted windows protecting their identities and smiled. This wouldn't take long, he thought, as another tree fell into the forest in a cloud of smoke.

'How useful has the new data been?'

'Very. One project the Robertson woman was working on in particular. It's filled in a few blanks in our own semantic web projects. I doubt she knew the full potential of what she had, all other things considered. I suspect SW Technologies envisaged it as some neat application for people too stupid to remember their passwords, online personal details and digital footprint. Instead, as we hoped, we're looking at a far more powerful, next-generation app. The possibilities are promising.'

Tate smiled from behind the rimless glasses, always peering over the top when someone else was speaking. Straightening his black silk tie, he considered Trevellion's information.

'And Langley's data?'

'Interesting in places. Not too much that our people didn't know, though. A couple of things to round off rough edges, one might say.'

'Good. Now we've taken care of Robertson and Langley, Phase I is complete. The sooner we get UKCitizensNet's headquarters built and the entire operation transferred to here, the better. My department has ensured maximum resources are available for the construction work. I want you based here in three months.'

Trevellion nodded as Tate pulled out his mobile to deliver an update on the protesters to Miles Winston in Whitehall.

Three months was plenty of time to have everything ready.

CHAPTER FOUR

THE DRIVER OF THE black Volvo estate floored the accelerator and pulled a dark green balaclava over his face. His passenger followed suit before removing a thick rubber baton from a canvas bag in the footwell.

The engine roared as the vehicle hurtled forward; lights switched to full beam to dazzle moments before it slammed into the back of the silver Citroen. The din of scraping metal and tyres screeching joined a fountain of orange sparks as the two cars melded together for a moment and then split apart as the Citroen veered into the right-hand lane.

With the left-hand lane now clear, the Volvo pulled up alongside the stricken Citroen, its bumper thudding on the tarmac as it hung off the back of the dented chassis. The Volvo smashed into the back of the car again with the impact of a bullet from a .44 Magnum. The force of the collision caused the Citroen to flip 180 degrees as it lost its grip on the road, rubber scorching the tarmac in a perfect arc.

For a split second, the two men in balaclavas were face to face with the opposing driver, Morgan Jones.

Jones' eyes were wide with panic, his arms a flailing blur as he wrestled the steering wheel in vain, unable to prevent the inevitable.

Brakes screeching, the Volvo ground to a halt on the quiet country road amidst a corridor of mature pine trees. The Citroen, still facing the wrong direction, had slid off the road. Perched at a precarious angle in a ditch on the opposite side, the nose of the car pointed upwards. The tangled metal from the rear embedded in the muddy bog.

Morgan Jones fought to rid himself of his seatbelt. His heart pounded in his ears, and a burning pain coursed through his back and neck from the impact of the crash. He knew what was coming.

The two men, dressed in black combat gear, emerged from the Volvo, their faces obscured by menacing balaclavas, evil intent burning in their eyes as they hauled open his car door.

The larger of the two men brought his baton down on Jones' right arm with a frightening force. Nausea welled up in him. For a moment, everything went black as unspeakable pain engulfed his body.

'On the fucking floor.' Jones fell out of the car and into the wet, muddy ditch. Prone on his back, too terrified to move, the two men stood above him, circling their prey, deciding which bones to break first.

A heavy Doc Martens boot clattered into his ribs, causing him to roll onto his side, adopting the foetal position as if this would somehow protect him. Bile rose in his throat and he was aware of one man bending down.

'I'm disappointed in you,' the guttural, threatening voice hissed. 'I would have thought after our last visit you'd have learnt your lesson and stopped poking your nose into things that are none of your fucking business. Was our last meeting in any way unclear?' A second kick hit the same ribs as before, and Jones was sure they'd broken at least one.

'Because you haven't left it alone, we're going to really hurt you this time. Don't think we're going to leave it there. We know all about your wife Margaret, and the family and children of your partners. They'd better look over their shoulders, if you know what I mean.'

Despite the searing pain in his ribs, Jones tried to sit up to protest, but a firm hand shoved him back to the ground.

'Get this straight, you dozy twat. This is your last warning. Either you leave well alone and keep your nose out of computers and the fucking internet, or being driven off the road will be the least of your worries. Do you understand me?'

Jones nodded, unable to speak from the weight pinning him to the ground.

As he looked into the eyes of his assailant through the narrow eye slits of the balaclava, he knew his ordeal wasn't over. The eyes were still full of aggression, sparkling with adrenaline, relishing the prospect of impending violence.

Jones watched, transfixed, as his attacker slipped his hand into the canvas bag his partner had been carrying. A long, thin knife with a serrated edge that caught the early evening sun paraded in front of his face, cutting the air as it moved backwards and forwards in front of his eyes.

Without warning, the man hauled Jones' arm upwards and turned his wrist as if being restrained. The second man grinned through the ragged mouth hole of his balaclava and yanked Jones' little finger outwards, almost dislocating it.

Jones' gaze followed the knife, now moved away from his face. The attacker holding the knife smiled, malice glinting in his eyes.

'Now this is going to hurt.'

Morgan Jones' eyes shot open, and the vicious memories receded. Despite his tiredness, he couldn't afford to go to sleep. Not tonight.

Hunched over his desk, a half-smoked cigarette hanging from his lips, he glanced at his computer's clock. The time was 11.34 p.m.

Twenty-six minutes left.

Jones' hand shook as it hovered over his keyboard, throbbing from where the knife had sliced through his flesh. Memories of all the pain he'd endured punctured his thoughts. A severed finger, four broken ribs and a ruptured spleen weren't injuries you forgot.

Most nights he'd wake up, his pulse racing, the darkness enveloping him, inducing the same sense of panic he'd felt when the men had restrained him before going to work on him.

Jones' gaze flitted from one part of the screen to another as he typed on the command line, the screen filling with code as he hacked deeper into one of the many government servers.

The system's security was appalling. For people like him and his three colleagues, former software engineers and security analysts, breaching the firewall was only a matter of minutes. If things had turned out differently, he might have been working for them, advising on weaknesses in their online security and how to beat the hackers. But not now.

To his right, his three partners sat at individual machines, all typing, committing any useful data they found in their searches to high-capacity flash drives. All four men were inside UK-GovNet—the government's internal network—accessing vulnerable document stores, servers, and individual computers still logged onto the network, looking for anything that could prove the imminent arrival of UKCitizensNet was a sham.

On the desk in front of him lay a well-thumbed edition of that day's *Guardian* newspaper, its headline as clear as it was stark:

Internet shutdown to begin as UKCitizensNet comes online

Jones looked at the clock again. 11.40 p.m. Just over twenty minutes away from the demise of the internet and freedom of online access and expression.

How has it come to this?

He stubbed his cigarette out in an empty coffee mug and shivered, rubbing his arms, attempting to rid his limbs of the cold and damp that seeped through the quiet, empty warehouse. A slight smell of solvents hung in the air, but the only thing it now contained were a dozen propane canisters fastened in the centre of the warehouse floor below them.

His attention moved from his screen as he peered down through the office window. The four of them had organised the canisters when they'd arrived earlier that evening, all too aware tonight was the night they'd most likely need to use them. But that was for later.

Once UKCitizensNet was up and running, they'd never be able to hack into internet sites in the same way again. The newspaper article confirmed that more robust security encryption was coming, and as skilled as the four men were, none of them knew how long it would take them to breach the system in the future.

To the right, a shorter, broader man was peering at his screen, also with a cigarette in his hand.

'Have you found the money yet, Brown?' his tone was serious, one eye on his own screen as another directory downloaded data.

John Brown frowned, taking a long drag on his cigarette before turning to face his colleague.

'No. They've frozen our separate account and the money's being drained from it. Fuck knows how they knew. There shouldn't have been any link back to us. And it's too well encrypted for me to hack into in the time we've got left to free up the money.'

The other two men, Stephen Smith and Richard Green, sitting at computers opposite, looked up.

'Then that's it, isn't it? We're fucked. They're onto us if they've shut down our account,' Green said, panic cracking his voice.

'It could be a coincidence,' Jones said with little conviction.

Somehow the masked men, whomever they worked for, had been trailing them and had discovered their discreet bank account in Geneva. It had been the only way to safeguard their resources in case of any unforeseen accidents. But now they were onto this.

Out of the corner of his eye, Jones glanced at the propane canisters on the warehouse floor below. He turned to Brown, who'd slumped back in his chair.

'Get into the CRB database and check to see if we've appeared in there. If they want to apply real leverage, the easiest way to get cooperation from all law enforcement agencies is to give us all a record. Check it out now, and bloody hurry.'

11.50 p.m.

Jones returned to his screen, searching one directory after another. His attention stopped on one area of a new server. His searching had taken him into a Defence Department directory. About halfway down the screen, he eyed a bland-looking report produced by the National e-Government Strategy Group—powerful commercial CEOs representing the UK computing industry and senior government ministers and civil servants. The report title suggested nothing more interesting than timetables for UKCitizensNet and its implementation throughout the country. He almost dismissed it as irrelevant, but at the last moment he noticed in the meta-data description of the document the name Miles Winston, the Secretary of State for Defence. Intrigued why he should have an interest in the network, he delved deeper into the Defence Department's directory.

Documents containing the names of covert operatives working in foreign countries, surveillance activities, and information collected from moles and informants scrolled past. Under different circumstances, most of this classified information would have been worth a discreet look. This evening he breezed straight past it.

He was now accessing a directory entitled "Networks," and as he waited impatiently, its contents began scrolling up on the screen. His gaze stopped on a folder named "CODEX." Casting a hasty glance at the clock, he began reading the files, hoping they contained something relevant to UKCitizensNet.

11.58 p.m.

Euphoria surged through him. Partway down the directory listing, one file stood out:

CODEX file OP09/ST—UKCitizensNet implementation and development.

Content his flash drive was secure in the USB port, he called up the PDF file, anxiety rising as it loaded.

Come on, come on. Load, damn you.

The Defence Department had issued the electronic file. The filename, also the title of the report, sat at the top of the screen.

What the hell is CODEX? And why is the Defence Department so interested in a new computer network? It doesn't add up.

The first few paragraphs stated the classified nature of the information before detailing the government's timetable for introducing the new network.

There's nothing new in this information. Why the hell is it covered by the Official Secrets Act?

11.59 p.m.

More information on the successful contractor for UKCitizensNet followed with details of key personnel. None of it seemed relevant. He could feel his frustration rising as he scrolled further into the document.

His eye caught the title of a paragraph: *Phase I—Primary Targets.* Three names featured on the page, and he began scanning the text.

Name: Colette Robertson
Position: Technical Director, SW Technologies
Skills: Semantic web technologies, financial management, broadband integration, legal and regulatory compliance
Dependants: Michael Robertson (husband); Clare Robertson (daughter)
Current personnel status: Colette Robertson (deceased), 16/9/10), Michael Robertson (active), Clare Robertson (deceased) 16/9/10)
Principal operatives: Sebastian Tate, CODEX Unit 2

Name: David Langley
Position: Technical Consultant, ACE Solutions

Before Jones could read any further, the information vanished. The same thing had happened to the other machines in the small office.

The computer clock read 12.00. Midnight.

A fresh message flashed up on all four monitors. As he read the words, he knew he'd missed his chance to save the document.

Access to the internet is no longer available in the UK. If you possess a UKCitizensNet activation code, please use this when UKCitizensNet becomes active at 9.00 a.m., 1 January 2011.

The four men looked at each other in silence. UKCitizensNet would begin in nine hours and online freedom would be no more.

Jones turned to Brown, who was now clutching a handful of papers that had just emerged from the printer.

'Did you get into the Criminal Records Bureau in time?'

Brown nodded, handing him the pile of papers.

The first sheet was a criminal record report in his name—his actual name. A surly looking mugshot and an array of personal details were at the top of the document.

Under "Arrests and Convictions" were many entries relating to electronic crimes, all in breach of the Computers Misuse Act: hacking offences, access to restricted data, and dissemination of confidential material. More alleged crimes followed relating to online extortion, identity theft, and correspondence with other criminal elements.

Brown glanced at the three other men and read the other criminal records, all lengthy and incriminating.

'There's going to be nowhere for any of us to hide now. You realise, don't you?' Brown was agitated.

Jones screwed up the printouts and tossed the paper balls towards the window behind his computer and slammed his fist on the table.

'Well, I guess that settles it. We've run out of time and I've got no proof. How many fucking hours have we spent looking for something, anything?'

The other three men shook their heads, fighting back their anger and disappointment.

'We mustn't lose our resolve now. We need to stick to the original plan. It's the only way we can safeguard our families and expose UKCitizensNet,' Jones said defiantly.

Silence met this statement as each of the men looked through the glass screen to the propane canisters below.

Brown looked defeated.

'It's odd thinking that while we're holed up here, our wives are currently leaving everything behind.'

The four men said nothing, tension creasing their faces.

'How did it come to this? It's so fucked up.'

Jones' expression was the first to harden.

'It was the only option to keep them safe. Are you all sure they've not told anyone where they were going? Not even you?' he said to the group.

Resigned nods followed the question.

'Good, because if we don't know where they've gone... If the worst happens, they can't use them as leverage against us. It's the only way.'

The implications of the sacrifices they were about to make hung heavily in the air as the men exchanged knowing looks.

With one last glance at the canisters, Jones turned back to his colleagues before pulling a small photograph of his wife from his shirt pocket. Margaret was smiling, as always. He loved that about her. She could always find the positive in every situation. How he needed her now.

Sorrow washed over him. He knew he'd never hold her again. But at least after tonight, she'd be safe—all their families would be. And for now, without the proof of the conspiracy threatening their lives, that was what mattered.

'If they know about the bank account, they'll know about this place, too. It won't be long before they get here. Gather up any information, flash drives or hard drives you've got and dispose of it as we agreed. Make sure you're back here in twenty minutes. I'll get things ready.'

Without another word, the three remaining men set about their task as the clock ticked on towards 12.20 a.m.

Jones reached into his pocket and pulled out a box of matches before heading towards the stairs that led to the warehouse below.

THE BLACK VOLVO ESTATE drifted along the access road to the desolated industrial park, its lights off as the driver searched for the warehouse. One unit after another slipped by, the premises empty apart from the odd delivery lorry with supplies for the following morning.

'Take a right up here,' the passenger said, glancing at the satnav.

After a right turn, a warehouse on the left-hand side at the far end of the road came into view, two upstairs windows illuminated. Drawing closer to the building, the silhouettes of figures passing backwards and forwards across the windows were visible.

The driver pulled into a car park of a unit halfway up the road, and the men exited their car, each holding a semi-automatic rifle. Both pulled black balaclavas over their heads before the driver pulled out an electronic device.

A schematic of the building appeared on the screen, and the men processed the building's entry points. There were two entrances, one on the far right of the building, the other on the opposite left side. A real-time infra-red satellite image of the building overlaid the schematic. Inside the boundaries of the warehouse, four red moving markers showed their targets were all present.

'You take the left entrance, I'll take the right,' the driver said, pointing at the building as they approached.

At the perimeter of the warehouse's car park, the two men separated. Before moving ten yards apart, the night sky was lit up as a searing fireball erupted from the warehouse, sending them sprawling to the ground.

Concrete and metal debris cascaded all around the car park as the two men rolled over to protect themselves from the blast. An orange and grey plume of smoke rose from where the warehouse had once been, rising into the sky as the fire raged below.

On their knees, the two men scrabbled to take cover behind a low brick wall, pushing their backs against the protective barrier as a second smaller explosion tore through what was remaining of the warehouse's aluminium structure.

'You OK?' the driver said, wiping away some of the debris from his black combat gear.

'Yeah, I think so.' He cast a look at the inferno behind them. 'What the fuck happened?'

'Beats me. The boss won't be happy, though. He doesn't like deviating from the plan. Not that it matters. No one could have survived that.'

The driver pulled his mobile from his pocket and dialled the number he needed.

'Is it done?' came the clipped, familiar voice at the end of the line.

'Yes, sir, Mr Tate, the job's complete and the warehouse destroyed... No, there are no survivors.'

CHAPTER FIVE

Michael Robertson woke in the familiar room—his cell for eighteen months.

He knew he'd be free soon. Free to return to the life he'd once had. Their words, not his.

He sat on the narrow, uncomfortable bed and ran his fingers through his untidy dark brown hair before shaking his head to purge the nightmare from his thoughts. It was the same nightmare he had every night—the moment he found Colette's mutilated body.

The duvet was on the floor at the foot of the bed. The sheets were stained crimson, with not a single spot of white remaining. Colette bound to the bed, her wrists fastened to the bedstead, her ankles taped together. Bloodied duct tape was pulled over her mouth, and a piece of rubber tubing hung from her swollen lips.

Every morning he'd wake up, cold sweat enveloping him, his heart racing until the images faded for another day.

What a joke. How can I ever return to the life I had?

They had butchered his wife in a most horrific way. And if that hadn't been bad enough, there was Clare's disappearance, and the discovery of their cat, Harry, in the back garden, bludgeoned to death.

On the night it all happened, the mother of one of Clare's friends had picked his daughter up from her ballet rehearsal, an extra session ahead of a performance at the weekend.

Michael's expression became more serious, and he frowned before exhaling, letting go of the anger. At the time all he could think of was that if the teacher hadn't organised an extra rehearsal, Clare wouldn't have been there to be taken. Maybe then she would've still been alive.

He knew this was a false hope. If she hadn't been at the rehearsal, she would've been at home with Colette, experiencing an even more unspeakable crime. As it was, the police had discovered her body in a shallow grave in woodland close to their home three days later. The cause of death was strangulation. There'd been no sexual assault or mutilations. One small thing to be thankful for, he'd convinced himself. It had been quick; a fate denied to Colette.

Since her murder he'd learnt the mother of Clare's friend, who was supposed to collect her that night, had received a phone call from a man claiming to be him, telling her he would collect his daughter. It was the reason no one had raised the alarm and why he hadn't found out she was missing until after the discovery of Colette's body.

But now was the time to return home, to what had been their family home. Two years on, he knew he was lucky he still had a house to return to. The mortgage company's patience had run out. Their Life Assurance policy hadn't been as comprehensive as he'd thought. He'd only discovered a few months earlier that both sets of parents had agreed to continue paying his mortgage until he recovered. He doubted they would've thought it would be over two years but was grateful for their help.

He scowled and clenched his fists, his muscles aching once more from the tension, as anger welled up again. There was nothing for him to return to except violent memories.

If the staff and counsellors at the care home called that freedom, they could damn well keep it.

Why hadn't they just let him die, released him from the torture of reliving what he'd seen in their bedroom?

Why, when they'd been pumping him full of sedatives and anti-depressants in his darkest hours, hadn't someone injected him with something that would have taken away the pain forever?

And why hadn't the monster who'd killed Colette and Clare taken him as well?

All these thoughts threatened to overwhelm him. He slapped himself across his left cheek. Were the staff at the care home to see him like this, they might reconsider their decision to discharge him.

Despite all the memories he would face, the thought of spending any more time here filled him with even greater dread. The atmosphere smothered him. It had done so from day one. The clinical white rooms and corridors, devoid of any personal objects or colour, and the bars on the windows to prevent the jumpers from escaping whatever trauma they'd experienced, only confirmed he hadn't been able to cope.

Who would have coped if they'd seen what I saw in our bedroom?

He clenched his eyes shut for a few lingering moments as the bloody images faded.

I'm better now. That's why I'm going home.

When he'd finished dressing, there was a knock on his door and Martin entered the small, austere room. A single bed occupied one end, with the clean lines of a Belfast sink opposite.

A saggy and faded, but comfortable tweed armchair was on one side of the bed next to a tall, but narrow pine wardrobe. Other than that, there were no ornaments, personal mementos, photographs, or pictures on the wall. Just the magnolia decor suffocating the warmth from the room. This nondescript cell was sucking the very life from Michael.

'Good morning, Michael. All set for your big day?'

Michael grunted in acknowledgement as his toothbrush entered his mouth.

Martin was a few years older than himself. Forty-three, he remembered him once saying. For all the time he'd spent in the care home, Martin had been his counsellor. At first, they'd spoken about anything but what had happened. He'd talked about his job in insurance, and then about Colette's in computing and web technologies. Details of how they'd first met, what had attracted him to her, their wedding, and the birth of Clare had helped fill the hours as he dodged the actual issues.

And for months he pushed what had happened, what he'd seen in their bedroom, to the back of his mind, the very edges of his thoughts. His denial was stubborn, and he hadn't spoken about it.

Until one Tuesday. He wasn't sure why it had been so special.

It was when he'd been ready, Martin had said.

When holding the memories back became too much, he blurted everything out in one torrential stream of consciousness. At first, it lifted a great weight from his mind. But within a few weeks, the black edges of his violent memories returned to every waking moment.

Martin had spent hour after hour for months working with him, helping him. But he always said the last step to recovery was one only he, Michael, could take. It was up to him to stay on this "lost road" or seek and find the way home.

Michael sighed, hoping this time he was on the right road.

'I'm ready,' he replied, gesturing to the suitcase sitting in the corner of the small white room.

Martin smiled. He had one of those faces that always seemed calm, on the brink of a warm smile, never troubled by anything. His tone was quiet, soothing, sometimes to the point of being soporific Michael had found. The closest comparison he could make was the contented feeling of someone who'd found religion, and whose faith seemed to have lifted their worries away.

They'd never discussed religion, so he didn't know if this assumption had any truth, or whether Martin's demeanour was just something you learnt when you trained to be a counsellor. It didn't matter. Martin had been his crutch, his support since he'd come to the care home. And without him, he knew he would still be under sedation and on suicide watch. Michael had a lot to thank him for.

'How have you been sleeping? Any recurrence of your nightmare?' Martin asked, glancing at the packed suitcase.

Michael turned away from his counsellor, supping some water from the sink as he pondered his response.

Since it had happened, sleep often eluded him. Instead, he would count each hour as it crept by through the night, every night. And when he could stay awake no longer, he never seemed to grab more than half an hour's sleep in one go. Insomnia had become a friend.

For the short time he slept, it was always the same—his recurring nightmare. Each night he rediscovered Colette, tied to their bed, butchered beyond recognition, her blood staining everything around her.

In his daily sessions with Martin, he'd always talked about the dreams, of some additional detail he'd noticed about the scene and his waking belief that he was hallucinating the entire ordeal: that Colette would be there beside him when he woke.

But she never is.

It was only after months of the same conversation and recollections with Martin that he'd realised they wouldn't discharge him, not whilst his nightmare persisted. Each day Martin noted it down, and that was putting him even further away from release.

In the end, he'd lied, telling Martin the nightmare was becoming less vivid, less frequent. And sure enough, when it "stopped" altogether, they began talking about him going home.

'I've been sleeping fine,' he lied. 'Haven't had the nightmare for months. I'd have told you if I had.'

Martin nodded; his smile constant.

'I'm glad,' he said, his gaze turning to the door. 'Are you ready?'

Michael nodded, his heart thumping at his deception as he reached for his case, his resolve never to return to this room as strong as ever.

'Let's go.'

At the bottom of the care home's grand staircase, Michael saw his parents shuffling in the foyer, looking at the floor, afraid to catch his eye. They'd promised to pick him up and take him home.

Michael's father, a man close to retirement, held out his hand, wearing a thin smile. Despite the bravado of the handshake, he knew the smile was as brittle as snow. His parents' strain was visible, despite the reassuring expressions.

Michael embraced his mother, looking into her ageing face that was trying so hard to look strong, a forced smile cracking her pale foundation.

Three of the staff who'd looked after him during his stay shuffled behind his parents, all wearing cheerful smiles.

They must have got their training, or religion, from the same place as Martin, he mused, smiling back. The four of them were the only people in the home he'd ever felt close to.

It was only Martin and the three other carers, Danny, Kate and Elizabeth, who he cared for in this pseudo-prison.

Danny, a young, athletic black man who was always working out, winked at Michael.

'We're going to miss you, mate.'

They would be the only ones, he thought with some bitterness as a surly male nurse walked by, throwing a familiar glare in his direction.

He couldn't blame him. He hadn't been a model patient. In fact, he'd been downright objectionable. He'd lost count of the number of times he'd resisted medication, hurling it across the room, demanding to be let out of his virtual cell. In the end, they'd grown tired of his antics and restrained him before pumping his arm full of anti-depressive cocktails. And despite slipping away into semi-unconsciousness whenever the drugs had taken effect, he'd never escaped from his personal hell. It was always there, lurking at the back of his mind.

If the male nurse had seen what he'd seen, what he'd witnessed in their bedroom, he'd have understood why Michael behaved as he did.

With some effort, he held back the bloody images of the past and turned back to his parents. Now wasn't the time for reflection.

He beamed a false smile. Now was the time to go home.

THE LIGHT BULB WAS still missing. Two years on and no one had replaced it, Michael thought, reaching his front door again.

He turned back to the car where his parents were sitting, and smiled in their direction, forcing the expression. They'd offered to come in with him, but he'd declined, telling them he needed to return home on his own.

The truth of it was he just wanted to be on his own. It was going to be hard enough to return to the scene of Colette's death. Trying to make small talk with his parents was something he could do without. At first, they'd tried to argue but had relented when he'd promised to ring them in a few days.

From the car, his mother and father both waved as the vehicle pulled away, leaving him alone on his front step. Martin's words rang in his ears. And Michael knew he was right.

'Only you can take the next step.'

The hallway was as he remembered it. The narrow hall table where it always had been. A few recent letters were stacked in a neat pile on the surface.

Just as Colette used to do.

Michael exhaled and was aware of an unfamiliar smell. For a few moments, his heart pounded in his ears, propelling him back to that night. He closed his eyes and concentrated, pushing the memories to the back of his mind. The smell was lavender, his mother's favourite.

Doubtless, she'd littered his house with various lavender air fresheners and potpourri. It was just like being a child again. He smiled wryly.

But in amongst the heavy smell of lavender, he was sure he could detect the slightest odour of disinfectant. The one remaining sign of what had happened in their house.

From the hall, he turned into the lounge. Dust sheets covered the furniture and, as his parents had explained, they had decorated the entire house.

New carpets. New wallpaper. And new furniture.

Although they'd never come out and said it, they'd hoped by stripping everything out of the house they could erase what had happened there. It was a kind idea, Michael thought, surveying the covered furniture.

If only it were that simple.

His apprehension rose as he retreated out of the lounge and headed for the stairs and their bedroom. The sooner he got it over with, the better. Then, maybe, he could get on with his life again.

At the top of the stairs, his breathing became more rapid as he stared at their closed bedroom door. Just as it had been the last time he'd come home.

With his heart pounding in his ears, Michael reached for the door handle. For a few long seconds, he just stood in the doorway, eyes clenched shut, unable to move.

Open your eyes and do it. She's gone. They're both gone.

Like the rest of the house, the bedroom was pristine from a fresh coat of paint. Another bowl of potpourri on the windowsill filled the room with a lavender scent. The cream colour of the bowl matched the walls and carpet and was just as bland.

Michael fought back the tears as he looked at the bed, remembering the horrific scene he'd discovered. Martin's words echoed through his mind as he admonished himself.

'Remember the good times with Colette. Remember the beautiful woman you fell in love with.'

He sat on the side of the bed and slid open a bedside drawer. A wooden picture frame was face down, and he couldn't stop himself from reaching for it.

The three of them were on a sandy beach in the Bahamas. Clare was smiling and laughing as she buried daddy further into the sand. Colette was standing behind them in her bikini, her dark brown hair blowing in the warm, gentle breeze. The most radiant woman on the beach.

'These images will save you. The violent ones will only destroy you.'

Michael clutched the picture frame to his chest and the first tears rolled down his reddened cheeks.

They'd taken everything from him.

CHAPTER SIX

2 August 2000

FIRST DATES WERE ALWAYS the worst. Everyone knew it. Excitement and apprehension all rolled into one. An emotional rollercoaster: you never knew whether you were going to be talking all night or hoping you could make your excuses because of some invented crisis after an hour.

Michael exhaled, and looking at his watch for the fourth time in the last two minutes, realised he didn't have a 'crisis' thought up should the need arise. Sighing, he knew he didn't understand the niceties of the dating game. He just hoped the same was true of Colette Matthews.

As her name crossed his mind, he felt the butterflies flutter in his stomach again. Butterflies for why this beautiful woman had agreed to go on a date with him. And butterflies over whether she'd turn up at all.

They'd been quite drunk when they'd met at a mutual friend's party the previous weekend. Maybe in the waking moments of her hangover the following morning, she'd realised her mistake, cursing her drunken stupidity of a date the following week.

It wouldn't be the first time he'd been stood up, he thought with a frown as the time moved on to 7.40 p.m. She was ten minutes late.

He closed his eyes for a moment, rubbing away the tiredness of another tedious day in insurance, and remembered what had attracted him to her. She'd been perfect. From the allure of subtle Chanel perfume and her sharp and articulate mind to the long, cascading dark brown hair that fell just below her shoulders.

In the four days since they'd first met, he still couldn't escape one inevitable question: why hadn't someone else snapped her up?

In contrast, the same question for him seemed far easier to answer. His last girlfriend had told him in no uncertain terms that he was too stubborn and possessive. He'd never quite been able to reconcile her exact description—clingy. In his mind, this just meant wanting to take care of her. Not to hide her away from friends and other potential suitors, as she'd implied.

It hadn't been working for a while, and maybe it was just an easy tag to use. But somewhere deep down, he worried whether she was right. Was he too clingy? And if so, would Colette Matthews see that in him? Would it put her off?

That was if she ever turned up. He sighed, looking around the quiet pub. Wednesdays were never busy in the Crown in Hersham. Just a handful of regulars propped up at the bar, wearing out the same bar seat year after year. Exchanging old anecdotes with the landlord as he wiped the damp bar top.

Michael took the last gulp from his half-pint of bitter and got up from his chair as the clock ticked onto 7.45 p.m. Second thoughts had won out, he decided, nodding thanks to the landlord as he headed for the exit.

As he reached the door, it swung inwards. A tall woman in her late twenties stood in the doorway, rain dripping off her long hair. Michael looked into Colette Matthew's large brown eyes, a look of concern glinting through a relieved smile.

'I'm so sorry I'm late,' she said, closing the door behind her, brushing the rain from her beige coat. 'The traffic was murder coming out of Guildford. I think there was an accident on the Hog's Back because of the rain, so there was gridlock.'

Michael took a step back and smiled, thrilled that she'd kept their date, but conscious not to seem too pleased. Not too "clingy".

I'm useless at this, he thought as Colette looked at him; her smile dropping.

'You weren't going, were you?'

Michael shuffled backwards, looking at the floor.

'Er, well, yes, I was. I thought you'd stood me up,' Michael said with some embarrassment. 'It wouldn't be the first time it's happened to me. I thought maybe you'd changed your mind. We were quite drunk at Gary's party.'

Colette touched Michael on the arm, her large brown eyes reflecting the smile beaming on her lips.

'Don't be silly. I wanted to see you again. You were by far the most interesting person there. It would have been a pretty poor party if you hadn't been there.'

Michael could feel the butterflies in his stomach dance again, the exhilaration. She was beautiful, and she found him interesting.

After buying the drinks, a pint of bitter for him and a white wine spritzer for Colette, the two of them sat at a low table in front of an open fire. The minutes seemed to fly by as they whistled through the small talk first, getting used to each other's company, before sharing sto-

ries about their mutual friends and the circumstances through which they'd met.

Gary, a colleague of Michael at the insurance firm, had been celebrating his birthday. Michael knew from experience that this always involved copious amounts of alcohol and food. On most occasions, Gary's parties were one of the social highlights of the year. But this party had been flat. The rumour going around was that Gary had been having an affair and that his wife had just found out. If it was true, they were both surprised Gary's wife, Linda, had agreed to the party. Never mind act as hostess. Maybe it was all just scurrilous gossip after all. Gary hadn't confided such a secret to him. But they both agreed there had been a definite atmosphere.

Amid this awkwardness, Michael had met Colette, invited by one of Linda's friends, Liz, whom she worked with. In Gary's back garden, next to a smoking barbecue, they'd got chatting. And here they were now, four days later, still talking.

'Come on then, I've got to ask,' Colette smiled wickedly. 'The question everyone dreads on a first date. Why are you still single? I must admit you surprised me when you invited me for a drink. I felt sure you must have had a girlfriend stored away somewhere.'

Michael smiled in slight embarrassment at Colette's forwardness.

'Well, I was seeing someone until last summer. We'd been together for four years. It was a long-distance relationship as I was living and working down here. She was working in Manchester, so we only saw each other on weekends. The crunch came when I suggested maybe I should look for a job up North and that we consider moving in together. Let's just say the prospect of that made her reconsider her options and us. Not long after we split.'

Colette nodded, sipping her white wine spritzer.

'Do you think she was seeing someone else up there?' she said, putting the glass down on the table.

Michael raised an involuntary eyebrow, surprised at the directness of the question. Colette read his expression and leant forward.

'Oops, I'm sorry. One of my biggest faults, as my last boyfriend liked to remind me, is that sometimes I can be a bit too direct. I hope you're not offended. It can be useful when I'm at work. But sometimes I think I should leave it there.'

Michael grinned broadly as he looked into her face, her light skin contrasting with the darkness of her hair, which she'd pushed back behind her ears. Despite all his male urges telling him to do so, he kept his gaze on her face, resisting the temptation to peer into her cleavage, which was on display since she'd leant in.

'No, it's OK. It's a fair question. I don't think so. But who knows? She never gave me any reason to think so.'

Colette leaned back in her chair.

'I'm pleased. The only reason I ask is that my previous boyfriend was seeing someone behind my back. He always denied it. But I knew. The woman always does. It was over once I realised. I can put up with a lot of things, but I can't stand secrecy. I think I could have almost forgiven the affair. At least that's what I told myself in more charitable moments. It was the secrets I couldn't stand. I've always felt like that about things.'

Michael became worried: had the conversation veered into failed relationships? At least they seemed on a similar footing relationship-wise, he thought, looking into her deep-brown eyes. In his mind, he traced an imaginary line down her pale skin from her eyes to her mouth. He watched her lips as she spoke, wondering whether he'd ever kiss them.

He snapped himself out of his silent appreciation and moved the subject onto something else.

'So, tell me a bit more about your job. At the party you said it was something to do with computers. I must be honest; I can't remember much more than that.'

Colette laughed, fiddling with her hair as she leant in again.

'That's OK. Not even my oldest friends understand what I do. I'm a project manager for a company called SW Technologies, or Semantic Web Technologies if you want it in full. We develop software and hardware that uses semantic web technologies.'

Michael tried to take it all in, but his expression couldn't hide his lack of understanding.

Colette smiled, holding his gaze for a few moments.

'OK, the simple version is that the semantic web applies intelligence to information that you can read and share, for example, via social networking tools on the internet. Long term, this means things like web pages, applications and databases will link more intuitively, allowing for better and more useful and personalised information to be made available to web users. It's an exciting area. One that is going to change a lot in the coming years. And if this new guy, Marcus McCoy, ever becomes Prime Minister, then things are going to change. We can say goodbye to the internet as we know it, as he'll ban it if you believe what you read.'

Michael nodded, reaching for his pint. The new leader of the opposition, Dr Marcus McCoy, had been all over the news for weeks. Since his victory, he'd started hinting at what his manifesto pledges were likely to be. Top of the list was banning access to the internet because of the increasing level of illegal sites popping up everywhere, and the surge of terrorist cells using the web to recruit members. Tomorrow's suicide bombers.

There was logic in the pledge, but no detail about how to replace it. Just the findings of a political think tank recommending an overhaul of online access in the UK.

'It makes insurance brokering sound very dull in comparison,' he said, sipping from his glass.

Colette laughed, pushing her hair back behind her ears again.

'Well, maybe. But we all need insurance, don't we?'

'Yes, I suppose so. At least I understand the world of insurance. I'm ashamed to say computers and the internet are a bit of a mystery to me.'

'I'll have to teach you then.' For a lingering moment, they held each other's gaze, both processing the commitment beyond the first date she'd just made.

'Would you like another drink?' Michael said, breaking the moment.

'Just tonic water.' Colette reached for her handbag, before adding, 'I'll be back in a minute.'

Michael approached the bar, watching Colette as she headed for the toilet. His gaze traced a line up her legs as he took in her full figure. Smiling, he turned to the barman, confident this wouldn't be their last date.

CHAPTER SEVEN

THE SCREEN FLICKERED FOR a moment and snapped into life. Michael sat in his chair, the instruction manual in his lap. The TV had been a coming home present from both sets of parents. Their old TV had been on the blink for months before Colette had been...

He stopped himself going down that road again and picked up the manual.

It was a nice thought. But this was no ordinary TV, as the manual was at pains to point out. This was eCitTV. In fact, halfway through the manual, Michael realised he'd only read the word TV once, and that was on the cover. The rest of the guide promoted the benefits of "content" and "integration" and, of course, the 5GSW platform. Michael read from the page open in his lap:

After your 5GSW device connects, and you have registered your details and interests, customised content will download to your secure personal device portal.

Michael frowned at the alien language: *5GSW, downloading, personal device portal.* It was clear using TV in the product name and the cover of the manual was only to provide something recognisable and less intimidating for the digitally uninitiated like himself. He could handle the concept of TV, even digital TV channels, but *personal device portals* and *customised content* rather than channels all seemed too much. None of this had been possible before Colette's death and his stay in the care home.

Michael looked at the slimline flat screen, reading the large white lettering that appeared.

> **Please enter your IP address and registration serial code.**

He looked at the screen with a quizzical look.

What the hell is an IP address?

Halfway down the second page of the manual, he found both.

He'd always been one of those annoying people who wanted to know and understand everything. He'd been a child who had always asked one more question than anyone else. Even when the teacher had exhausted their explanation, he would always be the one dissenting voice.

But why does it do that?

What does that mean?

Several paragraphs later in the manual, he found what he was after.

Consider the IP address as your Intranet telephone number. This, for example, allows web pages and email to know where to go.

He frowned a little, frustrated at how vague and patronising the explanation was. Turning back to the IP address and serial code, Michael reached for the sophisticated glossy black control panel that accompanied the TV.

Before *it* had happened, there had been remote controls. That had all changed. The remote was now a hi-tech, all-purpose, eCitTV control panel. The black console resembled a tablet computer with elegant curves at the edges and a responsive screen that you just had to stroke to get the desired response. A number pad on the screen was where the content selection was to be made.

Above the alphabet keys were further buttons which read: "Web," "Email," "Music," "Video," "Social Networking," "Shopping" and "Your Money."

Was "TV programmes" under "Video?" he wondered, confused.

From instinct rather than confidence, he pointed the control panel at the screen and keyed in his eight-digit IP address and registration serial code. The black screen flickered again, and the message changed.

Please complete the following details to initialise your UKCitizensNet email set-up.

Further boxes appeared on the screen asking for the number of users connecting to UKCitizensNet, their full names, and National Insurance numbers.

With a tap on the "Enter" key on the console, Michael watched as his details vanished from the screen. The screen went blank.

Great, the damn thing's not working.

He flicked through the instruction manual for the Troubleshooting section. But before he could find the page, the screen sprang to life.

> Hello and welcome to UKCitizensNet, the UK's new online network. The network by and for the people of this country, brought to you via eCitTV.

Michael looked up to see the smiling face of a woman dressed in a smart business suit. Long, dark hair framed her young, tanned features. Behind her was a wall of screens. A kaleidoscope of the UKCitizensNet logo and various channels pumping out their 24-hour content. The smiling woman continued.

> You have entered the age of integrated, fifth-generation semantic web-enabled online digital entertainment. Come with us and discover how you can take advantage of what UKCitizensNet offers you.

The woman paused; her smile unaltered.

> Please be ready to take down the email addresses of everyone you have registered with us.

Still smiling into the camera, and with no discernible break in the promotional announcement, she revealed Michael's UKCitizensNet email address.

> Thank you, Michael Robertson. Your UKCitizensNet email address is mrobertson@ser56.ecit.

Michael's jaw dropped as he scribbled down the address as it scrolled along the bottom of the screen.

That was pretty clever, he thought, putting his pen down. How on earth could the woman in this pre-recorded video know his name? Say his name? And then add it to a new email address?

But then there was a lot he didn't understand about the wonders of digital and online technologies. Or this recent phenomenon that seemed to be everywhere—fifth-generation semantic web, or 5GSW for short.

At the bottom of the screen, two further options appeared: "Learn more about UKCitizensNet" and "Select content channel."

By now, UKCitizensNet had his attention. In his mind, he couldn't be sure whether it was loyalty to Colette as her work had been internet related. Or maybe it was sheer wonder at new technology?

Without even considering, he opted to learn more about UKCitizensNet and the smiling woman reappeared on the screen.

> Welcome to the next part of your virtual tour around UKCitizensNet, funded by UK taxpayers' money, and developed by UK company Sem-ComNet on the national 5GSW platform. UKCitizensNet bridges the multimedia divide by offering all the country's favourite content channels with integrated semantic web facilities. No longer is online technology only the domain of computer specialists; eCitTV breaks down the technological barriers and offers the easiest medium for receiving content and integrated UKCitizensNet information.

The smiling woman's image faded and her almost hypnotic voice continued as archived footage of the BBC's Six O'clock news appeared on the screen.

> With UKCitizensNet and eCitTV we transform the way you receive your content, whether it's news, films, music, games or social networking. When watching any programme, pressing the 'Web' button on your control panel will bring up the UKCitizensNet toolbar at the bottom of your screen. From here, you can access further information about the news, see more pictures,

or link to previous reports on the same subject. By pressing the "Email" button on your control panel, you can contact the BBC, request further information, or air your opinions on one of the many social networks UKCitizensNet offers. All while, the original broadcast is still taking place. Available at the touch of a button.

The woman continued her smooth monologue, and the pictures changed, an array of smiling users typing emails, sharing links and commenting on social networks flashed by.

Michael attempted to absorb the implications of the new technology as the smiling woman's tone lightened.

Once you've finished checking the latest news headlines, why not sit back and watch your favourite film? eCitTV's many film channels, categorised by style, and with semantic integration with UKCitizensNet, offer the most interactive cinematic experience. Whether you want a romance, action, historical, thriller, comedy or children's film channel, UKCitizensNet's web-based information is always available. Just press the "Web" button on your control panel. The UKCitizensNet toolbar can then lead you on a tour of filmographies of the actors involved, clips from their other films, reviews from acclaimed film critics and links to other relevant websites on UKCitizensNet.

Again, the woman's face melted away to be replaced by clips from *Star Wars III*. The toolbar blinked at the foot of the screen as an imaginary user searched for a filmography before downloading a ten-second clip from *The Empire Strikes Back*.

Michael sighed and then scowled. All the talk of 5GSW technologies and 'semantic integration' just reminded him of how isolated he'd been the last two years. He didn't understand it, and that irritated and frustrated him.

He pushed the thought away and watched as the woman's focus changed to the network's online content.

> By pressing and holding the "Web" button on your control panel, you can jump from the dual interaction of eCitTV onto UKCitizensNet. A sprawling universe of exciting websites, blogging facilities, social networking services, shared video streaming and email services are at your fingertips. All sites and services are safe and approved thanks to our simple content and age rating system. Now you can surf with confidence and security. UKCitizensNet transforms the delivery of important everyday information for everyone, thanks to our 5G semantic web technologies.

Before Michael could take in all the information, a box in the top right corner of the screen appeared. The annoying UKCitizensNet representative bleated on.

From the UKCitizensNet homepage, you can control your entire life. By selecting our news content icon, you can order daily, national or regional news feeds straight to your personal portal. Your email will display your favourite news content through the UKCitizensNet browser on eCitTV.

Using the newest and most secure encryption, you can operate all your financial transactions safely through UKCitizensNet. Manage your mortgage, all national and local taxes, utilities, insurance and other bills securely via your UKCitizensNet email with no logging into third-party sites. All national banks, insurers, and businesses are part of UKCitizensNet's Financial Services Alliance; management of your money has never been easier. With your personal banking information available at the touch of the button, UKCitizensNet offers you a complete online financial service.

Michael had heard enough.

He pressed the "Video" button on the control panel, and the smiling woman vanished. BBC daytime content invaded the screen.

A smarmy game-show host with a fake tan was attempting to extract embarrassing secrets from a nervous-looking woman. The next channel showed manic chefs cracking jokes instead of eggs.

On another channel, a bad Australian actor was apparently failing at his marriage. Then came the news, archived sport, a futuristic cartoon, adverts, arrogant presenters, boring financial analysis, and trashy American soap operas with canned laughter.

How many of these awful content channels are there?

Before he could find out, the noise of the letterbox and a dull thud distracted him. At least some things were still normal and hadn't sucked into UKCitizensNet he figured.

The post comprised a glossy double-glazing brochure, an AA membership renewal form, even though his membership had expired eighteen months ago, and a letter. Only the letter didn't find its way to the bin.

The family solicitor conveyed his sincerest condolences. But then who hadn't? He was writing to discuss the contents of the will.

Michael already knew Colette had left most of her estate to him, with a few items left to her parents, sister, and other remaining relatives. Out of respect for him, those named in the will had agreed not to claim anything until he had fully recovered, as his solicitor had put it.

Fully recovered?

Not after what he'd seen.

Michael looked up from the depressing letter and his eyes widened a little as he looked at the smooth blank screen of his eCitTV set. The bottom of the screen was changing from its sharp, defined black edge to a blurred red colour.

Inside the screen, something was bubbling, boiling almost.

Michael's heart missed a beat. A cold sweat enveloped him, and his pulse quickened. The vicious red tide lapped against the inside of the glass screen. His jaw dropped as the ebbing mass withdrew from the screen like a wave moving out to sea. Then, with thunderous ferocity, the bloody tide exploded out through the screen as if it were as brittle as matchwood. The blast cascaded into Michael, whipping up the chair, sending it soaring backwards. Warm blood streaked across his body. Glass splinters tore at his face. Shards of glass embedded in his skin like an overused pincushion.

The back of the blood-drenched chair crashed into the wall. He heard glass crack and his eyelids shot open. There was no blood, and he was where he should have been, in his armchair. To his left, the eCitTV control was lying face down on the expensive glass coffee table, two yawning cracks running in opposite directions.

He frowned, inspecting the damage.

But as he leant over, gleaming globules of sweat dripped from his forehead, spreading on the cracked glass. For a brief instant, the eCitTV set was bubbling red again. He was reliving the nightmare that tormented him every night, as his heart pounded like a hammer in his chest.

Every night, it was the same.

Climbing the stairs.

Opening their bedroom door.

Colette tied to the bed.

Blood staining everything.

Nausea.

Clare.

At least he knew when he woke each morning that it had been a dream. But this was the first time he'd faced such an experience—a hallucination—whilst awake.

He took a deep breath, pushed his chest out as far as it would go, and exhaled. The words "fully recovered" reverberated around in his head.

He would see his solicitor as soon as possible.

CHAPTER EIGHT

THE FADED GREEN BOX file sat on the dining room table. Michael just stared at it, scratching his chin. He thought he knew everything about her. They had no secrets.

He'd been wrong.

He didn't know the box file existed. And he didn't know about the Post Office box either.

His visit to the solicitors had been pretty routine to start with. As he'd expected, they'd all been shocked and deeply saddened by Colette and Clare's deaths. His expression hardened and his forehead creased with tension.

Well, they would, wouldn't they? Gives you a bit more to do. A few more clients to bill.

There had been no major surprises in the will. Most of Colette's estate went to him. Although, some of it would have gone to Clare if she'd still been alive.

Her parents, sister, and some distant cousins had received family items of sentimental value. There were no surprises.

Not until the solicitor handed him the Post Office key that was with the will for safekeeping.

He could still see the embarrassed surprise etched on the solicitor's face. He wondered how many other times unexpected benefactors received an item they didn't know existed.

Michael touched the top of the box. It was comforting to know that Colette had once handled it. One of the few things left in the house she would have touched, he thought, gazing through the ornate patio doors onto the tidy lawn.

Since the parents had re-decorated and re-furnished, everything was new, untouched by Colette and Clare. He didn't know what was worse—knowing their presence wasn't there or having all the memories to remind him.

He looked around the pristine room and frowned. It was all too new. It no longer seemed like his home anymore. Without a second thought, he flicked the box file open, unsure what it might contain.

Or what it would reveal.

In the Post Office, when he first discovered the box file, he'd clung to the hope that maybe it contained clues to find their killers. But then reality struck. How would Colette have known someone wanted to kill her, to kill Clare? Unless there was something more sinister that he didn't know about.

No, he knew Colette. He would have sensed if she'd been keeping something important hidden from him.

The box file sat on the table. He hadn't known about that.

With shaking hands, he pulled the open box file towards him. His gaze rested on a stack of papers sealed by transparent plastic wallets. With reverential care, he picked up the bundle and read the titles of each set of documents.

"State Network Tender," "Intranet Development Plan," "fifth Generation Semantic Web," "Advanced App development," "Cookies" and "Data Storage Devices."

State Network Tender.

For several moments, he stared at the plastic wallet, re-reading the title. Sordid newspaper headlines came rushing back to him.

Computer company executives slain.
Green activists blamed for brutal double murder.

The familiar numbness when reminded of their murders engulfed him. He closed his eyes to fight back the dark shadows of his subconscious.

Michael rose and, clasping the plastic folder tight to his chest, crossed over to the eCitTV set. As the picture snapped into life, he slumped into the dark blue armchair. The new furniture was not to his taste.

As daytime content smothered the screen, he reached for the control panel.

Let's see just how useful and informative eCitTV can be. If Colette helped to develop this technology, it must be pretty damn good.

With a tap of the "Web" button on the console screen, the familiar UKCitizensNet toolbar appeared, clinging to the bottom of the screen. Pressing the 'Search' icon, the pictures vanished as the red, white and blue logo appeared on a fresh page.

He typed, his fingers perspiring.

Colette AND Clare Robertson

Within an instant, the search was complete, and the screen blinked again. A pale-grey screen advertising various information channels on UKCitizensNet slid down the right side.

Your search has returned 231 matches for "Colette AND Clare Robertson"

.

The information came in sections. On the left was an ordered list of 'Topic folders,' and as he scanned the titles, he ignored the mixture of emotions seeping through his body.

Robertson case

Police investigations

Anti-net campaigners

The right of the screen presented the entire depressing list of the 231 news articles on the murders. All the grisly facts and theories, preserved for posterity somewhere in the depths of cyberspace. Or at least in the depths of UKCitizensNet.
One article stabbed at his consciousness as he read the title.

Green activists implicated in double murder.

The small cursor hovered over the link. Within seconds, the news story from the *Independent Online* filled the screen. To the right was a picture of the front of their house. Police tape cordoned off access, preventing the hungry hacks from absorbing the horror beyond.

Michael read the painful text, his mouth getting drier with every word. He'd selected this story because he knew he couldn't face the crass sensationalism of one of the online tabloids.

The tone of the *Independent*'s news coverage was far more sombre, and a smiling photo of Colette and Clare taken on their last holiday to St. Tropez accompanied the piece. Michael didn't know how they'd got hold of the picture. He hadn't provided it to the press.

The ongoing investigation into the murders of Colette and Clare Robertson in Hersham took a new twist yesterday. Forensic details released by Surrey Police have revealed the discovery of fingerprints other than the victims at the crime scene.

Forensic experts have also taken samples of a distinctive soil type exhibiting particular pH levels and nutrient contents only found in certain parts of Surrey owing to historic farming methods once used in the area.

As part of a widening investigation, Surrey Police are keen to speak to Green activists who have been protesting at the proposed destruction of local woodland in nearby Brookwood. The site is to become the headquarters for UK company SemComNet which secured the tender for the new national state network. Colette Robertson, before her murder, worked for a rival company, SW Technologies, which had also bid for the same contract. Surrey Police have confirmed that a set of fingerprints found at the crime scene belong to a known Green activist, arrested for many public order offences in the past. Although refusing to name their suspect at this stage, a warrant is out for his arrest.

Michael's gaze dropped to the smiling faces of Colette and Clare. In his mind, he heard their laughter as pleasant, sun-drenched memories of their holiday came flooding back. When they ebbed away, Michael re-read the date at the top of the screen. It was well over two years since the warrant and still, they hadn't caught the butcher. He shook his head, feeling tears well up again. As they rolled down his cheek, he steered the cursor to a link at the foot of the article: 'Related stories.'

With one click, the screen blinked, and more macabre reminders appeared. The endless stream of news coverage careered off the bottom of the screen.

He scanned the words without registering their meaning.

Why am I torturing myself like this?

His gaze fell on one headline:

Profile of police suspect

The screen changed again. A mugshot of a man taken at a road-building protest at Twyford Down near Winchester some years before appeared. The protest had been about the motorway carving its path through the hills at Twyford Down. To the right of the picture was a history of the man Surrey Police had provided to the media.

> Name: David (Davey) Wilkes
> Also known as Digger
> Age: c. 40
> Qualifications: 1 O-Level – Woodwork
> Job history: none
> Political affiliations: environmental activist and campaigner – known involvement with environmental protests at road developments at Newbury, Winchester and Leytonstone
> Previous convictions: multiple arrests for disturbance of the peace, affray and grievous bodily harm
> Custodial sentences: three

Michael held his head and winced. The air in his lungs felt as if it was being sucked away by an oppressive force as he exhaled.

Davey Wilkes. Digger. Davey Wilkes.

The name thrashed about in the confines of his mind. The monster had killed his wife and daughter and the police still hadn't caught him.

He slumped back in his chair, sighing, Colette's folder in his lap.

"State Network Tender."

His forehead creased.

Only a few of the articles he'd forced himself to read referred to her company's work in bidding for the State Network Tender.

That was, after all, the brainchild of the Prime Minister; the project Colette had taken the lead on and spent so many hours working on before her death. Hadn't that been Digger's motive? The same reason for David Langley's murder. As his thoughts wandered, his gaze fell back on the police profile of Digger.

Qualifications: 1 O-Level–Woodwork.

When his anger receded, he flicked through Colette's folders. There were pages and pages of technical diagrams. Intricate samples of computer code and other incomprehensible information.

Would a man with little education have the technical knowledge to render Colette's computer unusable, and steal encrypted information? Wouldn't a hefty Doc Martens boot or a hammer through the hard disk have been sufficient? And what could Digger use any information he'd stolen for?

Michael looked at the page again. He didn't even understand it. He scoured the other articles. Some of the news feed and content sources mulled over the possibility of an accomplice. Two headlines leapt off the screen at him:

Police seek second suspect in Hersham blood-bath case.

Robertson murder case investigates possibility
of an accomplice.

Despite the hypotheses, nowhere in the abundance of coverage was a suspect profile to support this, as with Digger.

He stopped browsing the news archive and gathered his thoughts, analysing all he'd read. Green activists, and especially Digger, were the suspects in the murder of David Langley, IT Director at ACE Solutions, and the attempted murder of Vincent Trevellion, Vice President at SemComNet.

But there was no mention of the theft of any information from them. Not that he could prove that was the case with Colette.

He rubbed his eyes, overcome by tiredness. He couldn't get away from that nagging doubt that Green activists angry at technology would have ransacked a computer, and not out a meticulous format of the hard disk. It just didn't ring true.

Anxiety now consumed him; he closed his eyes and tried to slow his breathing. Was his paranoia inventing conspiracy theories? Wouldn't it just be easier to accept, like everyone else had, including the police, that Digger and maybe an accomplice had butchered his wife and daughter?

But it ran deeper than that, much deeper. He didn't just need to know who had killed them, although it was his mission to find them. He needed to know *why* for his sanity: to bury his demons.

On the screen, the UKCitizensNet logo emblazoned in the top left corner. His gaze rested on one name. He needed to see Vincent Trevellion.

CHAPTER NINE

THE TELEPHONE CONVERSATION WAS brief.

'I'd like to see Mr Vincent Trevellion, please.'

'I'm sorry, Mr Trevellion is unavailable at the moment.'

'Can I make an appointment?'

'He's a very busy man. Can I ask what it's about?'

'It's very important and personal. I don't wish to discuss this over the phone.'

'I'm sorry, but without the details, I cannot arrange a meeting. I'm sure you understand.'

'No, you don't understand. I have to see Vincent Trevellion. Tell him Michael Robertson wishes to see him, Colette Robertson's husband.'

Long pause.

Distant sounds of a man and woman's voices talking in the background.

'Would two o'clock on Tuesday be acceptable?'

'That will be fine, thank you.'

IT WAS LIKE ENTERING a secret government project where knowledge was on a need-to-know basis, Michael thought as the burly, unsmiling security guard waved him through the mechanical gate. In the car's rear-view mirror, he watched the security gate descend, sealing off SemComNet's headquarters once more.

The road carved its way through the countryside like a snake gliding through long grass. In front of Michael, sprawling woodland cascaded down either side of a small hill as far as the eye could see. The road cut straight through the middle of the thick woods, over the top of the hill and beyond, the trees enveloping him, forming a natural tunnel where the long branches met.

On the other side of the peaceful woods, SemComNet's headquarters soon came into view. He glanced at his dashboard; the time was a quarter to two. Parking close to the main entrance, he took a deep breath, closing his eyes, fearing the pain of what was to come.

Michael got out of the car and studied the building before him. A tall, imposing structure, looking more like a greenhouse than a place of work. SemComNet's headquarters were impressive.

The modern building, whose construction had caused such controversy because of the protected heathland and forest removed to accommodate it, glinted in the sunlight. A grid of tinted glass wrapped its entire width. A distinctive atrium ran through the centre of the building, adding to its splendour, providing the way in.

At the foot of the atrium, a set of marble steps led up to revolving doors.

Inside the building, he approached the main reception where the attractive blonde receptionist pointed him in the lift's direction. No sooner had the doors snapped shut than he seemed to be on the third floor. Trevellion's office was at the end of the corridor.

Vincent Trevellion's secretary was just as he had envisaged: stern-looking, her jet-black hair tied back in an austere ponytail. The metallic name badge on the desk read: Mrs Margaret Martin.

Quite a beautiful woman, although a smile would have helped, he thought, with little interest.

His thoughts about Mrs Martin faded as the door to Vincent Trevellion's office clicked open. The apprehension in his stomach rose to the back of his throat as a tall figure approached him. Michael stood and shook the welcoming hand. For a few seconds, there was an awkward silence. Hands locked. Gazes fixed.

'Thank you for seeing me,' he said, struggling to get the words out.

Trevellion seemed to smile in response, although his eyes remained free of emotion, and Michael was sure his lower lip never moved.

'It's good to meet you, Mr Robertson,' came the clipped reply.

Michael followed him into the office, noticing the plaque on the office door.

"Vincent Trevellion, Vice President"

Michael sat in the black leather-bound chair in front of the desk. It was like being sent to the head teacher's office to receive a punishment. He only felt about three-foot tall as he looked at the files and arranged paperwork on the desk. An impressive-looking computer with a slim black monitor sat on one corner of the surface. Trevellion's leather chair pointed in his direction.

An ornate globe in a corner caught his attention. A secret drinks cabinet, he wondered, or just an expensive ornament? Several paintings hung on the cream walls. He knew little about art, but if the rest of the building was anything to go by, they would be originals. And if he wasn't mistaken, Trevellion was wearing a crisp Armani suit that locked as if today was its first outing.

He licked his lips, unsure why he was so nervous of Trevellion.

'Coffee?' Trevellion asked from the table that ran against the adjacent wall.

His words were quiet but uttered with the assured manner of the strictest general.

Michael nodded, watching as he poured the coffee into a bone china cup. He wished Trevellion would just sit down so he could begin talking and find out what he knew about Colette and Clare's deaths. He didn't oblige. As Michael opened his mouth to speak, Trevellion eased himself into his chair, lifting his cup to his lips.

Michael estimated he was end thirty. Although, the trimmed goatee may have added a few years. He seemed quite young to hold such a senior position in a major blue-chip company.

'So, what can I do for you?' Trevellion asked, breaking the uneasy silence. A thin smile passed over his lips.

Michael shuffled in his chair.

'I was hoping you could shed some light on the deaths of my wife and daughter.'

Trevellion's authoritative, detached expression remained unaltered.

'Er... I mean, I was wondering if there was anything else, anything at all you might know which would help me better understand why they are dead.'

He felt himself choke, and forced back tears, stopping for a moment to regain his composure.

'Just something the police might not have told me.'

This time, he couldn't fight back his emotion. The tears streamed down his cheeks.

Trevellion slid open his desk drawer, pulled out a handkerchief, his initials sewn in one corner, and handed it to Michael. He rose from his chair and placed a hand on his shoulder.

'Just take your time.'

When Michael had regained his composure, Trevellion spoke.

'I'll tell you what I know, Mr Robertson. Whether it's of any use, well, I don't know.'

He paused, the few lines on his face tightening.

'Three years ago, the government put out a tender for the development, establishment and maintenance of our online state network. The only three companies with the relevant experience, R&D pipelines, and sufficient knowledge to make bids were SemCom-Net, ACE Solutions, and SW Technologies. However, a series of militant Green, anti-net activists began protesting when the plans became public. At SemComNet, we began receiving threatening letters. Staff faced abuse and intimidation. Objectionable items such as mobile devices and flash drives smeared in faeces sent to colleagues were a regular occurrence. It seems not everyone is in favour of technological advancement. Some have to be dragged kicking and screaming into the future. But as we know to our cost, it didn't stop there. People died in the name of the anti-net campaign.'

Trevellion paused and looked Michael in the face, his gaze boring into his own.

'One of them attacked me at home with a machete.'

Trevellion rolled up his sleeve, revealing a well-toned shoulder. Michael's gaze traced the line of the inch-thick scar that ran from just below the elbow to the armpit.

'I raised the alarm before my attacker could kill me. Your wife, David Langley, and I were the respective project leads for the state network tender bids. I was the lucky one.'

Michael inhaled, pushing his demons to the back of his mind.

'I identified my attacker from police photographs. Davey Wilkes was his name. A veteran Green campaigner. I'll never forget the name, or his face, as he stood over me with that machete.'

For the first time since being introduced, Michael saw a glint of emotion cross Trevellion's sombre features as he reflected on his ordeal.

Trevellion spoke again, this time more softly.

'He said he was going to cut out my insides to create a message nobody would ever forget.'

'Don't go on. I know how painful it must be for you.'

Trevellion leant back in his leather chair, a serious expression on his face.

'The police have never caught the man who scarred me and killed David Langley and your...'

The sentence trailed off as their eyes met. Images of Davey Wilkes on UKCitizensNet came rushing back. He was still out there, somewhere.

'I know this might sound strange, but around the time of the attacks, was any company information stolen or destroyed?'

Trevellion looked thoughtful, crossing his arms as his brow furrowed a little.

'There was an arson attack on our old premises, resulting in some data loss. Although we retrieved it through our disaster recovery protocols. Why do you ask?'

'I discovered around the time of my wife's death there was a break-in at SW Technologies' offices with information stolen and computers destroyed. Of course, I don't know what it relates to. They formatted Colette's computer and wiped off all its information. I saw the police profile of Davey Wilkes on UKCitizensNet. Let's just say he wasn't the sharpest tool in the box. I think the police profile of this man is all wrong. Would he know to wipe the data from a computer in that way? Why not smash it up with a hammer or something?'

Trevellion's expression changed to one of interest.

'What are you saying?'

'I'm not sure. I just think maybe this butcher is cleverer than we're all giving him credit for.'

Trevellion mulled over the idea.

'Perhaps we're just not giving the police enough credit. I'm sure they only release enough information to the public so as not to hamper their investigation.'

Michael nodded, somewhat surprised and disappointed at Trevellion's dismissal of his conspiracy theory.

'Yes, I suppose that's possible. I just hoped talking to you would help me understand better. I think it has to some extent.'

Trevellion nodded and smiled, although his eyes didn't.

'Well, if they were trying to destroy all the information to stop the work you're trying to do, at least they didn't get all of it.'

Trevellion had moved to the percolator to pour himself another cup of coffee.

'How do you mean?' he asked.

'Colette had some other files relating to her work. I suppose I ought to return them to SW Technologies. They belong to them.'

Trevellion's outstretched hand never got to the coffee jug as he turned back to face Michael.

'I guess it's out of date by now, anyway. Colette always said the IT market never stood still for very long.'

Trevellion grunted as he returned to sit at his desk.

'Yes, well, I hope our chat has helped,' he said, his tone more serious and formal than before. 'I'm due in a meeting, so I must ask you to leave now. You don't mind showing yourself out, do you?'

Michael watched as all compassion on Trevellion's face vanished. Was it being reminded of the horrific events of the past, he wondered.

Aware Trevellion was going to say nothing further, he rose, shook Trevellion's hand, and slipped from the office.

As the door closed, Trevellion reached for his phone and dialled.

'Put me through to Sebastian Tate,' he said, as a woman's voice answered. 'Tell him it's Trevellion.'

The line went dead as the secretary redirected his call.

'Tate.'

'It's me. There's an issue regarding the Robertson woman. Something important. When can we meet?'

CHAPTER TEN

MICHAEL BROUGHT HIS ROVER to a halt on the soft gravel of David Langley's drive, gazing in awe at the impressive mock-Georgian facade. It was at least six, maybe seven, bedrooms, he figured.

Opposite Langley's house, a gleaming silver Aston Martin DB9 sat in front of a sparkling white art-deco homage. Straight and curved lines ran around the front of the sprawling house, interspersed with tinted black windows in aluminium frames that doubtless concealed greater luxury inside.

Michael imagined David Langley may have thought he was safe inside his home. Would the smell of disinfectant and scent air fresheners have removed the smell of death more successfully here?

In his own house, he still woke in the middle of the night, the rich metallic smell of blood thick in his nostrils, pervading his every thought. Deep down, he knew the smell wasn't there. He'd woken every night for eighteen months in the care home with the same feelings and the same smells.

A short, plump woman of about seventy with a red, sagging face answered the door at the fourth attempt, arthritis and slight deafness slowing her down as Michael soon learnt.

Through using UKCitizensNet's online user directory, he'd found David Langley's address. The house was now in the name of Vera Langley, his mother.

A quick email explaining who he was and asking if he could visit followed. And within a few minutes, a soothing voice on his eCitTV informed him that an email from Vera Langley was waiting.

After using UKCitizensNet and eCitTV a few times he now appreciated the benefits and convenience of these integrated technologies.

'Can I get you a cup of tea or coffee?' Vera asked, leading Michael into what he expected was one of many sitting rooms.

'Coffee, please, black.'

When Vera disappeared to whichever wing of the house the kitchen was in, Michael surveyed his surroundings. The house was no less impressive on the inside. Varnished wooden beams criss-crossed the ceiling, meeting at a well-defined apex. An antique clock hung above the ornate wood-burning stove opposite him.

Michael had sighed with relief when he entered the house. None of the familiar malodorous scents of his own home was here. Instead, there was the smell of succulent roast beef cooking. Cut flowers decorated the large reception area, and the atmosphere seemed almost normal.

Looking around the room again, it was clear ACE Solutions had paid David Langley well. If Vincent Trevellion's office and wardrobe were any indicators, Langley was on a similar salary.

Colette had been working for the wrong company, he thought. She had been on a good salary, better than his. But nothing on this scale.

It was one reason SW Technologies was close to going into receivership on a couple of occasions, and why the state network tender had been such an important project for them.

Redundancies had been looming if they didn't get the tender; he remembered Colette telling him. He never discovered whether anyone lost their job when SemComNet got the contract.

Michael's gaze fell upon a small framed photograph on the walnut table on the other side of the room. He crossed to the table and picked up the photograph. A chubby man was smiling. His arm was around Vera Langley, who was smiling back.

'That's my David,' Vera said with pride.

She carried a wooden tray laden with two cups of coffee and a plate of chocolate biscuits and placed it on the coffee table.

Michael turned to face the woman. She had a sorrowful look on her face as she stroked the photograph of her late son.

'Thank you for seeing me, Mrs Langley,' Michael said as he sat on one of the plump floral sofas.

'I told you to call me Vera, Michael.'

'Thank you, Vera. I know it can't be easy having all those memories brought back to you.'

'What's done is done,' she shrugged. 'Even if they ever catch who killed my David or your wife and daughter, it won't bring them back.'

'Were you living here when it happened?'

Vera shook her head as she sipped her coffee.

'No, I was living in Guildford. My husband, David's father, had just died. David had invited me to come and live with him. But I said no. It's not that I don't like Weybridge, it just wasn't my home. And what man in his forties wants to live with his mother, anyway?'

She smiled, a mischievous glint in her eye.

Michael sighed as Vera's tale of tragedy and loss unfolded. Like him, she'd lost her closest family in one fell swoop. But she was coping with it with more strength and humility than he'd ever shown. There was no bitterness or anger in her. And her loss had been as great as his.

'The house came to me in the will and I didn't have the heart to sell it. David so loved this house,' she beamed.

'I can see why,' Michael acknowledged, reaching for a chocolate biscuit.

'In the end, I sold my house and moved here.'

'I'm sorry for your loss.'

'I know you can sympathise.'

'Yes, everybody's been very sympathetic. Even my employer.'

'How so?'

'I'm signed off work on full pay and pension until *I'm* ready to return.'

'That's nice,' Vera replied. 'David's employer was very supportive, as well. I suppose there are some decent people, after all.'

Michael forced a thin smile. Yes, there were some. But the evil monster who killed his family was still out there.

'Vera, I know this might sound strange, but did David have a computer at home, or keep any files relating to his work here?'

'Come with me,' Vera said, easing herself up from the sofa.

Michael followed Vera into a hallway and through the drawing room. She led the way into a tidy study. There was no colour in the room, no cut flowers, no life. The walls were a pale grey, lacking the style of the rest of the house. Michael feared the worse.

'I'll leave you to do whatever you need to do,' Vera said.

'Are you sure you don't mind me having a look around?'

'No, not at all.' As she reached the doorway, she turned back. 'Don't be too long. It happened in here.'

Before Michael could reply, Vera had left. He was alone in the cold, characterless room. A room that, like his own bedroom, had witnessed atrocity.

On the desk was a large touchscreen computer. On either side were two well-filled bookcases. He studied the assortment of computer manuals, project management guides, and business process methodologies, all crammed on sturdy-looking shelves. Titles of programming languages and terms he had never heard of ran up the spines in bright lettering. But as he looked around the room, he sighed at the lack of hard-copy files in the study.

The four drawers of the desk revealed nothing more than stationery, and yet another Java manual and a complicated-looking calculator.

Still no hard-copy files.

He frowned. Did everything have to be electronic these days? Forever consigned to some corner of cyberspace?

Michael wheeled the black, armless swivel chair out from under the desk. Sat in front of the dusty computer, he pressed the "On" button and waited, his pulse racing. Within a few moments, a message appeared.

Unformatted Primary Hard Disk. Please insert
System Disk and press Enter.

His stomach lurched, and his muscles ached from tension. That all too familiar sense of dread crept through him, and he leant back in the comfortable chair, scratching his chin.

The computer's hard disk had undergone formatting. Just like Colette's laptop.

Were both machines robbed of vital information relating to their work? Why not just delete the data from the machine?

From the depths of his patchy computer knowledge, he remembered the few basic lessons Colette had given him on their home computer.

'Never panic if you delete a file by accident. We can retrieve most files if you know how.'

Then had come the warning.

'Never, ever, deliberately or accidentally, try to format the hard disk. You won't be able to retrieve any information after that. Not unless you know what you're doing.'

Michael exhaled. If the intention was to make the data on the computer irretrievable, why not just take a hammer to the hard disk? Why be a butcher to the flesh, yet reverential in destroying technology, the proclaimed enemy of the anti-net activists' cause? It didn't add up.

Vera hobbled back into the characterless study, interrupting Michael's reflections.

'Any luck?' she asked.

'Not really,' Michael lied, not wanting to burden her with thoughts that even he didn't understand.

'I dug this out for you,' Vera said, passing Michael several typed sheets of stapled paper.

Minutes of confidential meeting between David
Langley (ACE Solutions) and Colette Robertson
(SW Technologies). Subject: Potential use of ad-
vanced Java applet technologies.

'I found it about a month after David died. It was amongst a pile
of newspapers in the drawing room.'

'Did you take this to the police?'

'There didn't seem any point. Mr Trevellion had already identified
David's killer. Besides, I didn't want the police going over every inch
of David's house again.'

Michael nodded and half-smiled.

'Do you want it? You can have it,' Vera continued.

'Thank you,' Michael said as he scanned the content.

The words on the page meant little to him. But at least it was a
small part of Colette. And at the moment, that was all he had.

CHAPTER ELEVEN

Vincent Trevellion sat on an uncomfortable wooden chair in the long, quiet corridor and reached for his mobile. *Why did all government buildings look this dull?* Long characterless corridors, door after door concealing nameless grey bureaucrats, cogs in the government wheel.

He looked at the door to Sebastian Tate's office before dialing the number of one of his project managers. He hated being kept waiting. In particular, when it was by Sebastian Tate, his government contact, and his boss for this project.

How many people knew what went on behind the doors in this hidden retreat, he wondered. From what Tate had told him, those in the know about CODEX were a very exclusive club indeed.

CODEX, or Covert Operations and Defence Exercises, had been set up by the current administration to conduct specific operations outside the normal defence and Secret Service arrangements. The Prime Minister sanctioned each operation, or CODEX project, with the Secretary of State for Defence; if they were ever to be classified in security terms, it would have been a long way north of Top Secret. From there, they went to Sebastian Tate and his small team to implement and run. That was as far as the knowledge went. A small group operating outside the normal mechanisms of law, scrutiny, or accountability.

Tate had told him the budgets for these selected projects came from a slush fund the Prime Minister had at his personal disposal. The Secretary of State would then suggest how to allocate the money. Tate had the job of spending it on resources and personnel.

A CODEX operative was often a former MI5 or MI6 agent, ex-SAS or Special Forces. Only in rare cases were recruits inducted from the civilian sector, depending on the project. Trevellion was one of the chosen few.

No other security group, police force, or army unit had any knowledge of CODEX. Not even MI5 or the Cabinet. CODEX was the strictest security definition of "need to know".

As Trevellion soon discovered, the UKCitizensNet plan, or at least parts of it, carried a CODEX project classification.

Tate had recruited Trevellion three years earlier from a software company supplying advanced logistical systems for the defence industry. When Tate had revealed in full what UKCitizensNet would deliver, Trevellion had taken no convincing to become part of the select team for this CODEX project. Patriotism and the chance to change the future with technology had been sufficient motivation.

Trevellion quickly learnt that Sebastian Tate could be very persuasive. A Cambridge education in law at Trinity College, a former visiting fellow of his Alma Mater, coupled with over twenty years of experience on the bench as Queen's Counsel and a direct approach, ensured things got done. And that the right people were recruited.

It was why he was so well-suited to join the project. Plain speaking and an iron determination defined his corporate rise. Tate saw himself in his young protégé. It wasn't a fact either man enjoyed, although they both recognised the similarities while never admitting it.

Over time, Trevellion discovered the circles Tate had moved in during his time as a barrister. It had brought Tate into contact with many interesting individuals within the government. It hadn't taken long before MI5 approached Tate to become a special advisor on covert operations. A large web of international contacts and a razor-sharp mind made him an obvious choice. Assignments in Iraq, Kosovo and Afghanistan soon followed; operations that never made the news. Projects that weren't an official part of the war effort.

Such was the success of Tate's work that when McCoy's new government had won its landslide electoral victory, an approach to enlist him followed soon after. Within months, the CODEX programme had begun and the UKCitizensNet plan was underway.

Once there was agreement on the CODEX blueprint for UKCitizensNet, a deputy's position became available. Trevellion had been the obvious choice.

Trevellion had easily gained the trust and admiration of his boss, Sir Donald Allison, and proved to play a key part in delivering UKCitizensNet on the 5G semantic web platform to the entire country.

Tate had stayed in the background but had watched developments with interest, waiting for his moment to pounce. And once they had taken care of Colette Robertson and David Langley, and SemComNet had secured the tender, the stakes rose. They always did with Tate. It had been that way from the first time they'd met in Tate's reclusive office.

Tate looked up from the thick paper file arranged on the desk in front of him. For a few long seconds, he didn't say a word, his gaze moving across Trevellion's face, taking in every detail, looking for the one weakness. One possible emotional vulnerability that somehow might get exploited at a crucial stage in the future, jeopardising the success of the entire project.

As hard as he looked between the details in the CODEX file and Trevellion's face, there was nothing. No discernible weakness. He was the ideal 'insider' to get infiltrated into SemComNet.

The sales pitch had been easy. People with Trevellion's ambitions and thirst for power never needed convincing. And so it had proved. There were just a few rules of the game his future prodigy needed to be aware of.

'So, Vincent, tell me, do you have a wife, girlfriend, boyfriend?'

Trevellion's eyes widened. For the last two hours, the discussion was on CODEX protocols and project deliverables once he was in place at SemComNet. The development needs for UKCitizensNet, who the targets were, and who were expendable, had been the topics of conversation. Every point was discussed at length. Every permutation had been analysed and then dismissed or recorded as required.

Now this question?

'What relevance does that have? You're not hiring me for my ability to sustain relationships, are you?'

Tate's cold, grey eyes narrowed, his brow furrowing as he leant forward.

'Just answer the question. I only ask questions I need to know the answer to.'

Trevellion scowled.

'There is a woman. A management consultant for a firm of venture capitalists.'

'Is it serious?'

'Well, if you call a year serious, then yes. But if you mean marriage, then no.'

Tate pulled open his desk drawer, pulling out a bottle of single malt whisky and a glass, not offering one to Trevellion.

'Does she have anything on you which could have blackmail potential?' Tate asked with a hawkish look over the top of his glasses.

Trevellion's features tightened as he absorbed the implications of the enquiry.

'There's nothing in the relationship, or any other that could be a source of embarrassment for me or you,' he replied, holding Tate's intent, inscrutable gaze.

A thin smile crossed Tate's face, but vanished before being observed.

'You have two choices then. Marry her or end it. CODEX projects demand all their operatives are 100% focused on the job. If you're trying to operate with your head fucked-up over some woman, then you'd be a bloody liability. And we can't afford to take that risk. Do you hear me?'

As opposed to addling your brain with whisky at ten in the morning, Trevellion thought, suppressing the urge to share his observation.

Trevellion nodded obediently, his thoughts wandering to the management consultant and their time together. It had been a good year. But they were both ambitious. That had been part of the attraction. More physical than emotional. An end to the relationship wouldn't be a big deal for either of them.

Priorities changed all the time in their respective businesses. In the last two hours, they had changed more than he could've ever imagined.

Tate was offering him a chance to shape the future. Who could turn that down?

Sebastian Tate's door opened, and he appeared in the doorway, beckoning for him to enter. Trevellion rose from his seat, delivering his orders to one of his project teams through his mobile, before breaking off the call.

'You sound agitated, Vincent. I trust everything is on track at SemComNet?'

'Some of the regional servers have experienced recent downtime.'

Trevellion moved into the large office overlooking the Houses of Parliament and the City of Westminster and sat in front of Tate's desk. Tate took the chair opposite.

'Nothing to worry about, I hope?'

He began polishing his glasses, holding Trevellion's gaze, unblinking and intense.

'No, nothing for *you* to worry about.'

'Unlike Michael Robertson though? What do we know about him?'

'He's left the care home where he's been for eighteen months following the dispatch of his wife and daughter.'

Trevellion clasped his left upper arm and smiled, although his lips did not seem to move. The scar on his arm he'd shown Robertson resulted from a nasty motorbike accident four years earlier. In his current condition, Robertson would have believed anything as he struggled to cope with his wife and daughter's deaths.

'I estimate it won't take too much to push him back over the edge again. Getting any further information he may have shouldn't be difficult.'

Tate nodded as he lit a Castella cigar before smoothing down his silver hair.

'Do you think the information he may possess is the missing link in the project?'

'We know Colette Robertson and David Langley were having secret meetings several months prior to the tender deadline. I have a feeling they were working on one component we've yet to perfect, a controllable app we can deliver via UKCitizensNet. A tool we can program for a very specific purpose. The only way SW Technologies and ACE Solutions could have created such an app was as a joint initiative. I think the app was their trump card.'

'Well, we'd better make sure we acquire any information Michael Robertson has then, had we not?'

Trevellion nodded, but resisted the urge to rise to Tate's condescension.

'How do you want it done?'

'With discretion. And this time, I don't want you or any of your henchmen involved. I know how you enjoy a hands-on approach. Robertson has been to see you so we don't want you anywhere near him.'

Trevellion looked disappointed.

'Perhaps a series of burglaries would be appropriate. Target the neighbourhood rather than just Robertson's house. That should prevent any suspicion on his part as to the motive of the burglary.'

Tate nodded, almost smiling.

'Yes, that sounds acceptable. I'll arrange for my department to deal with that straight away.'

Tate looked Trevellion in the eyes, his gaze hard and purposeful.

'So, tell me, just where are we in our development?'

Trevellion stiffened at the interrogatory tone.

'We can download the app to any standard network IP address or eCitTV set with no issues. It appears seamless, depending on what it's programmed to do. Our problem is we think we can only use the file to take control of isolated electronic applications. But not to the point yet that it's viable or reliable enough to deploy.'

'You *think* you can take control of the app in a limited capacity? I don't want to know whether you *think* it works. I want to know *if* it works. We need to have it working at full capacity for this project to succeed. A fact we rather took for granted when we recruited you. Whether through work at SemComNet and my department, or from the Robertson woman's files, I want this project fully operational, and soon. The Prime Minister and Secretary of State will not continue funding my department's work if they cannot see results.'

Trevellion fought back his irritation.

'I take I have the approval to test the app as outlined in Phase II?'

Tate nodded.

'You have my approval.'

'And the target remains the same?'

'Of course, that's integral to the project's success.'

A malicious smile crossed Trevellion's face.

'Don't worry, I'll take care of Phase II. Just bring me the rest of Colette Robertson's files.'

CHAPTER TWELVE

16 August 2002

Colette lay on the bed, blood staining the sheets, spreading like a slow crimson tide. Michael stood above her, his heart beating fast, pounding in his ears as he watched her pain. The beads of sweat on her face, trickling down her cheeks and into her hair, glistened from her exertions as she fought the agony burning inside her. He couldn't bear to see his wife in such pain.

He was sweating as the seconds ticked by. How much longer did she have to endure this? Detachment coursed through him as he watched her writhe on the bed, more blood soaking into the sheets. He didn't seem able to comprehend what was happening.

'If you could stand to one side, please,' a firm, authoritative voice spoke, filtering into his contemplations.

Snapping out of his trance, Michael looked back to Colette laying on the bed, crying out in pain. The middle-aged midwife eased past him, returning with a fresh set of towels.

Michael returned to Colette's side and squeezed her arm, smiling at her, hoping it would somehow help. Colette looked back at him, her eyes wide from excruciating pain and fear, the mask supplying gas and air clamped to her mouth.

'Remember, take slow, steady breaths.'

The midwife was mopping up the blood that had seeped out between Colette's legs. 'Keep it steady, otherwise you'll end up hyperventilating.'

Colette nodded, unable to speak as the contractions forced their way down from her womb.

'Now, when the next contraction comes, you've got to push harder than you've pushed so far. This little one is ready to come out. You can do it.'

Michael looked at the midwife's hand between Colette's legs, feeling the baby's position as it rested on the brink of being born.

The scream filled the small labour room as Colette pushed down into her pelvis when the next contraction shuddered through her. She sucked in as much gas and air as she could. Her muscles contracted as she pushed again, willing her baby to escape.

'That's right, keep pushing,' the midwife said, remaining upbeat. 'I can see the head. Do you want to feel?'

Colette rocked her head as Michael mopped her brow with yet an-other tissue. The waste bin would be full up at this rate, he thought, leaning forward to get a first sight of his child.

Through the midwife's fingers, placed on the tip of the head, Michael could see a patch of dark hair. For a moment, he could feel his adrenaline pumping as the prospect of being a father got ever closer.

It was a strange feeling, he realised as his gaze moved backwards and forwards between his wife and his child-to-be. He felt elation that soon he would hold his child, the moment they'd both longed for since they'd got married. But this sensation was grappling with the terror of watching Colette's pain.

She'd always said she couldn't wait until she could hold and touch her own baby. But as the moment approached, the pain seemed too much for her. The sooner the baby was out, the better.

Another contraction passed and the baby's head emerged a little further. Michael gripped Colette's hand. They were having a girl; they were sure of it, although had resisted the chance to find out when Colette had gone for her five-month scan. Tears had rolled down their cheeks. They had just sat in awe, laughing from joy as the radiographer scanned Colette and the baby's limbs became clear. They'd seen both arms and legs and for a long, lingering moment had looked into their baby's face. Of course, the image was grainy, but they could see a baby living, growing inside of Colette. Their baby.

Three more large contractions later and the baby's advance into the world was no nearer. Colette was still screaming in pain, her breathing rapid inside her gas mask as the midwife looked up. Attention moved to the monitor next to the bed. The three of them listened to the baby's heartbeat, rapid sounds echoing around the small room.

Michael felt the hairs on his neck stand up as more sweat ran down Colette's pale face, her long brown hair matted, pushed back off her face. The midwife got up, looking concerned.

'The baby is getting distressed. We need to get them out of there as soon as possible. I'm going to need an enormous effort from you Colette so we can get your baby out.'

Colette flung her head back on her pillow, taking another breath on the gas and air as another contraction bubbled up.

'I can't. I'm not doing this anymore.'

She cast a defiant glance at Michael.

The midwife's expression hardened. She had twenty-five years' experience of handling such a situation.

'Well, you have two options. We either stop here, all go home, and your baby dies. Or we carry on until they come out and you become a family. Which do you want?'

Michael looked utterly astonished at the midwife's bluntness. Yet, as he looked at her, he was sure she winked in his direction. Colette, often the one delivering the direct, matter-of-fact-type comment, half-smiled at the brutal honesty.

'Get me a bloody epidural,' she said, her words hoarse as she reached for the gas mask again.

'I'm afraid baby's too far advanced for that. We're going to do this the old-fashioned way. If your baby's not out in the next ten minutes, we'll have to give you an episiotomy.'

Spurred into life at the prospect of surgical intervention, Colette inhaled before letting out a deafening scream that the whole of the maternity unit must have heard. Michael watched her face turn purple as she pushed on the next contraction, remembering Colette's insistence that under no circumstances was she being 'snipped' during labour.

He half-smiled as the midwife got back into her former position. If there was any doubt Colette was stubborn, this proved it.

'That's much better. The head's out,' the midwife said. 'One more of those and I think we'll have a baby on our hands.'

Colette braced herself, and Michael readied himself for the ear-splitting scream. But as the noise filled the room, the sound ebbed away. He watched, transfixed, their baby sliding out of Colette and onto the bed.

Michael squeezed her hand, and they both leant forward as the midwife wrapped the crying baby in a towel, wiping its face, and making sure there was no fluid remaining in the lungs.

'Our baby,' Colette blurted out, the pain she'd been feeling only moments earlier ebbing away as quickly as it had rushed up on her.

The midwife smiled and handed the baby to Colette, resting her on her naked chest.

'Congratulations, you've got a baby girl.'

Michael stroked the baby's hair, tears ran down his cheeks as he took in her every detail. From the swollen eyes to the fingers and toes, which were still tinged with purple. Colette held her tight, pressing her daughter to her skin, feeling her warmth against her own. The hours of agony forgotten in an instant.

After several minutes, the midwife turned back to the new family.

'I'm going to weigh her and record a few details. Then she'll need a feed. Are you planning on breastfeeding or using a bottle?'

'I'm going to breastfeed,' Colette said, as her daughter cried for the second time.

The midwife nodded, tidying away the stained sheets.

'Have you decided on a name?' she asked, sliding the discarded sheets out of sight.

Michael and Colette both looked up from their daughter.

'We're going to call her Clare,' Michael said with a wide smile.

CHAPTER THIRTEEN

The short man scratched his face and shot nervous glances around him. He shuffled from one foot to the other and peered up Clarence Street in the middle of Kingston-upon-Thames's busy town centre. As far as the eye could see, there were shoppers, moving from one bargain to the next.

He reached for yet another cigarette, knowing it was madness being out in the open like this. He was sure one of those bastards was watching him, all of them. But despite the risks, he *had* to talk to Michael Robertson, warn him, and try to help him. Would he believe them? Did anyone they ever tried to help believe them?

With a frown, the small, nervy man peered through the crowd of bustling shoppers. It was too dangerous to be exposed like this. One of *them* could be anywhere.

MICHAEL EXITED THE BANK and slid his wallet into his jacket pocket. Memories came rushing back, happy reminisces. And for the first in a long time, he smiled.

Kingston-upon-Thames had been the last place the three of them had gone together on the weekend before it had happened. It had always been their favourite shopping centre. So many shops to choose from if you could stand the stress of the constant bustle in Clarence Street and the Bentall Centre.

On that last Saturday together, they'd bought Clare a blue fleece from Gap for Kids. He remembered her beaming smile as she wrapped her tiny arms around him when he bought it.

'Thank you, Daddy,' she'd whispered, as he stroked her hair.

He'd feared returning here might have been too painful. But to his surprise, it was therapeutic. There were no blood-drenched images associated with this place, only happy memories of family outings. Perhaps he was now coping with what had happened.

'Michael Robertson?' a male, agitated voice asked.

Michael turned and a sea of faces met him as shoppers forced their way up the street and into nearby shops. His gaze stopped on a small, unkempt man, who looked as if he hadn't slept for weeks.

'Michael Robertson?' the voice demanded again.

'Yes, can I help you?'

The man shuffled, casting wild glances all around him.

'I must speak with you. It's very important.'

Michael looked confused. The small man continued to look about him, the lines on his forehead taut with worry.

'What about?'

'Not here. It's too dangerous. Meet me by...'

'I'm not meeting you anywhere unless you tell me what's going on,' Michael interrupted, bemused that the man somehow knew his name.

'It's about your wife and daughter,' the man said, his uneasiness clearly growing.

Michael felt his breathing become rapid as an image of Colette tied to the bed flashed across his mind.

'Meet me at the far end of Kingston Bridge, the Hampton end, in half an hour.'

Michael opened his mouth to voice some protest. But before he could get the words out, the small, nervy little man had scurried away, soon lost amidst the sea of shoppers.

HALF AN HOUR HAD seemed like an eternity. From where Michael stood, the Hampton end of Kingston Bridge was only a five-minute walk. For the remaining time, he fiddled with DVDs and books he didn't want, scanning the storylines on the back of novels, not registering a word.

How could he think about anything as mundane as a book after the mysterious man had mentioned Colette and Clare? Did he know something about their deaths, a fact that might lead to catching their killer? Or was he somehow involved and now coming after him?

He dismissed the thought. The man wouldn't have approached him first if he intended to kill him. At least, that was what he hoped.

Michael waited at the end of the bridge. Heavy traffic raced in either direction. A hand gripped his shoulder, and he spun around, finding himself again face-to-face with the nervy little man.

'Not here,' the man whispered, leading the way down the bridge's steps and onto the Thames path.

'Look, you better talk soon' or I'm calling the police,' Michael said as they reached the path, pulling his mobile from his jacket pocket.

'Don't use one of those. Never use one of those. In fact, just turn it off, otherwise, they'll be triangulating your position,' the man's eyes were wide with fear as he put his hands up to stop Michael from dialing. 'They're the easiest things for them to detect us on.'

A little baffled, Michael put the phone away.

'Do you know who killed my wife and daughter?' he demanded.

'I have a fair idea,' the man replied.

Michael felt his pulse race. He still didn't know who this man was. 'Who? Tell me.'

'I'll come to that. There are other things you need to know first, facts that put this into a much wider context. But you must turn your phone off. Now.'

Michael frowned, but didn't protest, fearing to alienate the man. Pulling his phone again from his pocket, he turned the device off before turning back to the man.

'The first thing you have to know and understand is that UKCitizensNet and SemComNet are shams, from start to finish. Your wife and SW Technologies were putting together a bid to run the online state network. And a legitimate bid as well, I'm sure.'

'She was the Project Manager. Why, what are you getting at?'

'David Langley at ACE Solutions was also his company's project lead for the bid.'

Michael nodded.

'Did you ever ask yourself why they banned the internet here? Why a national state network replaced a strong international network that allowed unprecedented freedom of speech and information sharing?'

Michael thought back to when the government had banned internet access two years before, trying to remember Dr Marcus McCoy's parliamentary rhetoric.

'They said they wanted to reward UK enterprise and to deal with all the illegal websites and content. And broadband was too slow and companies providing it were fixing the price or something.'

The man scoffed.

'UK enterprise? What bollocks. Do you want to know the real reason they put web technology companies and ISPs out of business here? Because the internet was unregulated. They couldn't control it. So what did they do? They tell everyone that the internet is illegal, unreliable and slow. That it's got to go. How do they get away with this? Easy, they go in for a bit of patriotic US bashing by slagging off US browsers, social media websites, online applications, search engines, you name it. Soon, this spreads, and before you know it, the computer industries in North America, Asia, and the rest of Europe are Satan-incarnate. And we all just love to believe that British is best, don't we? A British-run replacement, a people's network, is the computing messiah this country's been waiting for.'

'But what has this got to do with my wife and daughter?'

The man ignored Michael and continued.

'The one message UKCitizensNet loves to preach is the greater freedom the people's network gives the country. It links us like never before, giving us more information than we've ever had. It's empowered us. Or so they would have us believe. UKCitizensNet is a sham and undemocratic, with no freedom of speech or expression.

'Did you know that if you want to have your blog or website on UKCitizensNet, your submission, which by the way is more complicated than completing an online self-assessment tax form, goes through three UKCitizensNet advisory committees before being approved? That's *if* you get approved. They refuse 80% of personal website applications on the most tenuous of grounds. On the old internet, any ISP would offer you web space to publish anything you wanted. Social media sites allowed freedom of expression and online communities. All with few questions asked. You can't do that today. Did you know?'

Michael didn't.

'And what about the fucking sham they call the UKCitizensNet social networks? They moderate every single network on UKCitizensNet. Do you know how many networks there are on UKCitizensNet? Hundreds of thousands. They vet every message created or shared within a group with sophisticated software, scanning for flagged terms or strings of related words that might be subversive.

'We're talking intelligence service-level of vetting of online chatter, just to scan the banality of people's lives. Nameless analysts working for SemComNet handle this surveillance. Just like personal website submissions, they veto 70% of social network messaging and remove it from UKCitizensNet within minutes of creation. And guess what? No one can do a thing about it. How can they? They voted McCoy and his puritan manifesto of online change into power, and now there's no alternative. Just goes to show that people should be careful what they wish for!'

The man paused for breath, wiping away a bead of sweat running down the left of his temple.

'Does that sound like democracy to you? Is that your definition of online privacy? Do you still feel empowered?'

'You said you knew something about my wife and daughter?' Michael said, attempting to absorb what the anonymous man had told him and what it had to do with his family's murders.

The man nodded, looking about him as if he expected to be arrested any moment.

'Ask yourself this, then. Do you think that a mere computer company like SemComNet, no matter how big, could impose such control over the information we receive every day without help from somewhere else?'

Michael looked back at the man, his expression confused, not sure whether he was expecting a reply.

'SemComNet, and therefore UKCitizensNet, are in the government's pocket. Maybe not openly in the corridors of power. But somewhere, from within the government, maybe even McCoy himself, this whole fucking state network project is being controlled.'

Michael looked incredulous.

'By the government? You can't be serious.'

'It's the only organisation big enough and powerful enough to run it. That's why they killed your wife and David Langley. To remove any competition with SemComNet's tender bid and to steal the project plans rival companies were developing.'

A thousand thoughts bombarded Michael's troubled mind.

'But why not just commission SemComNet to develop a network? Or have a nationalised intranet?'

The nervy man's expression became more sorrowful as his face sagged a little.

'The whole people's network tender was a sham. If they'd just commissioned SemComNet then the rest of the industry would have protested, UKCitizensNet would have got bad publicity and the project would have been doomed to fail. If McCoy nationalised a state network, he loses the opportunity to be jingoistic and stir up patriotism. Remember, this happened while the supposed tenders were being prepared. The illusion of a tender ensured other companies involved developed their web and IT R&D pipelines. Neither SemComNet nor the government had all the answers for this online technology. So what do they do? They kill the project leads and indulge in corporate espionage by stealing rival companies' information. Competition is now impotent and SemComNet is the only company that can meet the state network tender requirements. Quite a technological coup d'état, wouldn't you say?'

'No, it makes no sense,' Michael said. 'I don't believe the government killed my wife. Besides, Vincent Trevellion identified the man who attacked him, the man who killed my wife and daughter. His name is Wilkes, Davey Wilkes, an anti-net campaigner.'

The man scoffed again, looking around him.

'What? Those fucking illiterates? I don't think so. They don't care about the internet, they're Green anti-road protesters, and scapegoats for the killings.'

A terrible idea formed in Michael's head. The nervy man sensed what he was thinking.

'Who identified Davey Wilkes? It was Vincent Trevellion. Who does Vincent Trevellion work for? SemComNet. Who benefited the most from the deaths of your wife and David Langley? SemCom-Net.'

The man paused as Michael held his head in his hands.

'There is no doubt. SemComNet, Vincent Trevellion, or someone working for him, murdered your wife and daughter.'

'But why Clare? What did she have to do with the tender bid? She was only a child.'

The man frowned and shook his head.

'I don't know why they killed your daughter. Maybe they hoped the death of a child would condemn Davey Wilkes, and the supposed anti-net campaigners, in the eyes of the public.'

Michael looked up, his eyes narrowing, and aware one bit of information was missing.

'How do you know all this? And who the hell are you?'

The nervy man looked around again, his anxiety growing as Michael raised his voice.

'Keep your voice down,' he hissed, sitting down on a nearby bench. 'Me and some of my colleagues are what you might call internet patriots. We strive to keep the old internet alive, even though the government has banned it. Across the country, we've been re-establishing a communications structure by starting up servers, repairing routers, hubs and old broadband connections.

'We're an online splinter group trying to reconnect to the old principles of an online network. The only problem is the government knows about us and our activities.

'To start with, we got arrested, roughed up a bit, had our hardware and kit stolen, and given a caution.

'But when they realised we were probing into the very workings of UKCitizensNet and all its clandestine advisory committees, things got nasty. They ransacked our houses, threatened our friends and family, and froze our bank accounts. We had to go into hiding.

'For two years we've been hiding now, communicating with a handful of opponents to UKCitizensNet, or Fuck-the-Citizens-Net as we call it. We're always having to move the kit that connects us and the rest of the world to avoid detection from the authorities. But they've seized a lot of our hardware. It's put our plans of exposing them back by months.'

'Why haven't you gone to the police or the press?'

The man laughed dismissively.

'They'd pick us up in a matter of hours. This is the government and intelligence services we're talking about. They're always looking for us, watching us. They may be now. Don't think they're not monitoring you. If they think you know something about UKCitizensNet and its development, they'll be watching you. Why do you think I was so careful about where we met?'

Michael didn't hear the last sentence as an image of Colette's folder of files and the meeting minutes Vera had given him flashed through his mind.

'Can you prove who killed my wife and daughter?'

'Proof,' the man sneered. 'They're too clever for that. We only know what we established through hours of testing and probing UKCitizensNet, of being harassed by the police, of knowing that others like us are being sought by *them* for what they know.'

The man's disdain echoed in the cold air. Michael felt enraged.

'You've made me listen to this conspiracy theory rubbish, made me relive the horror of discovering my wife's mutilated body and identifying my daughter's corpse. All because of paranoid delusions so preposterous, I should have seen through them straight away.'

'Michael, believe me, they're not delusions. This is all real. Do I look like I'm fucking joking? Would I have been on the run for two years if this wasn't real?'

Michael rose from the bench, his face contorted in anger.

'Do you want to know what I think? I think you're some sort of sick voyeur who gets off on death and misery. I think you created this whole conspiracy in the hope I would reveal one detail about my wife and daughter's death that wasn't in the papers or on UKCitizensNet. A detail you could get off on. That's what I think.'

The man shook his head, agitated by the unwanted attention Michael's outburst could cause.

'No, you must listen to me, it's all...'

But he never completed the sentence as Michael pushed past him and headed back toward the steps leading onto Kingston Bridge.

The man shook his head, sighed, and thought about what to say to the others. He'd tried, but Michael hadn't wanted to listen.

But then he wasn't the first.

CHAPTER FOURTEEN

5 June 2009

We will ban access to the internet.

NO MATTER HOW MANY times Dr Marcus McCoy read it aloud, or recited the words in his head, he delighted in their inescapable truth. These words, his speech prepared for parliament, would be the defining moment of his premiership.

For months, he had been poring over the details he was about to reveal to the nation. All building up to this moment. The centrepiece of his party's manifesto pledge, which had helped him to the biggest electoral landslide in a generation. A majority of 196 in the House ensured he could push through anything in terms of change. The only unanswered questions were the details of his proposed reforms.

McCoy moved away from the window that overlooked the Thames, Westminster Bridge, and the London Eye, and returned to the desk in his spacious, comfortable office.

On the desk was a large computer screen, logged into the parliamentary network, a glass of water, and his pile of papers. Before any major speech to the House, he liked to have a few moments to himself, whilst the chamber filled, just to gather his thoughts.

The speech he was about to give was on the top of the neat pile of papers on his desk; he skimmed through the opening paragraph once more before moving it to one side.

Underneath, in a clear plastic wallet, was a further document, a report that Miles Winston, the Secretary of State for Defence, had given him in confidence, just days after the election victory.

His narrow, hawk-like blue eyes scanned the title, its meanings rumbling around in his mind: CODEX file OP09/ST—UK CitizensNet implementation and development. Pulling the report from the plastic wallet, he turned the first page and read. He'd viewed it before, more than once, and he knew all the meanings and implications. His speech today would lay the groundwork for a government project that would forever change the lives of every person living in the country. A move that would give him the means to pursue whatever political imperative he felt necessary.

After the first few pages, his gaze stopped on a list of names. Three people who, all in unique ways, were critical to the success of Phase I. Without them, the project could not succeed.

The first name on the list was Vincent Trevellion. McCoy read the brief biography. Trevellion was an ambitious regional director of a large software provider to the defence industry. He was qualified, familiar with the market, and driven by a thirst for advancement. An ideal candidate, he reflected, running his fingers through his greying hair, sweeping it into a tidy side-parting.

Before he could read the biography for the second name on the list, a gentle knock on the door disturbed his concentration. The door to the office opened. Nigel Braithwaite, his Private Secretary, stood in the doorway, bolt upright, efficient as ever.

'They're ready for you Prime Minister,' he said in a firm, authoritative tone. 'The House is very full today.'

McCoy nodded, gathering up his papers, taking one last sip from the glass of cool water on the desk.

'So it should be,' he replied, exiting the office to where two security personnel were waiting to escort him. 'My speech is going to change this country beyond recognition.'

Braithwaite nodded, already familiar with the contents of the speech, although unaware of the CODEX report accompanying the Prime Minister's papers. As the hour for McCoy's speech had approached, he'd prowled around the parliament building, monitoring everything that was going on. Conversations had taken place with the Chief Whip, ensuring all party members were in attendance. Although on a day like this, it would have been a job to keep them away.

Then there had been the press. Journalists were always bustling around the lobby at Westminster, trying to grab a word with a minister or senior backbencher. But in all his time, Braithwaite'd never seen so many hacks or political commentators congregated. Not only were the national media decked out in force, but reporters from what seemed every news desk on the planet were assembling.

It wasn't surprising. The ramifications of Dr McCoy's address to parliament would be far-reaching, impacting international markets and economies. All the major stock exchanges had been jittery since McCoy's ascent to power.

The once buoyant international IT market, and in particular the shares of semantic web technology companies and the growing social media giants, had been riding the crest of a financial wave for the last few years. But once the party's manifesto was public, and McCoy started fleshing out some of his ambitions, the share prices of US, Asian and European software companies had fallen. After today, they were likely to go through the floor.

The press was pursuing the story. The phones in the Number Ten press office hadn't stopped ringing and email boxes were forever full as journalists and social and cultural commentators kept bombarding his office with requests for information, clarifications, or interviews.

Until McCoy had made his speech, and the details, publicly known, the only answer would be "no comment". McCoy had been quite clear about that. He wasn't a man to be crossed, as many political opponents had discovered.

'After this session, tell Miles I want to see him,' McCoy said as they reached the doors to the chamber, the hum of chattering inside seeping out through the closed door.

Braithwaite nodded as McCoy strode with confidence into the expectant political arena.

When he emerged into the House of Commons, an excited murmur filtered around the chamber. McCoy's party members, many newly elected, filling row upon row of the benches, broke into rapturous applause as he approached his seat close to the Speaker of the House.

The size of his victory and the parliamentary majority had even taken him by surprise, despite over twenty years in politics. That time was in local politics, running an inner-city council beset by social deprivation and racial tension. From there, his elevation as an MP had been only in parliamentary opposition, climbing the ranks of his party, being a spokesperson for online developments and defence, before becoming the Shadow Defence Secretary.

Only after his party's electoral defeat had he at last risen to the role many political commentators said he was born for: leader of his party. Careful manipulation of the political scene and the turmoil of a governing party in decline had allowed him to stamp his mark on the future direction of his party.

When the election had come, at the latest date the former Prime Minister could cling on to, the polls had predicted an easy victory.

Not on this scale, though. Exit polls had predicted a majority of around 140. That would have been cause to celebrate. But 196?

McCoy smiled as he recalled that famous night. It was his crowning moment: returning his party to power. They claimed seat after seat from opposition MPs as the size of his victory grew. His policies and pledge to arrest what he had described as 'the moral and social decline of this great country,' had struck a chord with voters. His populist campaign transformed traditional voting patterns and swept away opposition party strongholds as the number of his own MPs rose.

Television cameras, picking up every angle of parliament, every expression on government and opposition party faces, all focused on McCoy as he acknowledged the applause of his party and the drowned-out heckling from the benches opposite with a smile. A location in the house he'd occupied not so long before.

McCoy took his seat and looked around at the sea of faces. This was his government, and they would listen to the promises he was going to deliver on. The MPs, the country, and the rest of the world.

Especially the rest of the world.

With the Prime Minister in place, the Speaker of the House rose from her elevated seat overlooking the opposing benches. Like a fearsome headmistress, a hush descended on the assembled masses as the respected Margaret Appleton, a former vocal backbencher on social reforms, addressed the benches.

Although everyone in the House knew the purpose of the parliamentary session, the Speaker gave the Prime Minister his introductions before resuming her seat. Rising to his feet, McCoy cast a slow glance at the party opposite and their new leader, before turning to his prepared speech.

'Honourable friends, when elected to lead this party, there were many challenges I wanted to address. These will now define the legacy of this government. Our vision will arrest the moral and social decline of this great country which the members opposite so efficiently oversaw.'

Derisive laughter filled the house as McCoy's MPs cheered his rallying cry, mocking the dwindling numbers of the opposition parties.

'One area more than any other signalled this decline. An area so important to the fabric of this country, and to the people who live under our laws, that I made it my top manifesto pledge in the general election. On that mandate, I came into this office. I will deliver on my pledge to address the political, social and moral corruption that now defines the internet.

'In the years of the previous government, UK websites, internet chat rooms, social media networks, and online services have risen exponentially. Yet what did the previous government do to ensure responsible governing of this vast information network? The answer is nothing. In their twelve years in power, the amount of illegal pornographic websites, threatening the safety and welfare of our children and our fam-

ilies, rose by over 600%. The latest figures from the National Crime Unit show new websites containing illegal images come online every thirty minutes in the UK alone. What did the former government do about this? Nothing. Neither has the industry that has been complicit in making it easy for sexual predators to create new obscene websites. This cannot continue.'

Spontaneous applause erupted from the backbenches as McCoy paused, shuffling his papers as the cheers faded.

'And what about the threat each of our citizens faces every day? Every time they get on a train, bus or plane. The threat of terrorism has never been more real than today. In these times of heightened security and threat, the internet is the single largest breeding ground for terrorists of all extractions. The number of laws extremist websites flout is too many to list. Our previous government put in place no enforceable safeguards to stop these messages from being transmitted, or to stop impressionable youths from being subverted by individuals whose only aim is to cause bloodshed and panic. The prevailing policy seems to have been "publish and be damned and never mind the consequences". How many lives have we lost thanks to this policy? This will not continue.

'Information is at the very heart of our lives and must continue to be so. Every day more and more people are connected to the internet. Yet for every new online user, there is a virus or malicious scam trying to steal personal information or destroy your computer. The number of online identity thefts is at the highest level it has ever been. Illegal scams trying to sell you everything from a timeshare that doesn't exist to pharmaceuticals without a prescription. This trend, and lack of action against it, has risen at the fastest rate ever seen in the last three

years—all under the previous government. We will not allow this to continue.

'And what about the industry? What incentives have we given them to clean up their act, to support the people of this country to get the most out of their online experience? The answer is none. We have never compelled them with enforceable legislation. Why should they care what's being published on webspace they can sell at premium prices when there's an insatiable demand and no questions asked? Also, let us not forget the recent independent review into broadband price-fixing by Sir David Michaels that I instigated when I came into office. The findings of this review, published today, confirm without question that internet service providers have been fixing the price of broadband whilst keeping the speed of access artificially slow so to encourage longer online usage. The result: larger bills for consumers and a bigger bottom line for these companies. Let me say now: we will punish all of those companies implicated in Sir David's review for their involvement in this scandal.

'This sorry litany of issues leads to one inescapable fact: our current online environment is not sustainable. This government will not allow a system that allows criminals to engage in illegal activity without consequences to continue. Therefore...'

McCoy paused, looking up at his counterpart on the opposing bench, and then to the camera suspended from the public gallery opposite. Adrenaline pumped through him as he prepared to deliver his coup d'état.

'In eighteen months, from 1 January, we will ban access to the internet in the UK. In its place comes a network for the people of this country, UKCitizensNet. The information tool of the future. And, in order to reward UK enterprises, the contract to run UKCitizensNet

will only be available to UK companies. They will build the infrastructure, tools and software able to deliver UKCitizensNet to every household, every computer and every mobile device. UKCitizensNet, the people's network, will be a crime-free online system. It will enhance this country, not threaten it.'

As wave after wave of applause echoed from the backbenches, McCoy provided more details of how he would implement UKCitizensNet. On the opposing bench, the leader of the opposition, Nathan Drew, made copious notes. Around him, his colleagues attempted to jeer and heckle McCoy's vision of the online future. They were drowned out by the overwhelming numbers of government MPs.

After the disastrous election result, the party had been quick to elect a new leader in Drew. As he sat opposite the baying, gloating, victorious rabble of MPs now in power, the sheer size of his task was all too clear. How could they compete against a parliamentary majority of 196?

McCoy finished his speech, resumed his place on the front bench, and the Speaker rose from her seat before looking in Drew's direction.

'Nathan Drew,' Margaret Appleton bellowed across the chamber, as he rose from his seat.

Although McCoy's pledge to ban access to the internet had been explicit in his election campaign, until his speech, no one had known just how far his planned reforms would go.

It was fortunate Drew had always been a quick thinker, with an articulate tongue to match. Officers' training at the Sandhurst Royal Military Academy and a rapid rise to the rank of Major had honed his natural leadership skills. As a decorated war hero and a gifted orator, his talents propelled him throughout his political career.

'Madame Speaker, we have listened to my right honourable friend's speech of national pride. I'm sure my colleagues will join me in express-

ing their surprise that he intends to deliver on an actual manifesto pledge. In his time in opposition, his record of changing his mind to suit his own agenda was almost second to none.'

Once more, a cacophonous din from McCoy's MPs drowned out sounds of the opposition party's jeers as they waved copies of his speech in the air in a sign of unquestioning loyalty.

'However, I feel I should be the one to point out the obvious flaw in what the Prime Minister is proposing. In banning access to the internet, and barring non-UK companies from bidding for its replacement, many companies will re-evaluate their priorities on these shores. This will only result in mass redundancies for the workforce he claims to protect, never mind the contravention of countless trade and labour laws. How can wholesale unemployment in the largest market sector in the country, and isolation from the rest of the online world, be for the good of either the people or the country?'

McCoy rose from his seat, a sneer across his ageing, sagging features, as he addressed his rival.

'Madame Speaker, first let me congratulate my right honourable friend on his new appointment. It's not a job that I'd relish.'

A ripple of laughter crossed the government benches as opposition party MPs squirmed in their seats.

'I fear he may have already shown he is out of his depth on this issue. As I have explained, safeguarding the political and social future of this country is at the heart of this change. Let me be quite clear when I say anyone working for a company that loses business because of this will be eligible for parachute redundancy payments and placed on a preferential register for a job within the UKCitizensNet infrastructure once built. No one is going to be disadvantaged by these reforms. UKCitizensNet will benefit everyone.'

For the next hour, McCoy fielded question after question, as he revealed more details of UKCitizensNet. In the main parliamentary lobby, journalists scribbled down every word that was said, broadcasting back to their studios what UKCitizensNet would mean.

As the parliamentary session ended, McCoy, accompanied by his two-security staff, exited the house, stealing away from waiting reporters, but having time to shake the hands of his delighted party members, revelling in their collective glory.

Once back in his temporary office, McCoy returned to the window, gazing out on the Thames. He would have a few moments to himself before returning to No. 10 to review the media coverage and the responses to his speech. From there, it would be a case of coordinating responses to likely questions and arranging interviews with his Director of Communications.

As he watched the traffic from the office window, aware people in their cars, in front of the television, and, with a hint of irony, listening via the internet, had tuned in to his address, he knew the media didn't matter. His election victory was on the back of his pledge to end crimes associated with the current internet. Now, he was delivering on his promise. In eighteen months, there would no longer be internet in the UK; by implementing UKCitizensNet, the CODEX proposal Miles Winston had submitted to him could come into place.

The door to the office opened and Miles Winston stood in the doorway, beaming as he waddled into the room. His oversized belly, trapped in a tight shirt, wobbled as he walked.

'Prime Minister, that was masterful,' he said, facing his leader across the table.

McCoy nodded, knowing how well he'd handled the debate, parrying away all the awkward questions, answering the obvious ones with ease.

His gaze dropped to his papers on the table and he pulled the CODEX file from its plastic wallet. Winston waited as he perused their contents once more.

'I want this CODEX project operational before the end of the day. Is that clear?'

Winston nodded, reaching into his jacket pocket for his mobile phone.

McCoy's gaze had once again stopped on the list of three names in the report.

'Are your sources sure these are the right people?'

Winston nodded, wiping a bead of perspiration from his brow, a result of his exertions of climbing the stairs to reach McCoy's temporary office.

'Without question. The preliminary CODEX team has done all the background checks. These are the initial targets.'

McCoy smiled, placing the report on the desk before returning to his appreciation of the river.

'Well, you'd better ensure your team starts the preparatory work then.'

Winston nodded.

With one last glance at the report, McCoy looked Winston in the face.

'Get me Sebastian Tate.'

CHAPTER FIFTEEN

MICHAEL KNEW IT WAS a burglary the moment he opened his front door. He always kept the doors to the kitchen and lounge at the end of his long hallway shut when he went out. This afternoon they were open. An untidy mass of papers marked a trail out of the lounge. As he rushed into the kitchen, he failed to notice the kitchen drawer pulled from its unit and laying on the floor. His left foot caught one side of the drawer, and Michael slid, thudding onto his backside. His right elbow caught a glancing blow on the front of the dishwasher.

He was sitting in a scattered line of glass. Cursing, he looked at his gashed hands. In front of him, he could see a hole in the back door pane, just above the door handle.

Michael rose and ran his bloodied hand under the tap, surveying the mess in his kitchen. His breathing became more rapid and constrained as images of Colette bound to the bed came flooding back. The last time there had been a break-in was that fateful day. Splashing cold water onto his face, he pushed the images to the back of his mind. He was alone now. No one else was here.

The kitchen and conservatory were both in a mess. Drawers and cupboards were gaping open. Damaged crockery and saucepans had been smashed.

The filing cabinet in the conservatory lay on its side amidst a sea of papers. Years of bank statements, mortgage details, and insurance policies covered every inch of floor space.

The lounge and dining room were no better. The coffee table, which had a small shelf storing the most recent mail, was thrown over. And the glass top had cracked even further than before. Against the longest wall was a pine sideboard, its contents rummaged through. Ornaments, Colette's ornaments, littered the carpet. Drawers and cupboards hung open, and more papers, books, and magazines littered the floor.

Michael's gaze dropped to the glass cabinet below his eCitTV unit, its doors half open. His DVD recorder was missing. So far, it was the only thing he could say with any certainty that was gone.

With a scowl, he took a step forward, kicking a pile of papers at his feet, watching as they cascaded into the far wall. He shook his head at the intrusion into his house.

All for a DVD recorder.

There were some twisted people out there, he scowled, looking at Colette's discarded ornaments. But then he'd known that for some time.

Michael leant down to pick up the ornaments and remembered what the crackpot in Kingston had told him.

'They're almost certainly watching you. If they think you know anything about UKCitizensNet and its development, they'll be watching you.'

Michael frowned as the words reverberated around his head. The man had said so much. Yet he couldn't prove a word of it. His hopes of catching Colette and Clare's killer were fleeting because there wasn't a shred of tangible proof. He'd thought the whole thing was preposterous paranoia.

Yet, a nagging doubt about the anti-net activists not just smashing up Colette and David Langley's computers had persuaded him to take a simple precaution. His intention had been to prove the anonymous man wrong. So, he'd put Colette's file back in the postal box for temporary safekeeping.

He shook his head and frowned.

The man couldn't have been right in his twisted theories. Could he?

Michael picked up a cracked crystal ornament from the carpet and heard a firm knock on his front door. His pulse raced as paranoia gripped him. Was he being watched as the man had predicted?

With a deep breath, he walked into the hallway. A silhouette of a man loomed in the frosted door panes.

His paranoia receded as he opened the door and recognised Jack Wilson, a retired accountant who lived opposite.

'Sorry to bother you, Mike,' Jack said in his strong Geordie accent. 'It's just that several of us in the street have had our houses broken into. I was wondering whether you might have seen anyone suspicious hanging around?'

Despite his fury at the burglary, Michael felt relief wash over him. This was no conspiracy. Nobody had been watching him, trying to find out if he knew anything about UKCitizensNet's operations. It was just a bunch of local thieves who'd gone on the rampage.

'I'm afraid they've done my house as well,' he replied, trying to sound angry rather than relieved.

Jack sighed; his wrinkled face flushed with anger.

'Oh Mike, I'm sorry. The bastards have been busy. Yours is the fourth house in the street, then. I've called the police. When they turn up, I'll send them over. I'm sure...'

Jack's sentence trailed off as the telephone in the lounge started ringing.

'Look, I need to go,' Michael said. 'I'll come over and we can talk about it later.'

Michael jogged back into the lounge to answer the telephone.

'Do you believe me now?' the voice at the end of the line asked.

'What?' Michael said with slight trepidation as the familiar voice spoke again.

'They've been to your house, haven't they? Turned it upside down, looking for anything you might know about them.'

'Why don't you just leave me alone,' Michael mumbled, pulling the net curtains in his lounge away from the window.

He looked up and down the street, hoping to see the man watching him. He could see no one. And there were no vantage points. He felt his pulse quicken. He hadn't checked upstairs yet. Was the man up there, he thought before dismissing it as ridiculous.

'It's just a burglary,' Michael said, raising his voice in anger. 'It's not your damn cyber police, you paranoid freak.'

'That's what they want you to think,' the man persisted. 'Check with your neighbours. Yours won't be the only burglary. It's how they work, to make it look like a spate of ordinary thefts. It's what they did to us when they ransacked our houses.'

Michael's pulse wasn't getting any slower, and his gaze dropped to one of the sideboard drawers. The drawer he'd placed the meeting minutes Vera had given him.

'Hold on a minute,' he said, placing the receiver down on the sofa arm.

A quick search of the drawer produced nothing, and dropping to his knees, he rummaged through the pile of papers strewn there, his heart racing. The minutes had gone. A thousand thoughts and endless theories, his own and the anonymous man's, raced through his mind.

Michael picked the receiver up again.

'Are you still there?'

'I'm still here. What have you found?'

'It's more what I haven't found. You say you and your colleagues are good with computers and all that?'

'We like to think so,' the man replied.

Michael's heart was pounding as he stood on the threshold of possible insanity and utter paranoia. But he was determined.

'Good. Because I've got something I want you to look at.'

CHAPTER SIXTEEN

Trevellion looked up from the stolen meeting minutes and smiled. He'd been right about the Robertson woman and Langley. But he'd been wrong, too.

The confidential minutes proved that both Colette Robertson and David Langley had been having secret meetings.

His error had been in underestimating them. Although, even now, he doubted they'd seen the complete picture, or had glimpsed the future. All it would have needed was a bit of fine-tuning of their companies' plans. But it had never got that far before their deaths.

Trevellion leant back, frowning deeply. Despite this information, SemComNet still couldn't administer this fine-tuning either. And they weren't getting any closer. Colette Robertson's hidden information had to be the last piece of the jigsaw. But the search had yielded nothing. They'd turned the house upside down—to no avail.

Michael Robertson had moved the important information. That was clear. Would he have destroyed it because it evoked too many memories? Trevellion shook his head, dismissing the possibility.

Robertson wanted to know why his wife and daughter had been murdered. He must have concealed the files somewhere.

The discovery of the confidential minutes had been unexpected, though. They confirmed what he already suspected but how had Robertson gotten hold of David Langley's copy? Could Langley's mother have given them to him? She was his only remaining relative. They would have to pay Langley's house another visit, ensure no other papers were still in circulation.

As Trevellion continued to turn the pages of the minutes, the telephone on his desk rang.

He snatched up the receiver and snapped down the line.

'I said no calls."

"I know, sir, but it's Mr Tate. And you said if he ever rang,' Mrs Martin said.

Trevellion paused. It was fortuitous Sebastian Tate had rung. He would need an update.

'Put him through.'

The line went dead before clicking into life again.

'Trevellion.'

'Do you have any news for me, Vincent?'

Tate spoke in his normal condescending manner, knowing the answer to the question already. It was a style he'd developed from twenty years of being a Queen's Counsel. A good barrister never asked a question he didn't know the answer to.

After three years of working with Tate, Trevellion had learnt not to get riled by his manner and subtle, sometimes petty, psychological games.

'After your men ransacked Robertson's house, I've received something of interest from them; not the files we were looking for though. He seems to have moved these.'

'That's unfortunate. And the item you recovered?'

'Robertson came into possession of confidential minutes from a meeting between his wife and David Langley, just before their deaths. They confirm a secret collaboration between the two, outside of their companies SW Technologies and ACE Solutions. They allude to a Java-based app controllable from a remote server. One which would have wireless capabilities and would operate on the 5GSW platform. However, we didn't find the documents referred to in the minutes. Nor are they part of the information we retrieved two years ago.'

'I presume these are files in Michael Robertson's possession? The files which he has now stored elsewhere?'

'I believe so.'

'Robertson is proving to be more troublesome than we envisaged.'

Trevellion always knew when Tate was holding information back. He enjoyed taunting him by holding the upper hand in a conversation, to make sure he knew who was in charge.

'I assume you've received some additional data on Robertson?'

'On your suggestion, we've been watching him for the past few days. It seems one of our subversive friends approached him.'

'Which one?'

'Brown, in Kingston-Upon-Thames.'

'Did your people apprehend him?'

'No. He evaded them in the shopping centre.'

'How careless. Your people aren't doing very well at the moment, what with losing Brown and not knowing where Robertson has moved the files to. That won't look good in your report to McCoy and Winston, will it?'

There was a long pause as Trevellion waited for a retort. There was only so much of Sebastian Tate's supercilious *"I'm a Cambridge Don"* attitude he would tolerate.

Tate's tone was a little more conciliatory.

'Yes, well, my people are aware of what I think.'

He was sure they would be. Tate could be an even bigger bastard than him when needed.

'The progress of this project supersedes any bickering between us. I want to know how you propose to get these files from Robertson. Discretion is of the utmost importance now, as Brown will have filled his head with conspiracy theories that make Kennedy's assassination lock straightforward.'

Trevellion smiled thinly.

'Keep your people watching him. He might lead them to the files and Brown and other sympathisers. I have another idea that might prove persuasive. Robertson's close to the edge. It won't take much to push him over.'

'What do you have in mind?'

'I think it might be time to introduce Michael Robertson to ANNA. But a version of my making. And I know just what will appeal.'

'Do whatever you have to. We need those files.'

The line clicked dead.

Trevellion's gaze fell on the confidential minutes before he turned to his computer touchscreen, elevated at a 45-degree angle.

He had a special version of ANNA in mind for Michael Robertson. He tapped an icon on the left side of his desktop and waited for the application to load.

Welcome to ANNA, the Advance Nano Network
Application version 2.01.

The message dissolved into a set of options. One of Trevellion's team had developed ANNA the year before. The software was in beta-testing for further use on UKCitizensNet.

Within SemComNet, developers described it as a "personalised and customisable animated 3D greeting card," developed on the fifth-generation semantic web platform. Trevellion doubted his developers ever had his use for it in mind when they were programming it.

A new message appeared.

Please select the gender of ANNA.

Trevellion slid his finger over "Female" and tapped the screen. Beginning at the feet, an icon about three inches high formed. In a parallel grid, the figure of a woman appeared. Lines ran vertically and horizontally through the body outline. When the grid was complete, he selected a fresh option.

Please select ANNA vocal and tonal capacity.

With a click of a flashing button underneath the woman's figure, a monotone female voice began reciting a pre-programmed phrase, "The quick brown fox jumped over the lazy dog," over and over.

For a few moments, Trevellion adjusted the tonal settings. The voice was as near as he could match to the one recorded on the video they had taken.

The screen asked:

Please enter sample dialogue.

He grinned as he typed a message into the provided box.

Trevellion looked back at the monitor and moved his finger over the last option before stroking the screen.

Please select the designated ANNA image file.

Trevellion browsed his files for the image.

Do you want to preview ANNA settings?

Trevellion leant back in his chair, tapping "Enter" on the screen.

A familiar woman's image appeared on the screen and words filled his office.

'Michael, is that you? Are you there, Michael?' the voice said on repeat.

The woman's body turned on the screen as she spoke. She had the face of Colette Robertson.

CHAPTER SEVENTEEN

Michael shivered as he exited the quiet, rural railway station. The station comprised two platforms and some covered seating on either side. There was no ticket office. The only other passenger departing the clunking slam-door train at Ash Vale was a tired-looking mother, who carefully negotiated the steep steps leading to the road with her pushchair.

On the pavement outside the station, he pulled his jacket tighter and looked at his watch. A little before three. At least he wasn't late.

It was a surprise he was on time at all for his meeting with the mysterious man, apparently called Brown, and his friends. Brown had warned him they, "the bastards at Fuck-the-CitizensNet" as he'd put it, would almost certainly be watching him. He had to ensure no one followed him.

At first, he'd protested when Brown had insisted he'd come by train. A car was too easy to locate. Brown had also ordered him to go into London first, to lose anyone monitoring his activities. Michael's complaints disappeared into a sea of paranoid assertion.

'We can't risk exposure by you being careless and leading them straight to us. We've spent over two years, keeping ourselves concealed from the authorities. Besides, you want our help. It's in your interests to cooperate,' Brown had told him in no uncertain terms.

In the end, Michael had grown weary of arguing with the man who, despite his conspiratorial paranoia, might be the only one who could help him.

Following the complicated instructions, Michael had walked to Hersham railway station. From there he'd taken a fast train to London Waterloo. Brown had told him to get off the train at the first available moment and run to one of the underground entrances on the platform. Instead of getting on the tube, Michael was to come back out of the underground and into Waterloo's main concourse. The bustle there would give him sufficient cover if his assailants were still close. He was then to catch a fast train to Wimbledon, where he would change to the District Line and take the tube to Richmond. At Richmond, he would pick up his final train to Ash Vale.

The entire journey had lasted almost three hours. Michael was certain nobody had followed him. On the train from Hersham, only two other passengers had joined the train, travelling all the way to Waterloo. And unless the woman with the pushchair was working for *them,* his presence here had been unobserved.

Michael frowned as another chill wind battered him. He was thinking like Brown, with thoughts of "*them*" and "*us*". He just hoped his trust in Brown hadn't been a mistake.

As he shivered again, a man emerged from a boarded-up shop doorway across the road. It was Brown, looking as furtive as ever, casting anxious glances around.

'Did you follow my instructions?' he asked, peering up the urine-smelling steps that led to the station platform.

'To the word,' Michael replied, tired from the journey.

Brown didn't reply. Instead, he scratched his chin nervously, his head bobbing up and down.

'Is that it?' he asked, his gaze dropping to the black canvas bag Michael was clutching.

Michael nodded and reached for the zip.

'Not here,' Brown hissed. 'Later.'

Fifteen minutes later, Michael arrived at the outskirts of Aldershot. The car trundled into what he could only describe as a derelict mobile home park.

Michael watched as they slipped by an old stone warehouse that had once housed God knows what. Now, the doors hung from their rusted hinges, glass from the shattered panes decorating the surrounding park.

Beyond the warehouse were about twenty dilapidated mobile homes, each in differing states of disrepair and decay. Michael frowned. The smell of the place matched its appearance. An odour of damp rotting wood and stale toilets hung in the air.

'You've got to be joking,' he said, closing the car door.

'It's this way,' Brown mumbled, striding across the mass of broken masonry and rotting weeds covering the area.

A deserted-looking caravan to their left seemed to be their destiny; Michael followed. It was too late to back out now.

The caravan itself was about thirty feet long. Additional black coverings on the inside covered the cracked, grimy windowpanes. Brown knocked four times on the caravan's stained door.

The door opened, revealing another anxious, dishevelled-looking man. He was in his late thirties, Michael thought, taking in his appearance. The weeks of stubble, the black bags under his eyes and the mass of grey hair swept back, revealing a high temple, made the man look twenty years older. Maybe more. And just like Brown, he had the same paranoid haunted look to his every expression.

'Everything go all right?' the man asked, betraying a strong Welsh accent.

Brown nodded.

'Yeah, fine. Let's get inside, it's fucking brass monkeys out here.'

The door to the caravan was shut, bolted and then padlocked. Michael was struck by the contrast between the inside and outside of the caravan. Blackened windows blocked the array of lights fastened along the entire ceiling.

Piled high along the full length of the caravan opposite the door were items of computer hardware; Michael could only guess at their purpose. There were ten to twenty monitors amongst the equipment, each projecting a different image. Further up the caravan the familiar UKCitizensNet logo appeared, flashed, disappeared and re-appeared on one screen. Two other monitors were scrolling endless pages of unintelligible code.

Whether it was chattering printers or the hypnotic bleating of UKCitizensNet's army of PR professionals, the hum was unerring.

Further down the caravan, sitting at a homemade constructed desk, Michael could see Brown's other colleagues pointing at another monitor, and from time to time typing commands into a keyboard.

As Brown approached, they looked up from their heated discussion.

'You made it, then?' the first man said, his eyes scanning Michael's frame.

An awkward silence hung in the air as the four of them looked at Michael, unsure as to their next move, their next words.

'Look, how about some introductions?' Michael suggested, looking at the man who had spoken.

'Stephen Smith.'

'Morgan Jones.'

'Richard Green.'

'John Brown.'

Amusement spread across Michael's face.

'You're having a laugh, right? Smith? Jones? Brown?'

'It's safer for everyone if you don't know our real names. Just call us by these,' said Smith, the first man who had spoken.

Michael frowned as thoughts of his dark purpose with these men resurfaced. Jones, who had unlocked the door to the caravan upon their arrival, guessed what Michael was thinking.

'The one thing you must understand, Michael, can I call you Michael? We are on your side. We all have something in common. The creation of UKCitizensNet, and the demise of the old internet as we know it, destroyed all our lives. We need each other. Our strength is in togetherness.'

Michael smiled weakly. How could five men oppose a government-backed project, if it was that?

'You said you wanted to show us something?' Jones continued, his gaze on Michael's black canvas bag.

Michael unzipped the bag and removed the contents.

'For whatever reason, my wife kept files and disks hidden in a Post Office box. Why they weren't at SW Technologies or at home,

I don't know. I've been thinking long and hard as to her motives. Perhaps she recognised the significance of her work. Was this her insurance? I am sure, though, that they must be important. Although I didn't believe what Brown told me in Kingston, I hid the files for safekeeping. It's lucky for you I did.'

Brown shuffled on the spot, forcing an awkward grin.

'Let's hope it's lucky for us all,' Jones said as Michael handed over the neat box file.

'I've had a quick look at the files. They mean little to me.'

A look of excitement spread across the men's faces as Jones clicked the box open. Green, who had until now remained silent, turned to Michael.

'There's a kettle and some biscuits. Not the chocolate digestives, they're mine. Make yourself comfortable. This could take a while.'

Green turned back to the box file. Michael guessed he was in his mid-forties, although the tidy combed side-parting and thick-set glasses which he was forever setting and resetting on his nose made him look much older. Like the others, he carried the same wide-eyed, fearful expression of someone who'd foreseen his own demise.

Green looked as if he ought to be a computer science or physics lecturer, Michael thought as he brought a mug of coffee to his lips a few minutes later, sitting on a torn sofa, watching the four men's activities. Maybe he had been. But then who knew what any of them had been before their lives had changed and they'd ended up in this desolate mobile home park.

His life had changed beyond recognition; sitting in a derelict mobile home park in the middle of nowhere was proof enough.

All around, the montage of computer monitors processed endless amounts of data, sometimes catching his attention as he tried listening to the four strange men's conversation. Every so often, a heated argument would erupt as language flew before excited exclamations. Another discovery would bring everything back to order.

Four hours of hot coffee and listening to strained conversations ticked by and Michael's eyes grew heavy as boredom set in. Before he could close his eyes, he heard the men approaching him.

Despite all the theories Brown had revealed to him in Kingston, Jones was the obvious leader of the four men. He sat in a swivel chair opposite Michael as the remaining men leaned against the stacked hardware. From what Brown had already told him, Michael surmised this was only a proportion of the servers, hubs and routers they used to keep the old internet alive. Although, what servers, hubs and routers were still wasn't clear to him.

Jones ran his fingers through his hair and his eyes were wide, pupils dilated, as he shuffled in his seat. His expression was a curious mix of excitement and fear.

'Is it important?' Michael asked, although sure that it was.

Jones laughed without smiling.

'Oh yes, it's important. And it's terrifying. No wonder they want it. Will kill for it.'

Jones paused, aware that much of the technical detail in the files would be beyond Michael's grasp.

'Your wife and David Langley were developing the most advanced Java app any of us have ever seen.'

Michael looked confused.

'OK, let me explain,' Jones continued, undeterred.

'A Java app is a small application, a piece of code that gets buried or used within a wider system, web page, computer platform. It could run a computer program of some sort on a UKCitizensNet page. For example, a Java app will run a clock within a UKCitizensNet page.'

Michael nodded, appreciating the explanation.

'The aim of this next-generation app, which was to be developed on the fifth-generation semantic web platform, I'm sure you must have heard of it, was to act as a help tool with some added perks. And not just for you and I, but for the sick, the disabled, the elderly, children, you name it. Anything where you can offer or need some type of help. Somebody who is elderly might program the app, through a simple interface, to turn all the house lights on at a certain time so they wouldn't have to grope around in the dark and risk injuries. Perhaps a mother might use the app to activate intercoms around the house at set times when she knows her baby will be in its cot. Or to operate the microwave at a certain time to warm the baby's milk. Perhaps someone living alone, feeling vulnerable, wants to have the burglar alarm automatically set at the same time each night.

'This way, they don't have to remember to do it or need the technical prowess to know how to set it. The manual goes out the window. Never again would you have to learn how to set the timer for your household appliance. The app does it for you.'

Jones stopped as Michael crinkled his forehead.

'Hang on, hang on. This app is a file from UKCitizensNet that is accessed through eCitTV? How the hell does it control your water and your lights and electricity?'

Jones exhaled, rocking on the rusted swivel chair.

'As I'm sure you remember, not long after the current government took power, McCoy banned access to the internet. Straight after, he re-nationalised all the utilities. Believe me, this was no coincidence. He got rid of privatisation in an instant. And because of this, the government now operates and controls the entire telecoms infrastructure, the gas pipelines, the electricity network and the water system. They control it all.

'The vision of UKCitizensNet that your wife's company and, of course, SemComNet, envisaged, was a complete and integrated national network. Not just an information network, but a network incorporating and controlling all the utilities as well. All being delivered via the existing infrastructures. All control was to be centralised.

'By now, I expect everything is on the network. Every computerised item at home or in the workplace carries an IP address. The infrastructure that brings your electricity and telephone connection can link to UKCitizensNet.

'That's what the fifth-generation semantic web platform has given us, a common integrated means to link every networked application. All derived and controlled from one source—UKCitizensNet.'

Michael nodded, although still unclear on many points.

'With this app, UKCitizensNet's users could control any networked application they have going into their home or business. This could include setting the lights to come on or turning up the heating when you want. Every user's eCitTV unit has an individual IP address or internet protocol address. In simple terms, the IP address is your UKCitizensNet ID number. It identifies where you are geographically and your precise position within the state network. You would then enter the manufacturer's serial number for the appliance you wanted to control. All of this information would be sufficient for the servers of the state network operator to get UKCitizensNet to automate the flicking of the required switch at the right time. So, if you want the TV to come at 7 p.m., UKCitizensNet, via its massive infrastructure, will turn your TV on at that time.'

Jones paused, reaching for a pack of opened cigarettes lying on top of a monitor.

'So they killed Colette and Clare to get their hands on a piece of technology that would help people?' Michael asked, unable to take it all in.

Jones rubbed his chin, his expression thoughtful once more.

'Yes, and no.'

Michael felt his muscles ache and twitch as his body tensed. His heart rate was quickening as he looked into the faces of the four men. The whole thing was so complicated. His head throbbed as he tried to make sense of it.

'What do you mean?'

'Yes, they wanted the technology. But no, they didn't want to help anyone with it. Imagine you control the entire country's networked utilities and household and other appliances. eCitTV is the easiest means to deliver it because everyone has a TV. Why do you think the government made them so cheap? But it's not the only means to deliver UKCitizensNet or their plans for the app. Don't forget your home computer, your mobile phone, and your iPod. So, imagine if somebody buys a thousand cigarettes online via one of the UKCitizensNet shopping arcades because it's cheaper than the corner shop. They've now got a record of your purchase and that you're a committed smoker.'

Jones stubbed his cigarette out beneath his heel.

'Then, in the middle of the night, using the app, they turn on the gas from your cooker because the gas service is on their network and your meter has its unique IP address. Joe Public wakes up the next morning, lights a cigarette and...'

Jones let the sentence trail off as Michael's face turned pale.

'What if they decide to alter the makeup of the gas piped through to your cooker to carbon monoxide? A discreet leak in the middle of the night and nobody will ever wake up. What about causing a small, innocuous electrical fire that soon engulfs an entire building? It doesn't have to be limited to one house or building. UKCitizensNet comes through regional servers, covering large local areas. You could cause any disaster you could dream up, silently and without a trace. Imagine if...'

'OK, OK. I get the picture,' Michael interrupted, as Jones' fervour threatened to get the better of him.

The enthusiasm at the technical milestone they'd just discovered receded as Jones continued more sombrely.

'It's the ultimate weapon. You don't know it's coming. You can't see it's coming. And when it's struck, you don't know where it came from. That's why they want it. And that's why they killed your wife and daughter, and David Langley.'

'Are you sure?' Michael asked, fearing the truth, but needing to know.

Jones nodded.

'I'm afraid so. It's all in your wife's files. Although the more sinister conclusions are our own. But there's no question why they want your files. They're incredibly valuable—to us and them.'

Michael leant back and watched a new expression on Jones's face. It was almost indiscernible, the slightest flicker in his eyes, gone as quickly as he saw it, but leaving him with the feeling that they held something back.

'What aren't you telling me?'

Jones chewed his bottom lip as he shuffled in his seat, casting a glance at the other three men. He exhaled and leant forward.

'Almost two years ago, on the night before they banned access to the internet, we got into several government databases via the old network, looking for anything that could expose what was happening. We didn't find what we were looking for.

'Whilst we were doing this, I glimpsed a confidential Defence Department file about a project called CODEX, which mentioned establishing UKCitizensNet. I couldn't understand why the Defence Department was interested in the network. But now it all makes sense. Thanks to your wife's files.'

Michael also chewed his bottom lip as he took in what Jones had just revealed, knowing he still didn't have the complete picture.

One key fact was missing.

'You're not telling me that's what you were holding back, are you? Why would I care about a Defence Department file unless it had something to do with Colette? What else did the file say?'

Jones hesitated, averting Michael's eyes.

'Just before they took the connection to the internet down, I came across a section in the file which talked about "Primary Targets." Your wife's details were there, along with David Langley's. Before I lost the connection, I didn't find any evidence CODEX, whatever it is, had anything to do with their deaths. But they mentioned both your wife and daughter. Why would the Defence Department or the government be interested in that?'

Michael could feel the knot in his stomach tightening. His heart thumped as he processed this new information.

'So, where is this file? That must be a starting point for talking to a private investigator or someone who could dig deeper?'

Jones looked down, and Michael knew what he was going to say.

'You don't have it, do you?'

Silence filled the mobile home as Michael waited for the inevitable confirmation the four men were reluctant to reveal.

'No, we don't. They disabled the network connection before we could save or print a copy. It's my fault. I got caught up in the document, hoping and praying it would give us some proof of what was going on with UKCitizensNet. I just forgot to save it before time ran out.'

He fiddled with his fingers, trying to evade Michael's gaze.

Michael could see Jones' deflation, his forehead knotted with tension; the other men's harrowed expressions showed resignation. There was no point in getting angry; anything he might have said, they would have already thought.

He stood up from the warm sofa and began pacing the grimy floor.

'What are we going to do? What can we do? As you've said, we can't go to the police, can we?'

The four men shook their heads.

'And with no evidence, private investigators are out as well,' Brown said from where he perched on a desk behind Jones.

'With arrest warrants out for all of us, investigators must hand over any detail to the police. They'd pick us up within hours.'

'Our biggest potential weapon is their biggest weapon, the app and UKCitizensNet,' Smith said, breaking the gathering gloom, and turning to a monitor that was scrolling code at an incomprehensible speed.

'What are you saying?' Michael asked, desperate to find something that might offer the chance of avenging Colette and Clare's murders.

Or was it revenge he was after? His troubled, angry thoughts had become so blurred he could no longer distinguish between revenge and comprehension of the situation.

Smith traced a line up and down the glowing screen as more text and numbers appeared and then disappeared on the screen.

'For months we've been trying to hack into the UKCitizensNet system, get into their databases, into their information. If we can get in, maybe we can find some piece of evidence to expose them or broadcast our evidence over UKCitizensNet. That would be the ultimate fucking coup, wouldn't it?'

A ripple of approval spread amongst the four men.

'But you've not been able to hack their system yet?'

Green shook his head, looking extremely annoyed.

'The bastards have rock-solid gigabit encryption on their system.'"

'Which means what?'

'Which means their network is fucking well protected. We've gone past several levels of security, but never into the actual system, never into its heart. Besides, we've had to move about quite a lot. We've had to leave equipment in places and the fuckers have found bits of our kit in their pursuit of us.'

Michael tapped the screen that was still carrying on with its operations.

'So what's this?'

'It's an encryption-breaker tool. It's trying to crack their system's security and punch a big hole in their firewall.'

Michael sighed, sinking back on the sofa, cradling his head in his hands.

'We can't prove they killed my wife and daughter, can we?'

Jones placed a comforting hand on his shoulder.

'They've been after us for two years and they haven't got us yet.'

Michael looked up, tears in his eyes. Horrific images and disturbing memories rushed through him.

'No, they haven't. But look at all of you. You look like refugees, and you're hiding in rotting caravans in the middle of nowhere.'

Jones ignored Michael's outburst. They'd all felt the same frustration, the same despair at having their lives stolen.

'Michael, the files you've given us also cover data encryption techniques because of the need for security the app would have required if developed. So far, UKCitizensNet isn't using this sort of functionality. And we know SemComNet hasn't perfected it yet because they want your files. Gigabit encryption is the most advanced there is. These files might just be able to help us crack it.'

'Might? Might? It's all "mights" and "maybes" with you. Never anything definite or real.'

Tears were streaming down Michael's face.

'Michael, we need to study these files longer to understand them better. We can help each other.'

Michael wiped away his tears.

How had it come to this?

Why did his only hope lie with four men he didn't know in a rotting hole in the middle of nowhere?

As he pondered this desperate thought, the monotonous words of UKCitizensNet's female presenter came back to him. She'd been right, he thought, frowning. It had changed his life forever.

CHAPTER EIGHTEEN

IT WAS 10.30 P.M. before Michael got back to his quiet house in Hersham. The journey back had only taken just over an hour, but it seemed like a tortured eternity as disturbing thoughts raced through his mind.

He was still confused as he attempted to grapple with the magnitude of what faced them. At least after spending several hours with these internet outlaws, he no longer doubted their sincerity. The dejected tiredness etched in their faces was all too genuine.

Despite the confusion, he felt in trying to understand how the app worked, he would find justice for Colette and Clare...

He'd already spoken to the insurance brokers to tell them he still wasn't fit to return. They'd understood so far. A little longer shouldn't be a problem.

He decided to take a long hot bath to ease his aches and pains. If nothing else, he wanted to get the damp, rotting smell of that caravan, which seemed to cling to his every pore, washed away.

Despite his cleansing bath, his mind was still an agitated maelstrom of troubled thoughts. He knew he wouldn't be able to sleep for several hours despite the crushing weariness he felt.

To compound things, he'd spent a full half-hour checking and double-checking every window and door—ensuring he didn't miss a single lock or bolt. His descent into the same paranoid state as his four allies was a rapid one, he thought, peering through the lounge curtains, surveying the quiet street outside.

If they came for him in the night, they wouldn't find anything. The files were no longer in his possession. He would never reveal their whereabouts. No matter what they did to him. What could they threaten him with, anyway? They'd already taken everything from him.

Michael returned to the lounge and slumped into an armchair in just a pair of tatty boxer shorts. Reaching across to the coffee table, he picked up the console for his eCitTV unit before switching it on. Within a few seconds, clichéd dialogue from a trashy American film filled the room. He clicked for another channel, and another, and another. Was there nothing interesting to watch, he wondered, as snooker highlights appeared.

He stared at the large eCitTV screen and thought back to what Jones had said to him, how they had to find a weak point in UKCitizensNet's operations. Without thinking, he pressed the 'Web' button on his console and the screen melted into the familiar red, white and blue UKCitizensNet logo.

The image disappeared to be replaced by UKCitizensNet's opening menu and he scanned the on-screen content. There had to be a weak point somewhere. Colette and Clare's memory demanded it.

Trevellion looked up from a memo he was typing as his monitor beeped an alert. A flashing red message appeared in the application's window.

> User mrobertson@ser56.ecit (IP address 56.2 4.89.10) has connected to UKCitizensNet.

'About fucking time,' Trevellion muttered, looking at his office clock, showing 11.45 p.m. He was the only one in the East Wing of SemComNet's headquarters, except for the army of security guards.

Trevellion slid his left index finger over the smooth screen and tapped the icon he needed for his task.

> Welcome to Advanced Nano Network Application (ANNA) version 2.01.

Trevellion's expression broke into a malicious sneer.

The welcoming message disappeared as he retrieved his special file—cr1.ana. With a further tap, a fresh dialogue box appeared:

> Send to: (please enter IP address).

Trevellion typed, watching as 56.24.89.10 appeared on the screen. His lizard-like features, almost indiscernibly, formed a thin smile as his finger glided over the "OK" button.

> Cr1.ana sent to 56.24.89.10. Intranet Relay Chat channel open.

Trevellion leant back in his chair and stretched his tired limbs. 'OK, Michael, it's time to play.'

Is there no end to the number of online channels of information? Michael sighed in annoyance as another screen of marketing rhetoric about UKCitizensNet whizzed by. Brown called it "brainwashing by saturation of misinformation." Being fed the same marketing drivel day in day out, your brain becomes so overloaded and desensitised you end up believing it all. And with the public's insatiable appetite for data, the distinction between information and misinformation soon becomes blurred.

His train of thought halted as a face flashed up on the screen before being replaced by the next UKCitizensNet promotional page.

His jaw dropped as he selected the "Back" button on the screen. The previous page of UKCitizensNet re-appeared. He rubbed his eyes. Perhaps he was more tired than he thought?

The second time it happened, he jumped in his seat. This time, the face was there longer, looking at him, into his very soul.

Almost before he could register the image, it had gone. UKCitizensNet's online service returned. He scowled. UKCitizensNet had never disappeared like that before. His mind was playing its familiar tricks on him and tempting him back to the welcoming arms of despair and tortured oblivion.

As the face appeared again, Michael broke into a cold sweat and his breathing became more rapid. This time, it was more than a face. It was the image of a woman facing him on the screen. It couldn't be. He knew it couldn't be. The face, that beautiful face. It was Colette.

As he slid off the sofa onto his hands and knees, struggling to the eCitTV screen, the image faded again.

'Colette,' he whispered in despair.

Michael reached out and stroked the screen as it melted back into UKCitizensNet.

'Damn you. Why didn't you take me as well?' he screamed as the UKCitizensNet logo and its annoying little jingle filled the darkened room.

He looked away from the image symbolising the destruction of his life and hung his head, trying to suppress the bloody images threatening his consciousness.

'Michael,' a female voice said.

His blood froze. The distant voice echoed throughout the room. Now he knew he was imagining things.

'Michael,' the voice said again as he snapped his gaze onto the screen.

In front of him, the vision of a woman stood in a nondescript grey dress. Michael could suppress his tears no longer as he looked into Colette's beautiful face. She shimmered against the jet-black background of the screen.

'Are you there, Michael?' the ghostly voice asked as he reached out to touch the screen, afraid the image would fade.

His jaw dropped, and he watched dumbstruck as Colette's mouth moved. The divine lips he had savoured so often began speaking.

He closed his eyes as, for the first time in two years, he heard her voice. Not that he could ever forget how she sounded.

'I'm here,' Michael whispered, hot tears rolling down his reddened cheeks.

'I'll always be here, Michael,' the woman's voice said. 'Here to guide you, to show you the way.'

He stroked the screen as Colette's lips moved. Lost to her and lost without her. Enveloped by every word she uttered as it rekindled a thousand memories, blissful and violent.

'The great dragon was hurled down—that ancient serpent called the Devil or Satan, who leads the world astray. He was hurled to the earth, and his angels with him,' she said.

Michael stared at the screen.

There was a brief pause as the woman's image faded, her hand outstretched to him.

'The great dragon was hurled down—that ancient serpent called the Devil or Satan, who leads the world astray. He was hurled to the earth, and his angels with him,' she repeated as the image flickered.

As Michael touched the screen, teetering on unconsciousness as shock and grief welled up, he heard a sharp cracking noise. Stirred from his wavering position in front of the screen, his eyes shot open.

He heard a drunken male teenage voice scream as another stone bounced off his lounge window.

The feeling of hyperventilating grew, and he wiped the cold sweat from his face, trying to take deep breaths. The sound of teenage laughter faded as the culprits scurried away.

I imagined it. I must have.

In the back of his mind, he knew what he'd seen and heard had to be tricks of his imagination. He felt the acid taste of nausea rise as he recalled his hallucination of the blood erupting from the screen.

This is just the same. A hallucination. Images brought on by the stress and grief of all I've heard and learnt today.

He held his head in his hands as he tried to breathe, fighting the waves of nausea and dizziness threatening to engulf him.

Yet at the back of his mind, he could still hear those words. Words that he didn't know, nor had any idea where they had come from.

'The great dragon was hurled down—that ancient serpent called the Devil or Satan, who leads the world astray. He was hurled to the earth, and his angels with him.'

CHAPTER NINETEEN

THE LIFT DOOR SLID shut, and Trevellion leant towards the retinal scanner on the right wall. Within a few moments, a green light bleeped a confirmatory tone and Trevellion pressed the button for the East Wing's basement, the heart of the R&D laboratories. An impromptu visit downstairs was always a good way to start a rumour, even if there wasn't any gossip.

Besides, and this was the best part, it scared the shit out of the programmers and engineers: it would cause a spurt in productivity and help improve the company's R&D pipeline.

The "Pit," as the staff referred to the labs, comprised of two distinct sections, broken up into specific project groups.

On one side were the network hardware engineers. They maintained the company's vast equipment infrastructure of high-speed servers, routers, hubs, and, of course, the eCitTV unit itself.

On the other side were programmers and analysts—the surveillance teams and software people. A mix of staff diagnosing and treating UKCitizensNet software problems, advanced programmers looking to create and perfect the next big-selling application, and the monitors of UKCitizensNet's online content.

It was the advanced programmers Trevellion wanted to see.

A ripple of acknowledgement spread through the Pit as Trevellion exited the lift, striding into the busy lab. Computer staff, young and old, cast nervous glances at Trevellion as his gaze scanned the large open-plan area.

A compliment from Trevellion was always a bonus. But more often than not, an interrogation had led to a sharp rebuke. On the odd occasion, his visit had resulted in staff being sacked. Everyone in the room held their breath.

He walked through the crisscrossed aisles without uttering a word, raising an inquisitive eyebrow toward some project sections.

Trevellion reached the closed door at the back of the Pit, that displayed a small but well-observed sign, "Authorised Personnel Only." The fingerprint ID pad verified his identity, and the door clicked open.

A collective sigh of relief filled the Pit as Trevellion left the busy lab.

The security door led down a narrow white corridor with individual offices on either side. Each office managed an individual confidential project. And he had picked each project team himself.

At the last door, Trevellion slipped into the illuminated office. A small man with rounded glasses and a lengthening widow's peak looked up from the monitor, rising to his feet upon seeing his visitor.

'Where's Wainwright?' Trevellion asked abruptly, looking around the large office where three other staff were typing on laptops.

'I think he's gone to get some coffee, sir,' the man replied, wishing Wainwright had been in the office.

As he curled his lip in annoyance at his most important project manager's absence, the office door swung open. Andrew Wainwright appeared holding two cups of coffee. The second cup had been for Paul Davis, who was still standing opposite Trevellion.

'Coffee?' he said, offering Trevellion the second cup as Davis sank back, looking relieved.

Trevellion took the cup.

Wainwright beckoned him towards his desk.

'I was going to call you. I think we may have something.'"

Andrew Wainwright was one of the few people at SemComNet not overawed by Vincent Trevellion's mere presence. He had worked for the Ministry of Defence before and had encountered many fearsome characters. Whilst you never quite got used to having orders barked at you, he'd reconciled there was nothing personal in the delivery. You just got on with the job.

A glint of interest sparkled in Trevellion's dark eyes. Sebastian Tate had been breathing down his neck all week. They needed results.

With a few instructions keyed into the computer, the screen changed, splitting into two sections. On the left was an ordered mass of Java code. On the right, a complicated network diagram of lines and hardware hierarchies within the UKCitizensNet system. With enthusiastic prods on the screen, Wainwright turned to face Trevellion.

'In the past, we could get the app to download to any designated IP address. As long as the user completes the registration form, which, of course, they have to in order to use UKCitizensNet, we can pinpoint their geographical location through their IP address. The problem we've had has been a network clash, getting the app to interface with other networked utility applications that are separate and developed outside of UKCitizensNet. Our remote system hasn't been able to isolate designated applications in other networks consistently. Bottom line, we don't know whether the app is operating the toaster, the home computer, or turning the heating on.'

Trevellion frowned.

'Yes, I know all of this,' he said, his tone impatient.

'Until now,' Wainwright continued. 'We went back and spent days re-evaluating the software and the code. But in the end, we realised it was a problem within UKCitizensNet.'

Wainwright pointed fervently at the right side of the screen.

'We're sure that it's a network configuration problem on the UKCitizensNet side that's causing our baby to be less than co-operative.'

A smile slid across Trevellion's reptilian features.

'So, how long will it take to re-write the code and reconfigure the system?'

'A couple of days, considering the variations on the regional server clusters.'

'You've got twenty-four hours.'

Wainwright's face dropped.

Trevellion patted his arm.

'You've done a good job. Just get this thing working for me.'

Wainwright forced a grin. It wasn't often someone received praise from Vincent Trevellion.

Trevellion studied the screen intensely as he felt a surge of triumph course through his veins. If this was the solution, then half of the lingering problems with the app were close to being solved.

But there was still one more issue that needed to be completed before the project could proceed any further.

'So, tell me about the wireless deployment of the app?'

Wainwright rubbed his chin thoughtfully, fearing Trevellion's previous praise would disappear upon hearing his next remarks.

'Wireless deployment is proving more problematic. We know that the problem with the network coding errors has been hampering the app in any environment. But there's still a problem with the wireless handlers and that's making the wireless network flaky. More often than not, the system isn't robust enough. It's experiencing far too much downtime. And that's assuming the app has deployed at all to a remote wireless IP address, which is not guaranteed at the moment. All the regional hubs are being upgraded and diagnostic testing is taking place whilst we re-examine the handlers at our end.'

Trevellion nodded but didn't reply. He watched as Wainwright brought up more on-screen diagrams, although he didn't hear a word as his thoughts mulled over the problem.

Once they sorted this, they could move to Phase III, the most decisive and defining moment of the entire project. They could still progress to Phase II without the wireless component being at its full operational level. But Tate had demanded a quick resolution to all the technical problems slowing the project down before they went after their next target.

Andrew Wainwright was an outstanding programmer, Trevellion thought as his colleague explained how they would solve the problem of wireless deployment of the app. But despite his work on the project, Wainwright didn't see the complete picture. Nor was he briefed on the real purpose of the app—only members of the CODEX project team were privy to the contents of file *OP09/ST*. Like everyone in the office, Wainwright was working under the impression that the app was a user-friendly network application, a tool offering the user even greater interaction with UKCitizensNet. A mechanism to make life easier and less complicated—the complete migration to a networked world.

Trevellion smiled thinly. Wainwright and his programmers didn't need to know. Only a select few were aware of the CODEX status and what that meant. He just needed to get the bloody thing working.

As Wainwright brought up yet another screen of network diagrams for the regional server clusters, Trevellion's mobile began ringing. He pulled the narrow, state-of-the-art device and read the display:

Sebastian Tate calling. Answer?

'Keep me informed,' Trevellion ordered, exiting the office and slipping back into the quiet corridor.

'Trevellion,' he said, answering the call.

'Vincent, we need to meet. And I hope there's good news to report.'

Trevellion's expression broke into a smile.

'Things are progressing well.'

'Good. Contact my secretary and make an appointment to see me as soon as Phase II is complete."

CHAPTER TWENTY

Sir Donald Allison gently brought his Jaguar XJS convertible to a halt, the soft gravel swishing noisily beneath the tyres. As he exited his car, he stood for a moment, admiring their home. Light shone through the Victorian latticed window frames, illuminating the grand facade against the evening sky.

They'd moved to Elvetham seven years earlier from their expensive flat in Mayfair, although they still kept it if they needed to stay over in town. But this was their home now, not the city.

The house boasted six bedrooms, adjoining stables and three acres of land in leafy Hampshire.

Margo had had enough of living in London and wanted a quiet retreat in the country as she had put it. And once SemComNet had moved from Croydon to purpose-built premises in Brookwood, the location in Elvetham seemed ideal.

He never tired of coming home to this house. It was a sign of their wealth, their success. Above all, it was out of the public eye.

Since SemComNet had secured the tender to run UKCitizen-sNet, his position as company president had thrust him into the limelight. There were meetings at Downing Street. Dr Marcus McCoy had, understandably, taken a keen hands-on interest in UKCitizensNet from day one, ensuring the state network delivered his national online vision. Then there were parliamentary sub-committees and strategy groups, and endless requests for interviews from the press. This was now a way of life. And they all wanted a piece of him.

But he knew it was worth it. He looked at the house again and across to the stables to the right of the building. It was definitely worth it.

As the great oak front door closed behind him, Sir Donald emerged into his expansive reception area. Margo appeared at the top of the marble staircase that snaked up the centre of the house.

'Ah, there you are darling,' she said crisply, fastening a diamond earring she'd bought that day. 'I wasn't sure whether you'd be back before I left.'

'Are you going out?' Sir Donald asked with disappointment, his gaze tracing the short, clinging black dress his younger wife shone in.

They'd been together for eleven years. A lot longer than most observers had predicted. The predictable snide comments about the beautiful gold digger had been whispered in most quarters. When they married six months after meeting, he'd been two months short of fifty and she'd been a young and voluptuous twenty-nine.

Despite all the underhand comments from supposed friends about Margo, she had good breeding. Good enough for him not to worry about a claim on his substantial estate after they got married. And to this day, he'd still been proved right about Margo.

Unsurprisingly, those supposed friends had been all too keen to rub shoulders with them again when SemComNet had won the UKCitizensNet tender. Bastards, all of them. He'd had to take many tough decisions in his business life, especially where UKCitizensNet had been concerned about making it financially viable.

But one decision he'd made in his life had been the easiest of them all—telling those two-faced wankers exactly what they could do with their false friendships and 'knowing the right people' attitudes.

He hadn't let them get away with snubbing his young wife, and he was proud of that. He was almost prouder of this than the tremendous success of UKCitizensNet. And he wasn't too big to admit that this business success owed a lot to the tireless efforts of his deputy, Vincent Trevellion.

Trevellion primarily looked after R&D developments and regulatory issues. In the two years UKCitizensNet had been operational, SemComNet hadn't been fined once for failing to meet the tender's service level agreement. The online feedback users were regularly encouraged to complete also showed a huge rise in consumer confidence. The integrated fifth-generation semantic web platform had transformed people's lives.

On the product front, Trevellion had successfully developed better and faster upgrades for the service. His devotion to UKCitizensNet and him would make Trevellion an excellent successor if he decided to retire. Not that he had any plans to do so for quite a few years yet. Margo doubted he could ever tear himself away from the industry he loved so much.

Margo gracefully descended the stairs, her long, wavy red hair cascading alluringly over her shoulders.

'It's the charity gala tonight at Highclere, darling. I did tell you last week.'

Sir Donald nodded, the vaguest recollection of their conversation coming back to him.

She kissed him tenderly on the cheek, her sweet perfume intoxicating his senses.

'I'll see you later. I'm going to take the sporty, OK?'

He chuckled. They'd bought the classic Aston Martin three years ago, but still, Margo affectionately referred to it as the sporty.

As the front door shut firmly behind her, Sir Donald sauntered into his study. Pouring himself a scotch, he flicked on his eCitTV unit and slumped onto the sofa. Selecting the "Web" button on the console, the channel output seamlessly melted into the UKCitizensNet logo. The symbol of his company's success gleamed in front of him.

Selecting the "Finance" channel, the screen again altered, displaying a fresh set of choices. Skipping the "Home banking" option, he clicked on the "Stock Market" link. Locating his reading glasses, Sir Donald hungrily scanned over the latest market predictions for SemComNet's shares.

As he nodded appreciatively at a modest rise in the share price, an alert on a remote system was being activated. An alert prompted the remote server to pinpoint an IP address, instructing the server to send a Java app file to that location.

Sufficiently satisfied SemComNet's shares weren't taking a battering because of uncertainty in the Asian markets and gloomy forecasts of a global recession, Sir Donald moved into the bathroom.

On the wall of the marbled bathroom was the electronic display controlling the water throughout the house. It had been a long day, he thought, casting his mind back to a heated meeting of the parliamentary sub-committee on IT infrastructure and development.

He'd had quite a job persuading the members that UKCitizensNet and eCitTV units were suitably compliant with the nationalised utilities networks. This interfacing to link the entire nationalised services structure together was pivotal to support the government's long-term strategy of a networked future. It would also secure future UKCitizensNet developments, providing more comfortable lives for everyone.

It had been a tough meeting. He needed a long soak, he concluded, punching a couple of buttons on the display. He didn't want to run out of hot water.

Returning to the master bedroom, he sat on the edge of the four-poster bed and slid open his bedside drawer to pull out the electric shaver. He quickly plugged the cable into the socket on the wall. Listening to the sound of the water slowly filling the bathtub, he brought the razor to rest on his throat.

As his finger began to ease the "On" switch into position, the telephone on Margo's dressing table rang. Lowering the razor, he considered answering before deciding the answerphone could take a message. If it were important, he'd ring them back.

As the machine clicked into life, his interest faded. The call was from one of Margo's horsey friends wanting to reschedule a dinner date.

The sound of water running filtered back through to the bedroom. Sir Donald decided to shave after his bath and put the razor down. He switched on the lamp on the bedside table. The light flickered into life and he rose from the bed and headed for the bathroom, flicking off the bedroom light.

Submerging himself into the fragrant bubble bath, he felt the worries and stress of his week float away. Closing his eyes for a lingering moment, an alien, acrid smell permeated his senses. Gently sniffing the air and almost expecting the odour to have vanished, his eyes quickly opened. The smell was growing stronger.

He sat up, the acrid smell thick in his nostrils. He could hear a sharp crackling noise from downstairs. And now he knew what the smell was. It was burning.

Leaping out of the bath as fast as his tired limbs would allow, he ran down the hallway until he reached the top of the stairs. His eyes widened in fear as spitting flames engulfed the first third of the wide staircase. Licking a rapid path up the wooden, recently lacquered wooden bannister, the flames ignited the paintings lining the wall next to the staircase. A long antique tapestry on the wall caught the path of the fire, hungrily sucking the flames up the wall and onto the upstairs of the house.

Sir Donald felt his breathing become more rapid as the thick black smoke seeped into his lungs. Coughing violently, he stepped slowly backwards, almost paralysed in disbelief.

Retreating sluggishly along the hallway, coughing from smoke inhalation, the wall of fire crept threateningly over the top of the stairs. Turning away in panic, he hurtled into his bedroom, slamming the door shut.

Racing across to the window, he roughly shoved the curtains back before throwing a glance at the bedroom door. His eyes widened as black smoke snaked mercilessly under the door and filled the room.

The crackling noise overwhelmed his senses as the bedroom door was slowly but surely eaten up by the flames.

He began coughing again, but worse than before, as he weakly tried to open the latticed windows.

Open, damn you, open.

Pulling frantically at the window, he fought in vain to open the firmly secured window lock. He'd always made security a top priority in their dream house.

What a bloody irony.

Turning back into the room, he coughed more violently, peering through the intensely hot gloom of the smoke-filled room. He could feel dizziness rising within him as he doubled up in a coughing fit.

Unconsciousness threatened. He sluggishly reached for the small stool in front of Margo's dressing table. He needed something, anything, to break that bloody window.

As he moved towards the stool, a thunderous crackling noise deafened the fire-consumed room. The bedroom door disintegrated like brittle matchwood. He barely heard the sound or saw the persistent flames as they shot over the bed linen and up the frame of the four-poster bed.

Sir Donald screamed as the fire engulfed him, burning his flesh away in a few murderous seconds.

His screams were rapidly drowned out as the fire consumed the entire room and everything else in its path.

CHAPTER TWENTY ONE

MICHAEL CLOSED HIS FRONT door and began to climb the stairs, suppressing the familiar feeling of nausea he felt every time he had to go to their bedroom. Dismissing the thought, he opened the door. Grabbing a bag, he began to pack his clothes.

Initially, his four allies had told him to return home. Jones said it would create the appearance of normality while they attempted to get the app operational.

But he knew despite not understanding how the technology worked, there was no way he could remain at home, twiddling his thumbs waiting for their call. Of course, they'd protested at first, fearing his presence would be a distraction. Eventually, they'd acquiesced. He'd virtually begged them. The only condition had been that he had to follow the same method for getting to Aldershot. If he had the remotest suspicion they had successfully followed him, he wasn't to go to the deserted mobile home park and risk compromising their security.

Reluctantly, he'd agreed as the prospect of another three-hour train journey loomed. It was still more tolerable than not knowing if any progress was being made.

Piling shirts, jumpers, underwear and anything else that looked suitable into his bag he was as confident as he could be that no one was watching his house. Nobody had been loitering on the street or watching avidly from a parked car or van. The only car parked on the street was old Mr Thomas's Robin Reliant. He doubted anybody would try and monitor his movements in that.

A fresh thought struck him and he moved to the window. Pressing his face to the glass, he peered through the net curtains. What if they were in one of the houses in the street, carefully concealed, watching his every move?

He shook his head, realising he was becoming as paranoid as Brown. There was nothing he could do about it even if they were camped in a house with intrusive telescopic lenses pointed at him. He would just have to stick to Jones's instructions.

Turning away from the steamed-up window the telephone in the lounge downstairs began to ring. Michael's pulse quickened expectantly.

Maybe they've got the app working already?

Racing down the stairs, he turned into the cold lounge and grabbed his telephone.

'Put eCitTV on,' a voice at the end of the line said. It was Jones.

Reaching for the eCitTV console Michael flicked the unit on and sat down in one of the armchairs.

'It's started,' Jones continued sullenly as the picture snapped into life.

On the screen, the BBC was broadcasting a news special. In the top right-hand corner was a photograph of a grey-haired man in his early sixties. The newsreader was talking in a sombre, reverential tone, listing the man's early career achievements. He'd clearly died Michael thought, hearing the name Sir Donald Allison.

'Who is he?' Michael asked, fearing the worst.

Jones exhaled loudly.

'He is, or rather he was, the President of SemComNet.'

Michael felt numbness spreading through him.

'How did he die?' he whispered; his mouth dry.

Jones did not attempt to hide the cynicism in his voice.

'Oh, it was an accident, of course.'

As the sentence trailed off Michael knew Jones was dying for him to ask the next question.

'What sort of accident?'

'An electrical fire of some sort at his house in Elvetham.'

A lump in Michael's throat made it unable for him to speak. His mind was locked in a state of confusion.

'Michael, they must have perfected the app. This is too much of a coincidence to have been an accident.'

Michael shook his head.

'But why would they kill the President of SemComNet? Who would kill him?'

'Who's the most to gain from this?' Jones asked firmly, already knowing the answer.

Michael said nothing, not wanting to hear what he knew was coming.

'Vincent Trevellion,' Jones continued sombrely. 'He's just been appointed as the new President by the company's board in an emergency meeting.'

Michael watched as the familiar face of Vincent Trevellion flashed up on the screen. He was leading the tributes that were pouring in for Sir Donald.

Looking into the emotionless face he'd sat opposite not so many days before, he heard Trevellion use eulogies such as 'online visionary' and 'leading pioneer.'

'Fucking hypocrite,' Jones hissed down the line as Trevellion talked about his sense of personal loss.

'Trevellion was the only one to survive an attack from the anti-net activists,' Michael said bitterly as he watched Trevellion speak, although failing to register a word he said.

'*If* he was attacked at all,' Jones added doubtfully.

'You've to get that app working,' Michael insisted, watching Trevellion's feigned grief.

What does he know about loss?

'We're still working on it. But testing is going to take a bit of time because we simply don't have the same resources that are available to UKCitizensNet.'

'Just get the damn thing working,' Michael replied angrily, flicking a button on the eCitTV console, any button just to get Trevellion off the screen. He turned away from the picture before noticing he'd inadvertently activated UKCitizensNet.

'We'll do our best. I'll talk to you later.'

Michael slumped into his armchair, head in his hands. For the first time since he'd left the care home, he didn't feel overcome by grief.

Nausea had gone. Anger had replaced the feelings of self-pity and loss. Raw, undiluted anger.

Despite all he'd read and had been told, there'd always been doubt clawing at the back of his mind.

Did anti-net activist Davey Wilkes really kill Colette and Clare?

The whole thing had been too clever for a campaigner who lived his life up a tree. In retrospect, the soil samples they'd found, allegedly from the Brookwood area, were just a little too convenient.

Again, an image of Trevellion flashed through his mind. No, someone or something much cleverer than Davey Wilkes was behind this. Something like SemComNet. And Trevellion himself.

Michael grimaced as UKCitizensNet's logo slithered silently across the screen. Closing his eyes, he let his troubled thoughts wander to a happier time and place.

In front of him, the swing in their garden was bobbing backwards and forwards, temptingly close to him. Colette gently pushed Clare back and forth. She giggled happily; the wind rushing through her hair as she went higher and higher. He watched in contentment as he gazed at the two women in his life.

Clare laughed again as the swing rushed upwards, leaving her dangling in the cool autumn air. Colette was laughing too, speaking to him from behind the swing. He could see the words forming, but they were lost in the autumnal wind. He leant forward slightly, straining to hear.

'Michael,' came the hollow voice. 'Michael, Michael, Michael...'

His eyes flicked open. He sat up with a jolt, sweat on his forehead.

'Michael,' said the familiar voice again, filling the quiet room.

'Colette?' he whispered as her image flashed up on the screen.

His pulse quickened as he watched. Colette stood motionless on a hill in rolling countryside stretching further than the eye could see. At the back of his mind, the voice of logic was telling him he was imagining the whole thing, imagining Colette. The black dress clinging to her shapely body and the rolling countryside simply couldn't be real.

But he could see it all on the screen. And he could hear her, hear her angelic tones.

'Michael, I'm with you. I'm here to guide you,' the voice said.

'Justice can be yours. You are the only one who can stop him.'

The voice paused.

'Stop who?' Michael spluttered.

'You must stop the only survivor. This is his will, his game. Our pain is his triumph. Please stop him. Please stop Vincent Trevellion.'

Michael's breathing became quicker. He rubbed his eyes as the image of Colette began to flicker and slowly faded.

'The great dragon was hurled down—that ancient serpent called the Devil or Satan, who leads the world astray. He was hurled to the Earth, and his angels with him,' the voice echoed as the UKCitizensNet logo melted back onto the screen.

Covering his eyes with his hands, Michael heard the words reverberate through his mind.

Is it real? Did I imagine it?

He didn't know how, and he didn't care either, but he was sure he'd seen and heard Colette.

She was dead. That was painfully real. But these weren't voices in his head telling him what to do, what to think.

His thoughts returned to the lonely care home. They'd pumped him full of drugs. Was this a mere side effect? He shook his head.

The one thing he knew for certain was that the words in Colette's message hadn't come from some piece of information picked up in the past and filed away in his unconsciousness. And now he'd heard her tell it to him twice. That was his reality now.

Reaching for the eCitTV console, Michael flicked the "Web" button and sat back in the chair. It was about time UKCitizensNet did something to help him. The origins of Colette's message surely had to be somewhere amongst the millions of UKCitizensNet pages.

When the UKCitizensNet search engine appeared on screen, he rapidly typed Colette's message whilst it was still fresh in his mind.

Images of Vincent Trevellion cluttered his thoughts. Colette had implicated him. Or was it all just in his head? Perhaps he'd listened too much to what Jones and the others had said. He'd never realised until this point how contagious paranoia could be.

Before another image of Trevellion could form in his mind, the screen changed and a list of matches to his search appeared. Moving his finger over the first item on the list, he clicked on the link and waited expectantly.

His eyes widened in surprise as a page entitled "Online Bible" appeared. Quickly scrolling down the page, he stopped as he saw Colette's words highlighted in red in the middle of a paragraph. To the right of the text in blue, it read: "Book of Revelation, 12:9."

The Book of Revelation?

Colette had never been the most devout person he knew. Although more so than him.

His eyes scanned the words again. But as he read it, it was her voice speaking the words.

'The great dragon was hurled down—that ancient serpent called the Devil or Satan, who leads the world astray. He was hurled to the Earth, and his angels with him.'

Michael screwed his eyes up, trying to find meaning in the words. Was UKCitizensNet the great dragon and Trevellion the Devil or Satan, leading the world astray? Was Trevellion the great dragon and the mysterious four men the angels who'd been sent to help him? Or was UKCitizensNet intended to signify the devil and Trevellion one of the devil's henchmen?

He clenched his fists. It was nonsense. It made little sense. None of it made any sense. Least of all Colette appearing before him, delivering obscure biblical references. His knowledge of the meanings of the Book of Revelation was patchy.

Shaking his head again, he began laughing wildly at the absurdity of it. Colette was dead, had been dead for nearly two years.

Maybe I'm falling apart again?

Maybe this was another step nearer to a total mental breakdown. But how had he known the extract from the Book of Revelation if it was all just in his head? He'd barely received religious schooling as a child.

Flicking the "Video" button, the picture returned to yet another interview Trevellion was giving following Sir Donald Allison's "accidental" death. He looked into his face and the ever-present ice-cool exterior.

Voices or no voices in his head, he was sure Vincent Trevellion had somehow been involved in Colette and Clare's murders.

And he wouldn't rest until their deaths had been avenged.

CHAPTER TWENTY TWO

25 March 2010

The waiting was over. Standing expectantly outside the main doors a hum of excited chatter filtered up the queue of those waiting. From inside the hall, the sound of music blaring from speakers on the stage slipped through the door, adding to the anticipation. Any moment now they'd be let inside.

For the girls, it was a matter of pride to make sure they locked their best. Hours had been spent in the toilets, making sure their hair and accessories were all present and correct. None of them wanted to be outshone by another girl. Particularly not at the St Winifred's Girls School Easter disco. And certainly not when the boys from St Mark's were there. Apart from the Summer and Christmas discos, this was the highlight of the school's social calendar.

Clare Robertson stood about a third of the way down the line of children, rubbing her bare arms where goosebumps had surfaced.

It might have been almost April, but there was still a chill wind—she didn't like the cold, just like her mother.

Knowing this, her mum had instructed her to take a coat. And despite several minutes of protestations, her coat had been neatly folded into her school bag. As she stood in the queue, it was still tucked in the bag.

Around her none of the other girls was wearing a coat, all showing off the latest trendy tops they'd bought especially for the disco. Why was it they were allowed to choose their clothes, whereas her parents always had to approve what she wanted? It wasn't fair.

She'd spent the whole week worrying that her white top, ornately decorated with a sunflower down the middle, and a pair of black jeans, although not as tight as the ones she wanted would look out of place compared to her friends. The competition to look good both in and out of class had been steadily getting more intense this school year as they'd all started to experiment with makeup and hair.

Thankfully, her friends had commented on how cool her top was. Feeling relieved, she was finally looking forward to the disco. The only thing she was more excited about was the prospect of seeing James Bartlett.

Ever since first seeing him at the Christmas disco, she'd had eyes for no one else. The only problem was being at an all-girls school meant she barely saw him. And even then, it was only as part of a group.

She wasn't even sure whether he'd ever noticed her. He always seemed to travel around with five other boys, including Giles Nelson, commonly acknowledged amongst her friends, and most of the other girls in her class, as the best-looking boy at St Mark's. Whenever Giles, the head of the pack, and his friends were near St Winifred's then all the other girls would hone in on him, fawning and flicking their hair in appreciation of Giles's corkscrew blond hair and square jaw. The other boys were almost always crowded out; she'd never managed to speak to James.

But maybe tonight would be her chance. Everyone knew Giles was coming, so that meant his group of friends would be there too. Her heart fluttered as she thought about James and his dark hair, slightly long, hanging around his ears.

Clare looked down at herself once more, hoping she looked pretty enough to finally attract his attention. She'd never told her friends about her crush on James. They were all far too wrapped up in Giles to notice she was indifferent to his charms. And that was fine. It was her secret, and she liked it that way.

The chatter that had been coming from the line of children waiting at the school hall rose to a crescendo of excitement when the doors finally opened. With a gentle push, the line moved forward, and Clare followed her friends into the hall.

On stage, as for previous discos, were two vast black speakers, each about six feet wide, normally used to support the orchestra when it was giving a concert. But tonight, they were playing the latest chart music. The DJ, a maths teacher who believed he was rather trendy, had selected an assortment of songs, all vetted to avoid unacceptable lyrics.

The hall filled and within a matter of minutes, two groups had formed. The girls stood on one side with the boys lined up opposite. A wry smile crossed the Head of Year's face as she surveyed the disco and the gender and school divide. Who was going to be the first to breach ranks?

Clare watched from where she stood with her four friends. All of them had their eyes firmly set on Giles Nelson, who was standing sideways nonchalantly, wearing a black shirt and faded blue jeans.

But next to Giles, laughing at something one of his friends had said, was James. She could feel her heart racing as she laid eyes on him for the first time in four months. He was even more gorgeous than she remembered. Black jeans and white trainers, the tongue riding up over the bottoms of the black denim offset a white T-shirt with a logo she couldn't read from across the hall.

The chattering group of girls fell silent as Giles strode out onto the dance floor, the first person at the disco to do so. Slowly walking towards the army of girls opposite, he was lit up by the light display emanating from the stage between the two speakers. He took his time looking up and down the line of girls, making his selection, revelling in the adoration he knew he commanded, before turning toward Clare's group.

Kelly, one of Clare's friends, thin, tall for her age, and with straight blonde hair halfway down her back, grabbed her arm and hissed under her breath.

'He's coming over here. Please, please let him pick me.'

Clare frowned as Kelly danced excitedly on the spot, a very different thought going through her mind.

'Oh God, don't let him pick me. I don't want James thinking I like Giles.'

Giles stopped in front of Kelly. Smiling broadly, his teeth lit up by the ultraviolet light spinning from the light display, causing them to glow unnaturally.

'Would you like to dance?' he asked, warmly but super-confident.

Clare was sure she heard Kelly squeal with delight as she let go of her arm and followed Giles onto the dance floor. Relief washed through her as she gazed longingly in James' direction.

Within a few minutes, inhibitions about being the first on the dance floor had receded. The disco had taken off. Clare danced with her group of friends, near to James, but not within talking distance. Despite all her best intentions, she couldn't quite pluck up the courage to move any closer to him. Instead, she willed him in her direction.

After half an hour of failing to coax James any closer, Clare left the dance floor, hungry and thirsty. With two of her friends, Rachel and Zoe, in tow, the three girls headed for the vending machine in the corridor outside the school hall.

'Kelly is going to be talking about this forever,' Zoe blurted out.

The other two girls giggled noisily, knowing it was true. The entire school would talk about it.

The vending machine had been restocked for the disco, but halfway through the evening, it was already almost empty of snacks. Virtually all the crisps had gone and cheese and onion was all that was left; the girls agreed it was because they were disgusting.

'It's going to have to be chocolate then,' Clare joked, inspecting what was left.

'I'm going to have a Snickers. I love peanuts,' Rachel said, slipping her money into the slot.

'Me too,' Zoe replied as Rachel retrieved her chocolate bar.

'Well, I'm not. I can't eat nuts. I'm going to have the last Mars bar.'

Having pressed the button for her snack, a male voice behind the girls interrupted their conversation.

'Oi, I wanted that last Mars bar. Give it to me, it's mine.'

The three girls turned as one and looked into the face of a short, overweight boy with cropped ginger hair. An empty Mars bar wrapper was clasped in his right hand.

'You've already eaten one,' Clare replied incredulously as the boy's glare alternated between her and the chocolate she was now holding.

'I'd already bagsied that one. Give it to me.'

Lunging for her hand, the plump boy lost his balance and tumbled onto the floor in front of the machine as Clare ducked.

'Serves you right, fatty,' Zoe laughed, and the three girls turned and hurried back towards the hall.

Hauling himself to his feet, Zack Richards kicked the base of the vending machine in disgust as the three girls disappeared out of view. It wouldn't be the last they'd see of him that night.

AN HOUR LATER AND the disco had finished. Clare and her friends were standing in the school's main foyer waiting for their parents to pick them up. Kelly was flushed with excitement and, as predicted, could talk of nothing but Giles.

Although pleased for her friend, Clare's thoughts had drifted off to James.

When she'd returned to the hall after that boy had tried to steal her Mars bar, she'd spent what had seemed like ages trying to locate him. Eventually, she'd found him, dancing with a pretty dark-haired girl whom she knew was called Maria, and who was particularly good at tennis.

She'd felt her heart ripped out, the tears rising, watching Maria smile at James as they danced together. She probably didn't even like him—not as she did. So why did Maria get to dance with James when it was her that had the crush on him?

Determined to keep her feelings and disappointment hidden, she'd made an excuse about going to the toilet where she'd spent fifteen minutes crying, leaving her friends to swoon over Giles and feel jealous about his interest in Kelly.

It had turned into a terrible evening. And as she'd sat in the toilet cubicle, she'd also realised she'd left her half-eaten chocolate in the hall, on one of the tables, just when she really needed it.

Now, having retrieved her Mars bar and standing in the school foyer, she couldn't wait to go home. The sooner her dad arrived to pick her up, the better. The prospect of seeing James appear with Maria was just too much.

But looking out the doors into the school car park, there was no sign of her dad's car. As she sighed, the familiar sound of Giles and his friends, laughing, always loud and boisterous, filled the corridor.

Turning involuntarily towards the sound, she reached into her jeans' pocket for her open Mars bar. Without a second thought, she took a big bite. The sweet taste of chocolate instantly made her feel better.

Giles and his friends strolled nonchalantly up the corridor, stopping in front of Kelly, the permanent grin on her face still in place. Munching on her chocolate bar, Clare ignored the conversation between the two, her view blocked by the other girls in front of her.

'Hi Clare,' a quiet voice said as she slipped the Mars back into her pocket.

Instantly looking up, she found herself gazing into James's eyes. His longish brown hair hung around his ears, slightly damp from the dancing.

Clare felt herself blush and she wished her mouth wasn't stuffed full of chocolate, although somehow it tasted different than it ought to have done. But that didn't matter now—James was talking to her.

With a slight shuffle and awkward look at the floor as he fiddled with his hair, James quickly looked her up and down. Unable to hold her stare, his gaze settled on Clare's blonde hair that hung just below her shoulders.

'I, er, wanted to ask you to dance earlier,' he stammered, thankful that Giles' attention was focused elsewhere. 'I thought you were looking very pretty tonight.'

Clare's blush instantly accelerated from a mild pink to a crimson red. She couldn't suppress a smile. Quickly swallowing the chocolate, she attempted to reply but before she could get the words out Giles was next to James and the group of boys dutifully followed as he sauntered off.

With her heart racing, Clare watched, her mouth open in shock, as James disappeared down the corridor. She was aware the Mars bar hadn't tasted quite right. Maybe it had been old and she shouldn't have eaten it, a voice in the back of her head was telling her. But none of that mattered. All of the tears and anxiety from earlier in the evening had vanished in an instant.

James Bartlett had spoken to her. And he thought she'd looked pretty.

Further down the corridor, Zack Richards stood contentedly eating his third Mars bar of the evening. Stealing it from the stupid girl with a flower on her T-shirt had been easy. Whilst everyone else had been looking at the dance floor, he'd slipped it out of the wrapper, replacing it with the Snickers bar he didn't want. No one had seen what he'd done. As the final mouthful slipped down his throat, he had no idea just how devious he had been.

Michael Robertson pulled his green, slightly muddy Rover into the school car park. Picking Clare up the previous night from Zoe's parents' farm always meant he had to take his vehicle to the car wash afterwards. Mud and who knows what else seemed to attract itself to his car like a magnet. It was the same every time.

And something else was the same tonight—he was picking Clare up from one of her many after-school activities.

Both he and Colette had recently commented how she had a better social life than they did. If it wasn't taking her to friends, it was ballet classes or school discos. Yet again it was dad who was the taxi. Colette was working late, as usual, another meeting of the management team at SW Technologies as they plotted their next move to try and secure the tender for UKCitizensNet.

The moment he'd got in his car, he'd turned the radio on, tuning into BBC Radio 4 with another discussion about the forthcoming demise of the internet in the UK. The journey to St Winifred's in Camberley normally took about half an hour, so he'd caught most of the debate as he'd weaved his way through the end of rush-hour traffic.

The current affairs programme had been focusing on the government's "Countdown to UKCitizensNet", the slogan they were now using to both promote and defend the online change. With just over nine months to the pulling of the plug on the internet, government ministers were all banging the same drum: UKCitizensNet is the future—safer, quicker, and better for Britain.

He was so tired of their rhetoric and Dr Marcus McCoy. If Colette's company hadn't been bidding, he would have boycotted any mention of it on TV or radio. But because of Colette, even though he didn't remotely understand the technical aspects her job entailed, he always paid attention to the "Countdown to UKCitizensNet".

Secretly, he hoped he might learn something that gave a clue as to weaknesses within the other companies likely to bid to run UKCitizensNet. Even though she'd never come out and said it, Colette was clearly anxious about what would happen to SW Technologies, its employees, and her job if they failed. If nothing else, the hours she worked were testament to that. The introduction of UKCitizensNet was already affecting their lives.

Pulling up in front of the main entrance to the school, Michael could see many of the children who'd been at the disco congregated in the foyer. Scanning the faces, he quickly located Kelly, one of his daughter's friends. And sure enough, in the accompanying crowd, he could see his daughter, beaming as she said goodbye to her friends.

'Was it a good disco?' he asked as the car door closed and Clare pulled her seat belt across her, locking it into place.

Clare's smile ran from ear to ear. She gave her father a quick nod before waving at one of her friends as the Rover pulled away.

Michael didn't push any further, knowing his daughter would want to share the details with her mother. Boys talk... he rolled his eyes. She was only seven and a half. Hopefully Colette would be home soon.

The traffic was light as Michael headed out of Camberley and Clare was unusually quiet. From all the smiles and hugs at the end of the disco, it looked as if she'd had a good time. But she wasn't normally this subdued, and they could always find something to chatter about as he drove them home.

'Are you all right?' he asked, glancing sideways.

The glare from a passing street lamp briefly lit her face and Michael was sure her complexion was pale, her expression drawn and slightly pained, her normal exuberance strangely absent.

'I'm not feeling well,' Clare mumbled, shifting in her seat.

'What's the matter? Are you feeling sick?'

Pulling quickly into a nearby layby, Michael looked into his daughter's face. Tears had trickled down her face, which had lost all colour and was ghostly white. With the radio turned off, the sound of Clare's breathing filled the car like bellows being pumped rapidly.

Panic rose in him, and he could feel his pulse racing. He knew he had to remain calm as a terrible thought formed in his mind.

Clare's chest visibly heaved as she fought for each breath.

'Daddy, I can't breathe,' she said, her eyes wide with fear.

Despite all the preparation for this moment, regardless of all the books they'd read about handling her allergy, Michael felt unprepared and alone. Why did this have to happen when Colette wasn't there?

'Clare, have you eaten nuts this evening? I'm not cross, but you've got to be honest with me. Did you eat any nuts at the disco?'

Clare's head lolled and her eyes rolled upwards as she fainted in her seat, her body limp, her pallor reflected in the nearby street lamp.

Turning to restart his car, Michael caught sight of a wrapper poking out of Clare's jeans pocket. The half-eaten Mars bar was melting and he almost dismissed it as irrelevant. But in his heightened anxiety, he opened the wrapper, looking for an explanation for his daughter's ailment. His heart thumped like a hammer in his chest as the realisation hit him with the force of a punch. He didn't understand why, but the half-eaten bar had peanuts in the middle and wasn't a Mars bar as shown on the wrapper. He knew Clare wouldn't have bought it on purpose. So why was it in her pocket?

Wiping the sweat from his hands, he screeched out of the layby and turned the Rover around, heading back in the direction he came.

Fortunately, he knew a shortcut that bypassed the centre of Camberley, which was always busy, and would get him to Frimley Park Hospital and the nearest A&E unit.

His daughter needed emergency treatment. He now knew what he needed to tell the doctors. His daughter had gone into anaphylactic shock.

Less than ten minutes later, Michael had abandoned his Rover in front of the entrance to A&E, thankful no ambulances bringing other emergencies were in his way. At least it wasn't Friday or Saturday, so hopefully, the medical staff wouldn't be short on the ground, occupied by angry drunks that had got into a fight. And if they were, he'd scream and shout until someone came and attended to his precious little girl.

Carrying his daughter in his arms, he barged through the doors, frantically looking around for help.

A doctor who was signing off on treatment for a teenager hit by a 4x4 turned in Michael's direction. The male doctor looked young, Michael thought, but had a commanding air. And what he needed most at the moment was someone to quickly treat his daughter.

'I think my daughter's eaten nuts. She's got a nut allergy and fainted in the car whilst complaining she couldn't breathe. Please do something for her,' Michael blurted out, trying not to let his panic get in the way.

The doctor nodded and pointed Michael toward a spare bed before turning to a male nurse who was in attendance.

'We've got suspected anaphylactic shock on a young girl. I need epinephrine, now.'

Laying Clare carefully onto the bed, the doctor felt her pulse. Michael stood back, shaking as he watched his daughter lying unconscious before him.

'Have you given her anything since she went into shock? An EpiPen or anything else?'

Michael shook his head, tension creasing deep furrows into his forehead.

'No, she doesn't have one. We were told she didn't need one.'

The doctor frowned, shaking his head as he monitored her pulse rate.

'Well, you might want to reconsider that in the future,' he said flatly as the nurse returned with the dose of epinephrine and a hypodermic needle. 'If you could stand back, please.'

Michael duly obliged, his breathing becoming shorter as he looked into Clare's pale face. All of her normal vitality washed away. Forcing back his tears and anger at how a peanut chocolate bar had been in the Mars wrapper, he was aware of how helpless he felt. There was nothing he could do other than to leave her in the hands of the medical team and hope she didn't slip away before him.

And what he needed most, other than his daughter being well again, was for Colette to be there with him. With them.

THE FIRST THING CLARE saw when she opened her eyes thirty minutes later was her mum's face, smiling, but anguished and reddened from crying. The last thing she remembered was feeling faint in the

car with her dad. She knew her mum was working late tonight, but here she was now by her bedside.

'You gave us a real scare, darling,' Colette said softly, squeezing her daughter's hand.

'I don't know what happened. Did I eat some nuts by mistake?'

Colette nodded, relieved the colour was returning to her daughter's cheeks. When she'd arrived, just after the doctor had administered the epinephrine, she was shocked at how white Clare had looked. If she hadn't been told otherwise, she might have thought her daughter had died there on the bed.

When Michael's emergency call had come through, her meeting was nearly over. Not that she'd have cared about what her colleagues would have said. Her daughter needed her; Clare's health came first.

She tried to show calmness to her daughter but was in turmoil. What the doctor had said had hit them both hard. The risk of future episodes of anaphylactic shock leading to major organ failure.

Colette let that terrible possibility trail off, not bearing to contemplate it.

'I'm sorry I wasn't with you when it happened,' Colette said, clutching her daughter's hand.

'That's OK, Mum.'

Colette's guilt had ridden up inside her to the point she was going to burst as she'd watched her daughter lying unconscious on a hospital bed. And then the doctor's warnings. All she needed now was to unload, reassure both her daughter and herself of what was important.

'Even though work has been really busy recently, you know I will always be there for you, don't you? No matter what.' Colette spoke softly as her tears streamed down her cheeks again.

'Of course I do, Mummy. It's not your fault.'

Colette embraced her daughter, holding her tight.

Michael was leaning against the bed for support. His relief had left him feeling exhausted and his limbs ached from the emotional trauma of the evening's events. He didn't even want to think about the long-term effects. Not now. He was glad they had been close to the hospital. If this had occurred the night before when he'd picked Clare up from Zoe's parents' farm, virtually in the middle of nowhere...

As he watched his wife and daughter, he knew he never wanted to feel this afraid again.

CHAPTER TWENTY THREE

THE EIGHTEEN MONTHS MICHAEL had spent in the care home had been confusing. Day after day they had pumped him full of sedatives and then forced to listen to counsellors trying to empathise with him. But it had nothing on this. Conspiracy and counter conspiracy. Renegade groups fearing for their lives hiding in the middle of nowhere. And now an app that could set fire to your house...

Sometimes he felt he would wake from this absurdness and discover it was just hallucinations. Paranoia induced by the drugs he'd been given.

He stepped out of Ash Vale station, which seemed permanently deserted. The cloying smell of urine on the steep steps hung sickeningly in the air. Casting one more furtive glance behind him, he relaxed. No one else had got off at this stop. If they'd been following him, he'd lost them somewhere along the line.

But then he'd seen no one hanging around suspiciously. Only the group's assertion that he was being watched kept up this onerous security pretence.

Within a few minutes of his arrival, Brown pulled up alongside Michael, opening the car door. Pulling his seatbelt across his chest, he noticed the bags under Brown's eyes seemed to have drooped a little further towards his top lip, if that was possible. The washed-out harrowed expression of a man on the run was still as clear as ever. But there was just the slightest glint of excitement behind the glassy eyes.

'Have you got it working yet?' Michael asked finally, getting impatient as Brown kept quiet as they followed the road towards Aldershot and their secret refuge.

For a few moments, Michael believed Brown hadn't heard him or was too tired to talk and drive.

'We're getting there. The others will tell you more when we arrive. They'll have the latest news.'

Brown sounded irritated as he kept his eyes firmly on the road ahead.

The latest news?

Michael guessed Brown's annoyance stemmed from being dragged away from his work and the inconvenience of picking him up from the station. He decided not to pursue it or attempt to engage Brown in any further conversation. They'd tell him soon enough.

Continuing in silence, Michael closed his eyes, letting his thoughts wander. In an instant, Colette was there on the TV screen, alive, talking to him, accusing Trevellion. And then those words which made little sense to him, being repeated in his mind. Over and over again until he could take it no more, until...

His eyes flicked open with a start as the car ground to a halt. They were in the derelict park in front of the dilapidated mobile homes. The windows were as ever blacked out to the world, concealing the secrets and fugitives inside.

The normally verbose Brown merely grunted as he opened his door and exited the car. His mind seemed elsewhere.

Probably a seething mass of code and questions to the problem Michael's information had set the group.

Following Brown to the door of the mobile home, Michael's heart rate quickened and his hands went clammy. He needed them to find the answers, to get the app working. Trevellion wasn't getting away with what he had done to Colette, to Clare, and him.

Taking deep breaths, he felt his anger and bitterness subside as he observed Brown knock four times on the door. He had to stay calm. He wouldn't be able to exact his revenge if he were the gibbering wreck he had been. His resilience would provide the strength to take his vengeance on Trevellion and all those with him.

The door to the mobile home clicked shut. Locks and bolts were re-applied. Michael quickly looked around him for any sign of the group's success in getting the app operable. Instead of answers, all he saw was the familiar screens, either scrolling unintelligible code at a ferocious rate, or showing the current lies and misinformation being pumped out by UKCitizensNet.

Green was sitting at one of the screens, a long burnt-out cigarette hanging limply from his bottom lip. Turning, he looked at Michael. But just like Brown, the harrowed-looking expression didn't reveal any secrets.

Before Michael could speak, Jones emerged from the dimly lit opposite end of the mobile home.

'Michael, good to see you,' he said, holding out a welcoming hand. 'Any problems getting here?'

Michael shook his head.

'Nobody was following. It was fine. But enough about that. Have you got it working yet? I've been going mad just sitting at home, waiting hour after hour to know whether we can use it against Trevellion and SemComNet.'

Jones raised a placating hand, beckoning for him to sit down.

'We've had some success,' he said slowly, picking his words carefully, knowing Michael was hanging on every possibility. 'We've only done a minimal amount of testing, but the app is working and seems operational.'

Michael's anxious expression turned into an encouraging smile.

'Don't get too excited,' Jones added cautiously. 'All we've done so far is upload the app with the changes we've made to a customised network we set up ourselves. We use it to test various ideas we want to try against UKCitizensNet if we ever get past its gigabit encryption. We've been able to manipulate the app to perform various tasks of our choosing but haven't yet successfully hacked into UKCitizensNet. That's what Green spends all hours of the day doing, looking for the slightest vulnerability in their system. And assuming we do get into the system, there's no way we can guarantee the app will work in the same way.'

Michael tried hard to hold back a feeling of deflation. At every turn, Trevellion still held the upper hand.

Sensing his disappointment, Jones leant forward, placing his hand gently on his arm.

'Michael, it's not all bad. The app is the biggest leap forward we've had since we went on the run. We now stand a chance of really being able to do something. Before, we were still groping around in the dark, waiting for something or someone, waiting for you.'

Michael grimaced, looking to Green, who was inspecting a print-out of unintelligible code which ran onto several pages.

'Do you stand any chance of hacking into UKCitizensNet? Or have I just given you a new toy to play with for a while before we all realise we're back to where we started?'

Jones sighed, determined to remain positive.

'Amongst your wife's papers was information on advanced encryption techniques. If UKCitizensNet is using one or any of the techniques mentioned in the papers, then yes, we stand a chance of breaking it. Whether that's tomorrow, next week, or in six months, I can't tell you.'

'You talk of *if* they used one of the techniques. What if they didn't use one? What if they used a new technique they created themselves? What if this is all for nothing?'

The incessant hum inside the mobile home came to an abrupt halt. The three other men turned away from their tasks to listen in on the unfolding discussion.

Jones chewed his bottom lip nervously. Pulling a small hip flask from his pocket, he handed it to Michael, who had slumped back in his chair.

'I won't say I understand what it feels like knowing what they did to your wife. But remember, we're all victims here. We all want this to work, and we're working our arses off here. None of us wants to be cooped up in this cold shithole in the middle of nowhere, wondering when they might finally locate us.

'We've had our lives taken away, too. Our families were torn from us. We've been made outlaws for opposing what *they a*re doing.

What do you think will happen to us if ever we're caught? We won't end up in some cosy prison cell with three square meals a day. We'll end up in a shallow grave in the middle of nowhere, just like your daughter. That's our reality. So don't you tell me this is for nothing.'

Michael saw the anger burning in Jones's eyes.

'I'm sorry. All I want is for Trevellion and all of those with him to suffer for what they've done to me.'

He paused, looking into the harrowed faces of the four men.

'For what he's done to all of us.'

Michael's renewed sense of togetherness immediately eased the tension in the room. Jones sighed.

Taking a swig from the flask, and handing it back to Jones, Michael looked him straight in the eye.

'Just promise me one thing. When you've cracked the encryption, we go after SemComNet.'

Jones nodded, but Michael hadn't finished.

'We go after SemComNet. But only after we've dealt with Trevellion first.'

CHAPTER TWENTY FOUR

Warm sunshine baked Michael's face as he squinted from the rays. His gaze dropped on the endless ocean before him. Sparkling aqua blue sea glinted in the morning sun. Not the dreary grey or green back home. This was the Caribbean Sea, where the beaches are white, and your feet burn on the fine sand.

About two hundred feet away, a glass-bottomed boat was making its way out into the quiet water, ready to show more tourists the wonders of the ocean. Multi-coloured marine life would dance beneath the glass, almost playing for the tourists as they gathered around, eager to see something of the beauty beneath the ocean's surface.

Colette was one of those tourists, armed with her new digital camera. One of their many wedding presents. Thankfully, this was the only one she'd brought on their honeymoon.

Michael smiled. Fortunately for him, she hadn't brought too much in the way of clothes. Not that you needed many during the day. And they didn't need any for the night either.

Yawning, he screwed up his eyes, trying to spot Colette on the nearby boat. But all he could see were a mass of blobs as one tourist melded into the next in the haze of the horizon.

They'd always wanted to go to Antigua. And when they'd finally set a date for their wedding, less than a year after they'd met, it had been the obvious choice. Two weeks of breathtaking scenery, laid-back locals, and all the indulgence you could manage. It was idyllic.

'Move your feet, will you,' a gruff male voice said, pushing his legs out of the way.

Michael sat bolt upright, instantly stirred from his light sleep. Lying back on the moth-eaten sofa, he'd stretched his legs out for comfort, but had only managed to block the walkway through the mobile home.

Brown sat down opposite him, a cup of coffee in one hand. A chocolate digestive in the other.

'Don't tell Green,' Brown whispered, pushing the biscuit into his mouth in one go.

Green was still busily typing away on one of the many computers at the far end of the mobile home. Hour after hour, he tried to find a vulnerability in UKCitizensNet's security, one window of opportunity. Smith had departed to one of the other caravans to get some much-needed sleep. Something all four men looked like they badly needed.

Out of the gloom at the far end, Jones appeared, the glint in his eye betraying excitement at their work. Dropping down next to Michael on the sofa, he yawned loudly, stretching his arms behind his head, interlocking his fingers.

'How do you cope, living like this, I mean?' Michael finally asked, looking from one man to the other.

'You'd be surprised how quickly you get used to it when your life depends on it,' Jones replied sourly. 'When the alternative is a shallow grave, this seems like a palace, believe me.'

'But what about your family? Your friends? There must be people out there who are wondering where you are, what you're doing?' Michael persisted.

'To all intents and purposes, we're dead. All four of us. It's easier for us. And it's easier for them. We chose to give up everything we had, including the people we love, to protect them.'

'But how? I could never have willingly given up Colette or Clare. Not for anything.'

Brown leant forward from his hard wooden seat.

'Look Michael, none of us could keep our former lives. The government and whichever part of it that supports SemComNet and UKCitizensNet came after all of us. At first, it was a bit of roughing up by unpleasant twenty-stone thugs. Then our bank accounts were drained. And then the death threats. All because we actively opposed UKCitizensNet. We believed in our cause. We still do. So we stood by our principles. But then they came after Jones, beat him almost to death and cut off his finger. As a warning... We knew our families would be next. They wanted to prevent us from hacking their system. If we wouldn't tell where our kit was, they'd break the legs of Smith's daughter. Or cut off Green's wife's wedding finger.'

Brown and Jones exchanged a glance as Michael listened intently.

'At that point, we all knew there was only one course of action to take. We had to disappear. Run. Effectively become fugitives in our country, even though we'd committed no crime other than to support freedom of speech and freedom of information exchange.'

'What did you do?' Michael asked, memories of his former life flashing before his eyes.

'We faked our deaths. It was the only thing we could do. The four of us were all friends, so it wasn't odd for us to be together. An explosion in a warehouse near to where we all used to live in London sufficed. And leaving around a few of our charred belongings convinced the authorities we'd all been killed. The blaze was so intense they'd never have found anything more than ash, anyway. It was the perfect cover. From then on, our families were left alone. They lost their bargaining power. We are under no illusion that they know, or at least suspect we're not dead but out here as objectors to UKCitizensNet. As long as they don't know who or where we are, our friends and family are safe.'

Michael looked at Jones, relieved to finally hear some personal details. Even if he didn't have his real name to match.

'Sorry to hear about your ordeal. So you're married?'

'Fourteen years next month,' Jones replied sorrowfully, looking down at the pale white, tan mark of where his wedding ring had been. Everything from their previous lives had had to go when they'd faked their deaths. 'It's funny, but despite all you've been through with the deaths of your family, we'd have given everything to have had the time you had with your daughter. How old was she when she...'

The sentence trailed off as the two men held each other's stare.

'She was eight,' Michael said quietly, as a picture of Clare dancing before him, her blonde hair swishing from side to side, filled his thoughts.

'We always wanted children. But Margaret wasn't able to. We tried everything. Even went through IVF four times, but it just wouldn't take. They told me it had nothing to do with my fertility. They didn't say it was Margaret, but then they didn't have to. It's just as well I was raking it in at Microsoft. God knows how we'd have afforded the IVF otherwise. Margaret would have been fifty if we'd waited for treatment on the NHS rather than going private.'

Not wishing to dwell on the issue of children, Michael chose another subject.

'What did you do for Microsoft?'

'I was one of their chief software engineers for six years, working primarily on their operating systems. It was good until that bastard McCoy banned access to the internet. The company's priorities changed. I think if I hadn't gone down the road I have, I would probably have been out of a job in two years anyway.'

Jones sighed and sank back on the sofa. The pain of telling it one more time didn't make it any easier. Michael's next question was all too predictable. And he had his answer ready.

'So, do you ever see your wife? Just to see what she's doing.'

Jones looked at the floor, clasping and unclasping his fingers as images of Margaret came rushing back. Images of her getting into her car and driving to her job. Images of her doing her weekly shopping at the supermarket. And images of taking flowers to his grave at the nearby cemetery.

His tombstone was always immaculately kept. It was the pride of the graveyard. Every month, on the twenty-third, the day of the month he had "died" she would visit. Without exception. Always with a fresh bunch of flowers, clearing away the dead remains of the previous offering.

Jones paused, casting a nervous glance at Brown, fearing his response.

'For the first few months, I discreetly kept an eye on her, following her around, out of sight. I think I hoped she would see me, but knew she couldn't. I so wanted to tell her I was alive, but knew that I couldn't. No matter how hard people try, no one can keep a secret. She would have told someone, who told someone else, who told someone else. And before long, that someone would be working at SemComNet and they'd be threatening to kill her. I couldn't put her through that, or myself. In the end, I just stopped. I let her go. I had to.'

Brown's jaw had dropped. He looked agitated.

'You fucking idiot. You could have got yourself killed. Again. You could have got all of us killed, including your wife.'

Jones raised a dismissive hand at Brown.

'Look, I said I wasn't doing it anymore. So don't lecture me.'

With the tension rising, Michael turned to Brown, whose face was flushed with anger.

'So what about you? What did you have to give up?'

Brown tried to calm down.

'Not as much as the others. I had someone whom I saw on and off. When we had to go into hiding, we were "off". I always guessed she thought I wanted that permanently. There was no emotional farewell. No trauma at my passing. I don't suppose she even knew. She was working in France at the time. She probably thinks I moved on. It was no big deal. The biggest sacrifice was the lack of freedom. I don't have any children and I don't have any family. No one misses me.'

'What about your job?' Jones replied acidly, still annoyed at Brown's admonishment. 'You lived for that.'

Brown scowled.

'All right, so I was pissed off I had to leave my job because of this. I worked for Google, developing their search algorithms. It was a fascinating job until fucking SemComNet ballsed things up.'

Michael raised his eyebrows. Knowledge of the computer industry wasn't one of his strong points. But knowing where they had worked certainly explained how they were able to take Colette's work and use it so readily.

'You'd have liked Colette,' Michael said quietly, with pride in his voice. 'Her ideals and yours aren't a million miles apart.'

An expression of doubt crossed Jones's face; Michael knew what he was thinking. How could she have sympathised when she worked for one of the companies the four men saw as their enemy?

'Colette was very much opposed to the banning of access to the internet. Even to where she gave serious consideration whether she could remain in her current job. But then, when the opportunity for her company to bid for its replacement came along, she saw it as a means to right the wrong she thought had committed. Believe me, if SW Technologies had won the tender for running UKCitizensNet it would be a very different beast from what SemComNet developed. Information wouldn't be censored and restricted. Colette would have made sure of that.'

Jones raised his eyebrows, the look of doubt still on his face as he tried to make his reply as tactful as possible.

'Look Michael, I don't challenge your wife's motives. I'm sure she was trying to do the right thing with the SW Technologies tender bid. But this was a dirty tender from the start. Even if it hadn't been contrived to give the contract to SemComNet, her company could have been corrupted. Everyone has a price.'

Michael wondered what Trevellion and SemComNet's price had been.

'So what about the others?' he asked, dismissing the thought and looking in Green's direction before turning to Jones.

'Well, Green worked for one of the big Japanese banks whose name I can't pronounce, up in London. He was some sort of financial security analyst. Whatever the bloody hell that is. He tried to explain once before I fell asleep. All I know is he's the best hacker I've ever come across. But I'm guessing he didn't learn that skill in high finance.'

'And Smith?'

'Smith is a chemist by trade and was working for one of the big pharma companies. Roche or GSK. I can't remember which one. Anyway, he's pretty nifty with any sort of chemical as well as being the biggest computing bore you can imagine.'

Jones and Brown laughed. Michael pointed an accusing finger at Brown.

'What, more than you, with your computing conspiracy theories?'

Brown's expression dropped whilst Jones laughed even harder.

'Well, I was right, wasn't I?' he replied indignantly.

Regaining his composure, Jones continued more sombrely.

'Smith was married, but she left him after a few years. Probably for being so bloody boring, I shouldn't wonder. But they had a daughter together. She'd be about five now, I suppose. He hasn't seen her since he's been hiding. Her name's Charlotte.'

'Good for him,' Michael said quietly, trying to remember what it felt like to hold Clare. As hard as he tried, he couldn't recall the feeling. 'Let's hope one day he can see her again and tell her who he is.'

The three men nodded, contemplating their predicaments. Would any of them ever hold a loved one again? Or enjoy a beer with friends? Or just enjoy the freedom to travel anywhere without the fear that their name and passport would get them arrested?

Images of the Antiguan coastline, the perfect blue sea, and a little glass-bottomed boat flooded Michael's thoughts. Would he ever feel that way again? He was certain he wouldn't, not without Colette or Clare. All he had now were memories. And he needed to hold on to them. But until he found out why they'd been taken from him, he'd never be able to truly enjoy them.

Rising from his seat as the images threatened to overwhelm him, he turned toward the unused bed at the far end of the mobile home.

'I'm sorry, but I'm going to bed.'

In an instant, he was gone.

Jones and Brown stared, not uttering a word as they let him go. Although unspoken, both men were left grappling with the same terrible question. A question they feared they already knew the answer to.

Would any of them ever get back what they'd lost?

CHAPTER TWENTY FIVE

THE DOOR SLID SILENTLY open, and Trevellion exited the elevator. Grimacing, he pulled his expensive suit jacket tighter across his chest and proceeded towards Sebastian Tate's office.

He knew the route well. He'd been here for various clandestine meetings. And each time he returned, this part of the building was as silent as a tomb. Considering the importance of what was decided behind the doors he passed, there was always calmness about the approach. A calmness at odds with what CODEX was undertaking.

Trevellion cast a glance at his watch as he reached Sebastian Tate's door and stopped. He hated being summoned to see Tate at the best of times. But especially when there were vital issues at SemComNet needing his immediate attention—issues such as Michael Robertson and his four accomplices. Although Tate wanted to discuss this, his time would be more usefully spent finding a solution to the problem rather than just talking about it.

He smiled wryly. That was the government bureaucracy for you, he thought, knocking on Tate's office door before entering.

Looking up over the top of his glasses, the silver-haired Tate motioned to Trevellion to take a seat. He didn't speak as he finished reading the confidential document SemComNet had sent him, another inclusion for CODEX file *OP09/ST*.

There was no computer on his leather upholstered desk, only papers. The rest of his department might be at the cutting edge of technology, but he preferred to read the written word from paper. With all Tate knew about SemComNet and the technological possibilities UKCitizensNet amongst other things provided, he trusted the integrity of a paper document. There were no secrets embedded here, no usage monitoring or targeted customised announcements. The only surprise came in the content itself, not the way it was delivered.

'Vincent, good of you to come,' he finally said, sliding the SemComNet document back into its folder.

Trevellion didn't reply as he tried to read Sebastian Tate's expression. He knew the small talk would end there.

'Congratulations on delivering Phase II of the project. Sir Donald's demise was timely. Needless to say, it was well received by the Prime Minister and Secretary of State, as was your inevitable promotion. It keeps things more or less on schedule, which is what they want to see. The question remains whether the app is sufficiently developed to deliver Phase III within its tight window of opportunity. Do we have success on that front yet?'

Tate placed the file on his desk.

'Wainwright and his team are working on the wireless deployment issues as we speak. There's still a problem with the wireless handlers; that's making the wireless network unreliable currently. The regional hubs are also being upgraded and diagnostic testing is taking place to...'

'Spare me the technical details, dear boy. That's your domain, not mine. However, I presume we no longer need the data in Robertson's possession?'

Trevellion frowned at the mention of the continuing irritation Michael Robertson had become.

'On the contrary. We need it more than ever. The last intelligence report from your department stated Robertson managed to lose his tail in London. The only reason he would have known he was being watched was if our friends had warned him.'

'So we get rid of him.'

'I believe he sought to lose your man because he was meeting Brown and the others. It's a stone-cold certainty they'll now have whatever information Robertson had. And let's not forget who these men are—experienced hardware and software developers.'

Tate frowned.

"If our assumptions are correct, Robertson's information might be the missing component to our wireless deployment problem. Let's not forget the importance of that in relation to Phase III."

'I thought you said Wainwright and his team were working on these issues?' Tate's top lip curled in annoyance at his lack of technical understanding that was giving Trevellion the upper hand in their conversation.

'Our programmers seem to have solved the deployment problem on the standard network. But they're not as advanced on the wireless side. That is precisely why Robertson's data is potentially vital. We cannot let up in trying to get hold of it.'

Tate looked thoughtful, pondering the continuing involvement of Robertson's able accomplices. Trevellion sensed what he was thinking.

'We cannot underestimate these four men and others like them. They've been on the run for two years. What better "fuck you" towards us would there be than to launch a version of the app to create havoc on UKCitizensNet. Or to aim the app specifically at us with the same purpose as we wish to use it for? If they have a wireless solution before us, we're potentially not safe anywhere. You'd better hope government IP addresses are sufficiently secure and not common knowledge.'

'They couldn't get to us,' Tate snapped. 'Could they?'

'The simple fact is we need to get hold of whatever they've developed from Colette Robertson's files. After all, as outstanding programmers, they may have improved upon it. In different circumstances, we would probably have recruited them to SemComNet.'

'What if they've done nothing with the files and aren't planning to launch anything?'

'Oh, they'll be planning something, trust me. I would if I were them.'

'So, what do you want to do about it?'

'We target Michael Robertson. He's the most vulnerable. The other four will have acclimatised to life on the run. Robertson still won't quite believe what's happening to him. He's the weak link.'

Tate nodded in agreement, running his finger over SemComNet's report in front of him.

'How exactly? Efforts so far don't seem to have been that productive, do they?'

'I think the little persuasion from the ANNA project will soon prove to be effective. She has implicated me for the deaths of his wife and daughter.'

Tate's eyebrows narrowed in surprise as he failed to see the direction Trevellion's thoughts were taking.

'Is that wise?'

'By implicating me, Robertson will undoubtedly want to come after me. What's the easiest way to do that? Launch the app against me.'

'How can you be so sure?'

'ANNA will be quite persuasive. Robertson will be easy to guide and manipulate. We then drop the security encryption on UKCitizensNet for a short period. Brown and the others will doubtless look for a way to hack into UKCitizensNet. So, we give it to them on a plate. The impression will be that they've got full access to the UKCitizensNet system. In reality, they'll be in a secure area, much like an extranet. The moment the app infiltrates the system, we restore full encryption and firewall security. We then simply isolate the app and get our hands on what they've developed from those files.'

Tate sneered as he sat forward in his chair.

'But my dear Vincent, is not the purpose of the app that it is undetectable and unstoppable once we have launched it at its target? Are we not compromising the integrity of the UKCitizensNet system with this approach and, less importantly, your safety if you're a target?'

'Your concern for my welfare is touching. You forget, we know what we're looking for. We've invested enormous R&D efforts in developing the app in a safe environment. We simply let the app access this secure area at an isolated IP address so it compromises none of the rest of the network.'

Tate mulled over every aspect of Trevellion's plan.

'All right, do it. But we can't afford any mistakes.'

Trevellion nodded confidently.

'There won't be any mistakes. And the other delightful part of this plan is the moment they upload a file from their equipment into UKCitizensNet we can run a satellite IP trace on exactly where the fuck they are.'

Tate nodded, but his expression remained dour.

'It occurs to me, though, that if this group yields no useful information, we are still left with deployment problems of the app that haven't been solved. Phase III is rapidly approaching. How long are you prepared to give your programmers to remedy this? Delays will not be easy to explain to the Prime Minister and Secretary of State.'

'The issue is time, not knowledge. Our R&D team will sort out the problem.'

'But Vincent, time is of the essence of the target for Phase III is to be removed. There will not be another window of opportunity we can exploit in such a way.'

Trevellion nodded.

'I have our R&D team on constant shifts around the clock, seven days a week, until the problem is sorted.

'Any knowledge Robertson and his accomplices have can expedite the process. But if they don't, we'll resolve the issue anyway and take care of this group so the timetable is unaffected.'

Tate removed his glasses and polished the lenses with his tie.

'This may be a CODEX project, but I have no taste for your methods of taking care of things. Nor do I have any interest in how you do it. All I want is an assurance that the job is done tidily and that nothing leads back to the project.'

'Don't worry, we have a scenario worked up that will give Michael Robertson nowhere to run. And believe me, no one will hide him. Thanks to UKCitizensNet, his face will be everywhere. He'll be the most wanted man in the country.'

Tate nodded, replacing his glasses.

'Any resources you need from my department are at your disposal. Don't disappoint me.'

Trevellion's expression tightened at the veiled threat. He could think of another target that would be worth testing the app on. But for the time being, he didn't need Sebastian Tate as his enemy.

Looking away, Tate re-opened the file in front of him. Sliding the report from the file, he quickly glanced down before looking back at Trevellion.

'So, let's talk about the Phase III target.'

CHAPTER TWENTY SIX

'SHUT THAT BLOODY CURTAIN,' a voice from behind said.

It was Brown. Turning to face him, Michael let the blackout curtain slip out of his hands, back into its original position.

'Those curtains are there for a reason, Michael. So they can't find us. And so any reconnaissance aircraft at night won't see any lights coming from this site.'

Michael's thoughts reverted to the plane he'd seen taking off from nearby Farnborough airport minutes earlier.

Surely they couldn't have seen anything on their take-off?

'What about infrared sensors that can detect heat? Wouldn't they be able to spot us?' he asked, although not wanting to learn they could be in this way.

Brown adjusted the blackout curtain, making sure it was correctly in place.

'Ordinarily, that would be true. But we've set up a homemade atmospheric device that disrupts temperature readings so they can't lock onto us. Any decent army will have been using similar devices for years. Although they'll have paid millions for the technology. Ignorant bloody cretins.'

Before Brown could continue, there was a loud shuffling from the other end of the mobile home. Green was sitting in front of a bank of terminals. Muttering inaudibly, he shuffled in his seat. His head bobbed up and down and from side to side as he looked rapidly from one screen to another.

'What is it?' Michael asked, approaching Green.

'Quiet,' Green hissed without looking up. 'Do not touch a fucking thing. In fact, do not move.'

Stopping in his tracks, Michael looked at the scrolling code moving across the screens in front of him.

Disturbed by the commotion, Jones and Smith appeared from the other end of the mobile home and stood with Brown behind Michael. Endless moments passed as they all held their breath.

Finally, Green stopped bobbing. His gaze settled on one screen just above him.

'Look there,' his voice quivered with excitement. 'Can you see it?'

Brown, Jones, and Smith barged past Michael and congregated around Green. The code on the screen had stopped scrolling, and a cursor flashed silently on the command line.

'Fuck me, I think we've done it,' Jones said finally.

Michael watched as the four men went into techno-babble overload, excitedly pointing at various parts of the screen. The nervous knot in his stomach, there since he'd first met Brown, was tightening. A feeling of nausea began welling up.

'What is it?' he managed to say. 'What have you done?'

Brown was the first to turn, a smile on his gaunt features.

'We've hacked a hole through the UKCitizensNet firewall. We've never achieved that before. Their encryption is gigabit and cutting edge.'

'Does that mean we've got access to launch the app against Trevellion?' he asked in a quivering voice.

An image of Trevellion, sitting at his desk—expressionless, emotionless, guilty—flashed through his mind.

'Give me time,' Green said, exasperated. 'I've only just got through the firewall. We don't even know Trevellion's IP location. Or whether it's running an active session at the moment. He may not even be there.'

Michael finally moved. Watching the screen intently, he moved alongside the computer hacker.

'Find him,' he hissed, watching the blur of Green typing at his keyboard.

Green turned and looked at Michael, saw the hatred and conviction in his face, and returned to his task with renewed purpose.

'OK, I'm in the personnel database,' he said, scrolling through pages of data. 'Let's call up all staff with a surname starting with T.'

The screen changed from unintelligible code to a directory listing names. Green scrolled down the long list until he reached "Trevellion, V."

Feeling his heart miss a beat, Michael exhaled loudly as Green called up Trevellion's record.

'Got you, you bastard,' Green finally said, his eyes quickly scanning and appraising the data.

At the very bottom of the personnel record were details of IP addresses assigned to Trevellion. Beneath the list was a button.

Check current IP activity status.

Green clicked on the button, and the screen changed again. There were three IP addresses, all corresponding to different computers. The first two were inactive. The third had been active since just before eight o'clock that morning.

Michael looked at the other men as they watched expectantly as Green trawled through the data.

'Can you lock down the physical location of the IP address?' Smith asked finally.

'I'm coming to that,' replied Green, annoyance in his voice. 'I just need to call up the network schematic to pinpoint the location.'

Michael watched as the personnel database disappeared to be replaced by complex network diagrams, identifying physical locations for the IP addresses overlaid on a schematic of the building. Hovering over Trevellion's active IP address on the diagram, Green clicked on the link.

'I've got him,' said Green triumphantly. 'The IP address is currently registering an active session. Trevellion must be there.'

The knot in Michael's stomach tightened. His moment of vengeance was near.

'Well, let's release it then. What are we waiting for?"

Even as the words were escaping from his mouth, Michael realised he didn't exactly know how the group was planning on using the app. Or what it would do once it was launched.

'Exactly how is this going to work? I want to know this is guaranteed to kill Trevellion,' he said finally, as the four men turned to face him.

Green avoided Michael's probing gaze and looked at Brown.

'This is your domain, my friend,' he said quietly, looking back at the screen, clearly uncomfortable.

Brown licked his lips, dry from the excitement of their breakthrough.

'As you know, everything technological is networked and has a unique IP address. Big companies such as SemComNet have enormous R&D units with huge technological and chemical resources at their disposal. I propose we divert some of the more dangerous elements of their chemical resources through their sprinkler system into Trevellion's office, which we've identified thanks to his active IP address.'

Michael processed the implications.

'So, you're going to gas him? Surely he'll flee the office as soon as he smells gas?'

Brown smiled wryly as he ran his fingers across his lengthening stubble.

'Yes, but as I said, everything at SemComNet is networked. Particularly their security system. If compromised, they can lock down any area of the premises in an instance. We simply lock down Trevellion's office whilst we deploy the gas.'

'What gas are you going to use?' Michael asked, feeling both nervous and excited as the prospect of vengeance rose.

Brown shrugged.

'It depends on what their R&D unit has in stock. But don't worry. Smith here is also a qualified chemist for his sins. He'll be able to devise a rather unpleasant cocktail for Trevellion.'

Michael's gaze moved from one man to the other. The excitement on their faces was evident as the prospect of their revenge loomed.

Was this the beginning of the end of UKCitizensNet and their isolation?

As Green delved deeper into the UKCitizensNet system, nervous chatter filled the mobile home. But it was Smith who detected the doubt on Jones's face.

'What's wrong with you?' he asked. 'We've been working towards this for months and you look as if you're about to be given the last rites.'

Jones exhaled loudly, running his fingers through his greasy, unkempt hair.

'Doesn't this strike you as a bit too easy? We've been trying to find a way into UKCitizensNet for months. Then the moment we find some vulnerability, we've suddenly got immediate access to Trevellion's location and his IP activity status. Surely SemComNet will have some form of countermeasures if they detected a system break-in? We've not seen any change in the system since we got in. Doesn't that strike you as odd?'

Green swivelled around in his chair, his face flushed with annoyance.

'Does it not occur to you, my friend, that maybe our undetected access has something to do with my prowess for getting in unseen by their system?'

Michael studied Green's expression. Was he seeing genuine irritation, or was it sheer desperation? A desire to believe he really had cracked it and might end their enforced nightmare.

Jones snorted his disdain.

'I don't like it. This seems like a trap.'

Michael was in no doubt surprising even himself with the force of his response.

'Now you listen to me. By your admission, this is the biggest break you've had in months. If not at all. Are we going to waste an opportunity and risk you won't hack into their system for another six months or a year? Trevellion is plugged into their network and we know where he is. What's more, we have the means to make him pay.'

Michael paused, composing himself as he felt his emotions threatening to take over. The image of Colette talking to him on screen swept across his mind.

'This may be my only chance to avenge my wife's and daughter's murders. Don't deny me this opportunity. Without you, I can't get to Trevellion and SemComNet. And I know you need this as much as I do.'

For a few long seconds, the bickering between the four men stopped as they exchanged anxious glances. Was this the moment they'd been waiting for?

'Fire up our secure FTP server,' Jones finally said determined, as the excitement of the moment took over.

A new screen whirred into life. Michael turned to Brown, struck by another thought.

'I realise I know little about this, but if we can see where they are, won't they also be able to see us? Pinpoint our location?'

Brown pointed at a narrow, tower-shaped box, about twelve inches high with a green LED that was permanently flickering.

A cable led from the back into the melee of other cables that disappeared behind the console Green was sitting at.

'This is our IP scrambler,' Brown said, tapping the green flashing LED. 'You see, with the old internet if you knew what you were doing, there was such a thing as "anonymous login" and you could cloak your IP address or reroute it to a machine somewhere in Eastern Europe with a bit of skill. Unfortunately, in the brave new world of UKCitizensNet, no one is remotely anonymous anymore, and SemComNet has developed techniques to prevent anonymous logins. But with this device, we can churn out half a billion IP combinations a second to prevent any locking onto our network position. As you say, we don't want SemComNet to know where this transmission is coming from. Don't worry, they haven't found us yet.'

Brown turned back to the screen.

Michael perched down on the desk next to Green.

'So how long is this going to take?'

Scratching his chin, Green scanned the data in front of him, gesturing at the screen.

'I need to do some configuration of the app with the data we've just extracted from the UKCitizensNet database. Changing some of the handler parameters is only going to take a few minutes. After that, we're ready.'

Green cast a glance at the secure FTP server next to him, which was now fully operational.

'Everything's in place to get Trevellion and UKCitizensNet.'

Vincent Trevellion glanced again at the digital clock on the wall opposite, the digits shining bright red. The time was 8.34 p.m. and the UKCitizensNet system had been open for fourteen minutes.

In front of him were two of SemComNet's most senior network security analysts. The two men were anxiously surveying a bank of four monitors running diagnostic checks on the security status of UKCitizensNet. These were the trusted two charged with isolating the app should Michael Robertson and his accomplices launch an attack. Trevellion was in no doubt Michael would want him dead after ANNA's extreme provocation.

Despite his conviction, they were still waiting for something major to happen. In the world of network security, fifteen minutes was a lifetime. In that time, competent hackers could unleash untold havoc.

As the clock moved to 8.35 p.m., Trevellion turned to the analysts, his mood worsening with every passing minute.

'Update me, damn it. What are those bastards up to?'

The first analyst, a young man in his mid-twenties, slightly balding with a long ponytail to compensate and who lived for code, looked startled at Trevellion's outburst. He was perspiring slightly, the hum of the computers in front of him drowned out by his fearsome boss.

'We've got some noise and data exchange around the periphery of the network, so we know they're active. We can also see they've accessed some of the file structure in the restricted area we opened up, despite their best efforts to cloak their movements.'

'What are they looking at?' Trevellion demanded impatiently.

'Well, they don't appear to be in the system anymore. But from what we can see they accessed personnel records and...'

'Whose records?' Trevellion interrupted.

The analyst quickly typed in several commands.

'Just the one, sir. Your record,' he replied, the sweat on his brow increasing as he feared Trevellion's reaction.

Trevallion smiled thinly.

'What else have they accessed?'

'They downloaded the false network schematics files and blueprints for this building,' the analyst replied hurriedly, scanning the screen. 'I think they're looking for you.'

Trevellion didn't reply. Turning away, he reached into his pocket for his mobile.

Flipping the device open, he called up Sebastian Tate's number. Within a few seconds, they were connected. Trevellion spoke first.

'Everything is on course and proceeding as I expected. We've opened the door and they're actively targeting me. We're waiting for them to attack the network in earnest, at which point we'll isolate the app.'

There was a brief pause before Tate replied. His tone was serious and official.

'We've invested far too much money in this project to allow a bunch of militant hackers to destabilise our objectives. If we don't have their app within twenty-five minutes, I want you to close the window. Is that understood?'

'Understood,' Trevellion replied curtly, flipping the phone shut.

He looked up at the clock. It was 7.37 p.m. Eight minutes until their window closed.

'The moment you detect any unusual activity, let me know,' he ordered.

Both analysts nodded obediently before returning to their screens with renewed vigour.

Trevellion wasn't a man to doubt his analysis. But there was a certain irony about putting himself up as a target for the weapon he'd helped shape. The purpose of this device was stealth and, as Tate had pointed out, they'd invested enormous time and effort in developing this app. The question remained whether the counter-measures SemComNet had developed to prevent an attack would work in a hostile situation rather than the simulated tests that had been run. If they didn't...

'Sir, I think I've found them,' the second analyst almost shouted as Trevellion stirred from his thoughts.

Trevellion studied the screen in front of the analyst.

'We've got adverse network traffic coming in on the hub we've opened,' the analyst continued, his fingers typing a blur of commands into his computer.

'Do not forget,' Trevellion said firmly, 'there are two objectives here: isolating the app and locating their IP address.'

The analysts didn't look up from their screens as they scanned the network activity.

'OK, something's inside the network,' the second analyst said, his head bobbing from side to side. 'I'm trying to lock onto its exact position to isolate its IP address.'

'Level 1 countermeasures have been launched to disrupt their deployment handlers and mask our IP address,' the first analyst blurted out, with growing sweat patches under his arms.

'Have you identified their IP address?' Trevellion barked, his gaze flitting from one screen to the next.

The second analyst, who was looking increasingly pale, shook his head anxiously.

'I can't get a lock. They're using some sort of IP scrambler.'

'Remind me again what I pay you for,' Trevellion uttered menacingly, looking up at the clock opposite.

The time was 7.42 p.m.

'You don't have much time. Find them.'

The second analyst turned back to his screen, casting a nervous glance at his colleague, who was looking equally pale and stressed.

The clock moved to 7.43 p.m.

A few moments later, the second analyst sat bolt upright and began pointing manically at his screen.

'I've got it. I've isolated their IP address.'

'Well don't just sit there congratulating yourself. Keep a record of it and help isolate the fucking app.'

The first analyst looked at his colleague and pointed at one of the monitors before them.

'Level 1 countermeasures have failed, our IP address is exposed, and they have shut down the scrambler. I'm launching level 2 and 3 countermeasures to restore our firewall. I need you to track their progress whilst I lock down the exposed network hubs.'

Without warning, a loud thud echoed around the office.

'What the fuck was that?' the second analyst whispered nervously.

'It sounded like the override on the security system and the doors being sealed,' his colleague replied, casting a glance at the door.

'Keep your fucking focus and isolate the app,' Trevellion ordered, rushing to the office door.

The analysts were correct. The office had been sealed.

"It's the app," the first analyst said, his voice cracking. "They know where we are."

Trevellion quickly looked around the room for another viable exit. There was none. His gaze moved to the ceiling and the sprinklers embedded in the ceiling panels. A bleak, fatal possibility crossed his mind.

The clock moved to 7.45 p.m.

Ignoring the worrying thought, he turned back to the monitors, acutely aware his twenty-five minutes were up. Tate's words echoed around his head. They *had* to isolate the app. It might provide the missing piece of the puzzle. But if he didn't close the window, the entire network could be compromised. The full power of the app, and whatever configuration Michael Robertson's group had given it, would be unleashed on him here in this office.

The clock moved to 7.46 p.m.

'Level 2 countermeasures have failed,' the first analyst said hoarsely, clearly panicking. 'It's getting deeper into the area we opened up. It will not be long before it downloads to our IP address location.'

'What success are we having with Level 3 countermeasures?' Trevellion asked, desperate to remain calm.

There was a pause as both analysts studied a new data stream that appeared on the screen. The pause seemed endless as they all waited and studied the screen.

'I think it's slowing down,' replied the second analyst. 'The countermeasures are blocking it from moving between hubs. The remaining hubs should lockdown in the next few seconds and block their access, stopping them in the system.'

He cast a glance at the monitor to his right and then pointed animatedly to the screen.

'Look, the remaining hubs have locked down, blocking access.'

Trevellion looked at the pale expressions of the men before him, trying to determine what was happening.

'Have we stopped it, and isolated it?' he said finally.

A fresh window appeared on the screen, flashing the message they'd all been hoping to see.

Level 3 countermeasures successful, designated network hubs secure.

The analysts sank back in their chairs, sweat pouring from their brows and staining their crisp shirts.

'We've stopped it, and isolated the app to a secure area. It's ours. We've got it.'

Trevellion looked at the ceiling and the glinting sprinklers. At that moment, the security override on the office door thudded again as the seal on the door was released.

'Fuck me, that was close,' the second analyst said. '"I thought I was going to have a fucking coronary.'

The first analyst nodded as they both turned to Trevellion for his approval. But Trevellion had moved away from the bank of screens and was already in contact with Sebastian Tate.

CHAPTER TWENTY SEVEN

TREVELLION'S BODY LAY IN the middle of the floor of his office at SemComNet. He was lying on his side, almost in the foetal position, his face slightly shielded. But even from this position, Michael could see his bloated and discoloured face as a result of the poison attack.

Michael moved towards the body, casting a glance at the sprinklers that had delivered his moment of vengeance. The noxious cocktail Smith had devised had dissipated from the air. Although Michael could still feel his skin tingling as he stood in Trevellion's silent office. Thoughts of Colette and Clare ran through his mind. Trevellion was dead. That was all that mattered. Their deaths had not been in vain.

Michael woke suddenly, his eyes shooting open as a cold sweat enveloped him. As his gaze became accustomed to the early morning light, he recognised the shapes of the mobile home. One of the blackout curtains was slightly ajar, allowing some light to stream into the room.

It was there the realisation he'd been dreaming about Trevellion's death struck him. But maybe he didn't need to dream it for too much longer. They'd successfully launched the app the night before and knew it had penetrated the hole they'd hacked into UKCitizensNet's system. The only question that remained was whether they'd successfully achieved their first objective—killing Trevellion.

For hours after they had launched the app, they'd watched UKCitizensNet coverage, waiting to see if anything was reported.

By 2 a.m., Michael finally succumbed to sleep, leaving just Brown at the bank of monitors looking for the smallest sign of their success.

He looked at his watch. It was a little after five o'clock. Brown was still sitting at the monitors, but Smith had joined him. Green and Jones were sleeping at the other end of the mobile home.

Stretching, he approached Brown and Smith. His pulse quickened, and the hairs on the back of his neck stood up. Their plan had to succeed.

'Has anything been reported?' Michael asked expectantly.

Brown and Smith jumped, unaware Michael had surfaced. Their faces were drawn from tiredness and stress. Behind the fatigue, Michael could see the verdict. Smith shook his head first.

'No, nothing. Fuck all about it. All we're seeing is continuous coverage about the Saudi President visiting the UK and how he's pissed off most of the world by nationalising the oil industry out there.'

'What?' Michael looked confused.

'They're blaming rising oil prices across the world on this nationalisation. They're also hacked off as so many oil companies had to leave the region because of it.'

Michael gestured for Smith to stop.

'No, no. That wasn't what I meant. You mean there's no mention at all of the attack on UKCitizensNet?'

It was Brown's turn to interrupt.

'My guess is they're trying to keep it quiet. But if we did get Trevellion, they won't be able to keep it a secret. Especially given how high profile he is now. And particularly not after the death of the former company president.'

'I told you it was too easy,' came a tired voice.

The three men turned to see Jones tucking in his crumpled shirt as he approached the monitors.

'They let us in. They wanted to see what we'd got. And now they know. We've got something that doesn't work yet. I told you we needed more time to test it.'

Michael felt the colour drain from his face.

'Look, we know nothing yet. Let's just wait. It's still early.'

Before Michael could continue, the news presenter on BBC News 24 caught their attention as he moved on to a new story.

Some breaking news just reached us. SemCom-Net, the operator of UKCitizensNet, is reporting a security breach into the state intranet last night by hackers trying to disrupt the UKCitizensNet service. The details are sketchy at the moment, but it appears anti-net campaigners were attempting to launch a virus against the network.

The presenter paused to listen to his earpiece.

I gather we can go over to our reporter, Becky Collins, outside the SemComNet headquarters. Becky, what can you tell us?

The five men in the mobile home fell silent, watching expectantly as the pictures on the screen moved from the BBC studio to the outside broadcast. An attractive brunette in a smart pin-striped suit stood under an umbrella. The perimeter fence to SemComNet loomed up behind her.

The latest news we've got is that at about eight o'clock last night, hackers breached the UKCitizensNet system intending to launch a virus that would have affected UKCitizensNet outputs. We gather they were unsuccessful. Here to give us the exact scale of the damage, is the new SemComNet President, Vincent Trevellion.'

Michael felt his legs weaken as the camera panned around from the attractive reporter to Trevellion in his crisp Armani suit. His expression was as impassive as ever. Without looking at the camera, his attention focused on the reporter as he answered the questions.

I'm pleased to report that, despite a security breach, the damage to UKCitizensNet was minimal and didn't result in any downtime. We're currently reviewing our security protocols to ensure this doesn't happen again. I'm confident UKCitizensNet will remain unaffected.

Do you have any idea who the hackers were? Could this be yet more work of anti-net campaigners? After all, they have targeted companies like yours in the past.

The four men in the mobile home all looked towards Michael. But his gaze was firmly on the screen, studying every movement Trevellion made.

We certainly haven't ruled it out," Trevellion continued. "It's too early to say at this point. But rest assured, whoever is responsible for this crime will be caught and brought to justice. We will help the police in any way we can.

Michael felt hatred rise in him. How dare Trevellion, of all people, speak of justice.

Where's the justice for Colette and Clare?

Or for David Langley?

Where's the justice for Davey Wilkes, who's been wrongly accused of their murders?

'Turn him off,' Michael finally said, sinking onto the sofa, tears of desperation welling up in his eyes.

Smith turned the sound down on the screen as the picture moved back from the SemComNet headquarters, returning to the news presenter in the studio. He watched as Michael sat, head in his hands. Jones was the first to break the uncomfortable silence.

'OK, so we didn't get him this time. It doesn't mean we can't find another way into UKCitizensNet and go after Trevellion again. Whilst we're all here, Trevellion will not be safe.'

Michael looked up, derision in his eyes.

'Trevellion isn't safe?' he said scornfully. 'Who is the one working for a state-of-the-art company in an Armani suit? And who are the ones living in a shithole in the middle of an abandoned caravan park? Are you telling me Trevellion has anything to worry about from us? He's untouchable. No one believes us anyway. What can the five of us do against him, against UKCitizensNet? Nothing. Absolutely nothing.'

Smith looked defeated, incapable of arguing with anything Michael had just said. It was Brown who took up the challenge.

'Look, Michael, we all knew more testing and development was needed on what you brought us. We took a chance by releasing the app early and it didn't work. It doesn't mean we can't get it working given a bit more time.'

Michael sank back in the chair despondently, shaking his head as Brown continued.

'There is one thing we haven't fully explored because we'd always assumed any attack would be on SemComNet.'

'And what's that?' Michael mumbled.

'In the app's code is an uncompleted handler for wireless deployment. It's by far and away the most complex element of the whole thing, which is probably why it's not complete. If we get that working, we don't have to target Trevellion at SemComNet alone.'

'Go on,' Michael replied.

'Every piece of technology we use these days is networked. Mobiles, handheld devices, iPads, satnavs, televisions. If we can send this app to a wireless device, Trevellion isn't safe anywhere, so long as we know where he is and can isolate his IP addresses.'

Michael sat up, more enthused now.

'Can you get it working?'

Brown nodded.

'Yes, I think so. You've got to trust us and give us some time.'

Michael looked back to the screen where Trevellion's image had been displayed minutes before. The BBC News 24 coverage had reverted to the trip of the Saudi President.

'I've got to get out of here,' Michael finally said. 'I'm going stir-crazy just waiting for something to happen. I'm going home. You ring me as soon as you've got anything, OK?'

Brown nodded reassuringly.

'Don't worry, Michael, it's not over yet. Not by a long way.'

CHAPTER TWENTY EIGHT

8 February 2010

The school hall at St Winifred's was humming as Michael, Colette and Clare walked up the wide corridor. On one side, children's drawings depicting the age of the Aztecs decorated what seemed like never-ending wall space. On the other, photographs of recent school trips showed children at a zoo and then an outside activity centre.

From the moment they'd entered the building, it was clear where the dance competition was being held. The sound of the children's excited chatter echoed down the corridors, hitting you the moment you come through the front door.

The car park had been like the M25 on a bad day. Virtual gridlock ensured parents were forced to park on the school field next to the normal car park. Parents, desperately trying to keep their animated children under control, strode across the school grounds in search of a seat in the hall.

'And to think I reckoned we were early,' Michael had commented. 'I didn't think this many kids would be interested in dance.'

Catching Clare's eye in the rear-view mirror, she'd shaken her head, reminding him how old and stupid he was if he didn't know that all children liked dancing. Colette smiled at him, trying not to laugh.

Decked out in her ballet outfit, both parents could barely contain their pride as Clare called out to one of her friends. She too was wearing an ivory, satin ballet dress. Michael was sure he'd seen the girl and her mother one time he'd picked her up from ballet practice, although he'd never caught her name. Keeping up with names was an ongoing problem with just the hordes of children, never mind their parents.

The sound of children laughing, running about, or shouting at their friends from across the hall rose to a cacophonous din as they approached the doors. Most of the chairs were already taken.

'We're going to be standing at the back at this rate,' said Colette as she pushed through the doors.

Casting a glance around the hall, all the parents and family ahead of them in the corridor had quickly snapped up the remaining seats. Michael and Colette were left standing in the aisle.

'Oh well,' Colette said, 'the wall it is.'

They moved to the back of the hall and leant against the climbing bars secured against the wall. Further down the room, Clare had turned, looking to see where her parents had gone. Spotting them at the back, she ran back up the aisle, a disapproving look on her pale features.

'Oh Mum,' she said with feigned annoyance. 'Why didn't you run to get a seat?'

Colette stroked her hair gently, leaning in for a hug.

'I can't run as fast as you these days,' she said. 'But don't worry, we'll be able to see your dance from here. I've got the video camera as well.'

Clare pulled a face at the prospect of her dance being filmed. Although secretly she was pleased. Especially if she'd win the competition.

With the dancing almost beginning, Michael casually looked around at the parents and children who sat, waiting for their moment of dance glory. His gaze stopped on a mother about six feet away, standing over her daughter, a serious expression on her face. What had her daughter done, he wondered as Colette followed his gaze.

Sharing the same thought, Michael and Colette strained to hear what the woman was saying to her daughter. Clare also turned, less subtle in trying to see what was so interesting.

'I want to see you concentrating and giving it everything you've got. If you don't, then all those dance lessons will have been for nothing. And you know how expensive they were, don't you? You're going to win this competition. You don't want to be a failure, do you?'

Michael's brow creased in astonishment at the mother's overbearing tone as she continued her "motivational" pep talk. Colette smirked.

Concerned, Clare looked up at her parents.

'You won't think I'm a failure if I don't win the competition, will you?' she asked, a little shaken.

'Oh, of course not,' Colette comforted her. 'Daddy and I will never think you're a failure. Not at anything.'

She turned to face Michael, who nodded reassuringly, squeezing Clare's hand gently.

'This is just a bit of fun,' Michael said. ' Go and enjoy yourself. It doesn't matter who wins. Don't listen to what the lady was saying.'

Clare nodded, wiping away a single tear rolling down her cheek. Feeling better about the competition again, she turned and ran off toward a friend.

Michael leant back against the wall, smiling as he looked sideways at Colette.

'What are you smirking about?' She elbowed him gently in the ribs.

'You're such a liar,' he laughed. 'You have just as high expectations for Clare as old "competitive mum" over there.'

Feigning a frown, Colette looked to where Clare was talking animatedly with a group of girls from her class.

'I know that, and you know that. But I will not let Clare know that and heap the same pressure on her. Not like that awful woman over there. Of course, I want Clare to succeed and be the best in everything. But she doesn't need us to set her up to fail with impossible standards.'

'Touched a nerve, did I?' Michael said playfully, moving his arms to prevent another probing elbow in the ribs.

'Oh sod off,' Colette said mockingly, flicking her long hair disdainfully.

Before Michael could retort, Colette's phone rang in her handbag. The smile on her face faded.

'Who can that be?' she said, irritated.

Pulling the phone from her bag, she read the name on the display before rolling her eyes in annoyance.

'It's work,' she hissed, pushing her hair behind her ears to answer the call.

Michael immediately looked to where Clare was finishing her conversation with her friends. Turning, she began to walk back towards her parents.

Colette spoke softly into her phone, uncomfortable at the interruption in the school hall, conscious of the glances she was getting from other parents.

'But I thought the pre-conference meeting was scheduled for tomorrow morning. I've got a train ticket for first thing in the morning... So what's the urgency? And they want to meet this evening?... Is there any flexibility on the time? ... I understand... No, it's not a problem. I'm leaving now. Bye.'

Michael could see Colette's eyes brimming with tears. Wiping them quickly away, she turned to face him, her face flushed with anger and disappointment.

'They've moved the pre-conference meeting from tomorrow morning to tonight. There seems to be some major crisis involving the state network tender only I can solve. The Chief Executive has asked for me personally, so it must be serious. They're getting twitchy about what might happen if we don't get it.'

'But what about Clare?' Michael said, as their daughter approached them.

'Look, I know,' Colette said angrily. 'Don't make this any harder.'

Putting his arm around Colette, he pulled her tightly to him, resting his head gently on hers.

'I know. I wasn't having a go at you. You shouldn't be so good at your job and indispensable to them. What would they do without you? Do you have to go now?'

Colette nodded, thankful she'd packed her overnight bag for the conference before they'd left for the competition. It would have to do for two nights now, she thought as Clare reached the pair of them.

'What's the matter, Mummy?' she asked, looking into her mother's reddened eyes.

Colette dropped down, gripped her daughter's hands, and looked straight into her wide blue eyes.

'You remember the conference that I'm going to tomorrow? Well, they've moved the time, and I've got to leave for it now.'

Clare looked utterly disappointed.

'What, now?' She fought to hold back the tears, determined not to show how she felt, knowing how important mummy's work was.

Colette nodded, pulling her daughter close, tears rolling down her cheeks.

'I'm so sorry, she whispered, feeling choked up.

Clare pulled away gently from the embrace to look her mother squarely in the face.

'It's OK. I understand,' she said. 'Daddy's told me how important your work is and how busy you are.' Gulping, determined not to cry, she added: 'There'll be other dance competitions.'

Colette squeezed Clare's hands before holding her tight again, proud of her daughter's response.

'You'd better go,' Michael said gently. 'The sooner you go, the sooner you can come home.'

Nodding, Colette rose to her feet and smiled warmly at Clare, wiping the tears from her face.

'I'll talk to you on the phone tomorrow. OK, darling?'

'I'd like that,' Clare said softly.

Turning, she ran quickly back down the aisle towards her friends, unable to stop her tears from streaming down her face.

CHAPTER TWENTY NINE

As the key slid into the lock of his front door, Michael cast a nonchalant look up and down his street, checking if he was being followed or watched. He knew he wasn't particularly adept at being subtle about these things. He certainly wasn't as well practised as his four counterparts in Aldershot. Perhaps there were some things he should be thankful for, he thought as nothing appeared suspicious about this quiet suburban street. But then nobody would have predicted a brutal murder to occur here...

Closing the door behind him, he felt pleasant warmth envelop him as the wonders of central heating filled the house. If nothing else, coming home was worth it for some comfort, despite the unpleasant memories lingering here.

A photograph of Clare taken at one of her ballet performances, hung on the hallway wall. Her radiant smile shone from the picture. The framed memory quickly doubled his determination. They had to succeed in what they were doing.

Walking over the pile of letters, flyers and newspapers scattered over his doormat Michael moved into his lounge, slumping onto his new sofa. Bills and pizza menus could wait.

As his television flickered into life and he reached for his console, he was aware at some subconscious level that his disposition had changed. Not so many days ago, the slightest mention of Colette and Clare's murders had made him want to seek refuge from the horror of the details, which always reduced him to sweaty waves of nausea.

But now he actively sought it out. Any detail or piece of information about them, about UKCitizensNet, about the anti-net campaigners, and even about Trevellion, needed to be absorbed, assimilated and rationalised. Only through understanding his quest for revenge would be truly sated. No detail could be ignored. No stone unturned, in case someone complicit escaped his wrath.

Gone, at least inwardly, was the mild-mannered husband and father. Their lives and deaths would count for something.

The UKCitizensNet logo appeared on the screen and Michael hit the "Video" button, typing in the channel number for BBC News 24. The news presenter might have been different from hours earlier, but the facts were still the same. Had the world not moved on in the last few hours?

A reporter, standing outside 10 Downing Street, was detailing the relevance of a mini-summit between the Saudi President and the Prime Minister.

Michael rolled his eyes in boredom and tapped the "Web" button. He blinked as the screen didn't melt into the familiar UKCitizensNet logo. Instead, it dissolved into an image of Colette, standing impassively, dressed in black as she had previously stood before him. Michael slid off the sofa and onto his knees.

Is this a dream?

Reaching forward, he touched the screen, running his finger across Colette's cheek. There was no human warmth. Just the cold sensation and static of the TV screen. Tears welled in his eyes.

'Don't cry, Michael,' the voice said as Colette's soft tones filled the room. 'You must be strong. Vengeance must be ours. Clare's death must be avenged. Only you can do that. You know what to do.'

Michael looked directly into Colette's unmoving eyes.

'Trevellion,' he whispered.

'The enemy is wider than you think,' Colette continued. 'Who foils the signs of false prophets and makes fools of diviners, who overthrows the learning of the wise and turns it into nonsense?'

Michael's expression changed from sadness to bewilderment.

Why are you still baffling me with obscure references I don't under-stand?

'Michael, you must read and understand the Books of Isaiah and Revelation. The truth lies within. The truth lies with the four Horsemen of the Apocalypse.'

Confused, Michael ran his fingers through his hair, scrabbling around for a pen and a piece of paper to note it down before he'd forget.

'After this I saw four angels standing at the four corners of the earth, holding back the four winds of the earth so no wind could blow on the earth, on the sea, or any tree. Then I saw another angel ascending from the east, who had the seal of the living God. He shouted out with a loud voice to the four angels who had been given permission to damage the earth and the sea.'

'Colette, I don't understand what these words mean or why they're important. What have they got to do with Trevellion? Who is the wider enemy? What do biblical references from the Books of Revelation and Isaiah and the four Horsemen of the Apocalypse have to do with anything? Or with your death or Clare's?'

I must be losing my mind. None of this makes the remotest sense. And how would Colette know about this? She was never religious, and certainly never quoted books from the Bible. I doubted she ever heard of the Book of Isaiah.

Slumping back against the sofa, Michael laughed. The sheer absurdity of the situation... Colette was dead, and he was talking to his TV screen.

I am hallucinating.

Closing his eyes for a second, he cleared his mind as best he could to get rid of the nonsense.

Will she still be there when I open them?

He opened his eyes. Colette was still looking at him from the screen. She was murmuring something about how she loved him and Clare, and how their killer must be caught. He watched as her face blinked intermittently. Her mouth barely moved, but the words kept coming.

'Find them, and take vengeance on them all. Do it for Clare. Our daughter,' the voice said dispassionately.

It was as if she had been brainwashed or was reading from an autocue, Michael thought, exhaling loudly, his chest rising heavily as the air rushed from his lungs.

Before he could reply, the screen was black again until a new image appeared. A box filled three-quarters of the screen, and what appeared to be a poorly shot home movie began to play. Michael watched, confused but transfixed.

It was dusk. Dark, malevolent-looking clouds filled the sky. A man in a smart, expensive-looking suit was trudging across a lush green field. His back was to the camera. In his left hand, he was holding a large brown canvas sack, drawstrings at the top pulled tightly shut. Every few steps across the slightly damp grass, he had to readjust his hold on the sack that clearly contained something heavy. The anonymous man was approaching a small wood. The person holding the camera quickly panned from side to side, looking to see if anyone was around before returning focus on the other man and the cumbersome sack. It was clear wherever they were was isolated. There were no signs of habitation or roads. Just rolling fields and trees for as far as the eye could see.

Reaching the wood, the smartly dressed man stopped, turning around to face the camera.

Come on, show me who you are.

But as the man turned, his face had been blurred out to prevent identification. No matter which way his head turned, the image remained blurred.

Turning back to face the wood, the camera continued to follow the man with his sack as he ventured into the trees. The visibility reduced slightly, but was still good enough for Michael to see what was happening.

In the back of his mind, a terrible sense of dread was growing. Nausea welled up inside. Less than a minute passed before the man stopped, dropping the sack to the floor where it lay crumpled and misshapen.

What had been out of shot previously came into view as the person holding the camera handed the smartly dressed man a long, black shovel. Michael clasped his hands to his mouth.

'No. No. Oh God, no.'

The face of the man remained blurred as the hole in the ground grew; the camera periodically moved around looking out for prying eyes. There were none in this diabolical place. Finally, the man placed the shovel against a nearby tree. The hole was deep enough.

Moving over, he picked up the sack, his left hand positioned next to the hole, so the drawstrings were next to it. Releasing the tension on the drawstrings, he moved to the other end of the sack. In one swift motion, he flipped it upwards and the contents spilled out, sliding into the ground.

Clare's lifeless body came to rest in the dark ground. Michael vomited. Clawing helplessly at the screen, he was oblivious to kneeling in his vomit.

'No, you sick bastards, leave her alone. No. Clare.'

He whimpered as he began to cry uncontrollably.

The pain of seeing Clare's body being so mercilessly dumped was excruciating. He hadn't been able to protect her, to save his little girl from these monsters.

And now, here they were on screen. Recording their crime for their perverted, voyeuristic pleasure.

What sort of animal does that to a little girl?

The smartly dressed man shoveled the dirt he'd removed over Clare's lifeless, broken body.

Collapsing to the floor, Michael lashed out in a blind, all-consuming rage, kicking the coffee table with his leg in one furious motion.

Instantly, the glass top shattered, spraying the floor below, covering his prone body. The noise of the breaking glass snapped Michael back to consciousness. Looking up, he pulled himself away from the shards of glass, his heart pounding in his ears.

Dragging his leg away, he was aware of a burning sensation in his right calf. A crimson stain spread across his trouser leg as a jagged shard of glass pointed upwards. Pulling the glass from his leg, he turned back to the screen. The man had finished covering the body. They were leaving the scene of their atrocity.

Once more, Michael looked at the blurred face as he walked away. As the man disappeared from the view of the camera, the film finished. The screen melted back to the image of Colette looking on impassively.

'A founder of sects, much trouble for the accuser: a beast in the theatre prepares the scene and plot. The author ennobled by acts of older times; the world is confused by schismatic sects.'

She paused long enough for Michael to scribble down a few of the cryptic words; her face blank and expressionless.

'For Clare,' she said finally before her image disappeared and BBC News 24 returned.

Instead of the news still focusing on the visit of the Saudi president, another story now had top billing. And this time, Michael was interested.

He scowled as he watched Vincent Trevellion sitting at a table. A high-ranking policeman with a resolute expression sat beside him. A gang of eager reporters sat before them, cameras poised, audio equipment recording their every word.

Trevellion was wearing yet another expensive suit. But this suit was different—and familiar. A suit that had crossed the field. A suit that had carried a sack. A suit that had dug a grave for his daughter.

Scrolling across the bottom of the screen was a new headline.

Police seek cyberterrorists.

The policeman was the first to speak.

> Following the well-publicised attack on UKCi-
> tizensNet, our officers have been working with
> SemComNet and Vincent Trevellion to identify
> the perpetrators of this act of cyberterrorism.
> We can now confirm we are looking for the
> following four individuals whom we believe are
> responsible for this crime.

A giant plasma display above Trevellion and the policeman flick-ered into life. Photographs of Michael's four accomplices appeared on the screen. Michael blinked as the faces were barely comparable to the haunted, tired faces he had spent days looking at. These were pictures of four well-groomed, energetic-looking men, far removed from the squalor of their current existence.

> We believe these men have been on the run and
> in hiding for some time, so their appearances
> may have changed. We advise the public not
> to approach the men as we consider them to
> be extremely dangerous. They are also wanted
> in connection with other related cybercrimes.
> We are also currently investigating whether any
> other individuals were involved in this terror-
> ism. If you have any information about this
> crime or their whereabouts, please email or

contact the police using the details on your
screen.

The policeman stopped talking. An email address and telephone
number flashed on the screen. Taking it as their prompt, the gathered reporters began their mad scrum to elicit more details.

The first question was aimed at Trevellion by a young reporter
who looked barely out of university.

'What can you tell us about the damage to
UKCitizensNet and the impact it might have on
the service?' he asked over the noisy hum of the
other reporters.
'UKCitizensNet have a robust system, using the
most sophisticated security measures in the
world. What we experienced by this anti-net
sect was nothing more than a scratch on the
surface. No damage was done. And no problems were experienced by any UKCitizensNet
users. All it has done is strengthen our resolve
to catch these cyberterrorists. SemComNet w ll
assist the police in whatever way it can.'

Michael snorted disdainfully at Trevellion's practised politician's
answer. He had to warn the other four they were now being publicly
sought by the authorities. They had to progress their plan more
swiftly now.

Despite this, something Trevellion had said bothered him.

'Anti-net sect.'

As the phrase reverberated in his head, his mind was filled with the image of Colette and her warnings about "schismatic sects".

He knew then he had to be more careful than ever. Not only from the authorities closing in on them but also from his four accomplices. The "wider enemy" could be anywhere.

CHAPTER THIRTY

'WHAT THE FUCK ARE we going to do?' Green said anxiously, chewing his bottom lip and rocking nervously from one foot to another.

The four men had seen the police news conference. Their faces had been splashed over all the screens, along with the assertion they were extremely dangerous. The irony might have been amusing if their situation wasn't so precarious.

Brown attempted to calm the situation.

'We've been able to hide away from the world for almost two years. No one has found us so far,' he said, surveying the bank of screens in front of them.

'But that was before our fucking pictures were broadcast over the entire internet, excuse me, UK-fucking-CitizensNet. So now we're sure they know we're not dead. How the hell could they have pieced together it was us is what I want to know?'

'Come on, let's not kid ourselves,' Smith said despondently. 'They're into everything. They'll have access to every semantic database out there.'

'Yes, but how did they specifically know it was us?' Green persisted. 'They couldn't have pinpointed where the attack came from because of our IP scrambler, and if they had, that doesn't tell them who we are. Someone must have tipped them off.'

Jones, who'd been avidly watching the broadcasts, turned around.

'You don't think Michael betrayed us, do you?' he said, his voice quivering as their faces again flashed up on the screen. The police force's email address and telephone number ran below.

'That's absurd,' Brown snapped. 'We all know what he's been through. He didn't make up the fact his wife and daughter were butchered, did he? There's no way he'd be working with UKCitizensNet or that bastard Trevellion.'

Jones looked down and shook his head.

'Well, how then?'

Before anyone could reply, a high-pitched alarm emitted from one of the screens. Like synchronised swimmers, the four men turned as one to look at a particular screen displaying a CCTV video feed from the perimeter of the deserted mobile home park.

'Oh fuck,' Green said. 'Someone's inside the perimeter and sprung one of the tripwires.'

'It could be an animal?' Jones said hopefully as Green tapped at a keyboard, changing the angle of the camera.

The four men exchanged glances. None of them believed in a stray animal roaming the area.

'I can't see anything,' Green said as the picture on the screen swung back, revealing no sinister cause for the alarm, which was still sounding. 'Maybe it was an animal after all.'

As the four men started to relax, the first swathe of bullets ripped through the thin walls of the mobile home, spraying ammunition throughout the confined area. Before he could move away from the screens, a bullet tore into Green's throat, severing his jugular and sending him back, crashing onto the desk of keyboards.

A second bullet careered through the frontal lobe, taking the top of his head clean off. Fragments of skull, brain and blood splattered the glowing screen behind, now showing Trevellion answering questions at the news conference.

The three other men crawled around on hands and knees, diving for cover. A deafening sound of automatic rifle fire filled the air. The smell of cordite permeated their nostrils. The gunfire stopped and a voice echoing through a loudhailer boomed in their direction.

'Come out of the caravan with your hands up. We have the area surrounded. Don't make it any more difficult than it has to be.'

'Oh shit, they're going to kill us all,' Jones panicked. 'If they wanted to arrest us, why shoot first? We're dead.'

Brown, who had scrabbled ahead, gestured to keep the noise down. Silently, he pointed to a bookcase rising from the floor to the ceiling, positioned against the sidewall. Realisation dawned on Smith and Jones. They quickly joined Brown, who was trying to pull the bookcase away from the wall. With the combined strength of the three men, the slightly dilapidated bookcase groaned as it moved, layers of dust dispersing into the air. With one final shove, the bookcase swivelled away from the wall, sending a few books careering to the floor with a loud thud.

The three men gazed expectantly at a now exposed second door into the caravan. Originally, the bookcase had been placed there to stop people from getting in other than through the one main door. They'd never considered they'd need it to escape.

As the voice from the loudhailer bellowed again, giving them one final warning, Brown pulled the blackout curtain back to peer out.

No one was in sight. They weren't surrounded. But the longer they took to expedite their escape, the more likely they would be.

'They haven't got this side of the caravan covered yet. If we can get out, we can try to lose them amongst the caravans.'

'How many of them are there?' Smith asked.

Brown shook his head, his heart pounding.

'I don't know, I can't see. But we can't stay in here much longer.'

Casting one last look around, Brown pushed the door open and jumped to the ground, dropping to his knees. Smith and Jones quickly joined him. Pushing the door closed, Brown quietly moved to the side of the caravan and peered around the side.

About forty feet away, facing away from him, he could see a soldier armed with an automatic rifle in conversation with another soldier. His finger hooked around the trigger of the gun.

Brown turned back to his colleagues, the fear etched on their faces, sweat patches staining their shirts. They kept looking behind them, expecting armed soldiers to appear.

'OK, I can spot a soldier talking to another soldier. They're turned away at the moment, so now's our chance. Follow me.'

Brown stole silently away from his covert position, moving behind the caravan opposite. Without a word, Jones slipped across the gap and stopped alongside Brown, panting.

The two men turned and looked at Smith, who was readying himself for a quick dash. But as he crossed the gap, he tripped on a protruding stone and crashed noisily onto his front, his chin smashing into the dirt. The sound of his fall echoed throughout the caravan park and the soldier who had been turned away shot round instantly in the direction of the noise.

'Oi, hold it there,' the voice shouted as the air reverberated to the heavy sound of army boots thudding in their direction.

Hauling himself to his feet, Smith broke into a run, following Brown and Jones, who had already begun their rapid escape. Reaching the far end of the adjacent caravan, he watched as Brown and Jones hurdled a small fence, disappearing between a small clump of trees. Before he could reach the fence, he heard a voice behind him and the clicking of a rifle.

'Don't you move another fucking inch,' the voice yelled fiercely.

Smith could feel the sweat pouring out of him and his bowels loosened in fear as he looked the soldier directly in the eye. Two further soldiers, also armed, appeared alongside him.

As he raised his arms, he saw an almost indiscernible twitch in the soldier's right hand. His gaze dropped to the soldier's hand, to the slowly tightening trigger finger. Before a cry of protest could escape his lips, the air was filled with the noise of gunfire. A volley of bullets tore into his stomach and chest, sending him hurtling backwards.

As he lay on the floor, blood erupting from his mouth, his consciousness rapidly fading, he was vaguely aware of the soldiers looking down on him. Closing his eyes in readiness, he allowed a mental picture of his young daughter to form. He was finally free of this life. Free of the running. And free of the burden of being a fugitive. For that, he was thankful.

But his feeling of calm was tinged with sadness. Never again would he hold his little girl, hear her laugh, see her grow into a woman, and experience everything life had to offer.

As the soldier who had fired at him raised his gun to his head, he just caught his words.

'Fucking anti-net scum.'

The last bullet shattered his skull, sending blood, brain, and tissue up the wall of the dilapidated caravan.

BROWN AND JONES RAN desperately through a clump of trees. With every step, a jagged branch gouged their skin, adding another laceration. They barely noticed the pain as they ran for their lives. After a few moments, they exited the trees and reached a six-foot wooden fence. Gasping for breath, they could hear the noise of army boots thudding somewhere behind and the loud hum of traffic noise.

'What now?' Jones said as he looked at the fence.

'We go over the fence,' Brown replied instantly.

'But that's the fucking Blackwater Valley Road. We'll get killed trying to cross that.'

'Well, if you want to stay here and get shot, that's up to you. I'm risking the road.'

Before Jones could reply, Brown had shinned up the fence and dropped over to the other side. As the sound of more gunfire echoed in the distance, and the sounds of the soldiers approaching grew louder, Jones turned and hauled himself over the fence.

As he descended on the other side, the bank rapidly dropped away into a steep incline and he slid uncontrollably down the grass, towards the busy dual carriageway below.

In front of him, he could see Brown also tumbling towards the tarmac, trying to put his arms out to stop his fall or grab anything solid.

Brown thudded to the bottom of the hill, throwing his hands out in front of him to stop his body from smashing heavily into the tarmac. He let out a cry of pain as his right elbow impacted the hard surface, his body rolling over onto the edge of the road.

Hauling himself to his feet, a car horn sounded nearby. Turning around, he leapt out of the way as a 4x4 jeep swerved out of the way and into the right-hand lane of the dual carriageway, narrowly missing a Mercedes, in the process of overtaking.

Turning away from the road, he saw Jones hurtling down the hill towards him, also trying, without success, to stop his descent. Just as Jones was about to reach the bottom of the hill and roll onto the road, he dived across to his right to stop his fall. The two men quickly jumped to their feet and looked back up the bank. A soldier was scrambling over the top of the fence, his rifle tucked under his arm.

'Come on,' Brown said, turning to face the oncoming traffic.

As the soldier began his descent, a small gap in the fast-flowing traffic opened up in front of the two fleeing men and they ran into the road, attempting to reach the central reservation barrier. The men clattered into the barrier; they could hear screeching brakes behind them. Quickly casting a glance to their right, Jones watched as a lorry crossed out of the left-hand lane, smashing into a Mini that was overtaking. The front wheels of the lorry easily crushed the back end of the Mini, which lost control and ploughed sideways into the central reservation. As the Mini became embedded in the metal barrier, the lorry rode up over the wreckage of the car and careered onto its side. Mounting the central reservation, it dropped into the carriageway on the opposite side of the road.

Now the lorry blocked both carriageways. Brakes were slammed upon, as the air was filled with more screeching brakes and smoke from the damaged lorry. Three cars that couldn't avoid the carnage crashed into the stationary lorry. As the first car exploded into a fierce fireball, Brown and Jones darted across the other side of the dual carriageway, trying to reach the grass bank opposite.

All the traffic was rapidly grinding to a halt in front of the mangled lorry and cars that had hit it, making their dash across the road relatively easily.

Reaching the other side of the road, they turned to see the soldier crashing heavily into the tarmac at the foot of the bank, his view of them obscured by smoke erupting from the flaming car.

Brown quickly climbed the grass bank. But before Jones could join him, he heard another screeching of brakes. He spun around to see a large motorbike bore down on him at great speed as it swerved away from the stationary traffic. Before he could move out of the way, the motorbike ploughed into Jones, lifting him temporarily off the ground before his body was dragged under the wheels.

For thirty yards, the tangled mess of Jones and the motorbike sped along the edge of the carriageway. Eventually, the bike toppled onto its side, sending the rider onto a car bonnet and the machine colliding with the wheels of a stationary car. Hearing the commotion behind, Brown turned, witnessing what had happened to his friend. Seeing the soldiers hadn't crossed the road, he rushed down to help.

Jones was lying prostrate on the ground, the motorbike a few feet away in a tangled mess.

Brown could see blood trickling from his ear. Kneeling, he looked into Jones' dazed face. He was still alive, despite his injuries.

'Can you stand?' Brown asked as drivers from the vehicles involved in the pile-up climbed out of their cars, all looking equally dazed.

'I'm not sure,' Jones said, lifting his head.

'Come on, I'll help you.' Brown carefully lifted Jones.

As he put the weight on his legs, Jones howled with pain, immediately lifting his left leg from the ground.

'I think it's broken,' he said as they turned to face the hill.

'This is going to hurt, but we've got to get up that hill before those soldiers catch us.'

Jones nodded, wincing as a burning pain cut through his side.

As fast as he could, Brown climbed the steep hill next to the road, hauling Jones with him until they slumped in a heap at the top. Quickly jumping to his feet, he pulled his injured friend away from the edge and into the trees that lined the top of the hill.

As he surveyed the carnage and smoke on the road beneath him, he couldn't see any of the soldiers.

They aren't going to risk exposure in a public place with so many witnesses.

As his gaze moved upward, he could see more smoke spiralling into the air. But this smoke wasn't coming from the mangled mess of cars. This was coming from the caravan park they had just fled from.

Not only had their hideaway been discovered, but all their work and resources had been destroyed.

CHAPTER THIRTY ONE

MICHAEL LOOKED NERVOUSLY AT his watch as the constant bustle of people on Clarence Street milled past him. Leaning against the lamppost opposite the Lloyds TSB in the centre of Kingston-upon-Thames, he watched all the faces passing by. Brown was almost half an hour late and he started to get concerned.

They'd arranged to meet so he could find out what progress they'd made on redeveloping the app for another attack on UKCitizensNet and Trevellion. They'd agreed that Michael needed to be seen at his house in case anyone was monitoring his movements.

Michael was under no illusions the four men were trying to safeguard their skins. Every trip he made to them meant possible disclosure. None of them had articulated this. They didn't need to. They hadn't eluded the authorities for two years without having developed a survival instinct.

Kingston was a good compromise. It was reachable and always busy. They hoped this would make avoiding capture easier. Since their four faces had been splashed all over UKCitizensNet, maybe a sea of people wasn't the best place to be. Despite these revelations the day before, Michael had heard nothing from Brown.

Maybe they've been captured? Is that why I've heard nothing? Or maybe the trains are running late?

Pulling his coat tighter, shielding himself from the chill wind and drizzle, Michael scanned once more up and down the street.

Dozens of faces whirled past in front of him. A priest. Two policemen. A group of oriental male tourists studying a map. A fraught mother pushing a double buggy with two hungry babies screaming for attention.

No sign of Brown.

Reaching into his pocket, Michael pulled out his mobile, flipping it over and over in the palm of his hand. If only Brown and the others used a mobile. At least then, he could put his mind at rest and find out where he was. Shaking his head, and rubbing the tiredness from his eyes, Michael looked the other way. His gaze fell upon the familiar UKCitizensNet sign which stood out above one of the many UKCitizensNet cybercafes now on every shopping street in the country. The risk of missing Brown wasn't as important as finding out if something had happened, he thought as he started to weave his way through the busy mass of shoppers.

The cybercafe was decorated in the familiar red, white and blue in keeping with its pervasive image. Michael grimaced when his shoes clicked noisily on the polished white floor as he approached the dark blue counter. Behind the handful of staff hastily preparing cappuccinos and lattes, the wall was pillar-box red, from floor to ceiling. The gaudy decor was vile.

'What can I get you?' a pretty brunette asked as she turned to face Michael

'Coffee.'

'Cappuccino, Latte, Espresso, Americano?'

'Just an ordinary coffee. Black.'

The brunette looked Michael up and down with a raised eyebrow at his sullen demeanour before turning to pour a filter coffee.

'That'll be £2.85 for the coffee and it's £6 an hour for using UKCitizensNet. Keep your receipt and pay on the way out,' she said cheerfully, ignoring his rudeness.

Michael smiled thinly, sliding the cup off the counter and heading for the nearest vacant computer.

As he sat down, a tubby-looking teenager wearing a Darth Vader T-shirt, tucking into a huge white chocolate muffin, eyed him suspiciously from the computer opposite. Stuffing another mouthful of cake into his mouth, he returned to the Star Wars chat room he was engrossed in.

At the back of the cybercafe, a huge plasma screen was erected on the wall displaying the UKCitizensNet homepage. Continuously changing and flashing new messages and headlines streaked across the screen.

Looking down at the terminal and the compact black touchscreen device, Michael slid his finger over the "Enter" key. The UKCitizensNet screensaver dissolved from the screen to show the all too familiar homepage, mirroring what was on the wall in front of him.

One click on the "Latest News" page revealed a full list of the headlines. The story about the four men being sought by the police for cyberterrorism was still high up there, alongside the latest updates on the Saudi president's visit. Selecting the previous day's article, Michael quickly scanned through the text and all its outrageous lies.

There was no mention of the capture of his accomplices.

Scratching his chin thoughtfully, he rocked back in his chair and stared at the ceiling, feeling relieved. Maybe Brown was just delayed after all. Or he'd just got panicky about appearing in such a public place. It wouldn't be a surprise.

He looked at his watch again, deciding he would return to their original rendezvous point. He'd wait for another half hour and then return home and wait for their call if Brown didn't appear. At least they hadn't been caught yet.

As he rose from his chair, Michael was aware the enormous UKCitizensNet screen at the back of the cybercafe had changed, flashing up a new message. His blood froze as he saw his own face looking back at him from the screen. Even from this distance, he could read the headline boldly displayed under his photograph, positioned alongside the four other men.

Fifth man sought in connection with an attack on UKCitizensNet – police suspect link with death of SemComNet chief.

He could feel his legs go numb. The colour drained from his face as he read the words in front of him. The chubby teenager opposite looked up from his typing, saw the desperate expression on Michael's face, and turned to look at what had stopped him in his tracks.

'Fuck me, you're a terrorist,' he bellowed.

The sudden outburst caused everyone in the cybercafe to look up from their screens and in Michael's direction as he stood motionless.

Two dozen eyes quickly turned to the large plasma screen and then back at Michael. Jaws dropped as recognition dawned.

The pretty brunette who had served Michael was the first to speak.

'Oh, my god. Someone call the police.'

Michael shot a glance at the girl, who quickly ducked down behind the counter. To his right, he was aware of several people rising from their seats to stay out of his way. The chubby teenager also quickly moved out of the way as Michael barged past him and ran for the exit.

Bursting onto Clarence Street, the sea of people still milling between shops met him. Without even thinking, he turned right, zig-zagging through the crowd as he ran. Looking back, he could see a congregation of people gathering at the front of the cybercafe. The two policemen he had seen earlier were approaching the café.

A few yards further, he turned again and saw the policemen had broken into a run, heading in his direction. He felt his heart beating as he shot glances from side to side, looking for a means to escape.

'You fucking wanker,' someone yelled as he bumped into a middle-aged blonde woman who was sent sprawling to the pavement. Michael turned to see a thin, elderly man helping her to her feet, still swearing at him.

Turning to his right, Michael raced through the doors of the imposing Bentalls shopping centre which dominated the street. Without breaking his run, he headed straight for the escalators at the front of the complex.

Barging through shoppers, Michael ran up the escalator, two steps at a time, until he reached the concourse of the first floor.

Stopping in front of the balcony overlooking the ground-floor shops, he caught sight of the two policemen who had followed him into the centre.

Spotting Michael from his elevated position, the policemen split up in their pursuit. The first officer headed for the elevator to block that escape route, whilst the second jumped into the nearby lift.

Feeling the sweat pouring off him, his breathing becoming more rapid, Michael continued running. Heading deeper into the centre and straight into the multi-level Bentalls store itself, an idea took shape.

Rushing through the clothes section, he looked around quickly, mentally noting the layout of the store. To his left, he noticed the in-store lift. As he pressed the button to call the lift, he glanced behind him; his pursuers were nowhere to be seen. The door opened. He slipped inside, pressing himself into one side of the lift, pushing the button for the ground floor. As the door slid shut, he caught sight of the two officers entering the store. He hoped they hadn't seen him.

After leaving the Bentalls store, Michael rushed to the ground floor and towards the sign for the Wood Street exit from the shopping centre. Slipping out into the cold air and the quieter Wood Street, he jogged back onto Clarence Street and walked briskly in the river's direction. Every few yards, he looked over his shoulder. He seemed to have shaken off the two policemen.

Turning into Market Square, he hastily headed for a narrow alleyway signposted to the river. As he reached the alleyway, he turned once more. Just coming into the Market Square were the two policemen, looking from side to side.

As he darted down the alleyway and broke into a run, he was positive they hadn't seen him. But he couldn't be certain.

A few strides later, the alleyway opened up onto the Thames path. Looking around, he turned left and headed for a medium-size boat, offering trips up the river.

A small group of Japanese tourists were handing over their money and walking onto the boat whilst chatting noisily and snapping photos of Kingston Bridge.

Michael sprinted as one of the cabin crew began to untie the boat's moorings, preparing to leave. Gasping for breath, he stopped alongside, reaching into his pocket for his wallet.

'Room for one more?'

The stocky young man, who looked no more than twenty, frowned but turned to look at his colleague, already stationed on the boat. Michael hoped his request hadn't sounded too desperate. The older man, who had rosy red cheeks on his haggard face and looked as if he'd spent most of his life outside, probably on the boat, nodded before returning to drinking his coffee from a flask.

Passing the required money, Michael slipped onto the boat. But unlike the Japanese tourists, he sat downstairs in the enclosed section, avoiding the open rooftop. The stocky young man threw a quizzical look in Michael's direction before finishing unmooring the boat, jumping aboard just as it pulled away from its jetty.

As the boat cruised noisily into the middle of the Thames, Michael peered through the boat's grubby Perspex window.

The two policemen appeared on the Thames path before turning in the other direction and towards the nearby Gazebo pub, milling with potential witnesses who might have seen a cyberterrorist running past.

Breathing a sigh of relief, Michael sank back in his chair before looking at his watch.

What the hell had happened to Brown?

He didn't want to risk heading back to the dilapidated mobile home park in Aldershot at the moment. Not if the police were now looking for the five of them.

If Brown or the others didn't get in contact, he was in this alone. How would he get to Trevellion then?

CHAPTER THIRTY TWO

Desperate situations called for desperate measures. As Michael watched the elderly woman pull another Tesco's shopping bag from the boot of her car and hobble back into her house, he knew this was one of them.

He'd been walking the streets for almost two hours now looking for a suitable opportunity. He could feel the proverbial net tightening around him. Since seeing his picture in the Kingston cybercafe he knew he couldn't go home. They'd either arrest him when he returned, or try to follow him from his house in the hope he'd lead them to his four accomplices. He had nowhere to go. And everyone who used UKCitizensNet or watched TV knew his face.

After his narrow escape up the Thames at Kingston, he'd exited the boat tour at Teddington and caught a taxi to Guildford from a bored-looking driver. Looking at his demeanour, Michael hoped he'd been working for several hours and hadn't seen his picture on the news yet.

The taxi driver, oblivious to the manhunt, dutifully and speedily took him to Guildford, dropping him in a quiet street away from the busy town centre.

And two hours later here he was, standing on the pavement, pretending to talk nonchalantly into his mobile phone, eyeing an unaccompanied car. The boot was open, exposing the remaining bags the woman had to carry into her house. The engine was still running so its elderly owner could park it in her garage after unloading her shopping. This was his opportunity.

Crossing the quiet street, Michael looked to the front door which was ajar. He could see the elderly woman silhouetted in the back of her house, attending to a waiting cat who had greeted her upon return.

Seeing the coast was clear he gently pushed the boot shut and slipped quietly into the driver's seat of the Ford. Sliding the gear stick into reverse, he eased the car off the gravel driveway and onto the road. Pulling away, hurrying through the gears, he looked in the rear-view mirror. There was no sign of the woman.

Relieved, he turned the radio on to UKCitizensNet's 24-hour digital talk radio station, eCIT-Talk, hoping to catch the latest news. As the news presenter was talking about the latest stage of the Saudi president's visit to London, Michael mentally tuned out as he drove around aimlessly.

Where will I go?

There was nowhere left. He couldn't risk going to the dilapidated mobile home park in Aldershot. That had probably been discovered already, he decided. He was running out of options. He looked at the dashboard, reading the digital display. It was 6.34 p.m. It would be dark soon. That would make things a little safer for him.

Eventually, he reached the busy centre of Guildford as he approached a large roundabout. A huge sign detailing the many options to take reared up from the centre. His gaze honed in on one of the place names; he knew he had to go there. Taking the exit signposted to Woking and Brookwood, the centre of Guildford melted away behind him. He was heading towards SemComNet.

The rush hour traffic had been heavy. It had taken Michael over an hour to travel the relatively short distance between Guildford and Brookwood. With the time approaching 8 p.m., at least it was almost dark, he thought, as the Ford meandered through the country lanes.

As the car swung around a gentle right corner, the entrance to SemComNet came into view. The same entrance he'd come through when he had visited Trevellion. As the car drifted past the entrance, three security guards were on duty. Obviously, the alert level had been raised in recent days as he recalled the solitary surly guard who had let him through previously. The security guards barely looked up as he drove past, following the road around the perimeter of the SemComNet complex.

About two hundred yards further, he pulled into a narrow layby overlooking a small arable field that had been recently ploughed. At the back of the field was a large wood that Michael knew from recollection spread onto the SemComNet complex. Checking no one else was around, he exited the car and climbed over a small wooden fence surrounding the field. Trudging across the recently disturbed soil, he looked from side to side, expecting security guards to pounce on him at any moment. But the only accompaniment in the field was a solitary crow, perched on a mound of recently turned soil, eyeing his every step.

Looking into the sky, Michael studied the almost full moon illuminating the field, allowing him to see where he was going. It was just as well, he thought, as he didn't have a torch. Although that would almost certainly have alerted the burly security guards to his presence.

A grim smile formed on his lips. He was so ill-prepared it was almost funny. He had no plan, no idea how he was going to breach SemComNet's security, or get to Trevellion.

He hadn't even sorted out a weapon to avenge Collette and Clare's deaths. He looked down at the hefty spanner in his left hand that he'd retrieved from the boot of the old woman's car. It might not be as conventional as a gun or a knife, but it would suffice to bludgeon the life out of Trevellion and anyone else who got in his way.

Reaching the wood at the back of the field, the moon's illumination quickly disappeared as he slipped between the trees. The gentle breeze which ensured the evening remained distinctly chilly, whistled through the trees, causing the branches to sway and creak, adding to Michael's already fragile nerves.

Moving quietly, he felt a sharp pain slash across his right cheek. Pulling his hand to his face, he could feel blood oozing through his fingers. A branch had gouged its way across his cheek.

Wiping his hand on his trousers, he groped around on the ground until he found a large stick, about six feet long. Holding the stick out in front of him, he used it as a makeshift guide to hack his way through the enveloping darkness.

Progressing at a greater speed, he soon noticed shards of light peeping through the trees in the distance. It had to be the lights from the SemComNet complex, he thought, forging forward with renewed vigour. In his haste through the gloom, he didn't see the large sign nailed to a tree, warning of an electric fence in close proximity.

The shards of light grew bigger as he approached the edge of the wood. Reaching out with his stick once more to swathe a way through the branches, he became aware of a rustling noise. Stopping instantly, he turned his head slowly, trying to make out any movement in the shadows. For a few long seconds, there was nothing.

Did I imagine it?

The only sound came from the trees as they swayed gently in the breeze. Then he heard a man coughing only a few feet away from him.

'Who's there?' he said, trepidation cracking his voice.

'Michael, is that you?' a voice whispered.

'Who are you, and where are you?'

There was movement to his right and what sounded like something heavy being dragged along.

'Michael, it's Brown,' the voice spoke again. 'Jones is with me. But he's hurt.'

A flashlight flicked on, illuminating the area, revealing their positions. Brown was holding the torch and standing next to Jones, who was leaning against a tree for support. The light flashed off again, barely on for more than a second or two. But even in that time, Michael could see Jones was injured.

Where are the others?

Quickly, he walked to the two men.

'What the hell are you doing here?' he asked as Jones spluttered again.

'They found us in Aldershot,' Brown replied, desperation resonating in his voice. 'Soldiers attacked the park and caught us by surprise. Green and Smith are dead. And Jones, well, he's.... we barely made it out of there alive. I only hoped they hadn't got to you. I guessed you'd come here and try to get into SemComNet when I didn't meet you in Kingston.'

'I had to come here. My face is all over UKCitizensNet as an accomplice to this mess. They're trying to make out I had something to do with the death of the head of SemComNet. That we all did.'

'We are so fucked,' Brown muttered, exhaling loudly.

'What about the app?' Michael asked as Jones gingerly eased himself into a sitting position against the tree.

'We'd uploaded the latest version of it onto one of our servers. But the soldiers that attacked us destroyed all our equipment.'

Michael felt the knot in his stomach tighten and numbness creep into his legs.

'Don't tell me we've lost everything?'

'No, we've still got it. As a security measure, in case we ever got captured, we always made copies of important work on a remote secure server.'

'Well, how are we going to get hold of it and attack Trevellion?'

Brown looked down and made out the silhouette of the heavy spanner Michael was clutching.

'You won't need that. The app is almost ready. I've almost sorted the wireless handlers which will give us more options to get at Trevellion.'

Michael swung his arm around, crashing the spanner into the trunk of the tree in a dull but satisfying thud. For a split second, he saw himself standing before Trevellion, watching as he rained down blow after blow on the man who had ruined his life.

'At least with this, I'll be able to see his face the moment he realises he hasn't got away with everything he's done to us.'

Brown raised a placating hand.

'Using that isn't the way. You'll never get close to Trevellion. The app is our best chance. Trust me.'

'So when can we launch it?' Michael asked, controlling his anger.

'There are a couple of safe houses I know of that we can probably use. They were set up for people like us to use only in an emergency, so we didn't expose the others. I can retrieve the app there and complete the remaining work.'

Michael looked quizzically at Brown as he absorbed this latest revelation.

'What do you mean, people like us?'

Brown was looking down at Jones, who was still slumped against the tree and had fallen into unconsciousness.

'We're not the only people trying to bring UKCitizensNet down. There are dozens of groups. But we all protect our identities to minimise betrayal and keep the opposition to UKCitizensNet alive.'

He broke off as both men noticed a shuffling noise behind them. Michael put his finger to his mouth, indicating for Brown to keep quiet. His grip on the spanner tightened as he shot glances around him, trying to pick out any movement in the gloom of the trees.

The shuffling noise was heard again. This time, it was considerably nearer and sounded like something being dragged across the ground. His eyes had become more accustomed to the wooded gloom.

Michael could now make out shapes moving amongst the tree. About twenty feet away, he could see the silhouette of a man walking slowly between the trees, dragging a bag behind him.

Without moving, Michael gestured at Brown to double back and come up behind the solitary man. He would wait until the man reached him, crouched behind one of the thick tree trunks. As Brown moved silently away, leaving Jones unconscious against another tree, and disappearing into the shadows, he waited silently, surprised he no longer felt fear. His sense of purpose seemed to have dulled this emotion. Survival instincts had taken over.

As the solitary man passed Michael, he leapt from his concealed position. Crashing heavily into the man's legs, he sent him to the ground. Without thinking, Michael brought the spanner down on the prone man's upper arm.

'Now,' yelled Michael as the man cried out in pain.

Behind him, he could hear the thud of Brown running to join him. In an instant, Brown's flashlight was on, pointed in the face of the man who squinted from the sudden illumination. His face was contorted in pain.

'I didn't do anything. Get the fuck off me,' he whimpered as Michael knelt on his heaving chest.

As he looked into his frightened eyes, it was immediately clear this man, who looked in his mid-thirties, hadn't been pursuing him. His face was dirty, slightly blackened by what appeared to be mud, and his hair was matted in thick, long dreadlocks that hung below his shoulders. He was wearing green combat trousers and a thick, but holey jumper that was stained and dirty.

'Who are you?' Michael demanded, releasing his grip on the man, allowing him to sit up and catch his breath.

Coughing and rubbing his upper arm, the man looked from Brown to Michael and Jones, slumped against a tree.

'Did you beat the crap out of him too?' he asked, looking at Jones's cuts and bruises and bloodied clothes.

'No, he's with us,' Michael replied more softly.

The man raised his eyebrows.

'Poor sod. He doesn't look as if he's going to make it. Why isn't he in the hospital?'

'Never mind him. I asked you a question.'

Before replying, the young man grabbed Brown's torch and flicked it off.

'Unless you want the whole of fucking SemComNet out here, turn that thing off,' he said disdainfully, tossing the torch back to Brown.

'My name is Davey Wilkes, although everyone calls me Digger. I live here.'

Michael felt the hairs on the back of his neck stand up. His eyes widened in disbelief.

'Did you say Davey Wilkes?'

The young man looked worried. He shuffled nervously.

'Yeah, why?'

'The police want you for the murder of Colette and Clare Robertson, don't they?'

Anger quickly replaced the fear as Digger sprang to his feet.

'That's fucking bollocks. I never killed anyone. They fucking set me up. They set us all up so they could build their fancy fucking building behind us.'

As a thought crossed his mind, his rant quickly trailed off.

'How do you know about the Robertsons? That was over two years ago.'

'I'm Michael Robertson,' Michael said slowly.

Digger took a step back, considering running before Brown blocked his path.

'I told you, I didn't fucking kill no one.'

'Sit down,' Michael ordered. 'I know it wasn't you.'

Digger looked suspiciously at the two men, not sure whether to believe or trust them.

'Whoever set you up is now setting us up, too. We're on the run, like you, which is why I came here. Vincent Trevellion is behind all of this. He's got to be stopped.'

Digger snorted disdainfully at the mention of Trevellion's name.

'Look, I'm sorry for what happened to your wife and daughter. I really am. All we wanted to do was to stop them from destroying the countryside. We never had any interest in the internet or killing people. It's all a fucking government conspiracy so they can do whatever they want.'

Michael looked grimly.

'You have no idea how true that is, or what they're doing in that building.'

Digger looked at the spanner Michael was still holding.

'Forget about trying to get in there. The entire building is surrounded by an electric fence and is patrolled by security guards and dogs. You ain't getting in there over the fence.'

'We won't need to,' Brown interrupted.

'What do you mean?'

'Let's just say we've been developing something that will make sure Trevellion gets what's coming to him.'

Digger smiled as he rubbed his throbbing arm.

'Well, whatever it is, add a "fuck you" from me. They killed my friends when they built this place. That's why I live in the tunnels now. Fucking ironic.2

'What did you say?' Brown said eagerly.

Digger looked confused.

'I said I live in the tunnels here. The tunnels we dug when we were trying to stop them from building on this historic site. Why?'

'Where exactly do the tunnels run?' Brown persisted.

'They're all over the place. There's one not far from where we're standing. All over the place.'

'Yes, but where do they end?'

Michael watched Brown's questioning, not entirely sure where he was going.

'Fuck me. You want to know if they go inside the SemComNet perimeter, don't you?'

'Well, do they?'

'Yeah, a couple of them do. But there are guards and dogs on the other side.'

'What are you thinking?' Michael interjected.

Brown rubbed his chin.

'When we tried to hack into UKCitizensNet before they somehow knew we were coming and could stop us. They were waiting for us to attack. That means they were monitoring external network traffic to UKCitizensNet.'

'You're losing me,' Michael replied tiredly.

'If we were inside SemComNet and launched the app, I'm positive they will never see it coming. Or not until it is too late for them.

They'd still be monitoring for an attack outside the network. We could get Trevellion and UKCitizensNet in one swoop.'

Michael felt his adrenaline pump.

Is it possible?

'Are you sure those tunnels go inside the electric fence?' Brown asked.

'Course I'm sure, I fucking dug 'em,' Digger replied indignantly.

'If we return here in a week, can you take us through the tunnels and inside SemComNet?'

'Anything that pays them back for Moley and the others has got to be worth it. I just hope you're not claustrophobic.'

Even through the gloom, the two men could see a wide grin on his grubby face.

'We need to get to our safe house and get Jones somewhere dry. I don't want him to die somewhere they can find him,' Brown said as he leant down to examine his condition.

'I've got a car,' Michael replied. 'Let's go.'

CHAPTER THIRTY THREE

THE FORD GROUND NOISILY to a halt on the gravel drive in front of a small bungalow. It had taken the three men just over an hour to drive from SemComNet's HQ in Brookwood to the nearest safe house Brown knew.

Michael had been careful not to draw any unwanted attention to the car, dutifully keeping to the speed limit and off the major roads. The car must have been reported stolen by now.

The safe house was in a tiny hamlet north of Alton, well off the beaten track. He'd certainly never heard of Blounce before. It seemed a good location. Exiting the main road which, eventually, would have taken them into the centre of Alton, they had driven for about a mile up a narrow dirt track before it opened up in front of the bungalow. All the lights were out, which was as expected, Brown said. This location was only used from time to time by fellow resisters to UKCitizensNet, who were travelling through.

In the back of the car, Jones had been coughing for most of the journey, howling in pain when Michael had taken a corner too fast or hit a bump in the road. As he turned the engine off, Jones coughed again. The metallic smell of dried blood filled the air inside the car. Michael was relieved to get some fresh air as he stepped out onto the gravel drive and surveyed the bungalow properly.

'You're sure we'll be safe here?'

Brown was helping a barely conscious Jones out of the car.

'I've used it once before. It should be fine. The most important thing is it's got a lot of the equipment I need to finish this bloody app since our own kit was destroyed.'

Looking around, Michael was struck by just how isolated the building was. Even allowing for it being late evening, he couldn't see a light from a house, a building, or a vehicle anywhere. The only sounds were nocturnal wildlife humming away in the background.

Brown had commented during the journey that the bungalow backed onto farmland. The farmhouse was several miles further east. The location was deserted. All he needed now was for Brown to access the backup copy of the app and get it working in time for their rendezvous with Digger in a week. At least being holed up here for a few days would be better than the crumbling mobile home, Michael thought, turning to help Brown carry Jones's ailing body.

As they approached the darkly panelled door, Brown loosened a paving stone that led to the doorway. Underneath was a key glinting in the moonlight. As the men slipped into the house and closed the door, Michael cast one last look behind him. He was sure they hadn't been followed.

As the light flooded into the house after they'd closed all the curtains, he helped Jones lie down on the sofa, his coughing becoming worse.

'Get him some water,' Brown said, gesturing to the kitchen at the back of a long, open-plan living area.

Pulling a handkerchief to his mouth, Jones coughed once more. The force was so great it caused his body to convulse and double up. As the pain tore through Jones, he cried out in agony.

His face was covered in sweat and drained of all colour, leaving a pale, sallow appearance. Dried blood was smeared around his mouth and cuts and bruises were strewn across his body. But it was the internal injuries that were rapidly sucking the life from him.

As the latest coughing fit subsided, Jones pulled the handkerchief from his mouth. Michael tried to remain expressionless, not betray what he was thinking. But when he saw the rag covered in blood, Jones read it in his face.

'Don't worry Michael. I know I haven't got long.'

'Brown is looking for a medical kit right now,' he replied as he handed Jones the glass of water. Brown had already begun rummaging through various draws and cupboards.

Jones grimaced, the dried blood around his lips cracking slightly.

'I'm fucked on the inside. You know it. I know it.'

Michael bowed his head. A ruptured spleen. Multiple broken ribs. A collapsed lung. These injuries would show no mercy on anyone, no matter how unjust their situation.

'Can I make you more comfortable?' he asked as Jones drifted in and out of consciousness.

Screwing his eyes up as another wave of pain coursed through him, Jones looked Michael squarely in the face, determined to share two final important requests with him.

'Tell Margaret that I always loved her, and I'm so sorry that it ended this way. Being apart from her was the hardest thing I've ever had to do. Please tell her she gave me the best days of my life. Find a way to get a message to her. Promise me you'll try.'

Michael nodded.

Jones closed his eyes, his pain briefly replaced by happy reminders of his wife's smile, her scent, her unquestioning loyalty through all their years together. As his life had been ripped apart and he was thrust headlong into becoming a fugitive, she had been there. Supporting him. Always by his side.

Opening his eyes again, a determined expression forced its way through the pain etched on his face.

'Promise me,' he replied, his voice barely more than a whisper. 'Make sure you get Trevellion. For your wife and daughter.'

Michael nodded, the perpetual knot in his stomach tightening.

'And for me, and the others, make sure you bring UKCitizensNet down. Don't let it all be for nothing.'

Brown had returned. His hunt for medical supplies had yielded nothing. He looked sorrowfully at Jones who was slipping away.

'They may think they have the power,' Jones continued, 'but they don't. They may think they can behave like gods and rule and control our lives, but they don't. They're false prophets. But we know and we must stop them. Others can help you. Get Brown to contact the RIG. You can't do it alone. You need their...'

Before he could finish, another surge of coughs erupted from his lungs. A mouthful of blood sprayed into the air before he doubled up in pain, toppling off the sofa and onto the floor. Michael stood motionless, unable to move. Brown dropped to his knees and rolled Jones onto his back, his face covered in fresh blood. As the last breaths passed his lips, Michael looked into his eyes. Two words burned a hole in his consciousness:

False prophets.

Images of Colette appearing before him came back.

'Who foils the signs of false prophets and makes fools of diviners, who overthrows the learning of the wise and turns it into nonsense.'

She had warned him the enemy was wider than he thought. In his last dying moments, had Jones inadvertently revealed his true self?

How could I have been so stupid? Colette has been trying to warn me all along. The four men must be involved with something they don't want me to know about, or worse, linked with UKCitizensNet. Linked with Trevellion. This is all a trap to fulfil their ends, or to get me caught so SemComNet can get rid of me.

He could feel his breathing quickening as adrenaline surged through him. He looked down at Brown, bent over Jones. Michael couldn't hear what he was saying to him. All he could hear was Colette's voice. Over and over again.

'Who foils the signs of false prophets and makes fools of diviners, who overthrows the learning of the wise and turns it into nonsense.'

Finally, Brown looked up, and Michael detected tears in his eyes.

'He's gone,' Brown said, wiping the small splatters of Jones's blood from his cheek and neck.

A million thoughts were rushing around in Michael's head. He ought to kill Brown right here and now. Before he had a chance to betray him. Or hand him over to Trevellion and his henchmen.

'Poor sod. I think he must have been hallucinating right at the end. I didn't understand all that crap about "false prophets". Did you?'

Michael could hear the question, could feel his anxiousness rising. The worst of all was that he needed Brown more than ever, now the others were dead. Without Brown, he had no completed app. No effective means to kill Trevellion and avenge Colette and Clare.

He looked into Brown's face. Now wasn't the moment. He needed to bide his time. And above all, he needed Brown to complete the app and help him to get it onto UKCitizensNet's system inside their complex. He would keep up the pretence for now, and deal with Brown's betrayal later. He'd beat it out of him if he had to.

'No, I've no idea what he was talking about.'

Remembering something else Jones had said, he added: 'Who or what is RIG?'

'Help me move Jones's body and I'll tell you,' Brown replied.

After carrying the body to the bedroom and laying him out on the bed, the two men returned to the lounge. Brown had discovered two beers in the cupboard, which, although warm, still went down well.

As they slumped tiredly into the worn armchairs, Brown explained.

'Do you remember me saying before there were other groups like us, all trying to bring UKCitizensNet down? Whilst we don't work together, the risk of betrayal and exposure is too great, we all acknowledge each other's existence. Unlike UKCitizensNet, which officially doesn't acknowledge any remains of the old internet or its infrastructure. But they know we're out there. Why do you think we've been living as we have for so long?

'Collectively, we call ourselves the Real Internet Guardians or RIG for short. Like us, these groups cropped up once UKCitizensNet had been established, and the government tore down and banned access to the old internet infrastructure. The groups mainly consists of academics and scientists. Men and women who still believe in the ideology of free access to information. Rather than the censored, regulated piece of shit UKCitizensNet is. I'm not sure how many groups we total these days, or even where the name came from. But there are certainly enough of us to keep UKCitizensNet's security specialists occupied.'

'Why did Jones want you to contact the RIG?' Michael asked, taking another gulp from his warm beer.

Brown looked thoughtful. He ran his fingers through his hair.

'I can only imagine he figured, since our numbers have gone from four to one, that we needed their help to get the app completed. It does make sense. I mean, I can look at the wireless handlers of the app, but I could do with some help on making some of the other components more stable.'

'Well, why aren't we contacting them?' Michael said forcefully, casting a glance at a door that led off from the main living space. He'd noticed stockpiled computer equipment in the room when they'd moved Jones's body to the bedroom.

'It's not the way we operate,' Brown replied slowly. 'For our safety, we don't meet or get involved with the other groups. If we were betrayed, the whole RIG movement could be wiped out. This way we guarantee the continuation of our opposition to UKCitizensNet.'

Michael couldn't conceal his frustration.

'Yes, but together, surely you stand a greater chance of bringing them down? Didn't you say the app was what you'd been waiting for? An opportunity to destroy UKCitizensNet. To get your lives back.'

'That's not much good for the others, though, is it?' Brown replied sourly.

'All the more reason to do this for them, then.'

'Look, if other groups had contacted us, we wouldn't have responded for fear of exposure. They'll all do the same.'

Frustrated, Michael leapt from his chair.

'We've got to try. I will not stay put knowing others can help us. I want to know how to contact them. Now.'

Brown rose, placing his empty bottle on the table.

'Look, we'll contact a sample of them individually, and see what response we get. I'm not sending it out to every contact I have and asking them to forward it to their contacts because they'll smell a fucking trap from the outset. We'll never hear from them again. And besides, for our own safety, one group doesn't have contact details for every other group. It's too risky.'

Michael made a conciliatory nod as Brown strode past and into a small room housing the computer equipment. It was a fraction of what the men had been using previously and looked distinctly archaic compared to the touch screen devices that everyone else seemed to use these days. He only hoped it sufficed to do the job.

As the ageing computer screen flicked into life, Michael sank in the chair next to Brown and watched as he typed a host of commands. After a few minutes of familiarising himself with the computer's setup, Brown finally turned to look at Michael.

'OK, I've established a link with a secure email server outside the UKCitizensNet domain. What do you want to say to the RIG?'

CHAPTER THIRTY FOUR

THE JAPANESE RESTAURANT ON Oxford Street was particularly busy this lunchtime. A delegation from Texas was in town for a pharmaceutical conference and had taken up about a third of the restaurant. Between them, they had ordered virtually everything on the menu. The kitchen staff were struggling to prepare their meals as quickly as the restaurant owner wanted. The owner had always prided himself in getting orders processed as quickly as possible. To get the next customer in and served.

But it wasn't this pressure that bothered the pretty young blonde waitress as she weaved her way through the tables with an expensive bottle of Bordeaux Margaux 1982. Walking past the party of noisy Texans, she ignored the admiring glances she was getting from at least three of the men who were beaming smiles at her. She just wanted to serve the wine and move on to the next customer.

She'd taken the order from the two men seated in the corner of the restaurant when they'd arrived. There was something about these two that disturbed her and she couldn't put her finger on it. She'd felt uncomfortable the moment they entered the restaurant. The hairs on the back of her neck had all stood up.

They hadn't been rude. They hadn't even tried to look down her shirt that was unbuttoned to just above her cleavage. But there had been something cold and detached about them. They'd had a presence. Maybe it was just they exuded importance, she'd wondered as she looked at the older man's expensive pinstripe suit.

Perhaps they were city stockbrokers or high-flying barristers? They had enough of them in here daily. But none of them had such a malevolent aura about them, she thought as she approached their table, their private conversation immediately ending.

Sebastian Tate looked over the top of his rimless glasses as the waitress approached. His face remained expressionless, disinterested, as she poured a sample of the wine for him to try.

'That'll be all,' Tate said dismissively, looking away and back to Vincent Trevellion, who was sitting opposite.

The waitress nodded, shivering involuntarily as she moved away from their table. Someone else could bring them their food.

Trevellion was the first to resume the conversation.

'As I predicted, our *friends* and Robertson launched an attack on the UKCitizensNet system with an advanced version of the app. They could only do this because we lowered the encryption and let them into a secure area within the system. There was never any danger of the infrastructure being compromised.'

The image of the two network analysts' attempts to stop the app's path briefly crossed Trevellion's thoughts.

'I told you they were amateurs. They were using some fairly sophisticated IP address scrambling techniques to try and cloak their position, though. But once the app was secured, we could pinpoint their location.'

Tate gave Trevellion a supercilious look as he sipped his glass of Bordeaux Margaux.

'Yes, but my dear Vincent, it's one thing knowing where these annoyances were. It's another thing actually capturing or eliminating them as a problem, isn't it? It would rather appear you failed in this respect.'

'As I recall,' Trevellion replied slowly, barely concealing the irritation burning in his dark eyes, 'you put the resources of *your* department at my disposal. Your men failed to resolve the problem.'

Tate waved dismissively before adjusting the position of his glasses on his nose.

'Semantics, dear boy. Now we have the app, I don't see why you want to spend so much energy on this minor irritation. They were unable to breach UKCitizensNet. Our position is invulnerable.'

Trevellion's scowl grew as he reached for his wineglass.

'I'm sure I don't need to remind you that whilst UKCitizensNet's security may be invulnerable, security elsewhere is not. You may currently enjoy quasi-ministerial perks; rest assured it won't last forever. I certainly don't intend to live within the confines of SemComNet. So, unless you want to risk these people, and many other groups like them, coming at you when you're taking a piss one day and your guard is down and your security personnel are nowhere to be seen, we need to resolve this problem. Yes, they're amateurs. And yes, we've crippled their capabilities by destroying some of their equipment after we retrieved their data stores. But they'll find a way. Let's not also forget what we had to do to get to this stage.'

He added, pointedly, 'I think all of us have invested far too much to risk it being sabotaged by some fucking amateurs. I would have thought that would be at the forefront of your thinking, given why we're sitting here today.'

Tate smiled as only he could.

'There's no need to get agitated, Vincent. You know you have my support. I trust you'll do what's necessary to remove Robertson and the remaining two from the equation. I just want assurances your focus will remain on the app and the target. My department will take care of Robertson if that's how you wish to use our resources. I gather they're scouring the area near Aldershot as we speak?'

Trevellion nodded.

Tate cast a glance around the restaurant. His security personnel were sitting at the two nearest tables, although not near enough to overhear their conversation. They were essentially cordoned off from the rest of the people dining in the restaurant.

'Let's get back to the matter at hand.'

'The app is almost ready?'

'R&D have taken what we retrieved from the failed attack on UKCitizensNet and what we obtained from Robertson's accomplices' machines. Some minor configurations need to be made to the wireless handlers in terms of IP synchronicity. Once that's completed, we're ready, which will be by the end of tomorrow. We'll then do some wireless testing in a controlled environment at SemComNet. After that, we're ready to go.'

'Good,' replied Tate, pouring another glass of Bordeaux Margaux. 'So we're still on schedule.'

He turned and looked out of the window and onto Oxford Street.

'Tell me about the route.'

'Security personnel will man the route throughout. Of course, they'll be looking out for snipers or anything suspicious on the route back to the airport. The car will travel in a convoy of five vehicles, made up entirely of their security personnel. Your men will be stationed at our wireless hubs from the hotel to the airport, ensuring the network isn't compromised at any point. We don't need one cluster to fail and lose our window of opportunity. Then at the appropriate moment...'

Trevellion trailed off as another waitress brought two portions of sushi to their table.

'Excellent,' Tate said, reaching for his perfectly polished fork.

'I understand their hotel isn't too far from here,' he added, as he tasted the first mouthful.

'Yes, they're based in Cavendish Square, so this is more or less the start of their route. We have this table booked for lunch on the day so we can observe their departure.'

Tate nodded, washing down the sushi with wine.

'And what a departure it will be.'

CHAPTER THIRTY FIVE

PARKING THE FORD IN a quiet side street, Michael enabled the central locking and walked briskly towards Odiham High Street two roads over. He hoped the combination of several days' stubble and a dark blue baseball cap he'd found in one of the bungalow's bedrooms would be sufficient to mask his identity. Whilst the bungalow was an ideal and safe location for Brown to complete the work on the app, they'd soon run out of food. And Michael had to be the one to get some more.

Initially, he had said it was too risky for him to walk into a supermarket and stock up on supplies. It was even too dangerous for him to risk visiting a local village shop. UKCitizensNet was in every shop, and the manhunt for the five of them was all over the news. There was no mention, of course, of the fact that Green, Smith and Jones had been killed. Not even a passing mention of the pile-up on the Blackwater Valley Road. So much for the wonderful free, non-manipulated press the rest of the country still believed it had.

In the end, Brown had come up with a compromise. Michael was slightly happier with it, although still very anxious at walking the streets during the day. Even in a sleepy village like Odiham.

Brown had suggested they order their food online with a fake credit card the four men had used previously when the situation demanded absolute secrecy. They would then get the order delivered to a fictitious address. When the delivery driver arrived and couldn't find the address, Michael would be on hand to explain the error and collect the food. It seemed simple. And Odiham had been a good choice. If there were any problems, it was far enough away from their bungalow in Blounce not to draw any suspicion.

Michael turned onto the high street and looked at his watch. It was just after 10.30 a.m. The street was quiet except for a few pensioners walking up to the nearby row of shops at the end of the street and a dog walker absorbed in the music coming from her iPod.

As the dog walker moved past on the opposite pavement, the delivery van came into sight, meandering down the road in Michael's direction. He watched as the driver read the house numbers carefully, unable to find the one he was looking for. Passing Michael, he did a U-turn, scanning the houses on the opposite side of the road in his search.

Michael looked around anxiously. But there was no one about. Eventually, as Brown had predicted, and after doing another U-turn, the delivery driver pulled up alongside him.

'Do you know where I can find 212a along here?' said a balding, slightly tubby middle-aged man leaning out the window. 'I've got High Street, Odiham, here, but I can't see 212a anywhere.'

Michael hoped Brown's ruse would work.

'There's no 212a along here. I live at 212 and the wife ordered some food on UKCitizensNet. She must have typed the wrong address accidentally. I'll take the food now if you like.'

The delivery driver gave Michael a quizzical look, reaching for his clipboard perched on the dashboard.

'What's the name?'

'Wilson. Mrs R. Wilson.'

Nodding, the driver jumped down from his van and opened the backdoors.

'I'll take them inside for you if you like.'

Neither Michael nor Brown had anticipated this.

'Er, that's OK. I've locked myself out of the house. I've phoned the wife. She's going to be back soon to let me in.'

The driver raised his eyebrows.

Michael felt his breathing become more rapid, hoping his story sounded plausible.

'What about your fresh stuff? You need to get that in the fridge.'

'She's only going to be five minutes. It'll be fine.'

Shrugging, the driver unloaded the three boxes of food onto the pavement.

Closing the back door of the van, the driver turned to Michael.

'I must rush. I've got four more deliveries to make. Although it looks like I'm going to be late, what with the roadblock they're putting up.'

Michael felt a twinge of apprehension.

'What roadblock?'

The driver pointed up the High Street towards the row of shops.

'When I came through, the army was setting up a roadblock. I only just got through myself. I'm not sure what they're doing. Always up to something round here, the bloody army. If it's not those bloody guns going off over on Ash Ranges, then it's something else. If you ask me, I reckon they could be looking for those cyberterrorists. There are lots of computer bods living around here. All those commuters. Don't understand it all myself.'

Michael could feel the colour drain from his face. The driver was quick to notice it.

'Are you all right mate?' he said, as Michael looked anxiously up the street.

Further up the street, a small company of soldiers, automatic rifles slung over their shoulders, were moving from building to building on either side of the road. Michael knew who they were looking for. Without picking up the grocery boxes, he turned and ran down the quiet side street toward his car.

The delivery driver stood next to his van looking bewildered before a realisation struck him. The image of a man shown on UKCitizensNet flashed back to him.

Leaving the boxes on the pavement, he turned and began to slowly jog in the direction of the armed soldiers.

CHAPTER THIRTY SIX

THE WEIGHT OF HIS rucksack was hurting Michael's back as the two men trudged across the recently ploughed field through the sprawling farmland. After spotting the soldiers in Odiham, he'd fled back to his car. Every road he'd taken to get out of the village had been blocked by either army or police cars as the forces worked effectively in tandem. They had completely sealed the area as the army conducted their house-to-house hunt. Finally, he'd spotted a gate into one of the many fields dominating the rural area and had turned the car off the road.

Following a narrow gravel track up the side of the field, he eventually exited on the outskirts of nearby South Warnborough. From there it had been a rapid four-mile journey back to Blounce. He knew it wouldn't be long before they discovered the safe house.

As they'd quickly packed up clothes from the bedroom in the bungalow, Brown had borrowed a few items of equipment from the computer room. Michael didn't have the faintest idea what they were, or why they were needed.

Brown had stored the work on the app on the secure RIG server for safekeeping, before moaning about how he needed more time to be sure it worked and was stable. It was the same rhetoric the four men had been giving him ever since he'd met them. But there was no more time. Not unless they wanted to get caught.

And he needed to watch Brown now, he knew the four men hadn't been all they seemed. If they'd been waiting for a moment to turn him over to the authorities, or even UKCitizensNet, just to save their skins and catch him unawares, then they'd missed their chance. He'd wised up to them. The only thing that mattered now was staying alive so he could complete his mission: avenge Colette and Clare.

Within ten minutes of returning to the bungalow, they'd packed up all the items they needed and could carry and had set off across the farm fields backing onto the bungalow's extensive garden. They'd had no choice but to leave Jones' body lying on the bed. In some ways, Michael was pleased to be leaving. The body was smelling.

They didn't have a map, so were unsure where they were heading. All they knew for certain was the house and the area weren't safe anymore. Brown hadn't disclosed the location of the other safe house, only that it wasn't nearby.

'Look,' Michael said, pausing for a breather and dropping the rucksack onto the churned soil.

In the distance, only half a mile away, a farmhouse and some outbuildings had come into view from behind a small wooded area. Brown nodded, reaching for a bottle of water and taking a much-needed swig.

'We need to be careful,' Michael continued, surveying the rolling fields. There was no sign of anyone working on the land.

'We don't need to be chased down by an irate farmer in his tractor. Let's head for the trees over there on the right and approach from there. We can then keep ourselves concealed from anyone on the farm or those bloody soldiers.'

Resuming their progress, Michael was struck by how he'd changed. A few weeks ago, when he was still convalescing at the care home, he knew he wouldn't have survived in this environment. He wouldn't have had the guts or the confidence to plot an escape cross-country. Never mind contemplate what they were planning for when they met up with Digger again.

Assuming we ever make it back to SemComNet again. How many soldiers and police are looking for us?

He let the thought slide away as they reached the small bank of trees, disappearing amongst them.

The farmhouse could just be seen through the trees as they carefully made their way to the other end of the wood. Crouching down before they reached the edge of the small wood, the two men scanned the grounds surrounding the quiet farmhouse.

There were no vehicles. No obvious sign of life anywhere. All the farmhouse windows were shut. And there was no sign of lights or movement inside. To the right of the farmhouse, three outbuildings, a milking station and a couple of grain silos were also deserted. Seemingly locked up.

'Looks deserted to me,' Brown finally said after five minutes of silent observation.

'Yeah, I reckon so. Let's head around the back and see if we can find a way in.'

'What do you want to break in for?'

'First, I want to know exactly what UKCitizensNet is reporting and why there are troops on the streets looking for us. Second, I don't know about you, but I'm bloody starving and we've got no food.'

As the two men stole out from where they were concealed, Brown followed Michael, who darted across the yard between the farmhouse and the outbuildings and round the back of the house. Turning the corner, Michael looked out onto a large back garden that was less than immaculately kept.

To his left, the large double kitchen window was closed. The back door was a little further on. Slowly, Michael moved around and peered through the kitchen window. In the middle of the room was a large wooden table with one chair. To the right was a large dresser, crammed full of books and folders. At the back of the kitchen was an impressive green Aga, dominating the room. Michael smiled at the stereotypical farmhouse kitchen. There was only one thing missing. And that, thankfully, was the farmer.

In the right-hand corner was a doorway leading into the house. Michael observed it for a full two minutes. There was no sign of movement. Moving past the window, he placed his hand on the back door handle. It was locked. His elbow smashed one of the glass panes in the kitchen door; he reached through and turned the key in the keyhole on the inside, hoping the house wasn't rigged with an alarm.

As the kitchen door creaked open and the two men stepped inside, they were met with silence. Brown heaved a sigh of relief, dumping the rucksack onto the kitchen table before slumping into a chair.

Passing him, Michael walked through the kitchen and into the dining room. Papers and files were sprawled across the table. He glanced down at a selection of sheets that caught his eye. There were numerous letters from a mortgage company and a bank demanding various payments. One letter threatened repossession of the farmhouse if the debts weren't settled. It seemed the farm wasn't doing well.

To his right, he could see a shotgun propped up against the wall.

Is that to stop the bailiffs getting in, or for the farmer to end it all if he doesn't turn a profit this harvest?

He exited the dining room to find himself in what appeared to be the main living area. In the centre of the room, against a long wall, was a television. As he'd been hoping, an eCitTV touchscreen console was in the armchair's seat.

The television flickered into life and Michael scowled when the familiar red, white and blue UKCitizensNet logo appeared on the screen. Sliding his finger over the "Web" icon the screen melted into the interactive area. Quickly clicking on the "News" link, he waited expectantly.

What are the lying bastards saying about me now? Can it get any worse than being branded a cyberterrorist?

Michael read the latest headline on UKCitizensNet and was thankful he was sitting down, as he feared he would have fallen. His face was again on the screen next to the offending headline.

Children's bodies discovered at house of cyberterrorist.

His hand was shaking as he absorbed the full grisly facts. He weeped as he read the terrible report that showed a picture of his back garden shrouded in police forensic tents.

Police report that they have discovered the bodies of at least eight children in the back garden of wanted cyberterrorist, Michael Robertson. The police were tipped off to this grisly discovery by a neighbour who reported he had regularly seen children coming to the house, even after the death of Michael Robertson's daughter two years ago.

Police had originally obtained a warrant to search the house following investigations which identified Michael Robertson as a potential cyberterrorist thought to have been involved in the death of Sem-ComNet President, Sir Donald Allison.

The macabre discoveries were made in the back garden of Robertson's house in Hersham, Surrey, where forensic detectives are still collecting evidence they hope will identify the children and help their investigation.

Police have also not ruled out the possibility that Michael Robertson may have been involved in the murder of his daughter two years ago. Initially, anti-net campaigner Davey Wilkes was charged with the killing, although police have never been able to apprehend Wilkes.

Chief Superintendent Miles Robson, who is overseeing this investigation, said the case would be reopened and examined in the light of these recent discoveries.'

Michael felt faint as waves of nausea spread through him. He could read the words in front of him, but he couldn't reconcile what they were saying. Anger replaced nausea as his muscles tensed and his colour returned.

Is there no depth to which SemComNet won't go to destroy me? Haven't you taken enough from me by killing Colette and Clare?

Holding his head in his hands, he didn't hear the Land Rover pulling up in the drive outside the house. Or the dull thud of footsteps approaching the front door.

As the key turned in the lock, Michael jumped up from the armchair in time to catch sight of a smartly dressed man in an Italian suit coming through the front door. He felt his pulse quicken. His heart was pounding. Vincent Trevellion strode into the lounge. Reeking of contempt.

Michael looked into his narrow, emotionless eyes, heard him say something, although he couldn't make out the words. Turning quickly, he darted into the dining room and grabbed the shotgun. Never mind what the farmer had in mind for the gun. It had a new purpose now.

With the confidence of the loaded shotgun, Michael strode purposefully back towards the main living area. Trevellion was standing in the doorway. Shouting something in his direction. Waving his arms around.

He couldn't hear the words. His mind was awash with images of Colette and Clare. Happy images of their time together as a family. Images of precious moments with his daughter when he took her to her ballet classes. Images of intimate moments he'd savoured with Colette. And bloody images of Colette lying tied to the same bed with that obscenity carved into her chest and scrawled onto the wall.

As Trevellion raised his palm, Michael pulled the trigger. The force of the explosion pushed him backwards, the butt of the shotgun thudding into his upper arm. The blast tore a hole in Trevellion's suit just below the sternum, but he remained standing.

There were still words coming from his mouth, his palm raised at Michael in some sort of defiant gesture.

The second cartridge smashed into Trevellion's side, sending him crashing into the large wooden fireplace. Blood splattered in an arc up the wall next to him.

The third shot blew a hole through Trevellion's heart, spinning his body around before it fell face-up onto the floor. A pool of blood rapidly stained the panelled wood floor as Michael stood in a trance over his nemesis's lifeless body.

'What the fuck have you done?' Brown shouted, rushing into the room.

The familiar sound of Brown's voice broke Michael's trance. He turned round in a daze.

'I've killed...,' the words wouldn't come as he felt his breathing tighten. 'I've killed Trevellion. He came here looking for me. But I killed him.'

Brown looked at the lifeless body of the middle-aged farmer laying in the spreading pool of blood at Michael's feet.

'You've shot the farmer, you fucking idiot. Don't you think we're in enough shit as it is? Why couldn't you have just tied him up until we'd got what we needed from this place?'

Michael looked bewildered as he turned back to look at the body. The farmer, who looked in his early fifties, was dressed in a pair of heavy walking boots, grubby jeans and a green Barbour jacket soaked in his blood.

'But it was Trevellion. I saw him come through the door. I reached for the gun and... I swear it was Trevellion I saw.'

Brown closed his eyes, running his fingers through his hair, exhaling loudly. Looking up, he caught sight of Michael's picture on the blood-spattered television screen and read the headline.

Children's bodies discovered at house of cyberterrorist.

'Oh no,' he exclaimed, walking past Michael, who was frozen in place.

He sank into the large sofa next to the armchair.

'Didn't I tell you when we first met what these people are capable of? What lengths they'll go to in order to protect their interests?'

'But it was him, I tell you,' Michael protested as he continued to stare disbelievingly at the body of the farmer.

'Listen, my friend, you're under enormous emotional stress. Sem-ComNet, and probably Trevellion, know exactly which buttons to push with you. The more they push you, the more you're likely to do something that exposes you and that gets us both caught.'

'You mean like shooting some poor guy who I thought was Trevellion?'

Brown looked at the floor, but his expression spoke volumes. In the distance, both men heard the distinctive noise of a helicopter. Rushing to the window, they watched as an army Chinook helicopter flew over the farm, heading north.

'That's probably supporting the searches in Odiham,' Brown said nervously as the helicopter disappeared.

'We've got to get out of here then,' Michael replied, casting another look at the dead farmer.

He was going to keep the shotgun with him. It would certainly be useful for when they returned to SemComNet. It was also added insurance against whatever Brown and the three other men had been up to. He would not let his guard down. And now Brown knew he wasn't afraid to use a weapon.

'Not yet,' Brown said, turning off the television. 'We don't need them to see what was being read on screen when they discover his body. There must also be a computer in this house. I need access to our secure email. And I don't mean through that bit of censored shit.'

He gestured in the direction of the eCitTV set.

'I haven't spotted one down here. Let's look upstairs.'

The ancient computer with its deep-backed monitor was in the second bedroom. Like most of the rest of the house, it was full of files and folders. The farmer didn't seem to have thrown away any piece of paper he'd ever received.

Brown opened up a DOS window and hastily typed a set of commands. A few moments later, a window opened on the screen. Michael watched as Brown accessed an email inbox.

'Don't blame me if no one replied,' Brown began. 'In their situation, I wouldn't.'

Eventually, the inbox loaded its content, revealing one solitary message. The sender's name was marked as Ephesus, and the email address ephesus@rig.uk.

As Brown opened the message, Michael noticed the recipient's email address: horsemen@rig.uk.

'We're known as the Four Horsemen of the Apocalypse in RIG circles,' Brown said proudly as the message popped up on the screen.

Michael took a step back as Colette's prophetic words came rushing back.

'After this I saw four angels standing at the four corners of the earth, holding back the four winds of the earth so no wind could blow on the earth, on the sea, or any tree. Then I saw another angel ascending from the east, who had the seal of the living God. He shouted out with a loud voice to the four angels who had been given permission to damage the earth and the sea.'

If there'd been any doubt before that the four men were pursuing their agenda and somehow using Michael, this proved it beyond all doubt. Colette had cryptically warned him about the Four Horsemen of the Apocalypse. This was why.

If only she'd revealed what their true plan was. Are they working for SemComNet or just trying to save their skins by using me and the knowledge I got from Colette's work? Whatever the reason, the shotgun would not leave his side. Nothing was going to distract him from his revenge.

Brown looked up from the computer and into Michael's stern face.

'Well, that sorts out where we're heading. I just hope we can get there before they find us.'

Michael nodded, turning his attention to the message on the screen.

> Thanks for contact. The sample of what you sent is intriguing. Keen to see more and help in any way we can.

This is more important than all of us. Meet outside Students' Union bar, main campus, South Downs University, 7.30 p.m. tomorrow. Mass of students will keep you concealed. Be careful. Ephesus.

Michael looked at Brown, who shut the computer down.

'Can they help us? Is it safe?'

'I don't know on either account. But if there's a chance they can help us complete the app, we've got to risk it.'

Michael nodded, gripping the gun he was holding a little tighter.

'Let's grab some food, and anything else useful. Then let's get going before those soldiers or that helicopter take an interest in this farm.'

CHAPTER THIRTY SEVEN

The main campus at South Downs University was teeming with students as the muddy Land Rover turned onto the access road before slipping into the pay-and-display car park nearby. It was the second vehicle Michael had stolen in almost as many days.

As they parked, Michael and Brown watched the steady stream of students heading towards the Students' Union at the other end of the campus. At least it wouldn't be difficult to find.

For the first time in a while, they'd been lucky. When they'd left the farm and the dead farmer, there were no army roadblocks in sight. And after negotiating the maze of country lanes, they'd found themselves on the outskirts of Alton and a relatively short journey down to the South Downs University campus.

Before making their trip to the university, the two men had needed to lie low. Brown had directed Michael to an isolated country park in nearby Winchester, where they'd parked up and got some much-needed sleep overnight. Their only distraction had been some drunken teenage boys banging on their windows just after midnight.

They'd run off into the darkness. The rest of the journey had, thankfully, been fairly uneventful.

Exiting the Land Rover, Michael caught sight of their reflections in a window. He knew they looked absurd, both wearing baseball caps and sporting several days' stubble. He had found a pair of sunglasses in the Land Rover and was wearing these.

A little ridicule from some raucous students would be worth it if they kept their identities concealed.

Merging into the stream of students heading for a noisy, drunken Friday night in the Union bar, Michael surveyed his surroundings. The campus was a combination of established red-bricked and concrete buildings built in the 1960s and 70s, and modern glassed-fronted buildings gleaming like mirrors in their midst.

Taking their lead from the mass of students, the two men crossed the wide road that bisected the campus past an imposing tinted glass structure. A similar-looking building was opposite, creating the impression of a large glass corridor leading into the heart of the campus. Crossing a landscaped patch of grass, they passed a tangled mass of distressed metal, one of the campus's many architectural statements, before reaching the Students' Union.

The crowds of students were queued back for almost two hundred yards as they waited patiently to get into the Union bar. The sound of music reverberating inside the building filled the air, mixing with the hum of excited students.

'Oi granddad, the bingo hall's in that direction,' a voice bellowed as the two men stood uncomfortably near the end of the queue.

Howls of laughter rippled up the line. The student who'd cracked the joke took another drag on his cigarette, slapping a high five with one of his friends.

Michael ignored the laughter, turning to survey the campus and the plethora of red-bricked buildings dominating his view.

'How do we know who we're looking for?' he finally asked.

Brown shrugged, rolling his eyes.

'Well, I'm guessing the contact will not be a student. This lot are far too young to be involved with RIG.'

Behind the line of students snaking along the side of the building, Michael caught sight of a sign next to a doorway that read 'Catering Services". In the doorway was a tall, thin man, with dark hair in a neat fringe. Michael estimated he was probably around forty. He stood silent and alone, wearing a smart pair of jeans and a black well-fitted shirt, smoking a cigarette.

Aware Michael had seen him, the man moved out of the doorway. Gliding through the crowd of students, he approached the two men. Looking them up and down, he took another drag of his cigarette.

'I assumed there'd be four of you?'

Michael tried to look nonchalant.

'I'm sorry, do I know you?'

The man rolled his eyes disdainfully.

'The Four Horsemen?'

Michael's nonchalance ebbed away as he studied the man's face. There was something strangely familiar about him as he looked into his dark eyes. He couldn't put his finger on it, but it bothered him.

'You emailed me, right?' the man continued. 'You sent me something also? Look, I took a big risk meeting with you, so I'd appreciate you not pissing me about.'

Brown nodded, raising a placating palm.

'Can we go somewhere private? It's not safe for us out here.'

The man looked confused. Then realisation dawned.

'Oh fuck, you're the cyberterrorists the police are after for hacking into UKCitizensNet. Why the hell did you contact us? This is madness. You know the risks to us all.'

He trailed off, looking at Michael, recalling the other crimes they were accused of.

'It's all crap,' Michael said, not moving an inch.

The man took a deep breath, looking nervously around him.

'Don't worry, you don't have to convince me of that. I know what SemComNet are capable of. You're right, though, we need to get out of here. Oh, and, no offence, but you look fucking ridiculous in those caps.'

Michael frowned before the man raised a placating hand.

'I should have made the connection. If I had, I would have suggested somewhere more private. Although, thinking about it, I probably wouldn't have come at all. None of us can be too careful when dealing with SemComNet. Still, you're here now. We can't talk here. Let's go for a walk.'

The tall man turned and walked toward the Students' Union and the long line of waiting students. Michael and Brown followed, ignoring the sarcastic wolf whistles from the crowd.

Passing the entrance to the Union building, manned by a couple of burly security guards, the campus opened up into a rolling landscaped green space. A stream ran through the middle, dropping gently down a hill populated by trees that rose back up the bank on the opposite side. All around, various academic buildings, a mixture of the familiar red-bricked buildings and grey concrete boxes, punctuated the landscape. Turning off the main campus pathway, the anonymous man followed a smaller path that slid away between the trees and bushes before revealing a large bench.

'We should be OK here. If you were followed, there are too many students around for anyone to try anything,' the man said as he sat down, swivelling round to face Michael and Brown.

'We weren't followed,' Brown said defiantly.

'I hope so for all our sakes. Now, what is this all about exactly? I've not been able to sleep or focus on anything since receiving your email and that bit of code. It looks very exciting.'

Brown opened his mouth. Michael interrupted him.

'How about some details from you first? You've told us nothing about who you are. We're not telling you anything until we're sure you are who you say you are.'

'OK, fair enough. I should point out that you've not told me anything about who you are yet. So either of us could be lying.'

Michael's expression became irritated.

'Two days ago the Ephesus group, of which I'm part, received an email to our secure RIG email account, ephesus@rig.uk. It was sent from the address horsemen@rig.uk. Only a select few people have access to these addresses. The email said you were in possession of an app that could potentially bring down UKCitizensNet. We were sent a segment of code with some of the most advanced deployment algorithms I've ever seen. We sent a reply telling you to meet us here this evening, which, I might add, puts us at great fucking risk.'

The anonymous man stopped, stubbing his cigarette out on the concrete path.

'Oh, and, by the way, you can call me Simon. As for you, even beneath the bloody stupid hats, I know you're Michael Robertson and you're John Brown. And from what I read on UKCitizensNet the five of you have been rather busy. So tell me, what is this all about?'

Satisfied the man was who he said, Michael relaxed as he looked around, half expecting soldiers to emerge from the bushes and arrest them.

'About two years ago, my wife and daughter were murdered. At the time, the police claimed it had been the work of anti-net campaigners. They publicly stated the person responsible was a man named Davey Wilkes. I had a nervous breakdown and spent a long time in care. When I finally came home, I discovered Colette, my wife, had kept some confidential files in a deposit box. These files related to work SW Technologies were doing on a tender to run the new state network, what became UKCitizensNet. But you know all this. Around the same time my wife died, a leading technology specialist and project lead at ACE Solutions was also brutally killed. There were similarities in the killings that pointed to the supposed anti-net campaigners. Not long after discovering the files Brown and the other Horsemen approached me and told me the truth about what happened to my wife and daughter, and what SemComNet is capable of. I passed on Colette's files and data to them. It seems what they were developing was incredibly important. And SemComNet is willing to kill and implicate anyone to get their hands on it. That's why we're on the run and need your help.'

Simon leant back, his forehead creasing as he absorbed what Michael had revealed.

'Let's be clear, SemComNet is in the government's pocket, or at least a government department, most probably Defence. They're able to do anything and mobilise any support they need to get their hands on what you possess. But the question is, what exactly do you possess? And, more importantly, why do you think it can bring down UKCitizensNet?'

Michael turned to Brown for a detailed explanation.

'SW Technologies had begun work on an advanced app with wireless capabilities, based on fifth generation semantic web technologies. I don't believe they ever envisaged it working as a weapon. It was a more advanced way to link networked functions. But SemComNet must have got wind of it and saw the real opportunity of using it as a covert weapon. What Michael gave us was an incomplete version of the app. The four of us got to work on it in an attempt to perfect it. Unfortunately, they found us before we could finish it so we had to run. Our equipment was destroyed and we don't have the necessary kit now to finish the work. That's why we desperately need RIG's help.'

Simon looked thoughtful.

'Am I guessing the recent attack against UKCitizensNet was done by you? And if so, what were you using if the app wasn't complete?'

'We had most of the app working, although, at the time, the wireless parameters weren't completed or configured properly. We punched a hole through the UKCitizensNet firewall. Although I think they let us in. It was all too easy.'

'So how is this going to bring UKCitizensNet down?'

'If we can get the app inside their system, we can use its destructive capabilities to launch attacks inside the network and from within SemComNet. They won't be expecting an assault to come from inside their system, so won't be looking for it.'

Simon scoffed, reaching into his shirt pocket for his packet of cigarettes.

'Come on, you're never going to get past UKCitizensNet's encryption and through the firewall. We've all been trying that for years with no success.'

Michael straightened up, looking into Simon's dark eyes.

'But in the past, you've never actually been inside SemComNet trying to hack into their system, have you? We will be.'

Simon's eyes widened as he lit a cigarette, exhaling a plume of smoke through his nostrils.

'You're the five most wanted men in the country at the moment. Do you think you're just going to walk straight into the SemCom-Net? You're in cloud-fucking-cuckoo-land.'

Michael gestured dismissively as he thought about their forthcoming liaison with Digger and the planned journey into his tunnels.

'Don't you worry about the how. We'll get inside and we'll bring UKCitizensNet and Trevellion down.'

Simon's dark eyes widened further, and Michael again couldn't shake the feeling that he was familiar. But he still didn't know why.

'You've dealt with Vincent Trevellion?' Simon asked, trying, but failing, to sound disinterested.

Brown cast a look at Michael before looking at the ground. Michael felt his fists clench involuntarily as images of Colette flashed through his mind as she accused Trevellion of his crimes.

'Vincent Trevellion is responsible for the deaths of my wife and daughter.'

'How do you know it was Trevellion? It could have been anyone at SemComNet. Or someone from whichever government department is supporting their activities.'

Colette's accusing voice rang in Michael's ears.

'I just know. And no one will convince me some countryside campaigner who spent his life living in trees was capable of their murders. Vincent Trevellion is going to pay for the lives he took from me.'

Simon inhaled deeply, shuffling uncomfortably. Noticing his apparent discomfort, Brown leant forward.

'So what's your interest in Vincent Trevellion?'

Simon looked the two men squarely in the face.

'He's my younger brother. I'm Dr Simon Trevellion.'

Michael felt the air being sucked from his lungs. From the moment he'd met Simon, there'd been something that had bothered him. The dark piercing eyes and slightly detached persona should have given it away. Now that he knew, he could see the family resemblance. Looking at a blood relative of the man who had butchered his family, he felt the permanent knot in his stomach tighten.

Michael turned to look at Brown, who looked bemused.

'But, how you can be Trevellion's brother? You're part of RIG? How can...' His voice trailed off.

Simon stubbed out his cigarette and reached for another.

'Look, Vincent and I have never been close. Not even as children. We always had different ideas about things. Ironically, our one area of common interest was computing. But our careers took us in different directions. I was interested in the free distribution of academic knowledge whereas Vincent rapidly got into, and became very adept at, commercialising computing technologies. I took my PhD in grid and pervasive computing techniques; he rapidly worked his way up the company ladder for parasitical companies wanting to stamp out academic freedom and exploit technologies for morally reprehensible motives. That's why SemComNet was a perfect fit for him. It's why RIG came into being. How much have your friends told you about the origins of RIG?'

'Not much,' Michael replied, glancing at Brown.

'Well, I can't speak for the Horsemen because I don't know a lot about them. Although I had heard of them, obviously. But, when the government put the state network out to tender and banned, and then dismantled the UK's old internet infrastructure, the creation of UKCitizensNet ended free online speech and the global sharing of content and ideas. UKCitizensNet users, and by definition, UK citizens, were unable to access internet-based information from other countries. Of course, McCoy defended this, claiming the internet was totally unregulated and fatally permeated with illegal websites.

'What UKCitizensNet and the government didn't bank on, though, was an increasing number of people, predominantly academics, prepared to defend this bastion of universal information flow. Between us, we stockpiled hoards of secure servers to preserve the real internet and the principles on which it stands. We have a limited, but vibrant network that still exists. Because of UKCitizensNet and SemComNet, the vast majority of normal people can't access it. The real internet is independently run by groups who are all part of RIG, or the Real Internet Guardians. The government and SemComNet know it exists. They've always tried to track us down and get rid of what they see as an illegal network. Ironic, considering all the illegalities surrounding UKCitizensNet. And I'm not just talking about basic civil liberties,' he said gloomily, finishing yet another cigarette.

'We're talking about murder, industrial sabotage, and God knows what else. If your app can bring UKCitizensNet down and open the way for the real internet to be restored, then *all* of RIG will be behind you. Just tell me what you want us to do.'

Brown scratched his chin thoughtfully. As he looked nervously through the bushes, a group of female students giggled their way past the men.

'I've been fiddling with the code of the app the best I can over the last couple of days. But since our equipment got destroyed, it's limited what I can do. The specific configuration I've given our version of the app is essentially untested and potentially unstable. We need your group, or any other RIG group, to test the app.'

Simon ran his fingers through his hair as he absorbed what they were contemplating. This was the best opportunity RIG had ever had to fatally damage the UKCitizensNet beast. But many issues were troubling him. Their involvement in such a high-profile assault on UKCitizensNet risked exposing the identities of other RIG groups and members. Would they all become fugitives like the Horsemen and Michael Robertson if they failed? Was that a risk worth taking to end the censorship and information sleight-of-hand UKCitizensNet had pulled on ordinary people? The Horsemen and Michael were testament to what would happen to them if they failed.

Images of his brother flashed through his head. The little respect he'd ever had for Vincent had more or less ebbed away over the years. Certainly since their father had died. He hadn't seen or spoken to his brother since.

Could Vincent really be responsible for such abhorrent crimes? He might be a shit, but could he have done this?

Vincent had always been a loner. Always had a steely determination to succeed. Simon knew he was ruthless. But a killer? Could he stand by and let Michael kill his brother in revenge?

MICHAEL WAITED PATIENTLY AS Brown and Simon Trevellion discussed the app. Brown certainly sounded persuasive in his assertions that RIG could be the final piece of the jigsaw. Giving them a genuine chance to bring down UKCitizensNet and Trevellion. Maybe it was the need to protect RIG that had been the Horsemen's real motivation all along? Had they been using him as a means to save the entire group?

But if so, why hadn't any of them mentioned the Real Internet Guardians earlier? Clearly, they weren't sure they could trust him.

The time they'd spent isolated from the rest of civilisation seemed to have redefined their paranoia. It was ironic given Michael no longer trusted Brown. He certainly didn't yet trust Dr Simon Trevellion given his blood ties. How could he? The Horsemen may have seen him as a means to an end. Maybe Simon Trevellion did too. Maybe they even saw him as expendable—one life in the pursuit of their academic freedom and sharing of knowledge and information.

But he was on to them all. And he would have to watch Simon Trevellion as closely as he was watching Brown. If they could help him get nearer to Vincent Trevellion he would play along with their charade—with his finger close to the trigger of the shotgun.

As the conversation between Brown and Trevellion moved back and forth, Michael caught the odd technological term. Most of it was lost on him as the two men explored the possibilities of the semantic web.

The only portion of the conversation vaguely understandable was the combined view that if the app were distributed to other RIG groups, a coordinated attack would be their best chance of success. To do this, they had to upload the app to a secure RIG FTP server so other groups could access their work and reconfigure the app.

'Are the rest of the Horsemen OK with the fact that you came to see me? We all know this sort of personal contact is a strict taboo within the groups. I wouldn't have come myself if you hadn't sent me that sample of code.'

'The other three are dead,' Michael said flatly.

Simon Trevellion's eyes widened. His hand trembled as he reached for another cigarette. The dangers of their undertaking became more apparent by the second.

Michael watched with interest as the hard-edged, disdainful persona Simon Trevellion had initially displayed eroded, revealing a softer, more vulnerable character. He wasn't as tough as his brother. And despite the dark, almost emotionless eyes, Michael could see a glimpse of the same insecurities the Horsemen had honed to a fine art in their time as fugitives.

Lighting his cigarette, Simon stood up from the bench, rubbing his back from where it had pressed into his spine.

'The equipment we need to look at the app and send to the others isn't on this campus. There's an office on the Med campus, a few minutes up the road, which we'll need to use. We'll have to wait until after 10 p.m. when the library closes. The building will be virtually deserted then, other than for a few of the night shift and security guards. But they won't bother us if you're with me.'

Michael and Brown nodded their approval as Simon shuffled past them on the narrow path and back toward the Students' Union bar.

'I don't know about you, but in the meantime, I need a drink.'

CHAPTER THIRTY EIGHT

13 September 2007

Douglas Trevellion's coffin sat to the left of the simple altar. A plain mahogany box with a subtle gold trim running around the lid, meeting on either side at the handles for the pallbearers. Standing on a sturdy metal frame, it was positioned at the same height as the altar.

The altar itself had a white cotton covering with a small blue cross embroidered on the front, facing the congregation. A simple chalice, lacking any form of decoration, stood in the middle of the altar. On either side, two large white candles dwarfed the vessel.

It was a simple scene. One his father would have approved of, Simon Trevellion reflected as he sat in the pews, his gaze fixed on the coffin. His father could hardly have been called a religious man, and a non-fussy Church of England funeral was far more in keeping with the man than the added pomp and idolatry of a Catholic church.

His father had been a quiet, unassuming man. Plain-speaking without question. But a man who didn't like a fuss to be made. Not in life, and certainly not in death.

Looking at his mother sitting to his right, a tissue firmly held in her hand and already moist from her tears, his gaze moved discreetly to his watch. The service would start in less than five minutes. But still, there was no sign of Vincent. His muscles tensed involuntarily, his anger simmering beneath the surface.

Not that he was surprised. Why break the habit of a lifetime?

Fighting back the scowl he didn't want his mother to see, on today of all days, he cast a look around the small village church and the assembled congregation. A combination of relatives and family friends filled the narrow aisles. Some of the people, Simon knew well. Others were casual acquaintances he'd seen at family functions over the years, although he couldn't place their names. But no sign of his brother.

During his father's long and painful illness he'd been there. Every step of the way. Through radiotherapy and chemotherapy. In the brief period of remission, when for a few weeks they'd dared to believe that maybe the aggressive cancer had been stopped. And then through the desolation of knowing it had spread and that there was no way back for his father. He'd been through all of it. Comforting his mother. Supporting his father.

Vincent's involvement had been rare. And the role of emotional crutch to both his parents had been down to him, Simon, alone. What irony.

His mother had, as always, taken a charitable view of his brother's actions. Choosing to believe he couldn't cope with the emotional stress of terminal illness and seeing his father fade away. He smiled bitterly. Even after all these years, and through this bereavement, his mother still believed nothing Vincent ever did was wrong or with bad intention.

Maybe being the baby of the family just reinforced this behaviour, he'd wondered on so many occasions. How could his mother not see his brother's interests were elsewhere? And always selfish. Vincent had never been a family man. He was too busy pursuing his career to care about what happened to any of them. It had always been that way.

It was only a chance meeting with a former acquaintance of his brother—Vincent didn't tend to keep friends long, and not after they'd served some use—that had given him some recent intelligence.

Apparently, his brother had just secured a major appointment at one of the biggest semantic computing companies in the country. The post of Vice President. Of course, he'd heard of SemComNet by reputation. Who hadn't? Another blue-chip company with a thirst for expansion. And as far as he was concerned one of the many enemies of freedom of information sharing.

Sadly, the appointment hadn't surprised him, just reinforced the gulf between their two ideological stances on computing and information delivery.

Needless to say, his parents had been full of it for weeks, telling everyone they knew about their successful son. Quite a different response to his PhD and post at the University. That had been merely met with the comment: 'Never mind, perhaps you'll make Professor one day.'

'Is Vincent here yet?' his mother asked softly, dabbing her eyes again as the vicar approached the altar.

'No, not yet,' Simon replied through gritted teeth.

'He's probably just very busy,' his mother said, smiling at the thought of her other son.

'I'm sure he is,' Simon replied caustically, unable to withhold his feelings any longer.

'Simon, please. If he could be here, he would.'

'This is dad's funeral. If he can't make it on this day, when can he?'

Turning to face his mother, Simon watched his mother's eyes brimming with tears. Not sure whether she was crying for the loss of her husband of forty-four years or Vincent's no-show, he put a comforting arm around her.

Squeezing her son's hand, she wiped away the tears, conscious the vicar had begun speaking to the gathered mourners.

Simon listened as the vicar eloquently and humorously talked about his father's life. From his early days as an engineer on the railways through to time spent designing wind tunnels, his journey had never been dull. And there was always a story to tell. Simon smiled as anecdotes were shared and the congregation laughed appreciatively as the vicar celebrated his father's life.

Drawing to its conclusion the vicar turned his attention to the family. Squeezing his hand, Simon's mother wiped away the tears again as he described the loving wife and their long marriage. Simon could feel his emotions rising, his sadness engulfing him as the vicar spoke of his father's pride and joy: his two sons.

But as he grappled with his grief and loss he felt his anger rise. Anger at the snub to his father. Anger that his brother couldn't find the time to attend their father's funeral.

As the vicar's word echoed around the small church Simon cast another look across the congregation. His sorrowful gaze stopped on the back row, just inside the church door. In the pews, wearing a smart dark suit, a black tie and sunglasses, Vincent sat, silently watching the service.

Confusion rushed through Simon. A mixture of surprise and anger at his brother. And a feeling of relief, however misplaced, for his mother. Whatever his opinion of his brother, he wanted everything to be right for her. Especially today.

As his brother sat, emotionless, another thought struck him. Were the sunglasses intended to hide his grief? Vincent was never one prone to sharing his emotions, even as a child. Or was it just a bizarre fashion statement? Another statement of his individuality. He was weary of trying to second-guess his brother's motives. He'd never really understood what made him tick. Why would now be any different?

Aware her son was distracted his mother turned also. A wide smile crossed her face and she raised a hand in acknowledgement to her younger son. Vincent turned, nodding in her direction, before turning back, seemingly listening to the vicar's continuing eulogy.

'I told you he'd be here,' his mother said quietly.

Scowling, Simon looked away also, focusing his attention back on his father's memory. He'd save what he had to say to his brother for later.

WITH THE SERVICE COMPLETED and the cremation carried out, the funeral party returned to the family home, a short car journey from the church and crematorium. Simon's mother had been busy, preparing a feast of food that would have fed twice the number of mourners.

His parents' house was a modest bungalow, with a long narrow back garden. If the weather hadn't been so favourable for early autumn it would have been a real push to get everyone inside, Simon reckoned.

But with the garden everyone could mingle easily and comfortably, stopping to pay their respects to his mother and himself. And to Vincent.

Suppressing the glower as mourners expressed their sympathy to his brother, Simon nodded his way through comment after comment.

Finally, with the vast majority of people standing in the garden, Simon approached his brother in the dining room, looking out onto the well-kept garden.

'Why did you bother coming? You couldn't spare the time when dad was dying. What's so different about today?'

Vincent turned, still sporting his dark sunglasses, a thin smile on his face.

'It's good to see you too Simon,' he said, ignoring the question.

'It broke Dad's heart that you stayed away when he was ill. You know that, don't you?'

'I saw him before he died. We said what we needed to each other. Don't assume you know anything about my relationship with our parents. You have yours. I have mine. I bet mother hasn't been complaining.'

Simon was sure he could see a sneer on his brother's face.

'Well, you know Mum. She doesn't think you can do a thing wrong. Dad didn't either. And how you took advantage of that.'

Somewhere in the back of his mind, he could hear the same mantras he'd heard since their childhood, gnawing at his thoughts:

'Stop lying Simon, Vincent wouldn't do that.'

'Why don't you behave like a real man, like your brother.'

'Vincent hasn't wasted his time on a meaningless degree. He's got a real job.'

'Simon, say sorry to your brother.'

The sneer on Vincent's face grew.

'Really, Simon, that sounds like sibling jealousy. And I thought it was the youngest son who is supposed to be the jealous one.'

'Don't flatter yourself. You chose your path in life and you can stay on it. I have no interest in it. You've sold your soul to the devil. At least I've still got my integrity.'

Vincent removed his sunglasses, placing them on the dining room table, before looking back to his brother, his eyes piercing as ever.

'And so speaks the great intellectual mind of the family. Is it any wonder our parents never had any interest in your career when you've wasted it so completely? Our father was a doer. He got his hands dirty actually making things happen, making things work. He didn't hypothesise the whole time, wondering how things might happen in some intellectual utopia. He went out and did the job. And that's what I do. That's why he didn't need the constant gratification of knowing I was here, in his face. Because he knew I was out there doing something. Not just talking or thinking.'

Simon felt his anger rising as his brother goaded him mocking the academic path he'd taken.

'Believe me, I'd take the same path every time rather than sell out to some parasitical company as you have.'

Vincent smirked watching his brother's face flush red with anger.

'So you've heard about my new job and promotion, then?'

Vincent had always known what buttons to push. Over the years, he'd been able to spot it. But no matter how hard he tried, despite his resolutions that he'd never rise to his provocations again, the red mist always came. And Vincent always ended up winning their psychological games. They didn't need to have a fistfight. His brother could hit him harder with a few well-chosen words. It was his natural talent.

'You disgust me. How can you possibly think a company like Sem-ComNet has anything other than its self-interest at heart? Remind me again, what's the slogan: 'Bringing the world to you.' What a pile of shit. Companies like that aren't interested in delivering any good. They'll just stamp on all the smaller companies developing proprietary software and using open standards, homogenising everything in its path. Why don't we all just say goodbye to creativity and free-thinking now and go home? Tell me, does your job description explicitly say 'shit on the competition at whatever cost'?'

Simon detected the merest hint of annoyance flash across his brother's eyes. He'd clearly touched a nerve. A minor victory. No one else would have been able to detect the indiscernible change in his expression. But this was his brother. He could still spot it.

'Well, who knows? We'll have to wait and see. Maybe one day we'll be able to get university computer research departments shut down when we launch our graduate scheme. What do you think will be more appealing? Twenty grand worth of tuition fees or a nice fat bursary to come and work and develop the future of semantic web technologies with SemComNet? Why don't you try computing that?'

Simon's mouth dropped open at the prospect of such a scheme as Vincent calmly replaced the sunglasses on his narrow nose. His veiled threat was the sort of scheme his brother would readily set up just to piss him off.

'I won't hold my breath waiting for a visit from you then,' he replied coldly, turning to see his mother returning from the garden. 'I'm sure you'd like the new premises we're going to have built. Very modern.'

And without another word, he was gone. After a quick exchange of pleasantries with his mother, Vincent had left the family home, staying barely long enough for the tea to get cold.

Exhaling deeply, attempting to calm himself down, Simon looked into the long garden, mentally noting who he should go and talk to next. It was hard to believe he was related to Vincent, so far apart were their beliefs and outlooks on life. If they hadn't looked alike, he might have thought one of them was adopted.

Distracting him from his musings, a slender arm slipped around his waist as Jenny leaned in against him. His wife had been the perfect host, guiding everyone through to the garden, loading them up with food, and saying all the right things befitting a wake. He was lucky to have her. A fact reinforced by his latest verbal spat with his brother.

'Are you OK?' she said softly. 'I saw you talking to your brother. I didn't want to interrupt. It looked a bit intense.'

Simon sighed.

'He's unbelievable, he really is. He doesn't show up at all during dad's illness, although he tried to tell me he did. Then he saunters in here and thinks he's going to get a warm reception.'

Jenny looked at him knowingly, raising a quizzical eyebrow.

'Are you sure that's all you talked about? You sure you didn't get on to his new job? You said you weren't going to...'

Simon bit his lip, frustrated at his transparency.

'I'm sorry I couldn't help it. I really didn't think he would turn up. Then he started goading me, I couldn't help myself. But it wasn't the only thing we talked about. I told him what a selfish shit he was. Well, I implied it at least.'

Jenny squeezed his arm.

'Look, I know how hard this is for you and your mum. Don't let Vincent make it any worse. OK?'

Simon nodded, knowing she was right. But as he watched his mother returning to the garden, talking to another distant cousin, he felt sad at her unflinching belief in his brother's motives. Why couldn't she see it? Surely everyone else could? But then maybe that was what being a mother was. Perhaps if he and Jenny ever had children, she could tell him if that were what it was like.

Whatever the truth, he was certain of one thing: he didn't want to see his brother again.

CHAPTER THIRTY NINE

Michael pulled the Land Rover into the quiet car park next to the angular building and looked around for signs of life. In the building to his left, the odd window was illuminated, bearing testament to an overburdened professor or researcher still working at this late hour.

The monolithic structure of the Medical Sciences Campus at South Downs University was set in gently rolling landscaped grounds surrounding the 1970s concrete structure. Concrete beams were evenly interspersed with tall windows running along the length of the building.

On the ground floor, a single light was on, housing two night security guards who were chatting and drinking cups of coffee.

As the three men exited the car, Simon Trevellion led the way, walking to the other side of the building where a slightly inclined ramp led to the building's main entrance. Through the electronic doors, they walked into the quiet foyer, where a further security guard sat behind a glass-windowed reception desk.

'Evening Bob,' Simon said, resting his elbows on the counter. 'It's quiet in here tonight.'

The security guard, a man nearing sixty, reading the sports pages of one of the day's newspapers, smiled.

"Yeah. Nothing much going on tonight. The Film Society was in here earlier, but they cleared out about half an hour ago."

Simon nodded, discreetly casting a glance at the screen behind the security guard showing a CCTV feed of the campus perimeter. The security guard currently had his back to the screen.

'I'm just heading up to see Ben with a couple of friends.'

He cocked his head toward Michael and Brown, who were pretending to be interested in the contents of a postgraduate student's notice board. The security guard glanced in their direction before nodding his acknowledgement and returning to his newspaper.

The three men filed past reception and past the cafeteria that was locked up for the night, towards the metal staircases, painted a vibrant red in contrast to the building's sombre magnolia colour.

Climbing up three levels, the men found themselves on a landing, laboratories signposted in either direction. Simon turned to his right and slipped through the double doors. To the left, a long corridor stretched as far as the eye could see. To the right was the entrance to a laboratory bathed in light.

Inside the lab, the many workspaces were interspersed with gas taps for Bunsen burners, specimen trays and an assortment of microscopes. In a corner, a metallic silver canister was propped up against the wall, rubber tubing running out the back of it into a connection in the wall. In large black letters, the words "Liquid Nitrogen–handle with care" ran across the canister.

Leading the way, Simon opened a door on the left-hand side of the lab. A long, narrow office intersected another lab running parallel to the one they were occupying. Another door on the right led to a further office.

Tapping gently on the door, Simon waited before it opened. A tall, grey-haired man in a white lab coat appeared. He had a slightly scruffy appearance, with long straggly hair that needed a cut and a comb. Surveying Michael and Brown suspiciously, he turned back to Simon.

'Are these the guys that contacted you?' he said as a younger man appeared in the doorway from the parallel lab.

Simon nodded, turning to face Michael and Brown.

'I told you about our group. These men can help you. Meet Ben and Wally.'

The two men nodded. Ben, the younger of the two, stepped forward to shake their hands. A look of recognition crossed his face as he shook Michael's.

'You're Michael Robertson, aren't you? I just knew the Horsemen were going to be the guys that had been all over UKCitizensNet. Pleased to meet you.'

Simon turned to Ben, a look of surprise mingled with annoyance on his face.

'You could have shared this revelation with me. I turned up to meet them without a fucking clue.'

Ben looked sheepish and stepped back.

'Well, it was just a hunch. I could have been wrong. I didn't want to freak you out before you had a chance to speak to them.'

Michael frowned, looking at Wally, who was still standing in his office doorway.

'Don't mind Wally, he doesn't say much. But he's kept our kit hidden away since we set up the Ephesus group.'

Ben had no such difficulties.

'So, are you going to tell us what's going on, then? Where did that amazing bit of code come from?'

'Let's step into the office and I can explain everything,' Michael replied.

THE CAMPUS CAR PARK was still deserted as the black Volvo estate pulled in next to the Land Rover. Two men in black combat clothing exited the car before walking quietly across the car park to the window of the security office. The solitary security guard was now listening to a late-night talk show on his pocket radio. Beyond the office, a corridor led away to one of the building's many stairwells.

Reaching the security office, the first man tapped on the window. The security guard raised a quizzical eyebrow as he looked up, surprised to see two men at this time of night.

'Can I help you gents?'

'Is this the Medical Sciences Campus for the University?' one of the men asked in a strong Welsh accent.

The security guard nodded. His hand slid discreetly under the desk to reach the alarm button, linked to the main university security office.

'Sorry to disturb you. We're from Safety at Home Security, sellers of home security systems. Some residents have called about suspicious-looking characters in the area. We're just checking it out. Probably nothing, but you can't be too careful. Have you seen anything suspicious?'

The man flashed an identification badge across the counter.

The security guard relaxed a little, moving his hand away from the alarm button.

'No, it's been really quiet here. One of the academics from the main campus dropped by about twenty minutes ago with a couple of guys. But apart from that, nothing.'

'Well, that's good then,' the man in black said.

Before the security guard could reply, the second man leant in, pulled out a handgun with a long silencer, and shot him between the eyes. As the guard fell, the first man slipped quickly around the side of the window and into the office. The first man dragged the dead security guard out of sight and into the empty office before pulling the door closed.

'Close that thing behind you,' he said to his partner, pointing to a half-open metal concertinaed door.

Turning around, the second man pulled the metal door shut before following his partner through the corridor into the stairwell.

WALLY'S OFFICE WOULD HAVE been comfortable; it could easily house all four men if it hadn't been full of computer equipment. From the floor to the ceiling, servers, routers, hubs and monitors, used and unused, lined the walls and occupied his desk. There was barely room to stand, never mind sit down. In front of the monitor on the desk, Wally and Brown stood. Michael and Simon leaned against a rack of servers humming away against one wall, lights flashing on and off.

'Is this kit all used by RIG?' Michael asked, looking at a poster of a family of insects on the wall opposite.

Simon shook his head.

'No, this is partly some of the kit for the department Wally works for. We've just camouflaged our kit amongst theirs. Nobody pays any attention. They wouldn't dare touch any of Wally's stuff. He has a bit of a reputation 'round here.'

Simon grinned as Wally looked up from his keyboard, scowling, before returning to what he was doing. From his pocket, Brown produced a 100-gigabyte flash drive, sliding it into the USB port at the front of Wally's computer.

'I split the app code into two sections. If we got caught, they wouldn't have all of the code. Half of it's on this drive. The other is on one of RIG's FTP servers.'

Opening a connection to the FTP servers, Wally turned to Brown. 'Which server did you upload the code to?'

'RIG37.'

As Wally typed, Simon chewed his fingernails nervously.

'We need to have a look at this and do some testing on it before next Monday, which is when Michael and Brown will try to get inside SemComNet.'

Ben couldn't hide his surprise and excitement. 'You guys are going to get inside?' Michael nodded shortly, his attention on Wally, who was bringing the two portions of code together in one location on a secure FTP server.

'We also need to get this out to the other RIG groups, explaining what we've got, and ask for their help. The more of us in possession of this, the greater our chance of bringing UKCitizensNet down.'

Simon stopped abruptly as Wally suddenly looked up from the computer.

"Did you hear that?" Wally asked quietly.

They all shook their heads.

'I've worked in these labs long enough to know all the sounds this building makes. And that was someone carefully opening the doors to 5E.'

His gaze moved to his office door and the lab off to the right, opposite the one they'd entered. Ben, nearest the office door, turned, careful not to knock any of the computer equipment. Peering around the corner into the front office, he could see into both labs. At the far end of 5E, just through the door, two men dressed in black combats were scanning the room.

'Fuck, we've got company,' he muttered as he felt panic rising.

'We need to go now,' Brown said, seeing the fear on Ben's face.

'I need a few more moments to complete this.' Wally was typing as quickly and quietly as he could.

'Wally, you need to go now.'

'Look, you go. Let me finish this. They don't know me. I'll get rid of them and join up with you later.'

Wally wasn't a man to be argued with, as many postgraduate students had discovered. Michael looked at him, realising it wasn't stubbornness burning in his eyes. It was commitment to their cause: to bring UKCitizensNet to task.

Silently, the four men slipped out of Wally's room into the front office, into 5W, the lab parallel to 5E.

As Wally rapidly typed in an attempt to contact the other RIG groups, he heard rubber-soled shoes on the front office floor. The two men in black combats appeared in the doorway.

'Can I help you? The labs aren't open this time of night.'

Out of the corner of his eye, he could see his connection to the secure RIG FTP server was still open. Under no circumstances could he let these men, whoever they were, access the RIG infrastructure. It would be the beginning of the end for the group.

The first man, who had shortly cropped ginger hair, looked contemptuously at Wally.

'Where are the others?' he asked.

'What others? I'm the only one working up here tonight.'

In the blink of an eye, the man pulled his gun, already fitted with a silencer, from beneath his jacket and shot Wally in the right shoulder. Agony shot through Wally as his collar bone fractured. The blast pushed him back into his chair.

As he clamped his left hand to the wound, he again caught sight of the open server connection on his screen. He knew they were going to kill him. But he wouldn't let them have the RIG.

'Where are they?' the man repeated calmly, his index finger still resting on the trigger.

Lurching forward, Wally hit the "Escape" key on his keyboard, immediately closing the FTP session. Before he could raise his finger from the keyboard, the second bullet fizzed through the side of his head, lodging in his throat. As his blood oozed onto the keyboard, the two men slipped out of the office and into Lab 5W.

Michael, Brown, Simon, and Ben quickly and noisily descended the metal staircase, dropping to the floor below.

'This building is a bloody maze,' Michael commented, looking around anxiously.

'Yeah, exactly,' Simon replied. 'And that's in our favour. Whoever those men are, they won't know it as well as we do.'

The four men looked up as they heard a door in the stairwell above crashing open. Without a word, Simon turned to his right, ducking into yet another long magnolia corridor. Another door later and they were in a further long lab decked out with long rows of workbenches, all fitted with gas taps and sinks. The only light was a small lamp, illuminating a far corner and giving off a dim, eerie glow. Reaching the double doors at the end of the lab, Simon caught sight of one of the men reaching the stairwell behind.

'Ben, take Michael and Brown and head down to Level 3 and through the Med labs. I'll meet you there.'

'Why? Aren't you coming with us?'

'I've got an idea. Now go, quickly.'

As the three men exited the lab, Simon ducked down behind the last row of workbenches. One of the men in black pushed his way through the doors at the opposite end. Underneath the workbenches were numerous cupboards stocked with equipment.

Opening one of the cupboard doors, Simon rummaged around until he found the longest piece of rubber tubing available.

Carefully, he raised himself to his knees so he could peer over the top of the workbench.

He could hear from the footsteps that the man in black was still at the far end of the lab. And as he peered over, he could see he was carefully scoping out each row of workbenches, a gun in hand.

Simon felt the acidic taste of bile rising in his throat as he sank back down behind the workbench. The sight of the gun burnt into his mind. His breathing became more rapid, and he perspired. Thoughts of Wally flooded his mind. These weren't the sort of men who would be easily fooled by someone playing dumb. His pulse raced as he feared for Wally's life.

Now wasn't the time for such reflections, he decided, hastily shoving the piece of rubber tubing onto the gas tap on the edge of the workbench before turning the tap on. He hoped his plan would work; if it failed, he wouldn't be getting out of the lab alive.

Crouching down, the rubber tubing in his left hand, trying not to cough from the gas as it escaped into the air, he waited as the footsteps got nearer. He could feel his heart pounding as each step brought the man in black closer.

When he saw feet appear at the end of the workbenches, he quickly flicked the switch on his cigarette lighter. As a flame appeared, he pushed it over the end of the rubber tubing, instantly lighting the escaping gas and fumes permeating the air around the man in black.

Simon rolled backwards, covering his face as the man erupted into a human fireball. His arms flailed wildly as he desperately fought the flames that savagely burnt away his skin and clothing.

In less than twenty seconds, the man had fallen to the floor between two rows of workbenches. The smell of burning flesh filled the air as Simon reached for the fire extinguisher on the wall, quickly extinguishing the flames. He didn't need the entire building going up in smoke.

As the flames died, Simon threw the fire extinguisher at the man's lifeless body in one final defiant gesture. For Wally, he thought before running out of the lab.

Michael, Brown and Ben had taken Simon's advice and dropped to Level 3, heading for the mortuary, which was used for anatomical training. In the past, Michael might have been squeamish about entering such a place. But now, in his current state, the thought didn't even cross his mind as they secretly slipped in.

Not that there was much to see. A mortuary table sat in the middle of the room. Several freezer compartments were in the wall behind, able to house up to six cadavers at any one time. Two rows of long shelves were mounted on another wall, stacked with specimen jars exhibiting various human organs.

The smell of embalming fluid hung in the air. Clinging to the walls, Michael could feel his stomach lurching as he tried not to breathe it in.

'I don't think it is a good idea just waiting here,' Brown said finally.

Michael nodded, fighting the gag reflex.

'If those men get to us first, we're buggered. Why aren't we heading for the car?'

Ben turned round angrily, raising his voice higher than was safe in the circumstances.

'Look, it was you that contacted us and dragged us into this shit. Simon leads our group and we're waiting. I suggest you get used to it.'

Before either man could reply, they all heard footsteps in the stairwell beyond the mortuary door. Michael scowled at Ben, annoyed that his outburst could have alerted the men to their presence.

They moved to the wall next to the door, ducking under the shelves in a vain effort to conceal themselves.

The door at the far end of the mortuary was too far away to escape through without being seen from the stairwell.

The door to the mortuary swung open. In a flash, Ben leapt from his concealed position, bringing the approaching figure crashing to the floor with a painful thud. Relief spread through him as he looked into Simon's face.

'Get off me,' Simon snapped. 'You could have broken my fucking arm.'

'We thought you were one of them.'

'Well, there's only one of them left now,' Simon grumbled, rubbing his arm.

Michael and Brown nodded approvingly, whilst Ben looked rather anxious.

'We need to get out of here now,' Michael said flatly, heading for the door at the far end of the mortuary.

As the door swung open, the four men ran down a further corridor before emerging on another stairwell that opened up onto a loading bay, leading back to the campus car park. Entering the stairwell, they could hear heavy footsteps running down the stairs above them. Michael peered up through the red-painted staircase. The second of the two men in black was descending the stairs rapidly, his gun clasped in his hand.

Without needing to spell out the danger, they ran. Using all his strength, Ben pulled back the metal concertinaed door far enough for them to slip through.

'Get the car started. I'll try and stop this one,' he said.

Watching the three men sprinting across the car park and towards the Land Rover, Ben could hear the footsteps of the man in black as he closed in on the loading bay door. As he reached the door, which Ben had pushed further across to prevent him from running straight through, he slammed the door shut, trapping the man between the door and wall. The man in black howled in pain as Ben withdrew the door before smashing it into him for a second and third time. The man fell to the floor, groaning.

Jumping down from the loading bay, Ben ran across the car park to join the others. They'd reached the car and were scrambling inside. The wheels squealed on the tarmac as the vehicle reversed, a low concrete wall preventing them from driving straight out. Ben reached the Land Rover, pulled the door open, and leapt inside.

Michael floored the accelerator and was aware of their pursuer to his right, stumbling across the car park in their direction, trying to cut them off.

A bullet smashed through the windscreen, flying inches from the left side of his face before exiting through the rear window, miraculously missing all of them. A second bullet hit the side of the car at the front of the vehicle as the gunman ran into the path of the oncoming Land Rover. His gun was raised again. Instinctively, Michael flicked the car's lights from normal to full beam, dazzling the gunman.

Michael didn't deviate and drove towards the gunman at full speed. A deafening crack. The sound of a body hitting the radiator grill before being tossed up into the air, onto the roof of the Land Rover and eventually smashing down onto the tarmac behind, filled the car as Michael raced towards the exit.

As they careered out of the campus and onto the quiet adjoining roads, Michael was the first to speak.

'Is everyone OK?'

The others murmured they were unhurt, absorbing what had just happened. Brown, unsurprisingly, looked the least shocked. But in the rear-view mirror, he could see Ben and Simon were visibly shaken. Their expressions pale and drawn.

Their lives had been tucked away, writing code, plotting ways to hurt UKCitizensNet. But *this* was the reality of their situation. This was SemComNet taking the fight to them. Something they'd never experienced before. They were now in this together.

CHAPTER FORTY

'ARE YOU SURE YOU want to do this?' Michael looked at Simon and Ben, sitting on a fallen tree trunk in the forest surrounding SemComNet's HQ.

The four of them had been lying low since the shootings at South Downs University. Discreetly, they'd been watching for news coverage on UKCitizensNet and other news wires. So far, no connections were being made between the four men.

A large amount of news coverage had reported the brutal killings of four men at the Medical Sciences campus. And that two university staff were currently missing. The police wanted to speak to Simon and Ben, to eliminate them from their enquiries.

Even though none of them had voiced it, they knew it was only a matter of time before Simon and Ben would be implicated in the alleged cyberterrorist activities.

Simon looked up from the cigarette he was silently smoking, the strain etched on his face. It was the same familiar drawn expression

Michael had seen when he first met the Horsemen. It seemed a lifetime ago.

'I don't see we've got a choice if we want our lives back.

'You've got to be in this one hundred per cent for us to succeed, otherwise someone's going to get killed,' Michael stated, enforced by his determination to see this through.

At the back of his mind, doubt lingered. Could Simon confront his brother and deal with what he had in store for Vincent Trevellion? He was still watching Brown. He didn't need Simon to be an added liability.

Michael looked at his watch. The time was approaching 10 p.m. There were still many lights on in the building. Digger had explained this was normal because of the various shifts SemComNet staff worked. However, he'd noticed that over the past few days, more people than normal were on the premises, round the clock. Something was going on.

Nodding to Digger that it was time to go, the four men followed. Weaving their way between the trees, seemingly not heading in any particular direction, the lights of the SemComNet building cast unusual shadows amongst the undergrowth.

Finally, Digger reached a small, barely discernible clearing amongst the trees and stopped. Gently, he kicked at the undergrowth as leaves and small twigs cleared a path on the ground. Shining a small torch on the earth, a concealed panel of wood was revealed from beneath the undergrowth.

Kneeling, he slid his fingers under one side of the square wooden panel, lifting it up. Carefully placing the panel close by, he shone his torch into the dark hole that had opened up before them.

The four men huddled around expectantly, silently impressed at Digger's knowledge of the woods and how he'd located this spot in virtual darkness. Just below the surface of the hole, a metal ladder was standing against one side of the tunnel, disappearing into the depths beneath.

'Take it slowly,' Digger murmured, climbing onto the top of the ladder and descending. 'This ladder can get bloody slippery. I'll be waiting at the bottom.'

Without another word, he slipped beneath the top of the tunnel and silently disappeared into the depths of the Green activists' tunnel network.

Michael was the first, feeling he ought to lead the way. Tentatively climbing onto the ladder, he felt it move slightly. Clinging on tightly to the cold metal, he pushed his weight forward to prevent the ladder from toppling backwards. But as he descended, he could just make out through the gloom that there were metal brackets at various points holding the ladder in place.

Moving down one step at a time, it occurred to him that Digger had not indicated how deep these tunnels went. How long was he going to be climbing downwards?

After what seemed like several minutes, which in reality he felt sure was probably only a single minute, he noticed a dull glow beneath him. It was Digger's torch. Looking down, he could just make out Digger's shadow.

Finally, the tunnel opened up into a small area, about six by six feet, and Michael felt his feet return to solid ground as he took his final step down. Above him, he was aware of one of the others beginning their descent as the ladder rocked and creaked slightly.

Less than five minutes later, the five men were all tightly huddled at the bottom of the tunnel. In front of them, they could see access to three separate tunnels, all running off in different directions. From his pocket, Digger produced a cigarette lighter and lit a thick, long white candle wedged into the side of the entrance to the middle tunnel. As the flame illuminated the area, the length of the tunnel became visible, disappearing away into further gloom. Digger could see the worried looks on the men's faces.

'Don't worry, there are candles all along the tunnels. You'll be able to see where you're going. And see the rats before they get you.'

He smiled, watching the looks of disgust on the four men's faces. Rats were the least of their problems, he thought as he strode off into the tunnel, ducking his head.

After a few minutes of walking through the silent, gloomy tunnel, they finally reached another area, opening up to a similar antechamber as before. In the middle of the space, a further metal ladder was embedded into the earth wall, pointing upwards, and leading back to the surface.

'I'll go up first and scope things out. You'll need to come up behind me as I'm not yelling down to you inside SemComNet's perimeter.'

The four men nodded as Digger rapidly and expertly ascended the ladder.

Michael again followed first, nervously inching his way up the ladder. He'd never enjoyed climbing ladders, always putting off jobs at home that required scaling up any distance. But now he didn't have a choice, he thought, trying to keep sight of Digger further up the ladder.

The climb began to take its toll on Michael's legs; he felt cold air blowing in his face. He was near the surface. And now inside SemComNet's perimeter. The knot in his stomach tightened as he thought about what he had to do.

Reaching the rim of the tunnel, Digger's face appeared from where he was lying on his front, peering into the tunnel.

'Come on, we need to be quick. The security patrol isn't on this side of the building at the moment. You should be able to get in close to the building before they return with their dogs. From there, it's up to you to work out how you get into this fucking place.'

Michael nodded, too exhausted to talk. Pulling himself out of the hole in the ground, he slumped down next to Digger.

Starting at the building before him, he recalled how Brown and Ben had been fiddling with some sort of electronic device earlier that evening. Something they claimed would give them access. He just hoped they were right. He, for one, certainly didn't fancy trying to outrun a snarling dog.

By the time he got his breath back, the other three had also emerged and were lying on the grass. They were about thirty feet away from the edge of the SemComNet building, never-ending rows of tinted glass windows before them. About two hundred yards behind, Michael could see the edge of the surrounding woodland.

Fortunately for them, there were no lights on in the offices behind. Not at all in this wing of the building. Digger had been true to his word, picking the most discreet tunnel for their approach.

'I'll see you back in the woods when you return,' Digger said as he descended back into the network of tunnels. 'Good luck.'

You'll need it, he thought as he slipped out of sight and pulled the grass-covered wooden panel concealing the entrance back into place.

Michael quickly scanned the area before he moved forward towards the impressive building, the three other men following closely behind. About halfway to the building, there was rapid movement to his right.

'Watch out,' Brown hissed.

Turning, his blood ran cold. A huge Dobermann was bearing down on him. Michael barely had time to register the dog's presence when it leapt at his torso, sending him crashing to the ground. Snarling jaws snapped at his upper body. The weight and strength of the animal were unbelievable as Michael grappled with the dog, his strength rapidly diminishing as the animal sunk its teeth into his left shoulder.

As the pain tore through his body, he was barely aware of a figure to his right speedily approaching the hungry Dobermann. Was this the accompanying security guard pursuing his prized partner?

The dog yelped as Brown's boot clattered into his side, although it remained firmly attached to Michael's torso. A second kick still failed to dislodge the dog, only making him snarl viciously in the direction of Brown before turning back to Michael.

Taking evasive action, Brown quickly manoeuvred himself behind the dog, grabbing the top of his head. Before Michael could blink, he heard the sickening sound of the dog's neck snapping as Brown twisted the Dobermann's head away from his face.

Instantly, he felt the animal's strength fade, as he turned on his side to roll the dog away from him. Rubbing his throat, and with his left shoulder throbbing painfully, he looked at Brown, who was crouching next to him.

'You OK?' he asked, concerned. 'Can you continue?'

Still gasping for breath, Michael nodded.

'Get yourself up to the building. I'll get rid of the dog down the tunnel. We don't need it found out here.'

Rubbing his arm, Michael watched as Brown dragged the lifeless body of the dog back towards the tunnel. This wasn't the first time his life had been seriously threatened in the past few weeks. But it was the first time someone had selflessly saved him from certain death.

Maybe he'd been wrong about Brown. He considered it as images of Colette's warning flooded back. Would he have saved him so readily if he had other motives?

If Brown planned to get his life back by bringing down UKCitizensNet, then he probably didn't need him anymore. They were now inside SemComNet and had received help from RIG over the app. Wasn't he, Michael, now expendable? If so, Brown could easily have let the Dobermann rip him to shreds.

Had his paranoia and obsession with Vincent Trevellion clouded his judgement?

He turned and watched as Brown replaced the cover to the tunnel and headed back in their direction. They really needed to get out of this spot and into the building.

As silently as they could, the four men reached the edge of the building, scurrying along the side of the premises. Simon had spotted a door about a hundred yards to the left. As they reached the door, all gasping for breath, Brown slipped a small oblong console from his pocket. A tiny screen glinted in the middle.

Michael watched as he took a little card out of the side of the console. On the door in front of them, he noticed a raised area intended for security card access.

Ben watched anxiously as Brown placed the tiny card into the cardholder on the door before typing in a series of commands on the console.

'We've been fiddling with the configuration of this over the last couple of days. SemComNet will change their access codes every twelve hours, probably every eight hours, to coincide with their staff's shift patterns. We had to adjust our algorithms a little to cater for this.'

Michael raised a quizzical eyebrow, barely understanding what Ben was talking about. As long as this device gave them access to the building, he couldn't care less about algorithms or shift patterns.

In the quiet of the night, the sound of the door clicking as the security code was accepted seemed to echo throughout the grounds. In the distance, they all heard one of the many Dobermanns barking. Was this one of the security guards and his dog looking for the one that Brown had killed? After all, Digger had told them the security guards were travelling around with two Dobermanns at a time. Or was it sufficiently far away to be coincidental? They all hoped so.

Turning the handle slowly, the door swung silently opened and the four men slipped inside the building before the sound of the dogs could get any nearer.

The door closed behind them. The four men realised they were in some storage room. All around the walls were boxes piled high with monitors, servers, and many cupboards. At the far end of the room was a further door.

Approaching the exit, Michael listened intently before turning the handle. He couldn't hear anything. As the light streamed into the room, his gaze fell upon a quiet, pristine white corridor. Deserted in both directions.

Scanning the corridor, he reflected on their plan. If they could get to a computer inside the SemComNet firewall, they would have access to both the UKCitizensNet infrastructure and to Vincent Trevellion's location on the network. And then his precious IP address.

Once SemComNet would realise the attack was coming from inside, the damage would be done. Michael hoped they were right.

To make it all work, they had to find a room with a computer linked to the network. How easy would that be?

'Well, this part of the building looks deserted,' he said finally after watching the corridor for a full two minutes. There were no security guards. No staff working the late shift. And, most importantly, no visible intrusive CCTV cameras monitoring the corridor.

Moving out into the long white corridor, which, save for the smell of disinfectant, felt like a hospital, the four men began their search for a SemComNet computer linked to the network.

The first two rooms were similar storage rooms, containing nothing useful. Michael could feel his anxiety rising as they got nearer and nearer to the double doors at the end of the corridor.

Who knew what was beyond? Was that where the night shift was based? Or where security guards were patrolling?

In the corridor they were currently roaming, there was only one room left to investigate.

As the door swung open and Michael flicked the light switch, he felt his pulse quicken. In front of him was a suite of computers, surrounded by various papers and folders, and clearly in active use.

'This looks like an R&D lab to me,' Simon commented, taking a quick sweep of the room, investigating computers, equipment, and files as he went.

Closing the door behind them, Michael watched as Brown and Ben sat down at the nearest machine. All the computers were turned on, a sign of the 24-hour shift patterns of SemComNet, but not logged onto the company's internal system.

'Give me a few seconds and I'll get past the security login,' Ben said confidently as Michael eyed the door carefully, listening for any sound of footsteps in the corridor.

'I've always wondered what the inside of SemComNet looked like,' Simon said, pacing about the room. 'From a personal point of view because of Vincent, and because it's so opposed to my views, what they do here. It's ironic, isn't it? Universities are trying to push the ideas of sharing knowledge, yet work in cramped, relatively archaic conditions. Whereas companies controlling the information flow and infringing civil liberties have multi-billion-dollar budgets and reek of wealth. There's something wrong with a system like that.'

'We're in,' Ben interrupted.

The four men watched expectantly as the screen booted up into the internal SemComNet system, providing various options organised by job role: analyst, contributor, editor, super-user, technical support.

Selecting "technical support", the next information screen presented a range of technical options beyond Michael's comprehension.

'With a few clever shortcuts, this should take us right to the kernel of the system, giving us access to UKCitizensNet's infrastructure—the ideal place to drop off our present. Where's the flash drive?'

Ben seemed to enjoy what he was doing, Michael thought as Brown produced the all-important drive storing the crucial app.

Despite the dangers, this was the first time the RIG had direct access within UKCitizensNet. Their plan had to work.

Sliding the flash drive into one of the USB ports on the front of the computer, they all watched expectantly as Ben entered various commands into the machine. Michael didn't understand or care what was happening as long as they could embed the app in the system. Every second brought him nearer to avenging Colette and Clare's deaths.

Ben exhaled loudly, sitting back heavily in his chair, suddenly aware of the magnitude of what he had just done.

'OK, the app is within the system. We just need to find relevant IP addresses to direct the app to. This may take a few minutes.'

'Make sure Vincent Trevellion's the first you find,' Michael said firmly, casting a sideways glance at Simon, who didn't say a word.

Before Ben could respond, they heard the deafening sound of an alarm going off. Michael could feel his eardrums throbbing from the force of the sound.

Had they discovered the body of the dead security dog? They surely couldn't have: Brown had closed up the hole to prevent that.

His pulse raced. None of the men moved as the sound of heavy boots running into the corridor punctuated the sound of the alarm. Sweat broke on Michael's brow as the sound moved past the lab before stopping. The four men looked at each other. Frozen in place. Fear etched on their faces.

With a further deafening crash, the door imploded into the room, damaged from the thunderous force of the butt of a semi-automatic rifle pounding into the structure. Within seconds, four armed security guards with raised weapons surrounded them. Their fingers threateningly poised on the triggers.

'Get on the fucking floor, hands on your head,' a security guard barked.

Without thinking, and with memories of the men in black from the campus firmly fixed in their minds, the men obediently dropped to the floor.

As Michael lay prostrated, his hands clamped to the top of his head, the alarm finally stopped. The sound of footsteps tapping up the corridor, heading for the lab, filled the air. A pair of polished, expensive-looking black shoes appeared in his vision.

Turning his gaze upwards, he looked straight into the impassive eyes of Vincent Trevellion. Despite his attitude, Michael felt sure he could detect satisfaction across Trevellion's sombre features.

Anger welled up inside him, frustration at being in such proximity to Trevellion, yet unable to execute his revenge. He noticed the sound of further footsteps. But these weren't coming from the corridor. These were from inside the lab itself. Michael watched in disbelief as Brown appeared alongside Trevellion. His hands weren't raised or on his head. And he wasn't under arrest.

'Good to see you're in one piece, John,' Trevellion remarked.

'I'm glad I am. There were occasions when that didn't seem likely.'

'We had to ensure neither Tate nor his men knew you were involved, otherwise their attempts to catch you and the others wouldn't have looked genuine.'

Brown nodded, a malevolent smile on his face.

Casting a look across the three men lying on the cold floor, Trevellion's gaze came to rest on his brother. Michael watched, expecting some sort of surprised reaction. Instead, all he saw was disgust, even loathing. A terrible thought struck him. Trevellion already knew about his brother's involvement.

'So, did everything go as planned?' Trevellion asked calmly.

'Signed, sealed and delivered,' Brown grinned, looking down contemptuously at Michael.

Michael felt raw, undiluted anger at this betrayal. But before he could scream his fury, Brown's boot thudded heavily into the side of his head, sending him into unconsciousness.

CHAPTER FORTY ONE

24 June 2010

THE PILE OF PRESENTS *sat on the coffee table in the middle of the lounge. A delicately arranged tower Clare had constructed, a glittery silver bow perching on top. She'd kept it, especially for this day.*

Michael smiled as he watched his daughter carefully arrange and rearrange the presents, making sure they looked as impressively tall as possible. If ever there was any doubt Clare was Colette's daughter, this should be proof enough. Never mind DNA testing, her attention to detail was second only to her mother's. Although he wondered for how much longer as she turned gifts over, repositioning them to make the mountain on the table look even more special.

Finally, taking a step back, having moved the silver bow once more, she turned to him.

'There. Now it's perfect,' she said, admiring her handiwork.

Michael stroked her blonde hair gently, nodding approvingly. There was only one thing missing from the birthday celebrations. Colette.

'When is Mummy going to open her presents?' Clare asked, not for the first time that morning.

Looking at his watch, Michael shook his head, still smiling at his daughter.

'Soon, I'm sure. Mummy has to finish some work first, which is very important. Otherwise, her nasty boss won't be happy on Monday.'

Clare's expression dropped; she sucked her lips in as she thought about the horrible man making her mummy work on a Saturday. But not just any Saturday. This was her mummy's birthday.

'In the meantime, though,' Michael continued, lightening the atmosphere, 'you can finish off your birthday surprise, can't you?'

Clare nodded enthusiastically, skipping toward the dining room and kitchen.

Looking back at the tower of presents, Michael sighed, gazing at the gold clock on their dark wood mantelpiece. The time was approaching midday and Colette had been stuck at her computer working since before 8 o'clock. On her birthday.

The insurance brokers he worked for were demanding, and long hours were sometimes part of the job. But it didn't compare with what Colette had to endure, particularly recently. SW Technologies certainly got their money out of her. Whether it was long hours at the office, at home, or nights and days away at various events or meetings. Her workload was immense.

Despite the pressure, Colette always found time for him, and most importantly, Clare. It was a sign of the strength of their marriage and her bond with their daughter. Never once had her work put a strain on their relationship. Somehow, she managed to balance being a mother, a wife, and a highly successful career woman. He didn't know how she did it. But it was one of the many things he loved about her.

In Clare, he could see the same determination and desire to succeed in everything. Whether it was excelling in her school work or just ensuring a pile of presents looked as impressive as they could. Her talents were clear.

They both knew she would eclipse any of their achievements as she grew into adulthood. Some parents might have felt threatened at the prospect of this. But not them. They wouldn't try to live through their daughter. They'd live it with her. Supporting her all the way. Emotionally. Financially. Whatever way she needed. She would always be their proudest achievement.

Climbing the stairs, Michael slipped into their bedroom, aware of Colette typing steadily at her keyboard in the study next door. Reaching into his bedside drawer, he pulled out a gift.

Softly knocking on the door to the study, he entered, keeping the present concealed behind his back.

'How are you getting on?' he asked quietly.

Colette looked concentrated; her long hair was drawn back in a ponytail, her brow furrowed as she pondered yet another technological issue. Folders glistening in plastic wallets were stacked up next to the keyboard. A green box file sat on a stool.

Looking up, she smiled wearily, rubbing the tiredness from her eyes.

'It's never-ending. It really is. I think I've solved one problem and then two more crop up. I'll be glad when this bloody tender is over and I can get some sleep.'

Michael squeezed her arm, looking into her tired face. Even with her hair scraped back and without make-up, she was still stunningly beau-

tiful. Her large brown eyes offset high cheekbones, normally framed by her luxurious hair. Her looks had mesmerised him since the first moment they met. Years of marriage hadn't dulled that.

'What exactly are you doing?' Michael asked, perusing the folders on the desk, their meanings largely lost on him.

Leaning back in the swivel chair, and fiddling with her ponytail, Colette tried to distil the information she'd been reviewing.

'You know the big tender we're bidding for. Well, if we don't get it, then huge parts of our core business are going to be automatically hoovered up by our competitors. And that means one of two things. Either mass redundancies and a major streamlining of the business and its operations, or SW Technologies go to the wall.'

'So you could lose your job?' Michael asked, concerned. He knew Colette was involved with a major IT project, but she'd not discussed it with him in these terms before.

'Potentially, yes. Although if I did, I'd get a very sizeable separation package, as I've been with the company for so long. We'd be OK, so don't worry. What I'm trying to do is work out a business plan that safeguards all the jobs at SW Technologies. And that means winning the tender.'

Michael nodded, absorbing his wife's problem. If anyone could write the appropriate business plan, it was Colette. And if they needed to entrust someone with saving jobs, she was exactly the person for the task. Direct when she needed to be, but also compassionate, always putting others first. It was one of the many things that had attracted him to her.

'Look, I know this is important, but why don't you take a break? It is your birthday, after all. You've been working the whole morning. And besides, Clare has a surprise for you which she's been working hard on.'

At the mention of Clare and her endeavours, the strain on Colette's face ebbed away. She smiled warmly. It was typical of Clare to do something like this, whatever the surprise was.

'OK, you're right. I probably do need a break. It'll help me clear my head. The rest of this can wait until tomorrow.'

Michael smiled mischievously as Colette rose from her seat. She eyed him suspiciously, suddenly aware he was holding something behind his back.

'What are you up to?' she said playfully, trying, unsuccessfully, to see what he was clasping.

'I wanted to give you this before you came down. It's not for Clare's eyes.'

Raising his eyebrows, he handed Colette the present, a soft item with a silver ribbon wrapped around it.

Quickly ripping the paper, Colette broke into an amused smile as she pulled out a black lace negligee.

'I was hoping I might get to see you in that later,' Michael whispered seductively, leaning in to kiss her.

'I bet you are,' Colette laughed wickedly, letting the garment unfold, revealing just how see-through it was.

'Come on, let's open the rest of the presents,' Michael said finally, as their long kiss ended.

Following him out of the room, Colette stashed the lace negligee in their bedroom before joining Michael in the lounge.

'I see someone's been busy,' she laughed as she looked at the tower of presents greeting her. 'I'm guessing you didn't do that.'

'No, that's far too organised for me,' Michael retorted as Clare stuck her head around the kitchen door.

'That's good timing, Mummy.' She beamed, a dash of icing sugar staining her left cheek.

'What have you been up to then?' Colette asked warmly, relieved to be away from her computer and all the problems of the tender.

Disappearing back into the kitchen, Clare returned, carefully carrying the birthday cake she had made and iced. Different coloured stars were arranged around the edge of the cake. In the middle was one large royal blue candle. Below it were words, jaggedly iced, reading: "Happy Birthday Mummy".

Colette could feel a lump in her throat, fearing she might cry at her daughter's handiwork.

'I've only put one candle on as I couldn't fit thirty-eight on there,' Clare said cheekily, her eyes sparkling.

'Who told you I was thirty-eight?' Colette protested playfully, casting a semi-accusing look at Michael.

After placing the cake on the coffee table, Colette pulled her daughter close, holding her tightly, as she admired her cake. Her daughter's talents never failed to amaze her.

Pulling away, Clare jumped onto the sofa, patting for her mother to sit beside her.

'Right. Come on then, Mummy. I want you to open my presents.'

Smiling, Colette did as ordered. Leaning forward, she reached for the biggest present in the pile and began to unwrap.

CHAPTER FORTY TWO

MICHAEL COULD FEEL THE sweat oozing from every pore. Each part of his body was on fire. His shoulder was throbbing from the Dobermann's bite. He was sure the wound was infected. Needless to say, the bastards at SemComNet hadn't attended to the wound. His head ached from Brown's vicious kick. And now the pain was radiating to the rest of his body.

He was going to die. He was certain. The others tied up next to him must also know. They would not get out of this alive. Their civil liberties couldn't be infringed in such a vile way with the prospect of being released afterwards.

He looked down at his heaving, sweaty body. Like Simon and Ben, he had been stripped naked and tied roughly to a chair bolted to the clinical white floor. His wrists and forearms were bound to the arm of the chair. His legs were spread and had also been restrained.

Despite everything, even he hadn't been prepared for what had happened next. Two of Trevellion's henchmen had punched him in the right kidney to subdue him, attaching two electrodes to his genitals. The wire from the electrodes led back to a small black unit resting on a table in front of the three captives. They'd all been tortured.

Now they were waiting. Waiting for whatever questioning and sick form of torment SemComNet could invent for them. Images of Colette's mutilated body filled his mind. He knew something diabolical was in store.

On the table opposite, next to the small black unit, was a pack of cigarettes. He wondered who they belonged to and who would carry out the questioning. Would it be Trevellion himself? When he saw Trevellion previously, he hadn't smoked, nor did his office have the stale smell of cigarettes.

SemComNet must have someone else for their dirty work, he thought, looking around their confined cell.

The room was painted completely white; floors, walls, and ceilings. There were no windows, computers, or phones. Only one electrical socket and a light switch inside the door and the table opposite. It was austere. And that was what bothered Michael most. Lacking feeling or emotion. Like their captors.

To his right, Simon and Ben were also sweating profusely, looking like death. How ironic, he thought bitterly, as he listened to Ben wheezing from hyperventilating when he'd been stripped and strapped to his chair. His breathing had calmed down. But he was in a bad way. They all were.

Without warning, and with no sound of approaching footsteps, the solitary door to the room swung open, revealing Brown and the two security guards who had restrained them earlier. The two guards stood to attention, staying outside as the door swung shut.

Brown perched himself on the edge of the shiny metallic table before reaching for the pack of cigarettes.

Michael looked contemptuously at him as he lit a cigarette.

'So how long have you been on Trevellion's payroll, you bastard?' he said venomously.

'Longer than you can imagine,' Brown replied, standing up and pacing menacingly in front of the three men.

'Did you really think you had any chance of getting to UKCitizensNet or Trevellion? We've been playing you from day one. We've known every move you've made. There was only ever going to be one outcome.'

Confusion spread across Michael's face as Brown eyed the other two men, his gaze tracing a path from the electrodes between their legs back to the unit on the table.

'But how? The soldiers who attacked your base could have killed you. The men at the Biomedical Campus were firing on our car and could also have killed you.'

Brown, exhaling a plume of smoke, smiled knowingly.

'I agree. There were certain risks of accompanying you on your revenge mission back to SemComNet. All the soldiers and teams that were pursuing us were briefed to shoot to kill. It had to look authentic to keep you on the right path back to us. And I was prepared to accept the risks to my own life because I believe in the cause. The end justified the means.'

'What cause?' Michael snapped indignantly.

'I think that's something for Trevellion to share if he feels it appropriate. Assuming you ever see him again, of course.'

Michael tried to fight back his fear as he again caught sight of the wires attached to him. He needed more answers. Needed to buy time before Brown began to work on them.

'So what was the point of playing me then? If you knew I was going to come back to SemComNet to try and kill Trevellion and destroy UKCitizensNet, why didn't you just get rid of me when you had the chance? Why this charade? Why waste your time with someone as inconsequential as me? Why pretend to help me?'

'"So many questions, Michael. You know, despite all you've been through, you still don't get it, do you? SemComNet had been working on this app for nearly two years without getting it to a satisfactory state to use it. Then one day in you walk to see Trevellion, telling him you've got some files of your wife that were previously lost. And what do you know, these files happen to address a lot of the knowledge gaps SemComNet had been trying to fill.

'SemComNet's role wasn't just to run UKCitizensNet. That's a piece of piss. They were also commissioned to use the network's infrastructure to develop a stealth weapon, deliverable over wireless and non-wireless networks. But then you know this part, don't you?

'Once we were aware the files existed, it was a simple matter of contacting you, filling your head with conspiracy theories about UKCitizensNet, most of which are actually true, by the way, and convincing you SemComNet and Trevellion were to blame for murdering your wife and daughter. Given your increasing thirst to avenge their deaths, it would not take much to make you believe anything we wanted.

'And so it proved. Trevellion told me how he deluded you with your wife, somehow communicating with you from beyond the grave. You fell for it hook, line, and sinker.'

Images of Colette and her words of warning flashed through Michael's mind.

'No, I saw her. *She* spoke to me. *She* warned me about Trevellion. *She* was guiding me, no one else.'

Brown scoffed, stubbing out his cigarette with his boot on the pristine white floor.

'Wake up Michael. How fucking stupid are you? She's dead. Trevellion staged everything. He sent the messages you received from Colette. We took some vaguely relevant sounding passages from the Books of Isaiah and Revelation and fed them to you. In your state, the more obscure they sounded, the more likely you were to look for the meanings we wanted you to. Haven't you learnt anything over the past few weeks about IP addresses? How they can give away your physical location? We sent those messages to you at your house to encourage you to try and attack Trevellion and SemComNet.'

'But I saw her. I saw her face.'

'You saw what we created. A simple illusion using advanced 3D modelling software. It's a pity I can't show you ANNA in action. Quite fascinating, really.'

'But why did you want me to come back here? What if I had succeeded in killing Trevellion?'

Brown smiled, returning to the table, within reach of the small black unit on the table and its array of buttons. Each one capable of unleashing unspeakable agony.

'It's very simple, Michael. You might have given the Horsemen the files from your wife. The other three weren't in on it, by the way. We were using them to infiltrate the RIG. But I'll come to that in a minute.'

He cast a menacing look at Simon and Ben, who shuddered, pushing involuntarily back in their seats.

'The one thing we couldn't be sure of was whether you were holding something back from us. A little insurance for yourself, perhaps. After all, you did not know who the Horsemen were when we contacted you. It would have made sense if you'd kept some of your wife's information concealed as a safeguard. Wouldn't it?'

Michael felt his heartbeat quicken as Brown's hand moved over the black unit.

'I held nothing back. I gave you everything. I swear.'

'I'm afraid I don't believe that, Michael. You see, once our analysts started looking at the data, it was clear some components and parameters were missing. Vital information relating to wireless protocols was omitted. Probably as a security measure on your wife's behalf. Sensible, really. We would have done the same if we'd been as advanced in our work as your wife and David Langley.'

There was a pause for what seemed like an eternity. Michael watched Brown's hand hover over the black unit.

'Where is the rest of the information?'

Michael gulped. Fear prevented him from speaking, from even moving.

As his scream filled the air of the small confined room, he experienced a feeling of detachment. He could hear his scream ringing in his ears; he felt the pain coursing through his genitals and his body as an electrical shock tore through him. But somehow, for a split second, he felt as if he'd left his body as he thrashed around in the chair. Through the haze of the pain, he could see Brown sitting on the table, a smirk on his face.

As the pain subsided to a dull throbbing, he watched anxiously, gasping for each breath, as Brown came to stand over him. He could feel his breath on his face as he leant in closer.

'The next one is going to hurt more,' he said menacingly. 'But before it does, I want to tell you something else. Something to show you the futility of resisting. I killed Colette and Clare. I rather enjoyed carving those words on her chest and using her blood to decorate your bedroom wall. Terrible wallpaper, by the way.'

Michael thrashed furiously in his chair, trying to fight his restraints, to get at Brown. No matter how hard he struggled, the restraints stayed firm. Sapping his strength as he fought them.

'Burying your little girl was easy too. She didn't struggle too much. Ironic, isn't it? You focused all your rage on Trevellion, and there I was in front of you the whole time. Don't get me wrong, though, he was there as well. And some of the finer touches were his suggestions. I think he's more creative than I am. The words on her chest were his idea. But hey, we can't all be good at everything, can we?'

As the video clip of Clare's body being deposited in the earth replayed in his head, Michael felt warm tears rolling down his cheeks. Anger mingled with regret. He'd come so close to avenging their deaths.

Brown moved back to the desk.

'I'll ask you again. Where is the remainder of the information?'

Michael swam in and out of unconsciousness as minutes turned into hours. Jolt after electrical jolt coursed through him, interspersed by savage blows. He wasn't sure how long Brown had been working on him. The entire ordeal had merged into one long punch and electrical shock as his head bobbed backwards and forwards from the pain.

Eventually, Brown stopped his assault, returning to the desk. He doubted Brown had run out of energy. Someone with psychopathic tendencies as he had exhibited in killing Colette and Clare, and also presumably David Langley, would always find that extra ounce of strength to elicit more pain.

Despite Brown's cruelty and the excruciating pain Michael had suffered, he had given nothing away. What could Brown or any of these bastards still take away from him? They'd already got his wife and daughter. And now they had his liberty, too. What else was there? What did he have to live for that was worth protecting by giving away anything they wanted to know? It wasn't as if they would let him go.

Michael watched as Brown pulled a dark handkerchief from his pocket and wiped the blood from his hand. His blood mainly. He cast a withering glare in Michael's direction as if to say: *'I haven't finished with you yet.'* Slowly, he turned his attention to Simon and Ben, still strapped to their seats, terrified.

Brown circled the two men, beginning another line of questioning. The two men shuddered involuntarily as he approached, sweat dripping from their naked bodies.

'Tell me about the Real Internet Guardians. How many groups exist? Where are they located and what contact details do you have? Where are their stockpiles of equipment housing the pathetic remnants of the old internet?'

The barrage of questions about the RIG continued. Michael realised something fundamental. Despite what Brown had said to him whilst they'd been fleeing across country, he actually had only limited knowledge and information about the groups. The few groups he knew about, which had included Ephesus, had obviously not been hunted down. They were a means to locate the rest of RIG and wipe them out for good.

He wondered how much the other Horsemen had known about the other groups. Had they been unwilling to share this knowledge with Brown? Or were the groups really that careful not to share their contact details for fear of betrayal?

'I only know about three of the groups,' Simon said, the fear in his voice evident.

With a sickening thud, Brown's fist impacted heavily on Simon's cheek and jaw, a stream of blood spurting from his mouth, spattering over Ben.

'Come on, you can do better than that,' Brown said threateningly, leaning over Simon's heaving body.

'They're the only ones I know or have any details of,' Simon protested, flinching in anticipation of a further blow. 'You know as well as I do, no group knows the details of all the groups. Each group only has access to three or four groups, who in turn, have access to three or four more groups. That way, no one group can compromise the whole network. It's not safe any other way. You know all of this.'

Brown turned away from Simon and appeared to move back in the table's direction. Simon readied himself for the agony of the electric shock. But instead, he watched as his hand slipped into his pocket, dragging an item out.

Turning back to face the two men, Brown took two steps forward and fired a handgun at point-blank range at the top of Ben's head. The thunderous noise echoed around the confined room, bouncing off the walls. The white wall behind turned into a kaleidoscopic mixture of blood, brain and tissue. Instantaneously, Simon vomited and hyperventilated as Brown pointed the gun squarely in his face.

'I swear, I know nothing else about the RIG groups. I can give you the IP address of all the secure servers I know of, not just the ones we accessed previously for the app. But I don't know anything else.'

Brown's finger twitched on the trigger. Michael felt his heart racing. He might have nothing to live for, but maybe Simon did. Maybe he had a family? A wife? Or a daughter? They'd never discussed it. But could he sit here and not try to help him? Perhaps he could bargain for Simon's life as his own life no longer had any meaning.

'Wait, I'll tell you what you want to know. Just leave him alone,' Michael yelled frantically.

Raising the gun away from Simon's face, Brown turned.

'I'm listening.'

'I'll tell you where the rest of the information is if you let him go,' Michael said, casting a glance in Simon's direction, who was wild-eyed with panic.

'You're not really in a position to bargain, are you?' Brown said menacingly, placing his gun down on the table and reaching for another cigarette.

'You need this information more than I need to give it,' Michael said defiantly as Brown lit his cigarette, tossing the lighter noisily on the metallic table.

After a brief pause, Brown looked up at Michael.

'OK, I'll talk to Trevellion,' he said calmly. 'You're right. We do need the information.'

Michael looked Brown up and down, knowing he couldn't trust him. But also knowing he had to try something to stop SemComNet from killing another innocent person.

'There's one further location I know of where Colette kept information relating to the State Network Tender and work on the app. The data are on a secure server. Its IP address is 16.08.23.28.'

Brown raised a quizzical eyebrow.

'That's an unusual IP address.'

'It's the date and time of our daughter's birth,' Michael replied quietly.

'And what exactly is this data? We're not interested in fucking boring meeting minutes. We need protocols. Real hard data.'

'The information relates to wireless deployment modules for the app. That's all I know.'

Michael watched as Brown's eyes lit up at the mention of what he'd just described.

'You had better be telling me the truth,' he said, moving towards the door before stopping.

Without warning, Brown turned back to Michael, cigarette in hand, menacingly approaching him. Michael flinched, expecting a fist or boot. Punishment for attempting to blackmail him into stopping his torture of Simon. But the reality was far worse.

Clamping his left hand on Michael's temple, Brown thrust his head back. With his right hand, he forced Michael's right eye wide open, pushing the eyelid upwards. Michael struggled violently as the lit cigarette was nearing his eyeball. His screams filled the confined room as Brown pushed the burning end firmly into his eye, the pupil and iris melding together, the soft eyeball burning.

Through his screams and desperate thrashing in the chair, Brown held the cigarette savagely in place. Unconsciousness overwhelmed Michael as his head swam from a mixture of pain, shock and fear.

Somewhere in the background, he heard the door opening. A familiar voice filled the room. Moments later he was aware of Brown moving away from him, the pressure on his head receding, but the fire of the pain in his eye still cruelly burning.

Through the haze of his left eye, he could just make out the figure of Vincent Trevellion.

'I want them kept alive. At least for now,' he heard Trevellion utter, just before he slipped into a welcome unconsciousness.

CHAPTER FORTY THREE

THE CAVALCADE OF FIVE black armoured limousines turned into Cavendish Square, like synchronised swimmers stopping as one in front of the Edwardian hotel. The middle car was neatly positioned in front of the ornate stone steps, leading into the opulent hotel foyer.

A series of beige marble archways, neatly offset by floral displays, antique wooden furniture that had barely aged despite its vintage, and countless paintings of rural landscapes, all originals, filled the bustling space.

In the foyer were a swarm of bodyguards, security officials, and media advisors, watching every door for the merest hint of danger.

Hotel managers were attentively ensuring the Saudi leader's stay had been as comfortable as possible, and that they had met his every whim.

Amid the bodyguards, President Mahmoud Khalefa Al-Haifi spoke rapidly in Arabic on a mobile phone to one of his senior advisors. The aide was waiting to greet him upon his arrival on his personal jet at Heathrow airport. And as usual, there were more reports to be read for the next leg of his European tour.

The sooner he left this cold country, the better Al-Haifi thought, ending the call, signalling to his bodyguards he wanted to leave. With all the pleasantries complete, the entourage exited the lavish hotel and headed for the waiting limousine.

President Al-Haifi was escorted to the centre car which sat, door held open, at the foot of the steps. As the car door closed, the procession of limousines began its slow exit from Cavendish Square towards Regent Street and out of London.

VINCENT TREVELLION AND SEBASTIAN Tate sat at their usual table in the Japanese restaurant, overlooking the busy Oxford Street below. Their food had been delivered, and they'd ordered no further interruptions.

At two tables nearby, four of Tate's security men sat menacingly, preventing any idle access to the table or their view. Tate spoke quietly into his mobile phone, listening intently.

A few seconds later, the call ended. Trevellion looked expectantly at Tate as he placed the phone down on the table.

'They're on their way,' he said assuredly.

'And the integrity of the network?'

'Everything is fully operational. We have carried out all the diagnostic tests, and again. The network is robust. As soon as they reach Whitehall, the app will be launched.'

A sneer crossed his ageing, distinguished face as he reached for his glass of white wine, turning to look out the window. His gaze rose to the rooftops of Oxford Street.

All along the route, security personnel from his department were stationed. Either on rooftops, in shop doorways, or in armoured cars. They had arranged the security details with the Saudi security force. The Saudis would protect their leader directly through their convoy of vehicles on the way to Heathrow. UK security forces would monitor the route to prevent any unfortunate incidents.

How ironic, Tate thought, catching sight of the convoy as it moved seamlessly up Oxford Street. Little did the Saudis know the details of the route had been passed on via Miles Winston, the Secretary of State for Defence, to CODEX.

The five black limousines glistened in the sunlight as they glided up the road. Passers-by stopped to look at the impressive sight, trying to peer in through the tinted windows to catch sight of who this important celebrity was.

The two men watched as the cars slipped past the restaurant below, continuing their journey toward Tottenham Court Road. On the rooftop opposite, Trevellion counted four snipers monitoring the progress of the convoy. Legitimate UK security personnel, all known and accounted for by the Saudi security force.

The procession drifted out of sight, and the two men returned to their previous positions. Tate placed his wine glass on the table, picking up his mobile. Glancing at his watch, he dialled a number. The phone was instantly answered.

'They're past us now, heading towards Tottenham Court Road. Keep me informed. I want to know if there are any deviations on the route.'

THE PETROL TANKER TURNED onto Westminster Bridge and began to cross the Thames, the London Eye and County Hall impressively rearing up on the river bank opposite. Glancing in his rear-view mirror, the driver was sure he hadn't been followed. The clock on the dashboard's digital display signalled he had little time.

Reaching the centre of the bridge, he turned off the tanker's ignition, letting the vehicle idle to a stop. In the same instance, he hit the button for the hazard lights, watching in his mirrors as the steady stream of traffic moved around the apparently stricken vehicle.

Reaching into his shirt pocket, he pulled out his phone and quickly dialled, anxiously glancing at the clock on the dashboard. A familiar male voice answered.

'I'm in position and about to exit the vehicle. Everything's set.'

Ending the call, the driver jumped down from the cabin onto the pavement that ran across the bridge.

'Everything OK?' an elderly passer-by asked.

'Bloody engine just died on me. Can't get the damn thing started. I'm going to have to call out the RAC, I think,' he replied cheerfully, reaching into his pocket for his mobile to validate his statement.

As the suited man continued his walk across the bridge, the driver looked around. No one was paying particular attention to him. Everyone was too eager to get to their destinations.

Putting the phone to his ear, he strolled up the pavement and away from the petrol tanker.

PRESIDENT AL-HAIFI LOOKED UP from his papers with minimal interest as the convoy moved slowly through Trafalgar Square, a series of roadworks on the route slowing their journey.

In the seats in front, two burly security guards sat with their earpieces securely in place so the entire team could communicate instantly at the sign of any threat. Not that he had any particular concerns. His security team's competence was never in question. And the security intelligence collated prior to his European tour hadn't indicated any potential threats.

The trip to the UK had been a great success. At least for his country. Following his election four years earlier, he'd energetically, even ruthlessly, pushed forward oil reforms. The nationalisation of the Saudi oil industry had been met with furious indignation from oil companies and nations worldwide.

Company after company had been forced to withdraw their operations from Saudi soil, and then suffer the indignity of paying higher premiums on exporting oil to service their own national needs.

It had been a painful deal for the countries, but universally popular in his homeland. Now, four years on, he was holding court with the leading European national leaders. Listening to them beg for reductions in the oil tariffs because it was crippling their economies.

Dr Marcus McCoy had been no different. He'd argued strongly, offering diplomatic concessions and deals elsewhere. Behind the media spin and national pride, McCoy was a vicious bully who'd tried every political trick in the book to intimidate him.

He was having none of it. When he'd pointed out fuel prices could be eased in this country by a reduction in fuel taxes, he was, unsurprisingly, met with little enthusiasm.

In the end, their mini-summit had reached a publicly amicable stalemate whilst further ministerial discussions took place. And now his attention turned to similar negotiations with the French President, another dour belligerent man who would also try to bully him into submission.

The convoy journeyed past Nelson's Column and turned into Whitehall. The elegant buildings of the Treasury, the Foreign, and Cabinet Office slipped by as the convoy sped on to its destination. The President smiled, imagining grey bureaucrats convening emergency meetings to discuss the lack of cooperation the Saudi nation was giving to their economy. Maybe if they came back with improved financial, military or diplomatic proposals, he might consider some sort of concession on the oil tariff. Without it, he wouldn't be moving his position.

ON THE CORNER OF Trafalgar Square and the entrance to Whitehall, a stocky man leant against a lamppost, talking into his mobile phone. He watched nonchalantly as the convoy of black limousines eased their way past him and onto Parliament Square, careful not to give the vehicles any attention.

As the convoy headed away, the man dropped his mobile into his shirt pocket and pulled a small black tablet computer from inside his jacket. The machine, already booted up, flashed several options on the screen. In the bottom corner, a status bar displayed the local wireless network's integrity. It was at a full 100%. With a few keystrokes and a quick tap of the "Enter" key, the screen went momentarily blank. The job was done.

A brief message flashed up on the screen.

Connection to remote IP address successful.
App successfully downloaded.

The man half-smiled, slipping the handheld computer back into his jacket pocket and retrieving his phone. He had to make his report.

Pulling out of Parliament Square the second of the five black armoured limousines turned onto Westminster Bridge. The leading vehicle was about twenty feet in front, the President's car a similar distance behind. The rest of the convoy came into sight in the rear-view mirrors as they also turned onto the famous bridge.

Four Saudi security officers occupied the leading car. All were armed and wired up on mobile earpieces linked to the head of the Saudi Security Force, who was also travelling in the President's car.

As the convoy eased along the bridge, the driver was struck by the impressive view over the River Thames. Driving on, he could see the London Eye as it made its slow journey around its axis. Tourists were pressed to the window of every capsule. Camera flashes reflected off the glass, lighting up the dreary lunchtime sky.

Part of him was disappointed they'd not had a chance to see the sights. But there had been no time. The schedule of their visit was too tight for such indulgences.

Without warning, his colleague in the passenger seat gesticulated at something up ahead, disturbing his thoughts. Looking beyond the leading limousine, a petrol tanker was blocking the left lane ahead, its hazard lights blinking. The driver watched as the first limousine pulled out into the right-hand lane to move past the stranded vehicle. But his attention was quickly brought back to his own vehicle. The digital display on the dashboard flashed violently as warning lights beamed on and off in unison. To the right, mounted on the dashboard, the satnav which was directing their journey was fading in and out before the screen went blank.

'What's going on?' the security guard next to him said anxiously, his right hand instinctively reaching for his gun inside his jacket.

'I don't know,' the driver replied frantically as the car veered from side to side.

Grappling with the steering wheel, the driver fought to keep the vehicle under control as it slid from the left lane to the right and back again.

'I can't control it,' he yelled as the petrol tanker loomed before them.

'Brake, use the brakes!' the second security guard yelled.

The driver's foot flattened the brake pedal. But instead of his car slowing, it increased in speed; the engine revving noisily in protest as it gathered pace. Grabbing the handbrake, pulling it as far upwards as he could, the driver started praying as the car hurtled forward at an ever-increasing speed, almost in front of the stationary petrol tanker.

The other three security guards were yelling instructions, desperately looking for a means to get the limousine under control. The second security guard leant over, grabbing the steering wheel in a vain attempt to stop the car's onward journey.

As the petrol tanker loomed large in the front windscreen, the driver looked at the photos of his wife and his young daughter fastened on the dashboard to the right of the steering wheel. He prayed he would see them again.

In the President's limousine, the security guards in the vehicle's front were watching anxiously as they viewed the swerving limousine close in on the tanker. The head of the security force was bellowing instructions into his phone, trying to communicate with the driver in front. Receiving no reply, he ordered the driver of the President's limousine to brake and take evasive action.

President Al-Haifi's papers, which had been sitting in his lap, spilled into the footwell. Gripping the light brown leather seat, he braced himself as the limousine slammed to a halt. Looking beyond his security guards to the scene in front, his eyes widened as the vehicle up ahead failed to slow, seeming to pick up speed as it approached the petrol tanker blocking the road.

The four men in the car flinched as the limousine ploughed into the back of the tanker with a deafening bang. For a second, there was nothing but silence. They all held their breath.

The tanker detonated in an immense explosion, which shook the whole of Westminster Bridge. A searing petrol fireball swallowed up the limousine that had hit the tanker, quickly spreading as the inferno ignited into a sprawling blaze, obliterating everything in its path.

The President saw the light from the fireball glow off the windows of his own limousine before it was blown into a thousand pieces. The explosion tore the reinforced metal apart, scattering debris onto the bridge and into the river before obliterating the limousine behind.

The driver of the final limousine felt the warmth of the explosion envelop his vehicle as he forced it into reverse. The wheels screeched loudly as the car hurtled backwards and out of the destructive path of the blast.

The vehicle came to an abrupt halt as it careered into the 4x4 Jeep that had been behind as they'd reached the bridge. The four security guards sat in silence, watching in disbelief as the tangled mass of metal burned fiercely. Barely metres away. Not one of them spoke.

As with everywhere else in proximity to Westminster Bridge, the explosion had been heard in the Japanese restaurant where Tate and Trevellion were finishing their meal.

Ignoring the four burly security guards, the restaurant's staff and other diners had rushed to the windows to see what had happened.

Black smoke rose into the cloudy midday London sky above the rooftops of Oxford Street. The acrid smell of burning fuel seeped into the restaurant as the babble of voices speculated about what had just happened.

'I think we should get you out of here, sir,' one of the security guards suggested, approaching Tate's table.

Tate nodded, casting a knowing glance at Trevellion.

'Yes, I agree. Bring the car around.'

As the security guard moved away from the table, the ringing of Tate's mobile phone punctuated the chatter of anxious voices in the restaurant. Picking it up, he exchanged glances with Trevellion before answering the call.

A familiar male voice was at the other end of the line.

'The target has been destroyed.'

CHAPTER FORTY FOUR

VINCENT TREVELLION STRODE PURPOSEFULLY through the white corridor, approaching the room where his brother and Michael were held captive. A tall, unfriendly looking soldier accompanied him as they reached the locked door. Trevellion stood back as the soldier unlocked the door, a baton held firmly in his right hand.

The two captives were at the back of the room. Simon sat on one of the three chairs, but this time he was fully clothed, not savagely restrained. Michael sat hunched on the floor, his back pressed against the cold white wall. Ben's blood still stained the adjacent wall where Brown had mercilessly executed him several days before.

Simon regarded the security guard warily; his face drawn and harrowed from the days of torture, fearing what might be next.

Michael looked up and in Trevellion's direction, remaining seated. His right eye was half closed from where Brown had blinded him with the cigarette. His skin and eyeball was swollen and blistered from the savage heat. His other eye burned equally with hatred for Trevellion and all he symbolised.

The soldier stood menacingly in front of Michael and Simon as Trevellion sat on the table, the same place Brown had been days before. Pulling a holstered handgun from his jacket, he held it purposefully in his left hand.

Smirking in Michael and Simon's direction, the soldier exited the room. The sound of his boots thudding down the corridor soon faded away, leaving the three men together in the windowless cell.

For what seemed like an eternity, none of them spoke. Mutual contempt hung in the air. Michael was the first to speak.

'You've come here to kill us then, have you?'

Trevellion looked Michael directly in the eye.

'Got every last bit of information out of us now, have you? Don't need us anymore?'

The slightest smile passed Trevellion's thin lips as his left index finger gently tapped the trigger of the handgun.

'Answer him, damn it,' Simon interrupted with equal hostility. 'Stop playing games.'

Trevellion turned to face his brother with clear contempt.

'But you know I like games, don't you?' he replied calmly. 'I always did. And I was always better at them than you.'

Simon scowled in anger and frustration. He knew it was true. Vincent had always been the more manipulative, the more conniving of the two of them. He'd always managed to wriggle his way out of problems far better than he had. In life, he seemed to have the upper hand. Now, in certain death, nothing had changed.

'It's ironic, isn't it,' Trevellion continued menacingly. 'The last time we met, you lectured me about your disgust at companies like SemComNet. And, as I recall, your moral opposition to their stance on unregulated information. Imagine how gratified I felt when I discovered my brother was a member of RIG. A group we've been hunting down for years. A rabble that stands for nothing more than anarchy and pathetic idealism. The irony was just too good.'

Trevellion paused, choosing his next words as carefully as a surgeon selects his scalpel.

'And then something else struck me, probably the greatest irony of all. I realised that maybe, just for once, father would probably have been proud of you. Finally, you were doing something you believed in. Not just lecturing or theorising about it. It's a pity this revelation didn't come when he was alive, isn't it?'

Trevellion smiled thinly as Simon's face flushed with anger. As usual, his brother knew exactly how to provoke him. But never before had he done so with a gun pointed at him.

'The RIG are over. We're locating more of your groups all the time, and becoming very adept at getting rid of them. And now we have your app too.'

'Oh yes, you're good,' Michael added, breaking the sibling hostility. He braced himself for what he was about to say, fearing the provocation might trigger Trevellion.

'Just tell me one thing. Why? Not why you brutally butchered my wife and daughter. I know you were stealing industrial secrets, and they were expendable and in your way. But why this app, this bit of fucking code? Why is it so important to you and SemComNet that you've killed God knows how many people in pursuit of it?'

Michael tentatively rubbed his blistering eye as it throbbed again, tears falling down his pale cheek.

'It's worth it, believe me. You don't understand the significance of what we now possess and what we can do with it. It's far beyond the comfortable confines of your previous, mundane urban lives.

You should have stayed in your quiet, boring existence and left this to people who are changing the world, not associating with losers trying to maintain some antiquated, unregulated old network. If you'd left it alone, you wouldn't be here now.'

Michael could feel his rage erupting.

'You brought me into this. You killed my wife and daughter. Did you think I'd just let that lie?'

'Yes, but we gave you a killer. There was no need to pursue this any further. You forced our hand when you came to see me, telling me your wife had further information. We couldn't let that lie, I'm afraid.'

'Davey Wilkes was innocent,' Michael said flatly.

Trevellion gestured dismissively, waving his handgun in front of him.

'A Green road protester who lives up trees and in tunnels. Hardly a loss to society, is he?'

'That's a matter of perspective, Vincent,' Simon interrupted.

Trevellion turned angrily to face his brother.

'Spare me your patronising intellectual reasoning. This is a ruthless business, and he was expendable.'

'The question remains: what is this business? This clearly goes beyond just computers. We've all seen the code and what it does. This is warfare.'

Trevellion smiled dismissively at his brother, content in the knowledge he was shortly going to end his life.

'You always were the smarter one, weren't you, Simon? It's a shame you didn't use that intellect in a more profitable way, rather than wasting it on academia and the freedom of ideas and information. What a waste of your life.'

'I'd stand up for that every time against the sham that's UKCitizensNet. That's worth dying for.

'Well, how ironic that you will die for your beliefs, then.'

Simon watched, surprised at how calm he was feeling. Vincent looked them up and down. His finger poised on the trigger.

Warfare?

Suddenly, he was struck by what Vincent had just said. The day before, they'd been moved out of the room they were being held in and taken to one of the many R&D computer labs. The purpose had been to check Michael's information about his wife's secretly stored away data.

Whilst in the lab, the various screens filling the room had been showing live UKCitizensNet feeds reporting the death of Saudi leader, President Mahmoud Khalefa Al-Haifi on Westminster Bridge in London. They blamed the tragedy on one of his drivers losing control of his vehicle and ploughing into a petrol tanker, causing a massive explosion, killing the President and leaving the bridge with enormous structural damage. A terrible thought crossed his mind.

'You used the app to kill the Saudi President, didn't you?' he said. In his epiphany about the motives for needing the app to work on a wireless network, his thoughts filled with theories and conspiracies.

Trevellion lowered his gun, relaxing his finger on the trigger, his eyes widening in surprise. A look of satisfaction crossed his face.

'You see? I told you your brain was wasted in a dusty university library.'

'But why? This country's not at war with Saudi Arabia. It never has been.'

His thoughts trailed off, struck by another idea.

'This is about oil, isn't it?'

Trevellion seemed to smile again, although his facial expression barely changed. He appeared to be enjoying the intellectual spat with his brother, Michael thought as he watched them.

'It's about oil this time. But it won't be the next time. This stealth weapon gives us control. The control to push through whatever policies this government sees fit that would be, let's say, less palatable to the average voter.'

Simon closed his eyes, trying to process all the facts bombarding him.

'So this is about the Saudi oil tariffs?'

'Go on.'

'The Saudi President has been touring European countries. They've all been trying to negotiate better deals on the oil tariff. Doubtless, they've been offering concessions to Saudi Arabia elsewhere?'

"Very good."

'But why kill him?'

Trevellion looked at Simon and Michael, and then at the gun he was holding, deciding how much information he was prepared to share. He had no interest in sharing anything with Michael Robertson—his purpose had been served. They'd squeezed everything they could out of him.

But with his brother, it was different. Academically, he'd always been superior to him. He would've made a professor.

What he lacked in intellect compared to Simon, he'd more than compensated with his determination. A ruthless spirit to see anything through to the end. No matter what the cost. The means always justified the end.

Here they were now. And for one of the few times in their lives, he held the upper hand intellectually. He understood the bigger picture. Had all the answers. Held the power. What a fitting scenario to end his brother's worthless pursuit of intellectual freedom and the sharing of ideas. Could their views be further apart?

'You've heard of Oil-NetCom, I presume?' Trevellion said.

Simon nodded. Michael, who was grappling with the pain in his eye, didn't respond. But somewhere at the back of his consciousness, the name was vaguely familiar.

'Oil-NetCom is one of SemComNet's sister companies and has refineries based in several oil-producing countries. Its biggest concentration of refineries was, however, in Saudi Arabia. Until four years ago when, as I'm sure you'll remember, the former Saudi royal family was ousted in a bloodless coup and exiled from the country. That was when President Al-Haifi and his cabinet came to power.'

Simon nodded, remembering the international coverage.

'One of the first things Al-Haifi did was to nationalise the oil industry in Saudi Arabia. The result was that all foreign oil companies were forced out of the country; the Saudi government claimed the wells for themselves. One of these companies was Oil-NetCom. Of course, there was outrage in the Western world, which only got worse when the Saudi government introduced the now infamous 'oil tariff.' Military action wasn't an option. It would have united the entire Arab world against the West. That was too high a price to risk. Instead, the cost of a barrel of oil immediately topped $100 and has been rising ever since. Before long, it will be over $200 a barrel. Oil-NetCom, like all the other companies forced to leave Saudi Arabia, incurred billions in losses. Some of these were cushioned by national governments. But not all. Not everyone in the Saudi cabinet supported the move to nationalisation, despite Al-Haifi forcing it through. This move to nationalisation was deliriously greeted in Riyadh and the rest of the country. A nice little 'fuck you' to the Western world.'

'So this is all about financial revenge because they forced UK companies out of the region and the price of oil went up?'

Trevellion smiled smugly at Simon's miscomprehension.

'If only it were that simplistic.'

Simon scowled at his brother's evident enjoyment of having the upper hand.

'Oil-NetCom and other UK companies affected, either directly or indirectly, by the oil tariff, all invested heavily in this country's defence R&D programme. Unsurprisingly, faced with billions of pounds' worth of debt and lost revenue, they were reluctant to commit to such expenditure in the future. But, with President Al-Haifi out of the way, his natural successor, Aymen Al-Hassany will come to power. And we're confident he will re-privatise the oil industry, restoring the former status quo.'

'You mean he's in this government's pocket?'

'Let's just say this government will make sufficient inducements to make it worth his while. Al-Haifi wasn't interested in the offer put to him. But that's immaterial now, isn't it?'

'So that's it? All these people killed, their lives ruined in pursuit of a better deal on the price of oil?'

'Please Simon, don't be so naïve. You know how important oil is. Countries will always go to war over it. But with the app, we don't need to go to war publicly over anything anymore or risk voters protesting about conflicts. More importantly, the use of the app runs far deeper than just getting a better deal over the oil tariff. Oil-NetCom will be back in the region.'

Simon watched as he saw excitement glint in Vincent's eyes, the realisation of what his brother had just said slapping him in the face. Michael looked bemused as his narrow gaze moved between the brothers, periodically stopping on the muzzle of the gun.

'Of course. You want access to the oil infrastructure's computer network. The wireless capability of the app could access any remote IP address within the oil system.'

Trevellion nodded knowingly, smiling thinly.

'I knew you'd be able to work it out eventually. Even if it took more than a little help from me.'

'I grant you that's brilliant. But are you telling me the real motives amount to nothing more than simple theft?'

'As you said before, that depends on your perspective, doesn't it? You've seen the code and what it can do. We have the leading network security protocols on our end through UKCitizensNet, with the most advanced means of hacking other systems' security via the app. Once Aymen Al-Hassany takes over as the new President and Oil-NetCom and the other companies return to the region, each company's network will reintegrate into the existing computer network in the region. Once we're connected to this again, we can deploy the app right across the oil network.'

'So you can then steal or siphon off oil production from one area or refinery into Oil-NetCom's reserves?'

'Exactly,' Trevellion exclaimed triumphantly. 'But more than that. The app's configuration will also be able to infiltrate the regions' banks, diverting money out of some of the less reputable business accounts stored there, and into our own secure Swiss bank accounts.'

'Divert? You're no more than common thieves,' Michael spat in disgust.

'As I said, you fail to see the bigger picture. The removal of the oil tariff and the appropriation of extra funds will allow this government to fund new national initiatives without having to raise taxes and incur the disappointment of the voters.'

'And the fact that these companies will reinvest in defence R&D again has nothing to do with it?' Simon added sarcastically.

'A fortunate by-product of the wider strategy. Context is everything, Simon.'

'You realise what the underlying irony of this whole 'strategy" is, don't you?' Simon said flatly. 'When Marcus McCoy banned connection to the old internet, they forced the big multi-national IT and web technology companies out of this country, all in the name of promoting "UK enterprise." As I recall, the Saudi President was supporting the "Saudi oil interest" when he nationalised the oil industry. There's no distinction between the two.'

Trevellion sighed, growing tired of his brother's continual intellectual rationalising.

'Politics is a dirty game. Each national government is only out for one thing: itself. We've simply been proactive. If you don't act first, someone will either do something to you, or beat you to the punch. It's dog-eat-dog in my world. Your academic values will never be able to reconcile that.'

'So how many people are going to have to die in pursuit of this government's less palatable policies?' Michael sneered, getting up to sit down on the chair next to Simon, Trevellion's gun pointing squarely at his chest.

'That's not really for me to say, now, is it? Suffice to say, SemCom-Net has developed the stealth technology allowing this government to keep their noses clean publicly whilst putting the app to use in whatever way is politically expedient. Although, I would like to thank you both for your input. And your lovely wife. She truly played a pivotal part in the success of this project.'

Without thinking Michael lunged at Trevellion, his rage boiling at the mention of Colette. Immediately recognising the danger, Trevellion moved gracefully to his right, swinging the muzzle of the gun towards Michael. The weapon cracked noisily on the side of his head as he fell to the floor at Trevellion's feet. Stepping back, he kicked Michael savagely in the ribs.

'Get the fuck over there,' Trevellion snarled as Michael groaned and hauled himself to his feet to slump back in the chair.

'The talking is over. All of you fucking RIG scum have been wasting my time for months. We'll be hunting down every last one of you. The Real Internet Guardians, and that pathetic old relic of the internet you're trying so desperately to preserve, will soon be gone.'

Raising the gun to head level, Michael and Simon braced themselves. An image of Colette and Clare from happier times, on his wife's last birthday as they opened presents together, laughing endlessly as they did so, raced through Michael's mind as Trevellion's left index finger moved over the gun's trigger.

The sound of an explosion in another part of the building echoed around the confined room. Trevellion quickly glanced at the door before returning his gaze to Michael and Simon. He listened intently, expecting the sound of running feet from the soldiers deployed at SemComNet. No sound came except that of a second explosion. And this time, the lights in the room flickered on and off for a split second.

Michael and Simon sensed their chance. When the lights flickered for a second time, the two men dived at Trevellion. As the lights came back on, the three men grappled over the table. Michael had gone for Trevellion's left hand and forearm, which was holding his gun. Simon had pushed his right hand into his brother's face, slamming the back of his head into the metal table with a sickening thud. Pulling his head up by the hair, he slammed it down again.

Trevellion snarled as he tried to fight off the two men. As Michael tried to dislodge the gun from his hand, his shoulder throbbing from where the Dobermann had bitten him, the gun went off, puncturing a hole in the wall behind. Moments later, Trevellion dropped the gun as Michael bent his hand back, almost breaking his wrist.

A third explosion rocked the building. The room shook before the three men rolled off the table in a tangle of bodies. Free from Simon's grip, Trevellion hauled himself up, viciously kicking his brother in the right kidney before swinging a fist at Michael's jaw.

Falling to the floor, Michael watched Trevellion clawing at the door handle before it flew open. Escaping up the corridor, his Armani suit jacket flapped behind him as he ran, disappearing out of sight.

Helping Simon to his feet, and picking up Trevellion's gun from the floor, the two men quickly exited the room into the corridor. Trevellion had disappeared through the double doors at the end of the corridor and into the maze that was the SemComNet building.

As the sound of another minor explosion somewhere behind them echoed through the corridor, the building's sprinklers kicked into life. Simon turned to Michael, who was nursing his swollen jaw.

'We need to get out of here. *Now.*'

CHAPTER FORTY FIVE

LUKEWARM WATER JETTING FROM the sprinklers filled the air as Michael and Simon made their way up the corridor to the set of double doors that had been Trevellion's escape. Listening at the exit, the pandemonium in the centre of the building became obvious. People were running and yelling, although the flurry of explosions seemed to have stopped. In the chaos that had erupted, they hoped no one would pay them attention.

Michael looked down at the gun he'd tucked in the top of his trousers. That should be very persuasive if anyone *did* take an interest in them, he thought, pushing through the double doors.

The doors opened up onto an expansively marbled balcony, revealing they were on the top floor of the building, in the heart of its atrium. The balcony ran all the way round in one enormous square. Four large corridors, ninety degrees apart, lead into each section of the building. Michael wasn't sure which wing they were in as he approached the edge of the balcony. Looking over the top, they could see people running, desperately attempting to escape whatever incident had taken place.

On all sides, he could see the images of worried staff reflected in the vast glass windows surrounding the atrium, running from floor to ceiling. It had looked impressive enough when he'd visited Trevellion in his office. But from this elevated position, it was breathtaking.

Mingled in amongst the startled workers were armed soldiers and SemComNet's security personnel. Withdrawing from the balcony, the two men stood, watching the commotion for a few seconds.

'I still want one more shot at Trevellion,' Michael said finally.

'Are you mad? In all this chaos, we'll easily be able to slip out of here and disappear into the woods. We might not get another chance once they've sorted out whatever the fuck is going on.'

'I'm not leaving until I find him,' Michael said defiantly, wiping away the sticky streak on his right cheek where his blistered eye was still weeping.

'Don't forget, he was going to kill you, too. Your brother. You can either help me or leave. I won't blame you if you decide to go. But make up your mind.'

Simon rolled his eyes in exasperation.

'All right, I'll help you.'

Looking around the balcony to the entrances to the other three wings of the building, Simon's gaze fell on the corridor opposite. The large sign attached to the far wall read: "Research and Development".

'Come on, I've got an idea,' he said, jogging in the corridor's direction.

Crashing through the double doors into the corridor, they were met by onrushing staff attempting to evacuate the building, heading for the staircases in the atrium.

'Where are you guys going?' a woman yelled as Michael and Simon barged past. 'We've all got to leave the building.'

The two men ignored her and kept on moving until the stream of worried workers had left the area. Now they were alone in a deserted white corridor. The only sound was the hum of servers processing somewhere nearby.

They stopped next to a door labelled "R&D Laboratory 6". Without a word, the two men slipped into the lab, closing the door behind them to conceal their presence.

'What have you got in mind?' Michael asked as Simon sat down at a desk.

The computer was still on from where the staff had hastily evacuated. It was still logged into SemComNet's internal computer system.

'These machines are still logged on, which means I haven't got to spend ages pissing about trying to hack a way in.'

Michael looked around anxiously as Simon closed down several applications before opening up an FTP connection window.

'Before we came here, I stored a copy of the app on one of RIG's secure FTP servers as a little insurance.'

Michael frowned, remembering the savage tortures.

'But you gave those details to Brown. They'll have deleted it, or taken it down now.'

'I didn't give them all the details. By the time you'd given them the IP details of where they could find your wife's information, they'd lost interest in the RIG servers. They're more interested in getting rid of the groups than in its infrastructure. This was the only bit of information I held onto.'

Michael nodded appreciatively at Simon's deception, watching as he opened another application on the screen.

'I'm going to download the app into the system. We can then try to use it against my brother. He must be somewhere in this maze. Doubtless in some secure location away from whatever's happening. I'm looking in SemComNet's logs to see if I can isolate his IP address so we know where to send the app to.'

As the app was downloaded from the RIG secure FTP server, Simon's eyes widened in surprise at the box at the bottom of the screen with information about the current network activity.

'Fuck me. I don't believe it,' he said, his jaw practically on his chest.

'What?' Michael replied, eager to know what was going on.

'The UKCitizensNet system is being bombarded by traffic outside the system. This sort of level of traffic and the complexity of what I'm reading here can only mean one thing. RIG groups are doing this.'

Simon paused, running his fingers through his unkempt hair as he tried to piece everything together.

'The only thing that makes any sense is that Wally managed to send the app out to our known RIG groups and they, in turn, must have distributed it to other groups. They're now attacking the UKCitizensNet system with it.'

Simon could feel his adrenaline pumping as he continued to delve deeper into SemComNet's files, determining the level of damage UKCitizensNet was sustaining.

Michael looked up at a large screen attached to the wall above the bank of desks and monitors. The display was showing the UKCitizensNet homepage. But this time it was different. Very different. He pulled at Simon's arm.

'Look. Look what's happening,' he said excitedly.

A large message had interrupted the normally well-ordered UKCitizensNet homepage, with its various options and menus all neatly laid out along the outer edges of the screen, in the centre.

Warning: UKCitizensNet is a sham. It is a government front controlling and restricting your lives and the news and information you receive. This is not democracy. Stand up against UKCitizensNet and discover the actual truth.

Simon punched the air in delight as he read the message boldly displayed on the screen. Never had he imagined this day would come. Looking back to his own screen, his smile broadened further as he pulled up a system report on the integrity of the UKCitizensNet system.

'"Shit, they've caused more damage than I thought. The combination of app attacks on the firewall has exposed the addresses of regional server clusters and individual IP addresses. With those details, they'll be able to launch apps against other parts of the infrastructure. Only a sustained attack from all the groups on the entire system can bring UKCitizensNet down. This is fucking fantastic. I can't believe it.'

The smile on Michael's face faded as his reality and sense of purpose hit him again.

'That's great, but find me Trevellion. If you've downloaded the app to here, I want to launch it against him. We have tried it before.

Smith had configured it so that it would release toxic gas through the sprinklers to his physical location. Can we do that again?'

Simon scratched his chin, typing a succession of commands.

'Give me a second whilst I just reprogram which parameters the app needs to use.'

'Don't waste your time,' a familiar voice came menacingly from behind.

Spinning around, the two men flinched involuntarily at the sight of their cruel torturer. Brown stood in the doorway to the lab, a handgun fitted with a silencer in his right hand, pointing at them.

'I should have killed you two pathetic shits when I had the chance. Only Trevellion wanted to keep you alive in case you had anything useful to tell us. Well, I think you've served your usefulness now. Don't you?'

Michael could feel the sweat dripping from his forehead as he watched Brown's trigger finger twitch.

'At least tell me your name,' Michael said defiantly.

A quizzical look crossed Brown's face as he kept the gun trained on Michael.

'Tell me the name of the man who killed my wife and daughter. You owe me that knowledge at least. Give me your real name, you bastard. You and the other Horsemen never told me who you really are.'

Brown smirked as he recalled the first time Michael had met the group.

'OK, for what it's worth. If that'll make dying any easier for you. I'm John Kennedy and I killed your wife and daughter. Satisfied? Feel better for knowing? Have you got your closure now?'

He sneered, waving his gun in front of Michael's face.

A look of calm crossed Michael's face as he processed the words. At least now, finally, he knew who'd been responsible.

As Kennedy lined the gun up with his head, Michael looked squarely into his assailant's eyes.

'Kill us and you won't be able to stop the attack on UKCitizensNet. If you don't believe me, look at the screen and your homepage. The RIG has hacked into your precious fucking system.'

Kennedy smiled wryly as he glanced at the screen.

'I should have known those useless soldiers were no fucking good. They assured us your colleague at the university hadn't had time to send the app before we killed him. Well, no matter, our teams are already out hunting down the RIG groups. This will only be short-lived. A minor victory, believe me. And besides, we'll be able to implicate the anti-net protesters for this. The same ones who savagely murdered your wife and daughter.'

As Kennedy smirked maliciously, a further explosion nearby shook the entire lab. The room shook and the door behind Kennedy slid open, knocking into the back of his legs.

The impact was sufficient for Kennedy to turn and see what had happened. In an instant, Michael seized his chance, quickly pulling his handgun. Seeing him reach for his gun, Kennedy fired, but lost his balance when his foot got caught in the door as he tried to kick it away.

Michael felt the bullet flash past his face before it impacted the white wall behind him. At the same moment, his finger tightened on the trigger. He felt the force of the gun explode in his hand and recoil before the bullet hit Kennedy squarely in the centre of his chest, sending him hurtling back into the door, shutting it with the force.

Before Kennedy could respond, Michael fired two more shots into his chest. Kennedy's body slid slowly down the door, blood streaking the white interior where the bullet had exited his body. Michael stood over Kennedy's slumped body, panting. Even through the pain and the blood bubbling from his mouth, Kennedy still smirked maniacally as he attempted to speak.

'I enjoyed killing them both,' he finally blurted out as Michael's finger tightened on the trigger.

'I know,' Michael said flatly. 'And I'm going to have to live with that.'

The gun recoiled again as a final bullet shot Kennedy through the top of the head, his body toppling over into a bloody pool blocking the door.

'That's for Colette and Clare,' Michael said quietly, looking back at Simon.

Turning to his computer, Simon typed a few more commands as the machine processed his request.

'I've accessed the login logs. I'm trying to isolate where my brother is logged in, if at all. He may have fled the building.'

'He'll still be here,' Michael said confidently. 'He's not going to leave. This is his project. He will not let it go up in flames without a fight.'

Simon watched as the SemComNet system scanned its logs for any sign of his brother being logged into the system, and where. Michael watched anxiously as the machine processed his request, fearing his opportunity could be lost.

'I've got him,' Simon finally said. 'He's logged into the system all right. I just need to cross-reference his login IP address with his physical location. Give me a moment.'

The sound of another explosion filled the air, going off in another part of the building.

'He's in the Data Warehouse on Level 3,' Simon said, as the information popped up on the screen.

Michael exhaled loudly, looking down at the gun he was still holding.

'That's where all the servers and infrastructure for UKCitizensNet will be stored.'

'He's trying to save it from the attack,' Michael said knowingly.

'You'll need a security code to override the retinal scanner to get in there,' Simon added, exiting the information on the screen and querying the security module for the SemComNet building.

Michael turned the handgun he was holding upside down in his hand and released the magazine from the butt of the gun. There were five bullets left. He hoped it was enough.

'OK, the security code for the Data Warehouse door is 190704.'

Without a word, Michael turned, heading for the door.

'Wait, I'll come with you.'

'No, you get yourself out of here. I'm going alone. I want to see the look on his face when he knows there's no escape. When he realises they've failed. I need to ensure Trevellion is in the room when the app strikes his location. I need you here to do that.'

Simon's eyes widened as he realised what Michael was saying, and the price he was willing to pay to avenge his wife and daughter.

'How long do you want before the app releases the gas into the Data Warehouse?'

'Fifteen minutes should be enough,' Michael replied, pondering his showdown with Trevellion.

'OK, I'll need to do a minor bit of reconfiguration, but that shouldn't take me long.'

Michael nodded.

'Good, and thank you. Just promise me when it's done and the app's gone that you get yourself out of this damn building.'

Simon nodded, looking at the determination burning in Michael's eyes.

In an instant, Michael left the room in search of the Data Warehouse on Level 3. Simon typed rapidly, configuring the app to send his brother to his death.

CHAPTER FORTY SIX

It took Simon less than five minutes to reprogram the app, ensuring the gas release settings Smith had originally programmed were used as the correct deployment handlers. The Horsemen had programmed potential scenarios for the app. But this was the one Michael had wanted, and he'd obliged.

He'd paused for a few brief seconds, debating whether he really could send the app to kill his brother. Memories of their childhood clouded his thoughts, dredging up the same pain and regret he'd felt at his father's funeral. And then his father's words rang in his ears once more. The irony was all too palpable.

'Why don't you behave like a real man, like your brother?'

'Simon, say sorry to your brother.'

The images of the torture ordeal Vincent had sanctioned and his intention to kill him came flooding back.

Blood isn't always thicker than water.

Without pausing, he slid his finger over the "Enter" key, initiating the app, and sending it to Vincent's location in the Data Warehouse.

Michael had fifteen minutes to get to his brother and trap him there until the app released the deadly cocktail Smith had manufactured.

Running from the quiet lab, Simon reached the balcony in the atrium. He looked over the top at the chaos below. People were still running about. All sense of calm had vanished as the building continued to rock from explosions. Sprinklers were going off in various parts of the complex in an attempt to salvage the premises.

Amidst the chaos, soldiers were attempting to direct the crowds. But in the general panic, it wasn't effective. This was Simon's best chance to escape.

Heading for the stairwell, he quickly descended from the fourth floor onto the ground floor in the centre of the atrium. Reaching the bottom of the steps, a group of armed soldiers hurrying past nearly sent him sprawling to the floor. They did not pay any attention to his dishevelled and beaten appearance.

A group of workers were pushing at the main doors of the building, struggling to escape. The soldiers had given up trying to control the situation at SemComNet's entrance. Without a second thought, Simon ran in the direction of the crowd, hoping to be lost in the anonymous hysterical mass.

THE THIRD-FLOOR CORRIDOR AND its offices were deserted as Michael ran purposefully in the direction of the Data Warehouse. The East Wing of the building was eerily quiet, apart from the constant hum of computer hardware permeating the building and the distant cries of workers trying to flee.

Turning another corner Michael stopped, his heart beating like a drum as he saw a sign on the wall: "Data Warehouse – authorised personnel only". On the wall next to the sealed door was the retinal scanner to only admit authorised personnel. The override keypad which required an access code was positioned beneath the scanner. Michael gulped, squeezing the handle of his handgun for confidence before punching the access code Simon had given him.

There was a brief pause before the door clicked. Tentatively he pushed it open, unsure where Trevellion would be or how potentially large the Data Warehouse was.

The door closed, and Michael stood in a narrow corridor leading into a much larger, long room. A few steps forward and the room opened up properly, and he found himself looking at row upon row of servers encased in gleaming metal cabinets. Multiple aisles filled the room. In between each row, there was sufficient space for a technician to work at a particular server if needed.

Without moving, he listened intently for the slightest sound of movement or activity that would give him Trevellion's exact position. There was nothing. The only sound was the persistent hum of the hardware, processing its required operations, despite the onslaught from RIG.

Looking around, he felt the knot in his stomach tighten as he scanned the equipment. It was the heart of UKCitizensNet's infrastructure, and the reason Colette and Clare had been murdered. All the lies, the deceit, and the attack on the country's freedom were symbolised in this mass of wires and microchips. He shivered as his gaze fell on the tall towers of machinery, unsure whether it was the cool temperature of the room or the sight in front of him that made him feel so cold.

Carefully, he walked down between the first row of servers, looking for any sign of Trevellion. Emerging at the end of the row, he was met with yet more aisles of servers. How many of these fucking things were there, he thought with disgust as they stretched out as far as the eye could see.

Still, there was no sound betraying Trevellion's location. Or the fact he was even in the Data Warehouse at all. Where could he be logged in, Michael wondered, slowly edging his way past the next row of machines.

Emerging again, he stopped as he reached rows of filing cabinets, the bank of servers finally ending. At least not everything in this building was electronic, he mused, gently running his hand over the cold metal cabinet directly in front of him.

Before he could progress any further, he heard the slightest sound to his right. The sound of someone opening a filing cabinet. His heart raced. His mouth was dry. And he moved from one row of filing cabinets to the next; his gun raised in anticipation of Trevellion.

The sound of his heart pounding rose to a deafening crescendo each time he turned to look discreetly down an aisle of filing cabinets. But each time, there was no sign of anyone.

Continuing forward, he could feel the sweat on his brow as he reached yet another row, turning to investigate. The air was sucked from his lungs as he saw Trevellion standing in the aisle, holding a paper file, looking down as he read its content.

Michael's grip on the handgun tightened as he slowly approached his nemesis.

It took a few agonising seconds before Trevellion finally looked up from the file. A thin, almost indiscernible smile crossed his distinctive features.

'You know, I didn't think you had it in you. Kennedy kept telling me you were close to cracking. But he still thought you'd see it through to the end. I must admit, I had my doubts.'

Michael continued walking until he was only ten feet away from Trevellion. The drawer of the filing cabinet, open at waist height, was the only thing between them. Michael pointed the gun at Trevellion's head.

'I would have walked to the end of the earth to find the one responsible for Colette and Clare's murders. The walk is over. You're all that's left now. Vengeance is mine.'

Surprise crossed Trevellion's face before his usual calm expression returned.

'You took care of Kennedy?'

Michael nodded, his right eye throbbing, still moist from where it was weeping.

'Pity. He was a dedicated follower. A believer of the cause. You don't find too many like him.'

'He was a sadistic bastard that deserved what he got.'

'That depends on your perspective, doesn't it?' Trevellion said patronisingly, looking into Michael's left eye, the fire of his hatred burning bright.

'Spare me your political rhetoric. There's no justification for this or what you and others have done. It's coming to an end. Tonight. UKCitizensNet is collapsing around you. The RIG has already hacked into the system and posted a statement on your homepage.

They are showing the country what a murderous sham this whole state network is. This is over. And so are you.'

'Yes, I noticed the Guardian's handiwork. Most irritating. But you are quite wrong about there being no justification for our actions. Our work is helping to preserve the best interests of this country. And there are plenty of us that believe in it—would die for it.'

'Nobody with any decent moral code would condone, never mind participate in this.'

Michael's finger slowly tightened on the trigger as he looked down the barrel of the gun pointed at Trevellion's head.

'Not even your wife?' Trevellion asked, watching Michael's trigger finger twitch.

'What did you say?' Michael was surprised.

'This has nothing to do with morality. This has to do with power. The power of this country to push its own agendas,' Trevellion continued quickly.

'What did you mean when you mentioned my wife?' Michael said angrily, waving his gun frantically at Trevellion's head.

'I knew you would come looking for me. It's quite fortunate really that the system backups and core infrastructure of UKCitizensNet are housed within our information archive. I've dug out a file with a few documents I thought you might be interested in.'

Michael looked confused; his gun remained pointed at Trevellion.

'The state network tender was never an open tender. It just had to *seem* that. In reality, only three companies could bid for the project: SemComNet, ACE Solutions, and SW Technologies. A year before we made the tender public, the government concocted a strategy to ensure SemCom had access to all the knowledge on 5G Semantic Web technologies it needed to succeed. Yes, we had some answers.

But ACE Solutions and SW Technologies had made substantial progress in other areas. We needed that knowledge and retrieved it through covert means.'

'What has any of this got to do with my wife?' Michael demanded angrily.

'Not just your wife, but David Langley as well. The covert team running this project for the government approached both your wife and David Langley, revealing the plans for the state network and how this would serve the national interest. At that point, they came over to work for us, secretly. For over a year, they have supplied us with important information about their own companies' R&D pipelines.'

Michael blinked in disbelief and fury.

'You're lying,' he shouted.

'Think about it. Those conferences and overnight stays Colette had to make, allegedly working for SW Technologies. They were all meetings and debriefs with SemComNet and Langley. If you don't believe me, read the reports she filed.'

Michael shook his head angrily, waving the gun maniacally in Trevellion's face. He recalled all the nights Colette had been away, allegedly working. And he remembered one night in particular. The evening she'd been called away from Clare's dance competition and the first prize she'd won. That had been for yet another conference.

Had it been all for them? For SemComNet?

'No. I read the meeting minutes Vera Langley gave me. SW Technologies and ACE Solutions were contemplating some sort of collaboration to strengthen their tender bid. Colette and Langley were leading on the tender bids for each company. That was why they were meeting. They weren't working for SemComNet.'

Trevellion sneered.

'The two companies themselves may have been planning that, but your wife and Langley fed us data about this potential partnership. Why do you think we chose them? They were perfectly placed within their own companies, only too willing to help. What we didn't know was that they were holding something back. The app they were developing. That got them killed. Well, and being a liability, of course.'

Trevellion shoved the paper file towards Michael. Stepping forward, but with his gun still raised, Michael read the incriminating file. Scanning the title, Jones' words in the mobile home came rushing back.

'I glimpsed at a confidential Defence Department file about a project called CODEX, which mentioned the establishment of UKCitizensNet. I couldn't understand why the Defence Department was interested in the network. Now it all makes sense. Thanks to your wife's files.'

The title on the cover of the file burned into Michael's memory of Colette and his head swam, nausea rushing through him, bile burning the back of his throat.

CODEX file OP09/ST – UKCitizensNet implementation and development.

Inside the file, which contained several hundred pages, Trevellion had turned over the top right corner of a specific document.

Memo from: Colette Robertson, Technical Director, SW Technologies
Recipient: CODEX
Subject: Update
Since the last CODEX meeting, the project team preparing SW Technologies' tender bid for the state network has met for the first time. Technical implementation issues are being examined by a separate working group which will report progress to the project team directly in due course.

The initial delineation of tasks is broken down as follows:
Project team:
Budgetary overview
Project deliverables
Project milestones
Redundancy estimates/scenarios
Regulatory framework
Ethical data collection

Technical team:
Bandwidth issues
Wireless access
IP synchronicity
Single network sign-on
Network services
Email services

The relevant project documents, including the Project Initiation Document (PID) and a preliminary Gantt chart detailing the first phase project milestones and deliverables, are attached. A more detailed brief of important issues discussed, but specifically not recorded in the event of a Freedom of Information request, will be provided at the next CODEX meeting.

Most of the technical detail was lost on Michael. But there was no doubt the report bore out Trevellion's assertion of industrial espionage. At the bottom of the page was Colette's familiar signature.

One phrase, in particular, struck deep inside him, into his soul, eroding his perfect image of Colette:

Redundancy estimates/scenarios

He could still remember the long hours she'd worked, even on her birthday. It had all been to safeguard the jobs at SW Technologies, she had assured him repeatedly.

She lied to me.

Stepping back from the file, he felt the tears welling up, his emotions threatening to overwhelm him. Everything he thought he'd known about Colette was disintegrating. The perfect woman with her perfect integrity. It had all been an illusion.

How could she have done this and not told him? He might have understood. Or he might have been able to persuade her not to do it. They would have found a way to deal with Clare's medical bills. He was an insurance broker, after all. Why hadn't Colette shared her concerns with him? Why the secrets? Everything he thought he knew and held dear was a lie. And the root of it was standing right in front of him.

He raised his gun again, tears rolling down his cheeks.

'She believed in the cause,' Trevellion said dismissively. 'That is until she realised she and Langley held the key. Then she wanted money. Don't talk to me about the morality of the project. This isn't about morality. It's about power and control. The former internet didn't allow it. UKCitizensNet does. It's as simple as that.'

Michael could hear a stream of questions that demanded answers in his head.

'But if she was so important to you, why did you have her killed?'

Trevellion didn't respond. He grinned.

Michael's finger squeezed the trigger. The bullet flashed past Trevellion's head, catching the side of his ear, puncturing a hole in the metal filing cabinet to his right.

Trevellion flinched before touching his ear. His fingers were coated with blood. The bullet had grazed his lobe on its way past his head. The aim had been closer than Michael had intended. But it had the desired effect.

'They betrayed us. They deserved what was coming. We couldn't afford any loose ends. If either she or David Langley had been exposed as passing on secrets to SemComNet our tender would have been over. And we were always very careful who she met at SemComNet. It wasn't desirable for her to meet with the senior team. Myself included. She only met trusted "go-betweens". Any risk or exposure and the project would have failed. There couldn't be anything leading back to us once UKCitizensNet was operational.'

'So she was expendable?' Michael was furious.

'She'd served her purpose,' Trevellion replied bluntly. 'She knew the risks. That's why she didn't want you to know. To protect you. What we hadn't counted on was her taking out a little insurance policy by storing information elsewhere rather than sharing it.'

'I guess she didn't quite trust you enough,' Michael sneered. 'Maybe her family came first. Clare came first.'

Trevellion scoffed.

'Don't kid yourself, Michael. She believed in it and she was prepared to see SW Technologies go to the wall. She fed us information because she understood the wider picture, and what we could do with UKCitizensNet. She was a patriot. Read the file, man. It's all in there.'

As Michael glanced down at the file again, Trevellion lunged at the end of the cabinet, thrusting it closed, smashing it into Michael's arm. Colette's incriminating files were thrown into the air as Michael fell to the ground. Trevellion turned and ran.

Pulling himself to his feet, Michael set off in pursuit, unable to lock his aim on Trevellion as the pair of them scurried down the aisle of filing cabinets. Eventually, their pursuit opened up into an office area. Michael grinned triumphantly as Trevellion ran into a cul-de-sac.

His nemesis stood behind a metallic desk, a single tablet computer on it, linked to a large screen on the wall opposite. Trevellion cursed at his wrong turn, glaring angrily at Michael.

'Just answer me one last question.' Michael spoke slowly, desperately trying to keep his rage and his trigger finger under control. 'Why film it? Why did you film what you did to my little girl?'

An almost indiscernible expression of guilt and concealment crossed Trevellion's face. Realisation hit him.

'You videoed that butcher killing Colette too, didn't you?' he yelled. Trevellion edged backwards, signs of fear showing on his sombre features, his eyes wide open.

'Answer me, you bastard,' Michael bellowed, enraged.

Before Trevellion could reply, Michael involuntarily pulled the trigger, and again, and again, and again, until the barrel stopped. The magazine was empty. The smell of cordite filled the air as smoke blurred his vision.

As the haze cleared, he blinked. Trevellion was standing motionless against the wall. Behind him, to the left of his head, there were four yawning craters. The bullets had impacted with the brick wall. Michael had missed his target. The magazine was empty. Turning to examine the holes in the wall, Trevellion smiled wryly.

'It looks as if you're out of ammunition. I think the odds have swung back in my favour.'

In an instant, Michael dropped the gun. Slipping his hand into his trouser pocket, he pulled a small hand grenade. Trevellion stopped in his tracks. He looked warily at Michael.

'I've got a bit of my own insurance,' Michael stated firmly. 'Something I picked up from one of your soldiers who didn't survive all the blasts here.'

Sliding his finger through the pin at the top of the grenade, he ordered Trevellion to sit down behind the desk.

'The question remains: why did you video their deaths?'

'We thought it would give us extra leverage should certain circumstances ever arise. And how right we were.'

'But why kill my little girl? She wasn't involved. Why kill an innocent child?'

Trevellion rolled his eyes, looking exasperated.

'Do you still not get it? We had to crucify Davey Wilkes publicly to ensure the public's appetite was satisfied in having someone—a monster—to blame for the killings. The murder of a child ensured that. I told you before, this is a dirty business. One you shouldn't even think of playing.'

Michael looked at the grenade in his hand.

'You're right. I don't want to play this game anymore. I'm going to end it. Here. Tonight.'

He looked at his watch. If Simon had kept his word, the launch of the app was less than two minutes away.

'Why do you keep looking at your watch?' Trevellion snapped impatiently. 'Do you need to be somewhere else?'

'I'm not going anywhere. Never again. I came down here looking for you for one reason and one reason only—to ensure you never leave this room. You see, in less than two minutes, this room is going to fill with a deadly gas cocktail from SemComNet's own resources. Ironic really. In less than a minute, you'll be dead amongst your prized computer network.'

Michael looked up at the sprinklers evenly distributed in the ceiling panels and smiled. Trevellion looked panic-stricken. Realisation struck him.

'Didn't Kennedy explain how we tried to kill you previously? I guess not.'

'But you'll be killed also,' Trevellion protested.

'What have I got to live for? You took everything from me. There's nothing for me to go back to. My wife and daughter are dead. The police and army are hunting me because they think I'm some sort of child-killing cyberterrorist. What could I possibly have to live for outside these walls? The only thing I have left is ensuring you die with me, and that UKCitizensNet ends here. Tonight. Your CODEX project has failed.'

Trevellion advanced on Michael, who held the grenade up in front of him.

'If you try to get past me, I will detonate the grenade. Not a pretty way to go. Although probably somewhat quicker. The choice is yours.'

He looked at his watch again. Thirty seconds to the gas dispersing.

Trevellion exhaled loudly, sitting back on the metallic desk, a reluctant smile on his face.

'I certainly underestimated you, didn't I?' he said resignedly, rubbing his hands.

Twenty seconds.

'There will be others to carry on this work. You know that, don't you? This CODEX project will continue.'

'It's over. The Real Internet Guardians are tearing UKCitizensNet to pieces. Look at the screen behind me.'

The large screen mounted on the wall displayed the UKCitizensNet homepage and the message the RIG had posted to the nation.

Ten seconds.

His index finger was firmly gripped around the pin of the hand grenade.

'You can't stop progress, no one can. It will...'

The thunderous explosion ripped through the East Wing of the building, swallowing everything. The walls crumbled, sending mountains of flying debris into the air. As the building heaved, the floors above the room collapsed, filling the area with more dust and masonry.

In the Data Warehouse, the room shook and everything went black as the lights were extinguished. Then there was silence.

CHAPTER FORTY SEVEN

THE FIRST EXPLOSION HAD woken Digger from his slumber in the hammock he'd erected forty feet up between two sturdy oak trees, above his observation platform. In a state of stirring consciousness, he'd laid in his hammock, unsure whether he'd dreamt the noise.

The sound had given him anxious flashbacks. As if the bastards were coming for them all over again. Like they had two years earlier. He could still hear the screams as the trees had fallen to the ground, taking his friends with them. They'd either been killed by the fall or beaten to death by the soldiers on the ground. No mercy had been shown that day. It still haunted him. Regularly he would wake up in the night in a cold sweat, the images haunting him, wondering why he'd been the only one to escape.

But this was different. Normally the sounds of the explosions were just in his dreams. This had been real. And this had come from within SemComNet.

When the second explosion shook the ground, he knew he wasn't dreaming.

Moving to the edge of his platform, he peered through the trees and the darkness. SemComNet was illuminated in the distance. Lights beaming through the gallery of windows punctuated the night, covering the imposing complex. Straining his hearing, he was sure he could hear screams and ensuing panic coming from the building.

The sound of another explosion filled the air and this time he could see flames licking at the inside of the right wing of the building as parts of the structure collapsed.

What the hell's happening?

Quickly, he began his descent. It was three days since Michael, Simon and Brown had entered the building, and failed to return. They'd obviously been captured. He'd presumed they would be dead now. He knew only too well how ruthless SemComNet was. If they'd been caught, no way they were coming out alive.

But he'd not been expecting this. It was surely no coincidence the building was under some form of attack.

Reaching the ground, he moved to the edge of the tree line, close to the entrance to the tunnel. Scratching his several days' stubble, he watched the chaos several hundred feet away. Frightened staff were frantically trying to escape from the main entrance in the atrium, their screams and cries filling the still night air.

Surely, there wasn't any prospect of the three of them escaping, he wondered, looking at the concealed entrance to the tunnel.

Kicking the leaves and foliage away, another thought struck him. Although virtually none of it had made any sense, he remembered discussions the three men had had before their covert advance on SemComNet. They had mentioned other groups being able to attack SemComNet if they could infiltrate UKCitizensNet.

As a stream of fire blew out a window about halfway up the building on the right side, he pondered this possibility. Could this be the attack they were talking about?

He didn't know. But there was one thing he was sure of. And without further hesitation, he pulled open the entrance to the tunnel and began to wait.

THE CANDLES IN THE tunnel had long since burnt cut. Simon's escape was slow and tortuous. Walking slowly through the tunnel, he groped at the walls for direction, fighting off claustrophobia as he looked into total blackness. He had no idea where he was in relation to the other end of the tunnel. He just had to keep on walking.

Several minutes later, he breathed a sigh of relief. His hands made contact with the base of the ladder which led out of the tunnel. Sweating, he wondered if Michael was behind him or whether he had stayed to the end as intended.

Climbing up the ladder, it took him a further two minutes before he felt the cool night air on his face. As his head poked out of the top of the tunnel entrance, he could hear the sounds of SemComNet burning, screams filling the air as staff attempted to flee the mayhem.

Pulling himself out, he crouched on the ground, his heart pounding. Before he could move, a vice-like grip surrounded his neck.

'Tell me who you are, or I'll break your fucking neck,' a gruff but familiar voice whispered.

'Get off me, it's Simon,' he gasped, trying in vain to pull the strong forearm away from his windpipe.

The grip loosened. Simon slumped forward as Digger grabbed his arm, hauling him to his feet.

'Sorry, mate,' he said. 'Can't be too careful. You could have been one of those fucking SemComNet bastards. Or one of those soldiers I've seen patrolling around.'

Rubbing his neck, Simon gestured for him not to worry. The main thing was, he was out of the building.

'Where are Michael and Brown?' Digger asked, watching the inferno that was SemComNet.

'Brown betrayed us,' Simon said angrily, images of his torture flooding back. 'He was working for SemComNet all along. The whole thing was a trap just to get us into the building so they could find out if we had useful information about the app.'

'Bastard,' Digger hissed. 'I hope he's burning alive in there.'

Simon sniggered.

'He's dead. Michael killed him.'

Digger smiled, pleased some justice had been done.

'What the hell's happening in there? What's causing all the explosions?'

Simon shook his head as he, too, turned to face the blazing building.

'It's the Real Internet Guardians. We must have succeeded in sending them the app before they caught us. They've managed to breach the UKCitizensNet firewall. They're attacking UKCitizensNet and SemComNet with it. The irony is almost poetic. UKCitizensNet has been exposed for what it is, a murderous sham. It's the end for them.'

More screams filled the air. Digger asked, concerned, 'What about Michael? Where is he?'

'He was going after my brother. We sent the app to kill him. I don't think he's coming back.'

Digger nodded, understanding what Simon had left unspoken.

Simon looked at his watch. The app would have had more than enough time to do its job. And if that had failed, the devastation of the East Wing of the building would have made an escape virtually impossible.

'To be honest, I'm not sure he was ever trying to escape. He only wanted vengeance for his wife and daughter. But if he's not dead, I just hope he can make it out.'

The two men fell silent, pondering Michael's potential fate. As another explosion ripped through SemComNet, their attention fell to the entrance of the tunnel at their feet. Michael's only possible route of escape.

MYTH TELLS US THAT Nero was fiddling while Rome burned. According to the legend, Nero seemed dismissive and arrogant at the devastation. As he now scrabbled across the grass, the flames of SemComNet illuminated the route of escape. There was nothing minor or dismissive about this devastation. He knew the scale of what was happening. They'd brought down UKCitizensNet.

Behind him, he could hear screams, terrible screams, as another blast ripped through the state-of-the-art complex. He felt the heat of the explosion and the flames that licked mercilessly from room to room warm his skin as he scurried away, looking for cover. Looking for his route out.

Pulling himself up, he turned back towards the burning complex, assessing the situation. The entire East Wing had been destroyed, reduced to a rubble inferno. The flames were rapidly gathering pace, spreading through the open-plan atrium and into the North Wing, which predominantly housed the management offices.

Amidst the crackling of the fire came the sound of shattering glass. A domino effect of people toppled through the shards of the breached atrium onto the ground outside, tumbling helplessly onto each other as they sought to escape. Bodies were lacerated on the shattered glass or crushed by the wave of people pouring from the point of escape.

He watched as one man trampled the rising mass of limbs, stumbling onto the gravel path running around the entire complex. His screams pierced the air as the flames burning away his hair spread down his body, sliding down his clothes in a terrifying instant. The man ran in a crazed zigzag as if this would somehow halt the furious path of the flames, before flinging himself to the floor, attempting to roll over and over. It was too late. The smell of burning flesh permeated the air as more screams shot from the ruptured atrium.

Turning away from the panicked cries, it occurred to him that the chaos and panic would surely make his escape easier. Looking from side to side, he moved forward, thoughtfully scanning the ground for the way they'd got into SemComNet avoiding the heavy perimeter security. Behind him, there was another deafening explosion. The ground shook from the force, sending him sprawling onto his front. His angular jaw thudded painfully into the earth.

The most recent blast lit up the ground in front of him. Fifteen feet ahead, he could see a hole in the ground. Reaching the entrance to the tunnel, he saw the ladder poking up from the yawning opening below. Casting one last glance around, he felt confident he hadn't been pursued. He quickly descended into the maze of tunnels below.

The light from the flames above slowly ebbed away, to be replaced by the enveloping gloom in the tunnels. He reached into his trouser pocket for his cigarette lighter. As the light flooded into the tunnel and lit the way out, Trevellion ran his fingers through his dark hair, contemplating his good fortune.

Even now he wasn't sure what had happened. The clock had been ticking down to the release of the noxious gas into the Data Warehouse. But an explosion had ripped through the room before that had happened.

Had Michael Robertson detonated the grenade?

Was it intentional or an accident?

Maybe the sight of sitting in front of the man responsible for the death of his wife and daughter had been too much? Maybe he simply couldn't wait any longer? Or, had the thunderous explosion that had sent him sprawling to the ground, fortuitously underneath a metal desk that had protected him, resulted from the RIGs' attack? Whatever the cause of the blast, it hadn't been his time. Fate had smiled on him this night.

Reaching into his jacket pocket for his mobile phone, he flicked the device open, calling up his phone book. Choosing a number, he grinned as the caller ID appeared on the screen.

S Tate mobile

A scowl soon replaced the smile. He had no signal. Not this far underground.

Never mind, he'd speak to Tate when he was out at the other end of the tunnel.

They might have succeeded in destroying SemComNet and destabilising UKCitizensNet, but he was alive. And that meant the CODEX project was still alive. And the project was bigger than all of them.

AT THE UKCITIZENSNET CYBERCAFE in Kingston-upon-Thames, the manager pulled the cafe's door shut, pressing the button on the digital display from "Open" to "Closed". It was only 9:10 a.m. But there would not be any customers today. And maybe not for a while if reports on UKCitizensNet's radio station, eCit-Talk, were to be believed.

Walking through the cafe, the manager grimaced. She turned off each monitor until the only one remaining was the large display screen attached to the far wall. Studying the message on the monitor, she wondered if this might cost her the job. Once again, she read the message that had been on every screen before flicking it off.

We regret UKCitizensNet is currently unavailable. We hope to restore service as soon as possible.

NOTE FROM THE AUTHOR

Thank you for reading *The Codex File*, I hope you enjoyed it, and that I scared you a little! Perhaps, you'll look at the internet through slightly different eyes now.

Would you also be able to take a moment to leave me a review on Goodreads and Amazon? I'd be very grateful.

Thanks again!
Miles Etherton

Connect with me:
Author Page on Publisher Website – citystonepress.com/Miles Etherton
Author Website - www.milesetherton.com
Twitter - twitter.com/milesetherton

ABOUT THE AUTHOR

Miles Etherton is a historian with a special interest in WWII and modern-day technologies.

He likes to explore the darker side of our existence, and in particular the murkier depths of the online world. He is an expert at melting intriguing facts into captivating fiction–not for the fainthearted–in his cyber thrillers.

Miles loves the internet and online world. What if one of the greatest technological advances we've made, would be misused? What if the freedom of the internet has turned on its users? Imagine devious minds having their way with our data... it makes for fascinating ideas to explore in writing.

If you love cyber and conspiracy thrillers then why not come along for the ride... Are you brave enough?

ALSO BY MILES ETHERTON

HEDON'S GATE TRILOGY

SHROUD OF DARKNESS
THE CAMPUS KILLER
REDEMPTION

Ambiticus journalist, Zahava Lee, is looking for her next big scoop.

Maybe she's just found it when former lover and private investigator, Bill McAllister, brings her details of Hedon's Gate, a deadly new designer drug from Eastern Europe.

While students are dying from overdoses, a lone student sets on a terrible path of revenge. The killer weaves his way through the hedonism of undergraduate life, with its cocktail of drink, debauchery, and the lethal designer drug Hedon's Gate. The murderer's weapon of choice.

His aim: revenge. His target: the beautiful siren, Claudia Devoy who relentlessly wrecks lives with her promiscuity. Through social media, he tracks her every move to close in on the woman he once loved.

Zahava Lee infiltrates the university... and walks headlong into London's newest serial murderer – the Campus Killer. Seeking publicity, the Campus Killer wants Zahava to voice the motives behind his murderous scheme. It will be the biggest story of her career.

Zahava's life is threatened when she crosses paths with London's narcotic underworld and a ruthless Russian drug gang on a killing spree. Caught between the Campus Killer and a vengeful Russian drug lord exacting violent retribution, Zahava faces demons from the past.

Can Zahava evade the murderous attention of the Russian drug gang and expose the truth behind Hedon's Gate and the Campus Killer? Will Zahava survive?

To be published in 2023 by <u>City Stone Publishing</u>. Check for the author's books on their website.

ABOUT CITY STONE PUBLISHING

A publisher with a passion for the written word and a heart that beats for indie authors

We are an imaginative and enthusiastic traditional publisher who also provide editorial services, author branding, website design and social media support.

Our ambition: to publish good books; to develop, work alongside, and support great writers through our publishing services.

We are not just about the books; we build relationships with our authors. Because we both write, we know what (indie) authors want. That is how we work: in cooperation and partnership with our authors.

From dark and gritty crime thrillers, entertaining and delightful women's fiction, and contemporary novels to interesting and insightful non-fiction, we publish it all.